To the Dewire family,
with best wishes
from
Tonye Thomas

The Last Spell

Also by Bryce Thomas

Rhamin

Rhamin II: Blue Tooth

❖ ❖ ❖

Lucy Lockhart: The Awakening

❖ ❖ ❖

Coming soon by Bryce Thomas

Lucy Lockhart: The Wall of Silence

The Last Spell

by
Bryce Thomas

THOMAS HAMILTON & CO.

This novel is entirely a work of fiction. The names, characters and incidents portrayed in it are the work of the author's imagination. Any resemblance to actual persons, living or dead; events; organizations including companies and domains formed during or after the writing and publication of this book; or localities is entirely coincidental.

First published in Great Britain 2012
Thomas Hamilton & Co Publishers
80 Warham Road, Harrow HA3 7HZ

Cover artwork by Neil Booth

A CIP catalogue record of this book is available from The British Library

ISBN: 978-1-907696-11-4

FIRST EDITION PAPERBACK
Printed and bound in the UK
by CPI Group (UK) Ltd, Croydon, CR0 4YY

www.thomashamilton.co.uk

To June

For many hours of patient support.

PROLOGUE
The Dark Angel

LOCATION: THE FIELD HOSPITAL CRIMEA - OCTOBER 1854

None of the men would make it off the battlefield. There was no point in transferring them. Most were hardly conscious, all were dying and none would survive the journey.

In all, twenty one men lay there, feet facing the centre of the circular bell tent, on thick blankets on a hard rock floor. Around them the sides of the tent flapped wildly as the dry, cold wind whipped and buffeted the canvas. A single lantern cast a dim, yellow light, making dancing shadows as it swung from side to side on its rope hanging loop.

The assistant field surgeon looked in on them every hour. He did what he could to help them die peacefully, dosing them with laudanum to ease the pain through their last mortal hours.

Marcus was one of the wounded. He was still conscious and, despite the opiates he had been given, he was in terrible pain. He knew he was dying. The stinking dressings on the wounds in his abdomen were soaked in blood and stained with other leaking liquids. The surgeon couldn't stop the fluids seeping out. The damage inside was too great to repair. He had tried but had given up. And so had Marcus. He had given up caring, given up trying to carry on living. He stared up at the canopy of the tent, just waiting for the end. He knew he would be dead before the next day dawned.

He grew colder as his life force, his strength and will to live, drained slowly from him. Drifting in and out of consciousness, he thought he saw an angel. But she wasn't what he had expected. He had always presumed that angels would be dressed in white flowing robes, and surrounded by an aura of bright light, reaching forward, offering a hand, inviting the dying into their other world. This one was not such an angel. This one was dark, as dark as the shadows, completely dressed in black as she emerged from the night. At first it was hard to make out whether it was just a shadow or a shrouded figure in a black cloak. But as he gradually focussed his eyes in the dim, shimmering light, Marcus could see that it *was* a figure, her head covered by a loose hood, her disembodied face like a pale mask, hovering in the blackness. A pale, ghostly hand suddenly emerged from the darkness beneath the face. It was remarkably clear to see as it hovered over his eyes and then touched his forehead.

Somehow the pain in his belly just eased away, fading into a warm comfortable feeling of euphoria. She carried no drugs as far as he could make out; she simply placed the palm of her hand on his brow and, suddenly and almost instantly, he relaxed. How she eased the pain, he did not know, but he was grateful for that. He watched her as she stood up and floated around the tent, looking closely at each of the other dying soldiers. At first, when he had seen her, he'd been afraid. There seemed to be something un-angelic, almost sinister, about this dark figure. One thing for sure, she couldn't have been a nurse. Females were not allowed on or near the battlefield. They were assigned to tend the wounded, moved each day to the rear lines, away from the battlefront. But as she took his pain away, he realized she was there to help him, whoever she was. She rose and went to inspect some of the other patients again, looking closely at their faces, and then returned and knelt once more beside him. She sat on her heels and took out a small pouch from under her dark cloak. She held it between her hands just above his chest as she watched and waited. She seemed in no hurry to go and Marcus was happy for her to stay. She was good company even though she never spoke. As he grew weaker and began to lose consciousness, the dark angel took his hand.

'Thank you,' he said not knowing why he said it.

Suddenly, a shuffling of the canvas and a slight brightening of the gloomy light indicated that someone was entering the tent with his own inadequate lantern. As the army chaplain secured the flap, the dark angel slipped silently to one side and away into the shadows, unseen by anyone but Marcus.

'I have one who has recovered,' the assistant told the surgeon. 'One of the dying?'

He said it as a question. He wasn't used to reporting that a man, who had been put in the tent for the mortally wounded, had somehow overcome his injury and begun to recover. He needed to know what to do.

'Recovered?' the field surgeon asked back.

'In tent four, Sir.'

The surgeon grunted. There had to be some mistake. He had dressed the wounds and operated on all of the people who had come in from the battlefield with injuries. He had seen every possible kind of injury in all stages of severity. He knew which patients would live and which would die. 'I'll have a look in a minute,' he said as he finished bandaging a man's head. His operating table was an old plank door set across two water barrels. Two lanterns suspended from the rail that held up the canopy gave out an inadequate light. 'Tent one,' he said and nodded to two orderlies. They lifted the casualty from the makeshift table onto a canvas stretcher, then, raising it carefully, they carried the wounded man out. The surgeon picked up a bucket of water and washed it over his table then, lifting one of the lanterns off its hook, he led the way.

Tent number four was nearest to his operating table. Mortally wounded soldiers, as patients, were not the majority of casualties. The really badly wounded had already died on the battlefield. So on the whole, as a proportion of all the injuries upon which he operated or for which he dressed their wounds, those soldiers that died were in a small minority. The fact remained however that, of those that survived and should continue to recover as a direct result of his work, over half their number would subsequently die of typhus, typhoid, cholera or other diseases related to unsanitary conditions at the military hospital in the old barracks where they were sent specifically to recuperate. It was deeply saddening. He held out very little hope for a mortally injured soldier who had refused to die.

Lifting the flap, the surgeon entered the tent and waited until his assistant had closed it again and was standing beside him. The assistant nodded to a pile of blankets about a third of the way around the side of the billowing canvas. The surgeon glanced at the other patients as he stepped carefully past them. A head wound that would go gangrenous because the bullet was still lodged deep inside the soldier's skull; a bayonet wound that had severed the intestines and the spleen would soon turn to septicaemia; amputees who had lost too much blood and who, even if they survived would be bled again by the doctors in the general hospital; bullet wounds that had severed vital organs. The new conical bullets had left soldiers damaged far more than the effects of the old round musket balls. There was nothing clean about war; and it was getting dirtier.

'Is this the one?' the surgeon asked as he bent over the soldier.

'Yes Sir.'

'What's his name?'

'Marcus MacKay, Sir,' the assistant replied, bending forward with his lantern also. He wanted to make sure he hadn't acted too hastily having perhaps brought the surgeon to look at a corpse. Sure enough, the soldier was alive and, although very pale, he was looking around, but at the moment, only by moving his eyes.

'Well soldier, how are you feeling?' It seemed a stupid question but he asked all his patients the same question whether they were recovering from a minor wound or screaming and dying in agony.

'Where am I?' the soldier asked. He coughed and a little drop of blood trickled from his nose.

'You've been wounded,' the surgeon explained. 'You are in the field hospital.'

'Field hospital?' It didn't make much sense.

'You took a bullet in the chest and another in the abdomen.' He wanted to explain that he couldn't repair the damage, but preferred to let the soldier die without such worries on his mind. What's the point of getting distraught over how you are dying? The result is just the same without the anxiety.

'Well I suppose I ought to thank you doctor,' the soldier said wheezily.

The surgeon put his hand on the soldier's arm. 'I did my best,' he said, trying to give the man some final words of comfort. 'Have you much pain?'

The soldier thought for a moment, waiting to see if his body was hurting really badly. Then his eyes showed a light of resolve as he realized what he would say as an answer. 'My chest hurts,' he said with a slight cough.

The surgeon was holding the soldier's wrist. 'Hmm, your pulse is much stronger. I suggest you get some sleep,' he said as he lay the man's hand down on the blanket. He gave a furtive glance at his assistant and stood up. 'We'd better check the rest,' he said and continued to walk amongst the other casualties. He pointed to a soldier who had just expired, and without a word, the assistant pulled the blanket over the man's face. Eventually they went out into the fresh air. The breeze was welcomely refreshing after the stale and putrid smell of death.

'He was dying,' the assistant insisted. 'I saw him only an hour ago and he didn't look like he would last another five minutes. I asked the chaplain to keep an eye on him, but when I went back to check him he seemed much better.'

'I thought he'd be dead by now,' the surgeon confirmed. 'He seems to be fighting well. The problem is, when septicaemia sets in, which it is bound to do, then we have nothing to combat it. He'll die of blood poisoning; mark my words.' He stood and looked up at a gap in the clouds where a few faint stars were the only light in the sky. 'Does that soldier know he's paralysed?' he asked eventually.

'No Sir. We didn't think it any use telling him.'

'That's fair enough,' said the surgeon. 'By the way, where is the chaplain?'

'I don't know. Possibly in one of the other tents.' He paused a second and then said, 'It's strange. MacKay's Scottish isn't he?'

The surgeon shook his head. He hadn't met any of the men before they appeared on his operating table.

'Well, I spoke to him earlier,' the assistant began to explain, 'only he had a broad Scottish accent.'

'Didn't sound like it to me,' the surgeon stated. 'Probably just slurring his speech.' He tilted his head towards the assistant's tent. 'Go get some rest. There'll be more work tomorrow.' With that he went to look in the other tents. It hadn't been a bad day. Thirteen dead and sixty four in the tents, of which forty two were expected to survive. Some days he and his assistant had over two hundred casualties to see to.

As the surgeon went on his rounds, the chaplain was nowhere to be seen. He left word with several guards that he was looking for him, and returned to his own meagre quarters, yet another tent with a hard rock floor. He hung up his lantern, slumped into an old folding chair, eased off his boots and dozed.

He was awakened by a voice.

'Doctor? You were looking for me?' It was the army chaplain. In the pale light, his head looked detached as his face peered through the flap of the tent.

'Huh? Oh yes. Have you talked to all the wounded soldiers?'

'I have indeed.'

'What about tent four?'

'I've talked to all that were conscious. I gave the last rites to those who looked like they would never regain consciousness.'

'Did you see a soldier called MacKay?'

'Abdominal and chest wounds. Yes, I did.'

'What did he say?'

'He died while I was holding his hand. Never regained consciousness.'

'No, I'm talking about MacKay.'

'There's only one MacKay in all of the tents,' the chaplain affirmed.

The surgeon pushed himself up out of the chair. 'No, I'll show you who I meant. I'd like you to keep an eye on him.' Wearily, he picked up the lantern and led the way.

A cold wind cut through their jackets as they walked out towards the flap of tent four. The rain clouds had smothered the sky completely. Only the yellow glow of the lantern gave them light by which to walk. As they entered the tent, the lantern threw a long shadow across the prone bodies. None lifted their heads to see who was entering. The surgeon stepped over to where MacKay was lying. The soldier opened his eyes as the lantern threw light upon his face.

'This is MacKay,' the surgeon stated. He turned to look at the chaplain.

Even in the dull light the chaplain's face had paled. 'I… I must have been mistaken,' he stammered, gazing into the eyes of the soldier, eyes he had closed as the patient passed out of this world. He nodded to him and then turned quickly away.

'What's the matter?' the soldier coughed and stretched as if waking from a long sleep.

Did he move his legs then? Surely not. The surgeon shook his head. He was too exhausted to think. 'You still Okay?' he asked.

The soldier nodded weakly. 'Who's MacKay?' he wheezed. His voice was barely a whisper. 'Where am I?'

'Don't worry about anything now. Get a good night's sleep,' the surgeon said. 'You are going to need it. Tomorrow you are being transported out of here. Istanbul, then home.'

'Istanbul!' the soldier grated. The bubbles in his lung made his voice rattle. 'So just exactly where am I?' he asked again, impatiently. 'Tell me.'

'The Crimea, of course,' the surgeon replied with a shake of his head. The poor soldier had lost his memory as well. He wondered why he hadn't seen any head trauma when he cleaned the man up before operating on him to get at the bullets. 'Just get some rest for now. You are going to be all right,' he lied as he tried to work out how this soldier was rallying so well. Despite his best efforts to save him, MacKay, in his opinion, should still have been beyond any medical help.

It was his intention, in the morning, to ship all the wounded soldiers from the front lines to Scutari Barracks, which were being used as a general military hospital. Now, however, the surgeon expected that, if MacKay continued to cheat death from the damage to his organs, tent four might not be the soldier's final destination after all. He would instead be transported straight back to England for spinal treatment. There, along with large numbers of other casualties he would be treated and then forced to spend the rest of his days in a wheel chair. The bullet that had entered his abdomen, after ripping through his bowel and his spleen, had lodged in his back, severing his spinal chord in the lumbar region. It was still there. If he was, by some miracle, going to recover from the terrible wounds to his abdomen as well as the bullet hole in his lung, then Marcus MacKay would, should still be left paralysed. He would never walk or fight again.

Exhausted and perplexed, and still holding out little hope for his patient, the surgeon stood up and turned away. As he looked up, a shadow at the far side of the tent caught the corner of his eye. He turned his head and strained to see what it was but there was nothing there. The flickering lantern was playing tricks on his tired eyes.

Knowing there would be more wounded, dead and dying soldiers tomorrow, and with a mind too exhausted for any more contemplation, wearily, he brushed his fingers through his hair, sighed deeply and left with a heavy heart.

PART ONE

The Witch

Chapter One

AUGUST 1854. ON THE RUN IN YEMARA

Footsteps thundered along the plank walk as a more than a dozen soldiers filed down to the dockside. No one could mistake the sound of their regimented footfalls as they trooped along the gloomy, lantern-lit waterfront. They were not ordinary soldiers serving in a regular army. They were mercenaries; private soldiers from a ruthless private army.

A commanding voice pierced the cool evening air. 'Check all the bars and all the inns. Leave no face unchecked!'

All. the roads out of the port had been blocked and checkpoints had been purposely set up to stop their quarry from escaping. No ships had sailed from the port of Yemara that day and only one ship was docked at the quayside now; *The Arinosta*. It was waiting to sail with the evening tide and Henri Dubois had less than two hours in which to get on board. In that time he had to avoid being caught by the soldiers of Abraham Drach.

Several of the militia burst into the bedrooms of the inn. Screams cut through the darkening sky as the occupants were pulled off the bed and inspected. Then as the men left one room for the next, the same happened again and then again.

More soldiers, carrying oil lamps, mulled through the tables and under the awnings, lifting each face up to the light to examine it closely enough to ensure there was no mistake. Everyone was suspect.

'Who's that man?' the commandant barked, kicking open a door and lifting his arm as he pointed to a shabbily dressed tramp of a fellow sitting in the shadows in the far corner of the dingy bar.

'Nobody,' a voice reported as a soldier, hand clasped on the man's shoulder, spun him around to face the lantern. The scruffy looking man had thick matted hair and was wearing a faded, heavy great coat that brushed against the dirt floor. In the dim light of the tavern his face looked crooked and distorted.

'Stand up!' the commandant ordered.

The man pushed back his jug of ale and reached for an old wooden crutch that leaned, waiting, against the wall. Unsteadily, he rose from his seat and placed the crutch under his left armpit.

'O right; o right!' he grumbled, more under his breath than to the irritating soldier. 'Giv us a minit!' Pressing one rough hand firmly on the table he managed to balance himself with the aid of the crutch and finally turned to face his inquisitor.

'Wat's up?' He asked in a gravelly, phlegmy voice. He cleared his throat and spat onto the sawdust covered floor. 'Watd'yer want?'

The commandant walked up to the man and, in the dim light, grasped his bristly chin and turned his face up to the light to examine him closely. His lip curled in disgust as he looked upon the thick matted hair and a mouthful of blackened teeth. He looked at the droopy eyelids, one of which was pulled tight as if badly scarred at some time. Even in the muted light of the tavern, he could see that the eyes behind the eyelids were bloodshot. The face was greasy and unshaven. He dropped his gaze down the length of the man's grimy great coat and stepped back to look at the one leg protruding beneath it.

'I suppose times are hard for one legged beggars!' he stated, smirking sadistically and pushing the man backwards. The man grabbed at the table as he tried to land on the chair, but staggered clumsily back against the wall and, amidst a flurry of curses from between his dirty clenched teeth, sank down onto the floor in the shadowy corner.

The commandant seemed greatly amused. 'Still afford to drink though,' he stated disapprovingly as he turned and signalled for his men to leave.

'Every man deserves a drink or two,' the old beggar called after them as he watched the men leaving in search of their quarry. Not until the sound of footsteps had long faded did he try to pull himself up off the floor. No one seemed to have noticed him lying there once the soldiers had left, except for a young lad sitting at a table with a group of sailors. His eyes met with Henri's but he quickly averted his gaze when Henri saw him watching, and the youngster went back to listening to the conversation around the table. Henri supposed he was probably a cabin boy on board *The Arinosta*.

For the moment, Henri Dubois was safe. Manoeuvring himself rather clumsily on his one leg, he settled on the chair, clasped the jug of ale, lifted it to his mouth and gulped the flat, bitter draught. He swilled it around his mouth and then, lifting it to his lips once more, he downed the remaining liquid in one gulp.

He waited a good half hour or so before rising from his seat and limping to the door. He only had a few hundred yards to go and had plenty of time to get where he was going. The ship had still well over an hour to wait for the high tide before sailing. He had bought his passage earlier, but he knew that the soldiers would have interrogated the crew. They would already know that the man they were looking for had booked passage, and if they hadn't found him already then they would not leave until after the ship had sailed. They would be watching the vessel, waiting for their quarry to try and get onto it. Only when it had sailed would the search party continue their hunt elsewhere.

As Henri shuffled through the door and onto the wooden walkway, he looked from side to side. Just as he had suspected, a small compliment of soldiers were stationed next to the gang plank of the ship. Nobody could get on board without being seen. But the rest of the search party had disappeared into the town. In the distance, he could still hear the screams of women and the harsh, raised, complaining voices as soldiers burst into bedrooms and disturbed the occupants. Henri turned and slowly made his way back along the quayside away from the bar and the ship. The shouting was fading, getting further away as he hobbled slowly and with no seemingly determined purpose to the far end of the dock. It was dark there. As he approached the old wharf, he could see no one in the shadows and he knew that once there himself, nobody would be able to see him either. It was the old end of the dock with a rickety old jetty where a rotting fishing boat and few rowing boats were moored.

Eventually, now feeling safer, he leaned against a stack of fishing nets and relaxed. Still, he kept a sharp watch out for any other person nearby, for often the dark shadows hid other people who wanted to escape from the light. He waited and listened for a long time before breathing a sigh of relief. When he was sure he was alone, he leaned the crutch up against the nets and, balancing on his one leg, took off his heavy coat and let it drop to the ground. Carefully he pulled at the end of some twine that was wrapped around his waist. It gave and the knot released. Slowly he began to untie the bonds that were strapped around his left upper thigh, careful not to release them too quickly. His knee and foot were throbbing and he knew he was going to suffer pain as the blood flowed back into his leg. Gradually, as the strings released, he let his bound leg drop to the floor. It felt dead and heavy and at first he wondered if he had left it bound up behind his thigh too long. He placed it on the ground but could feel nothing. It would take no weight. Clinging to the nets with both hands, he tried stamping his left foot on the ground. Still there was no feeling, only a dull ache in his knee. He turned and leaned against the nets again and then lifted the leg up with his hands and rubbed it vigourously, trying to get some circulation and feeling back into it. When he let go it flopped uselessly, his foot hitting the ground with a dull thud. It was then that he felt the pain. Something was happening. The leg was getting back feeling; but it was a feeling of sheer pain and agony. He felt like crying out but stifled it to a sharp gasp. Now he could feel his foot on the ground and, leaving go of the nets, he stood upright. But the leg regained none of its ability to sustain weight. He stumbled against the nets, grabbing at them to remain upright. More pain shot through his leg and up through his hip as the prickly, pins-and-needles feeling of blood circulation began to slowly replace the pain.

A good half hour passed while he regained his ability to

walk on two legs, during which time he pealed off a thin skin that pulled his eyelid out of shape. As a boy he had seen actors using the white of a seagull egg to alter their facial expressions, holding the skin taut as the albumin set. When dried, it held his eyelid down at one corner. Then he had rubbed sand and dust into his hair with the more of the egg white to leave his mop of black hair looking thick, greasy and dirty. The remainder of the cosmetic he used to dirty and darken his features, once again, rubbing dirt into his face and unshaven whiskers. At the moment he could do nothing more about the dirt and grime. As for his teeth which he had blackened with soot from the fireplace in the inn, they would soon clean themselves, for soot is an excellent cleaning agent for teeth, leaving them white once the soot is spat out or swallowed.

Henri carried an old hunter watch in the pocket of his trousers but he could see nothing in the darkness. He reckoned that he still had thirty minutes to make it to the ship. With his left leg still tingling, he was about to gather up his coat and make his way down the slippery green steps that led to the water's edge when, suddenly, voices approached. Carefully, he looked around the nets and out of the dark shadow, and by the light of the moon, he could make out three men coming down to the dockside, none carrying lanterns. A sudden panic welled up in Henri's chest. These men were not soldiers. The soldiers had been carrying lights, as do most of the people who walk the streets in the darkness of the night, for few people knew their way about in the dark and shadowy streets and alleys once nightfall had engulfed the town. These men were not such people, ordinary citizens going about their business. He had come across such men before. Or rather, they had come across

Henri for it was from such men that he had sustained a knife wound to his arm three months ago. He had just arrived in the town and they had tried to rob him. There had been four of them. But the robbers had underestimated the stranger. He was young and he was strong. As the man's knife had thrust at him, he had parried the blow with his arm and, grabbing the man's wrist, he had managed to twist the dagger back on his attacker. As the other three hesitated seeing their companion bleeding, Henri had run for his life.

The air was becoming chilled, but Henri dared not pick up his coat. For what seemed like forever, he watched and waited as the men prowled the dockside, chatting and laughing, looking for nothing in particular, but moving on only slowly.

Henri cursed under his breath. He couldn't stay in the country any longer, but neither could he risk confrontation with these men. Already there were signs of movement along the quayside. *The Arinosta* was getting ready to sail and still the men were wandering about in the shadows. But eventually, after what seemed like a long time to Henri as he stood and waited, the men started moving away at last. But he still waited and watched them for several more precious minutes before daring to slip out of the shadows and step lightly towards the quayside.

He had to move or he would miss the boat. Dragging his heavy great coat behind him, very slowly, he picked it up and pulled it on. He fastened it with a cord around his waist, glancing back constantly as he manoeuvred carefully past hanging nets and stacks of crates, towards the steps that led down to the water's edge. With a sigh of relief he found the small rowing boat still moored under a shabby tarpaulin where he had left it. He pulled back the sheet, climbed into it, checked that his own canvas bag of clean clothes was still stowed safely in the bottom, pulled the tie rope to release it, sat down and picked up the oars.

The sound of activity got louder as orders were called, preparing the ship to sail. The order was given to raise the gangplank and more voices broke into the night as the soldiers on watch gave up their vigil and, with no sense of urgency, began to walk back towards the inn.

Henri kept the boat close into the sea wall. Slowly and silently he rowed towards *The Arinosta*. But he feared he might have left his escape too late. A bell sounded, a final command was given and the crew began to rig the sails. The brig would begin to move any time now. He knew he had but a few more remaining minutes to get on board the ship. Desperate and determined to leave the port for ever, he began to row in earnest. He pulled and pulled again as his oars began to splash and make a noise, but the sound of activity on *The Arinosta* was now deadening any sound he made.

To get alongside the ship, he had to move away from the wall of the dock to row into clear water where the moon was trying its best to light up the sea like a new morning sun. Cursing the fine weather, he headed straight for the bow of the ship. *The Arinosta* was beginning to sway with the movement of the wind in its sails. Soon the anchor would be hauled in, the mooring ropes would be unlashed and his chance to escape would disappear with that wind. As the mooring ropes were being detached, he realized that he was still a hundred yards or more from the vessel. He rowed as fast as he could, pulling on each stroke with all the strength in his body. Despite the chill in the air, his back began to prickle with sweat. His arms began to ache with the sheer effort of getting to the ship, now without any regard to being seen. Twenty yards to go and the anchor was being weighed in. He was so close now that he could see every glistening link.

Then an outcry barked from the dockside. A soldier had seen his little rowboat and was calling for the ship to haul to and re-dock. But the captain was watching over the side. He too had seen Henri rowing towards the ship. And he too had no love or respect for the mercenaries of Abraham Drach. While in dock he would let them search his ship and pilfer apples from the stores, but now he was in command once again. The ship was twenty feet from the dockside and moving away slowly. Twenty five feet. The calls from the soldiers were now raising the alarm. Alerted by the calls, more soldiers were running down to join them. 'Haul to!' a voice demanded, but the captain shrugged and lifted his hands in a gesture of impotence against the strength of the wind now carrying the brig, yard by yard, on its way out to sea.

A shot rang out in the air. A musket ball passed over Henri's left shoulder. Another sank into the side of his rowing boat. Yet more shots were fired and desperately Henri pulled at his oars with the last of his strength. His arms burned with fatigue. Sweat poured down his face, streaking through the dirt he had rubbed on it to age his features. He had missed the chance to sail with *The Arinosta*.

More shots rang past his head as the ship moved towards him. And then the bow of the ship hit his rowing boat at an angle and, almost upending it, threw it to one side. In his effort to keep the boat upright, Henri let go of the oars and grabbed the sides of the boat with both hands. The sway of the little boat almost tossed him overboard. The oars disappeared into the dark water as the ship somehow drew the little boat around the bow. The boat was being washed along the starboard side. The Anchor was lifting out of the water only feet away from Henri's head. Now, out of sight of the soldiers and out of reach of their shot, he had but one chance. Desperately he stood up in the rocking boat and, placing one foot on the side, he pushed and jumped at the point of the anchor. The boat gave, rocking sideways beneath the pressure of his feet. His effort seemed to have little effect on his attempt to propel himself upward as the boat dipped down. When the tips of his fingers grabbed at the anchor, it was wet and slippery. No amount of strength would have enabled him to grab a hold of it. Helplessly, he realized he was falling into the black water. He hit it, landing on his side as the boat disappeared from beneath his feet.

Now he found himself caught in the wash of the ship; he was being carried alongside it like a cork, as *The Arinosta*'s weight and speed gained momentum. The heavy great coat began to weigh Henri down as it soaked in the water. Should he discard it? He knew it would kill him to keep it around his body. But then he knew that if he survived he would be caught by Drach's men and his fate was sealed in that direction.

And what about his possessions? The few he had were deep within the inside pockets of that coat and his remaining gold was sewn into the lining. His bag of clothes had already disappeared to the black murky depths of the dock with the rowing boat.

He began to sink. Kicking wildly with his feet, and gulping at the air as he went under the water, he managed to get his head above the surface. But his head cracked against the ship's bow as the thrust of the rushing bore dragged him under once again. In the black murky depths all he could see was a glistening ball that had been the moon, ripped to pieces by the rushing foam way above his head, and a solid, shadowy hull glancing past his shoulder. He swallowed water as he struggled to stay conscious. Frantically he pulled at the chord around his waist, desperate to free himself from his coat but something was caught against his hand and was pulling his arm away from his body and the string. The other hand alone could not loosen it. Struggling and kicking, and not knowing how, he rose once more to the surface. He took another gulp of air, knowing it would be his last one, for he knew he would not have the strength left to kick himself and the weight of his clothes back from the deep watery grave that awaited him.

But the thing that had tangled about his arm seemed to be pulling him now. Grasping at it, suddenly he found his head free of the water. His arm was outstretched above him. A dragging rope had somehow washed up against him and had wrapped around his wrist. No longer was he being washed alongside the ship, he was being carried along with it, the tension of the rope was lifting his shoulders out of the spume as the ship gained speed. As the angle of the rope increased he was lifted higher again. His legs were now skipping over the foam. He looked up at the side of the ship and could see the rigging towering above, but there was nobody that he could see on the deck. He had only himself and his own determination to help and save him. For a short while he just clung to the rope. The sheer exertion of rowing and then jumping and then half drowning had taken all his energy. He was safe for a while, dangling there. He could tell the ship was turning now, heading straight out to sea. He looked back along the ship towards the stern, and slowly the dockside and its occupants came into sight, now too far away to be able to see him or shoot at him. Their lanterns flickered in the darkness as they gathered at the water's edge looking for the body of the man who they were sure they had killed. Henri watched, for what seemed like ages, as the flickering lights and the land slowly but surely receded into the darkness of the night.

Henri didn't know how long he had clung to the rope. If it hadn't been wrapped around his wrist he would never have had the strength to hold onto it, but as it was, and with the sheer and utter feeling of relief of having escaped from Yemara, and watching the moonlight glinting like stardust on the rolling waves, he felt he could have clung there forever, skimming over the surface of the water as the ship ploughed on into the darkness and out into the open sea. Eventually, though, his strength returned. Slowly at first, he began to bend his arm and pull himself upwards. With his free hand he grabbed the rope a little higher and with that he pulled himself completely clear of the water. Now, still leaving the rope wrapped around the wrist of his right hand, he let go with his left hand and reached a little higher. Inch by inch, and dragging his heavy drenched coat, he hauled himself upwards, stopping every few feet to regain his strength.

Eventually he came to the top of the rope where it hung through the base of the rail that edged the wooden deck. The gap beneath the rail was too small to pull himself through. With the rope still firmly wrapped around his right wrist, he gripped it with the same hand, and then with his left hand he grasped at the loose rope below his arm and wrapped that part of the rope around his wrist once more to ensure he could not fall. He rested there for some considerable time, breathing in the cool night air and contemplating his next move. Somehow he had to get over the rail and when his strength had returned a little, once more he hauled himself upwards. Slowly, he managed to get his fingers onto one of the rail posts. Now he loosened the rope that had secured him and, gripping it in his right fist, he grabbed the post with his left hand and, with all his strength, pulled himself up to the top rail. As he tried to get his arm over it, he kicked with his legs, trying to get his feet onto the ridge beneath the rail. But with the weight of his clothes, and now having lost all his strength, he dangled helplessly from the side of the ship as, slowly, his arm began to slide back off the rail. With panic coursing through his whole body, he heaved again but his efforts seemed futile now. At some point he knew he would have to give up his struggle. His will to survive had pushed him so far, but he could do no more. He looked down, wondering if he could dangle there high above the water until his strength returned. He let his arm relax and began to slide down the outside of the rail when, suddenly, from out of the dark night air, a pale, thin hand brushed past his face and grabbed the collar of his coat. He kicked frantically again as another hand heaved at his sleeve, and with his last grains of energy, he pulled at the rail one last time as he was hauled over it onto the deck.

Spent of all his energy, he lay there face down on his belly for a long minute before turning onto his back to see who it was that had helped him. But the hands that had come to his aid had disappeared, and with them, their owner. He found himself completely alone and exhausted on the hard wooden deck. For what seemed like hours, but was only a matter of minutes he lay there gazing up into the star studded sky, relief washing through his cold bones. But the night air was warmer than the sea and, pulling off the rope from around his arm, and closing his eyes to rest, he soon began to dry off and regain some of his body heat.

Chapter Two

THE ARINOSTA

The kind of ship on which Henri had embarked, afforded little comfort for passengers. They were designed as cargo ships but had a small hold rigged out with rudimentary sleeping accommodation for all but the richest of passengers who would be afforded better accommodation in the way of a cabin on the upper deck. Henri was not such a passenger. He had booked his passage second class despite the fact that he had enough money to pay for better accommodation. He had travelled on ships many times and knew that the safest place for anyone was not in the cabins that were rigged for carrying the wealthy, for ships were not safe places. There were lots of scoundrels in the world, and many travelled on ships either as passengers or as part of the crew. They wore no signs telling who they were. There was little chance of escape if anyone was looking for you. Everyone watched everyone. And Henri knew he had to remain unnoticed for these ships rarely landed with the same complement of passengers as when they left port.

Although he had never travelled on this ship, he had travelled on many others, so Henri had a pretty good idea where the passenger hold was located. He knew very well that Cargo sailing ships were designed to carry freight not passengers and, in his experience, there was little effort to adapt them for passengers. Apart from bringing on provisions - flour, potatoes, oatmeal, bland biscuits, some salted fish, some dried meat and water - a captain merely would lay down a temporary deck over the cargo and construct narrow, flimsy berths that could be dismantled after the voyage. This steerage accommodation between the upper deck and the cargo hold would be a passenger's home for the duration of the voyage, and Henry hated it. In fact he hated everything about the sea. On some voyages, passengers had been packed so tightly, that they had had no more than a few square feet of space per person, and with little or no toilet facilities or windows, sanitation and ventilation were always serious problems. Conditions varied among vessels, of course, but nearly all passengers on cargo sailing ships, regardless of class, had to suffer overcrowding and disorder, seasickness, a foul atmosphere, and poor food. He wasn't looking forward to the journey.

For the time being at least, Henri was happy to prop himself between the rail and the capstan and sleep in the cool night air. There seemed little activity on deck and the ship was at full sail, in the dead of night, heading towards a distant, dark horizon.

There would be plenty of time to find his place in the hold, but he was careful not to be seen by any of the crew. He wanted to make the best of the time he had before descending into the crowded quarters. And besides, Henri knew that the captain would not have seen his name on the list of those passengers who had boarded the ship. Indeed, the captain had seen the soldiers firing guns at one of the men who presumably had booked a passage on this voyage, and he hadn't seen him board. Henri decided it would be best to announce his presence in the morning. In the meantime, now totally exhausted by his flight from the soldiers and his struggle up the side of the ship in his heavy clothes, Henri curled up against the coil of thick hemp rope that bound the capstan and, drawing his great coat around him, fell into a dreamless sleep.

'Passengers aren't allowed on deck at night,' a voice broke into Henri's deep slumber.

He opened one eye and, in the grey light of dawn, looked up into the face of the cabin boy dressed in a dark blue twill jacket and sail canvas pants.

'Better get down below before anybody sees you,' the lad stated matter of factly. He offered Henri his hand. Henri looked at it. It was small and white with long fingers with unusually clean nails for a sailor. It looked familiar, but the cabin boy looked far too puny to have been the one to haul him over the side rail. He showed no sign of recognition, as Henri looked into the boy's eyes, so, presuming he was mistaken, Henri extended his arm and took hold of the slender wrist, pulling himself up as the cabin boy braced himself for support by grabbing onto the side rail. He nodded his acknowledgement without a word.

'I'm Jack,' the cabin boy said before they released each other's hands.

'Henri,' said Henri, stretching his back as he released the hand and turned to walk along the deck.

'This way,' Jack instructed, leading Henri along the rail and towards the stern of the ship. 'Better get down there now,' he said, pointing to an open hatch. 'Good time to find an empty hammock and put your name on it, while everyone else is still asleep,' he explained. 'Just act as if you have been there all night.'

That sounded to Henri as if the boy at least knew he had embarked the unorthodox way, but he didn't push the question. He nodded his thanks and walked over to the hole in the deck. There was a coarse wooden stairway running down from the moonlit deck into the darkness of the hold. As he descended, he steadied himself against the beam that supported the deck and looked back at the thin waif of a cabin boy. Jack had already turned and was walking away.

Henri took his time climbing down onto the passenger deck. As he descended, his body blocked out what little light there was, but once he was on the flat boards of the deck, the light got past him and seemed to brighten as if lighting the way for him.

There were several empty hammocks. Obviously there were fewer passengers than the temporary deck had been designed to take, but it would still seem crowded. He picked a hammock that was as close to the hatch as possible and slumped into it. Already the atmosphere in the hold was stale and the open hatch afforded at least a little fresh air.

He lay and, for what seemed like hours, he watched the brightening sky through the opening. He thought about his escape from Abraham Drach and what had led to his hasty departure. Why had he come to this country in the first place? He wondered now whether it had just been his sense of adventure or whether there was more to it than that.

As the light increased and lit up the gloomy hold, Henri could just make out that the sleeping accommodation consisted of small, makeshift, open fronted cupboards that lined the walls of the hold. In each one hung a hammock except for six or so that he could make out in the dimly lit space that had some roughly made, flat, bench type cots in them. All the wooden beds were taken; the occupants huddled beneath rough canvas blankets. Of the hammocks, all but three were full. He counted, in all, twenty three passengers not including himself. No one seemed to be stirring. On a long, tedious and stressful journey, which this was sure to be, nobody wanted the days to begin and when they did, they wanted each long dragging hour to be over as soon as possible.

In the centre of the floor there were four heavy, wooden tables with a similarly heavy bench at each side, and over to the far side of the hold there was a flight of six roughly hewn oak steps that led to a boxed out section that no doubt served as the only sanitary accommodation for the passengers. Later he would explore the steerage deck and the toilet facilities, but he knew that now the accommodation, dank as it was, was as good as it would get. From hence on, the hold would become staler and smellier; and the lavatory would make up a great part of the stench that would ultimately fill the whole deck.

When Henri had booked his passage, it had been explained that passengers were rarely allowed on the upper deck. Passengers were a source of extra income, but in return for their fares, they got transport only. There would be little sightseeing on this journey.

As time passed, he eventually saw the other passengers stirring. Some looked better dressed than others; and of the others, Henri's attire was by far the shabbiest. The great coat was clean, especially after being pounded by the bore of the water rushing past the ship's hull, but the rest of his good clothes had been lost with the rowing boat. In the midst of his determined flight from the authorities, he had exchanged some of his good clothes with those of a willing tramp. But his appearance had improved a little with his dunking and his trip through the frothing waters of the ship's bow. He no longer had as much dirt in his hair or on his face. But the salt water had not washed him entirely clean. His hair still felt matted and the stubbly growth on the point of his chin was already beginning to lengthen into a wispy beard. There would be no washing facilities for passengers on this trip and Henri was content to think that, unlike the other passengers, his appearance was never going to get much worse. At the present, however, his dress code was going to work to his advantage. He didn't want to mix with the other passengers and, given his unkempt appearance, he thought that it would be unlikely that any of them would be inclined to socialize with him. But that wasn't the case.

As he considered the sanitary conditions, a whistle blew and slowly everybody moved towards the tables. Each passenger sat on one of the fixed benches and waited. Henri followed suit, for he had been absent when the captain or his bosun had explained the finer working of the cruise timetable. Obviously the whistle was the precursor to food being served, though "being served" was somewhat of an exaggeration, Henri was to discover as he sat at the table nearest to his hammock at the aft section of the deck.

Five minutes or so after the sound of the whistle, a hatch opened towards the front of the ship. For the first time, Henri saw in detail the far end of the deck which had hitherto been masked in darkness. Now, with the daylight from the open hatch he could see plainly the wooden steps leading to the upper deck. He sat at the table watching as a sailor who was wearing a yellow and white striped vest descended from the fore hatch to the floor level. In his hands he held in front of him a large enamelled bowl with a lid that rattled uneasily with each step he took down the stairs. The man was clean shaven and had long sideburns that ended at the angle of his jaw. On his head he wore a head scarf that was tied behind the nape of his neck. His dark eyes looked around and, with a face with less emotion on it than the lavatory door, he placed the tureen on the nearest of the tables and departed. Henri wondered if he was going to fetch anything with which the contents could be eaten, but soon he realized that each and every passenger had their own bowl and a knife and spoon with which to partake of the food. He watched as the nearest passenger to the tureen, an elderly, silver haired man who was perhaps the best dressed of all the passengers in his frilly shirt, a grey coat and clean looking grey wool trousers and, who Henri was to discover later, went by the name of Garside, took up the ladle from the bowl and dished out his own portion before handing the ladle to the next person on his table. Patiently, everyone waited their turn until the tureen was passed to them, and each in turn took food for themselves, and then passed on the container to the next person to them or to the one nearest on the next table.

Henri had no idea what he was going to do, for he had no spoon, nor had he anything from which to eat his share. However, the problem was not to resolve itself immediately as, when the tureen eventually got to the last table, the one at which Henri sat with only two other people, they found that the tureen was completely empty. Henri looked at the man seated opposite him, but he simply looked away. The other man at the table turned to Henri and said, 'Are you going or shall I?'

Since Henri had little idea what the procedure was in the case of a shortage of food, he nodded and pushed himself up from the table. He was about to find out. It was something to do and would at least break up a small part of the long day. He picked up the tureen and walked towards the still open hatch at the fore end of the deck. As he walked up the stairs and emerged on the upper deck, to his surprise, he noticed that there were few of the crew in sight. One man was at the base of the main mast, checking ropes and another was up on the yard arm, sitting astride it, doing something with part of a the sail that appeared to have snagged. He gave out a little sigh and proceeded to walk the length of the deck. He passed what he recognised as the rear hatch above his birth, the one through which he had entered the steerage. Beyond that there was another opening in the deck. He walked over to it and straight away he knew it led to the galley. The smell was unmistakable. The smell of warm and cooked food was not all it should have been to any ordinary person. It was a greasy, old-fat smell; it was the smell of cooking facilities that were either not clean, or where the cook or chef or whatever qualification he held, was using old and rancid fat. Or both.

Henri gritted his teeth. This voyage was going to be worse than he had expected. He descended into the galley and as his head cleared the beam that was the joist beneath the floor of the upper deck, he spotted the sailor's head scarf. The man had his back to Henri, bending over an old wooden and much worn hollowed-out trough.

'Hello,' Henri said in as confident a voice as he could.

He waited until the cook turned to see who had entered his domain.

'What do you want?' the man asked, seemingly annoyed at having his territory invaded.

'More food,' replied Henri, looking around at the utensils and knives hanging from the beam by the cook's head.

'None of that left. That was all I made.' The cook shrugged and carried on chopping up some salted fish.

'Got anything else for the three of us that didn't get any?' Henri asked disarmingly.

The cook sighed, rubbed his damp hands down the side of his canvas pants, wiped the end of his nose with the back of his hand and turned to a crate in the corner. Lifting the lid he pulled out three strips of leathery looking meat and handed them to Henri. 'That's all I've got till t'night,' he said, and returned to his bench without a further glance in Henri's direction.

'That'll do fine,' said Henri. He wasn't going to argue. He knew that the food would get worse as the voyage progressed, and making an enemy of the ship's cook was not on his list of do's-for-the-day. Without another word, he turned to go, but then he remembered something. 'Oh, by the way, where do I get a bowl and spoon?'

'Won't need them for that.' The cook chuckled as he nodded at the tough-looking meat in Henri's hand, but on seeing that Henri was not laughing, he grunted and bent down to reach under his worktop. He stood up and handed Henri a wooden bowl and a steel spoon and knife. 'You're the one that nearly missed your ride I suppose?' he stated rather than asked.

Henri nodded, surprised that anyone knew who he was or that he had made it onto the ship.

'Your friend told me,' said the cook, and turned back to his work.

'Friend?' said Henri, curious, but the cook was not anxious to strike up much of a conversation. He grunted again and just carried on as if Henri had already left.

Without another word, Henri returned to the passenger deck. All the passengers had finished their food by this time. The two people who had been at his table were now seated at other tables, chatting to the other passengers as if they had been old friends. They looked up at him furtively and the conversation seemed to dwindle away as he walked over and handed each of them a strip of the dried meat. Without a word, he went by and sat at the empty table, sure that the topic of conversation had been Henri himself. Slowly, what seemed like a fresh topic seemed to break into somebody's mind and once again, a low babble of interacting voices filled the gloomy space.

Though quite dull, the light from the two open hatches still lit the whole of the passenger deck enough to be able to see most of it, and, chewing on the tough meal, he began to take in every detail of the place that would be his and every other passenger's home for the next four weeks or so. In the corner by the side of the fore hatch from where the cook had emerged, was a barrel of fresh water and several ladles hanging by strings from a series of nails in the oak beam above. He knew from his previous journeys on boats that fresh water was only for drinking. There were no washing facilities for passengers on these sail ships. The latrine in the corner near to the rear hatch was still fresh from being washed down with chloride of lime, but that would soon begin to add rich texture to the atmosphere as it began to be used regularly by each and every person in the steerage section of the ship. The whole deck was plain and simply constructed. No unnecessary luxuries were added.

Henri hadn't been seated long when one of the men who had been at his table pushed himself up from his bench and meandered over in Henri's direction.

'John Blackwell's the name,' he stated as he introduced himself. He held out a thick fingered hand which Henri took a hold of and gave it a cursory shake.

'Cursed way to travel,' he said, placing his huge hands on the table and easing himself down onto the bench beside Henri. 'If only I'd been able to afford to travel on a proper passenger ship,' he added with a deep sigh.

'Moi aussi,' said Henri despondently and then in English, 'Me too.'

'You have no baggage, I see,' Blackwell said curiously, nodding in the direction of the hammock where Henri had slept. 'I have a couple of bags of clothes and my only few possessions over by my bunk.' He pointed to one of the few wooden framed beds. 'Have you got no spare clothes?'

Henri was on his guard. Not only did he know he looked like he needed a change of clothes, but he was sure that all the passengers would have known that he was the person at the centre of the commotion that took place during the night. The steerage section of the ship was too small a place for gossip to go untold. He wondered if any of the passengers had been watching from the upper deck. Possibly some had, but he wasn't sure whose hand had helped pull him over the rail and onto the deck. More than likely it was one of the crew. Perhaps it was the cabin boy, but he was such a wisp of a lad and the hand that pulled at his collar seemed to wield much more strength than he imagined the cabin boy possessed. One thing for sure, the hand wasn't that of Blackwell. This man's hands looked thick and heavy; hands that had done a lifetime's hard labour.

Henri shook his head. 'Only had enough money to pay for my passage home,' he stated blandly, trying to put the man off asking any more questions. Not wanting to be rude, he turned his head away in an attempt to avoid any more conversation.

'Oh, I managed to make a little money,' Blackwell said proudly. 'Not a lot, but enough to see me set up when I get back to England.'

'Good for you,' said Henri. He patted the man on his shoulder. It was the first time he had taken a good look at this new "friend". Blackwell had been clean shaven before the voyage began. Now he had a dark bristly shadow around his square jaw. His dark brown eyes looked black in the dim light. He smiled proudly, displaying well kept teeth.

But there was something unsettling about the man that made Henri reluctant to tell him anything about himself and how he came to be here. He hadn't planned on boarding the ship dressed in the tramp's shabby clothes, but at the moment, it seemed like a good idea to maintain the illusion. He placed his arms on the table and rested his head on them. 'I don't travel well,' he lied in a sickly voice and pretended to concentrate on keeping his meagre meal down.

'You'll get used to it.' Blackwell stated with the confidence of a seasoned traveller.

Henri heard him rise from the table and walk away. It wasn't long before he heard him talking to more passengers, asking the same questions and giving out the same information that he had imparted to Henri. For a man who gives the appearance of having travelled a lot, thought Henri, he certainly knew nothing about being careful about talking to strangers.

And so, for the next few days, Henri dozed at the table with his head on his arms. Only at meal times did he raise his head. If Blackwell or anybody else looked in his direction, he would nod an acknowledgement only if the man threw him a cursory wave or nodded a greeting at him. At first Blackwell persisted in coming over to Henri and trying to throw up some kind of conversation. Throughout the day he would return to the table and sit next to Henri, making reassuring phrases about how sea travel got easier as the days passed. But getting little or no response from Henri day after day, he began to lose interest and spent more and more time with any of the passengers who wanted to talk to him.

By the fifth day, most of the passengers had settled into small groups, possibly with something in common, but most just desperate to pass the time. Some played cards, some played dice, but few seemed to have the money to gamble. They were friendly games on the whole but Henri never joined in. If invited to join he would stand up, shaking his head, and stagger away into a corner with another attack of sea-sickness. Nobody persisted. Nobody wanted to be near him when he threw up. Few people, it seemed, were interested in him.

But somebody was curious.

Chapter Three

THE STORM

At night, Henri would lie awake, listening to the sound of people snoring and the sound of the sea washing against the hull of the ship and the wind whispering in the sails. The sixth night of the voyage was particularly dark. The hatch above his berth was still open, but the sky was thick and heavy with cloud and no light from stars or the moon penetrated the gloom of the hold. The sea was getting choppy and the wind was whistling over the upper deck. The ship was rolling and shouts from the crew could be heard up above as they rigged the sails for a storm.

Henri heard nothing down in the hold that could have alerted him. As he lay with his great coat wrapped tightly around him to keep out the damp, cold night air, the first thing he felt was a hand brushing against his shoulder; feeling, sensing where he was. Henri almost cried out, but something made him suppress his surprise. The hand stayed, hovering close to his face, waiting to see if the touch had awakened him; but something alerted him to a sinister danger. Forcing himself to breathe normally, Henri gave out a slight grunt, and pretended to snore, as he lay on his back, motionless in the hammock. He kept his head still, but his eyes were wide, searching the blackness for the intruder. Slowly, the hand began to lift sections of his great coat, gently feeling the fabric for the presence of anything inside the pockets. Henri snored a little louder. A cold blade of steel pressed against his throat as two hands began to search for his possessions. Henri's right hand was by his side, clenching a small, percussion cap pocket derringer pistol. His left hand was across his stomach, its fist tightly clenched around a piece of gold, an object he little understood.

There were two men there in the darkness, two thieves and for each Henri had a .27 lead ball in each barrel of his tiny pistol. But the knife was up against his throat and he was not sure how many more of these scoundrels were standing next to him in the darkness. He stayed his hand and let the search continue. After all, if they were going to kill him they would have done it by now. Careful not to stir, he maintained the rhythm of his breathing and eventually the search came to an end with nothing taken. The knife slipped away from his throat, and the surrounding blackness of the night continued with only the sound of the rising seas and the increasing wind.

He lay there motionless for what seemed hours, straining his ears to pick up any movement within the hold. But he heard nothing except, much later, the voices of men up on deck, shouting and receiving orders as they trimmed the sails and did whatever else they had to do when the ship headed into a storm. As the wind increased, the shouting got louder, and as the wind turned into a gale, the ship rolled from side to side and dipped from bow to stern. To Henri, it seemed as if a giant hand was lifting the vessel in the air and then letting it go, dropping it until, what seemed like ages later, another hand caught it and lifted it high again. Water began to spill down the steps from the upper deck, as the wind swept waves washed over the sides of the ship. Suddenly, with a startling thud, the hatch above was banged closed and the sound of hands working on lashing the ropes tight came faintly to his ears as the shutters were battened down, tightly sealed against the storm.

He pulled at the canvas sheet that had been draped over his legs and dragged it up over his shoulders. The air was beginning to chill him to the bone. He knew he would get little sleep this night, but clenching his small pistol in his right hand and the other most valuable possession, a golden cube, in the other, he closed his eyes and listened with strained ears as the storm rose and the ship rolled and tossed in the heavy seas.

Henri hadn't slept. It had been a long, long night, and it was hard to tell when morning actually arrived in the sealed hold in the centre of this vast cargo ship, but some people, sensing the night had passed, had stumbled about in the darkness looking for the door to the latrine. Some might have found it, slopping about ankle deep in water, and others probably didn't bother. The water about their feet stank anyway, much of it probably having made its way to the floor of the steerage section of the ship through the opening in the lavatory itself. Although, the passenger deck was so far down in the ship that there was always some leakage through the planking, the flooding most certainly was coming from an opening left somewhere unsecured. Somebody had left the door of the latrine unfastened and it slapped backwards and forwards with the movement of the ship, shedding only the thinnest sliver of grey light as it banged open against the wooden beam and then sinking the hold back into complete darkness as it slammed hard against its jamb. The latrine had been constructed in a makeshift cabin higher than the level of the deck floor so that a small porthole could be left un-shuttered. A bench no wider than the width of two men had been nailed across the small cabin, lower than the porthole and with a board nailed askew from the base of the bench sloping down to a long trough which captured the effluent, the contents of which had to be periodically shovelled out through the porthole. No one had thought to close the porthole, or at least nobody had ventured into the latrine to notice the hole was left open. The door slammed open and closed with every roll if the ship. Each time it swung open, a dim grey light revealed that the sea water that had already slopped its way through the porthole and in and out of the trough, was washing down the steps of the latrine like water in a rocky river.

He just closed his eyes and wished the storm to pass. For the first time on the voyage, he really didn't feel particularly well, unlike earlier in the trip when he had pretended to suffer from motion sickness simply to avoid being drawn into conversation with the other passengers. He knew before that night what sort of rogues travelled on these ships. He knew that if he had told anyone about his treasure, it was more than likely that he would be relieved of its burden before the voyage ended. But he hadn't expected the search last night. It was early in the voyage and most people were robbed only days or hours before a ship sailed into port, giving the victim or the crew little time to make any proper investigation before the passengers disembarked. Now, probably as a result of the events that had passed, as much as the motion of the vessel itself, his stomach churned and his head ached. He felt not the least inclination to rise from his hammock. The water could run into the hold as much as it wanted for all he cared. Someone else could close the porthole.

No sooner had the thought passed through his mind than, as if spirited up by his thoughts, one of the passengers came slopping through the water towards him. Not until he passed close to Henri's hammock could Henri make out that it was none other than Blackwell. But the man wasn't looking at Henri as he normally did, seeking conversation. This time he kept his gaze straight ahead and sploshed past, heading to the latrine. Seeming totally unaffected by the storm, it was Blackwell that ventured to close the wooden porthole, sinking the hold back into total darkness once again. Henri heard him returning to his bunk, splashing past him confidently in the blackness of the hold. It was a good thing that he could find his way about in the dark, Henri thought. Even above the sound of the seas and the churning of the stinking bilge, he heard Blackwell grunt as he settled back onto his makeshift bunk.

With the hatches battened down and the porthole closed the air in the hold would get staler. But Henri, somehow, felt a little safer. He pulled the canvas over his head, closed his eyes and, for the first time in endless hours, he managed to doze off into a troubled and fitful sleep.

When he next opened his eyes he was chilled through to his bones. The ship was still rolling on a wind-riven sea but it was hard to tell if the heavy rain had passed. The deck was still cloaked in darkness. Nobody had disturbed him and he doubted if anybody else had stirred much. With his pocket watch in his boot and no light by which to see it anyway, he had no idea whether it was night or day. Apart from the sound of rats squeaking to each other and scurrying about on the beams, there was little sound other than the creaking movement of the ship. There were a few people murmuring at the far end of the deck and voices could be heard on the upper deck as sailors, shouting above the noise of the storm, went about their job of keeping the ship steady and afloat. But he doubted if the cook had ventured down into this part of the ship. During a storm, access to the main deck was impossible as hatches were fastened down tightly. It was a time when all hands were on deck. Every able bodied seaman had to do his bit. The passengers reverted to being just another load of cargo. But he wasn't concerned about food. He could not have eaten any if it had been offered. But the cook was like a chiming church bell. You could set your watch by him. Every day, at the same time, he would appear in the late morning with the bare sustenance for the passengers, and the same thing again would happen exactly eight hours later; he would arrive with the second and final meal of the day, albeit oatmeal and water or just salted fish. But food was food and nobody complained. And of the crew, and although he spoke very little, the cook seemed the only affable person on the upper deck. Apart from the cabin boy that was, and Henri hadn't set eyes on him since his first arrival on board. To the rest of the crew, the passengers were just a paying cargo to whom never a word was spoken.

Since ventilation and light came only from the hatches when they were open, the air was becoming stale. The storm could last for a few days or even a week but the hatches would stay battened down. And worse, lights could not be used during the storm because of the danger of fires. So the lanterns remained secured and unlit and the passengers all remained like prisoners in total darkness, and if anyone wanted food they had to make do with the emergency ration of maggoty biscuits which were stored, to protect them from vermin, in a lidded barrel at the fore end of the deck. Most of the passengers preferred to go hungry.

❖

Chapter Four

THE WARNING

By Henri's calculation, this particular storm lasted more than three days and nights. The mere sight of daylight as the hatches were opened seemed to cheer everyone's heart, and, at that precise moment, the whiff of fresh sea air was better than the smell of his mother's home baked bread.

The rear hatch was the first to be opened and as two sailors came down into the hold the first one waved his hand in front of his face as if the smell was overpowering him. Henri felt sure it could possibly do that. The passengers had been cooped up with little ventilation for days and the air was toxic. The smell of the bilge water that had washed in through the lavatory had been sheered up and enhanced by vomit and effluent from the passengers. No one was feeling well.

The second sailor, a thin gangly man with a salt worn face and wearing a string tie to hold back his long greasy hair, stopped on the steps behind the first, bowed his head to look under the beam and stared at Henri before turning his glances to some of the other passengers nearer the hatch.

'You'd all better get up on deck,' the first sailor announced, stopping at the bottom of the stairway. His manner was brusque, his face unshaven for at least the duration of the storm. His dark eyes seemed to be smiling but his lips were compressed into thin lines across his face. 'Jump to it. We don't want you under our feet for long.'

A few passengers murmured curses at him but nothing audible, as they joined in the queue and waded through the water to the stairway. His hammock being nearest to the rear hatch, Henri was the first to follow the sailors back up the steps and emerge into the bright light of day.

It was pleasantly warm out on deck. Henri took deep breaths of the clean, fresh air that tasted as sweet as spring water. He held his face up to the sky and watched a distant skein of geese wing its way to the far-off horizon. Oh to be able to fly like a bird, he thought, but then reflected on the idea no more as a voice spoke behind him.

'They didn't find anything, then?' It was a question.

Henri turned to face the cabin boy. 'What?' He wasn't sure how to respond.

'There's bad folk on this ship,' Jack stated in a voice that had yet to break. 'I know they searched you. Be careful, that's all I can say.'

'Who searched me?' Henri asked, scowling at the lad. 'Who searched me? What do you know?'

Jack's eyes seemed to light up as he spoke again. 'I know more than you,' he said, and then turned to look around. 'Look, I can't be seen talking to you,' he said, turning back to face Henri. 'But somebody knows your secret. Be very careful.'

Then Jack turned and walked away without looking back.

Henri's eyes followed him as he climbed some steps and disappeared into the quarters where the captain lived.

Secret? He thought about Jack's words. *I know more than*

you. He put his hand deep in the pocket of his great coat and clenched the object he had held in his left hand every night since the voyage began. In his right hand he had always held his tiny little, double barrelled pistol. Nobody would take what he had in his left hand without facing death. But who could know? Who could have told anybody on the ship why he was fleeing from Drach's soldiers? Who knew why he had come to the country in the first place?

He looked about him. All the other passengers were filing onto the deck. None seemed very talkative. Some looked at the others suspiciously and several looked at the tramp who had just been talking to the cabin boy. Some of them had probably suffered the same indignity as he, he thought, being searched in total darkness at knife point. Or perhaps it was his imagination. Perhaps it was the sheer relief of getting through the storm alive, for soon the passengers began to chat between themselves, some laughing with relief, some cursing the foul conditions as their fears and torment subsided.

He looked at the sailors. Most of them were looking at the file of smelly passengers as they dispersed about the deck, but some were curiously looking up at the sky, leaning against the rail and pondering their fate as they looked out at the vast expanse of endless water.

The storm had blown itself out completely but the skies were not completely clear. Strangely, from the distant horizon to which they were heading, a purple sheet of cloud stretched with jagged fingers towards *The Arinosta* as if, having failed to sink it with the storm, it were reaching to take the ship and its inhabitants away with it in some other way. A shiver ran down Henri's spine but he couldn't work out why such an unusual phenomenon could affect him in such a way and feel so sinister that it chilled him to the bone. Some of the sailors had noticed the purple sky too and, the others, seeing their comrades distracted, then turned to regard the curious occurrence as well. Then, as Henri gazed at the purple sky, it seemed to suddenly and inexplicably dissipate into thin air leaving the skies clear and blue as, dragged away over the curvature of the earth, its last fingers clawed at the surface of the sea.

There was a very light wind in the huge sails, pushing the ship along at a moderate speed. Now the strange coloured air ahead of them had disappeared, the sky was almost void of clouds except for a few fluffy patches that had appeared astern from nowhere and appeared to be propping up the sky on the horizon from where the ship was sailing. Perhaps that was the rest of the storm that they had left behind and not the strange coloured sky he'd seen ahead of the ship, but whatever the puffy clouds signified, it was good to see them disappearing as *The Arinosta* headed directly away from them.

When Henri next looked around the ship, he saw the captain up on the poop deck above the stern, hands behind his back. Apart from Jack, he was the only member of the crew wearing any kind of uniform. He was dressed in a dark blue naval great coat, open at the front and was wearing a rather soiled frilled shirt that was tucked into his trousers behind a broad, brass-buckled belt that was pulled tight around a thick waist. He, too, looked as if the storm had taken something out of his appearance, for this was the same man Henri had paid for his passage three days before the ship had sailed, and then the captain had been spruce and spotless. From his position the captain could see the entire ship. He could see the sails and he could watch the crew going about their business, although at this particular time, the crew seemed more interested in watching the troubled passengers. The crew too had had a difficult time during the storm, for it was they, at the command of the captain, who had kept the ship safe and afloat.

The captain watched everyone and everything, but finally his gaze fell upon Henri's face. He showed no sign of recognition, nor any of surprise that Henri had made it on board from the little rowing boat that had been run down by the ship. He had obviously been informed of Henri's presence, probably by his cabin boy and so long as the person had paid his fare, then his presence was accepted and his looks, more shabbily dressed than the sprightly young man he had met on shore, seemed to be of little concern to him. He continued to look at Henri, neither giving any sign of a smile nor any other look of acknowledgement until the sound of shouting distracted his gaze.

Two passengers were arguing over something, and three sailors were holding them apart as they cursed at each other. But the spat soon subsided as the cook emerged from the galley with two large baskets of oatmeal bread. Behind him were two of the crew carrying similar goods. The baskets were placed on the deck and everyone was allowed to take what they wanted. Another member of the crew fetched two rope-handled, wooden pails of water and placed them on the deck beside the baskets of food, whilst another sailor fetched a handful of ladles with which the passengers could take the water to drink. Despite the plainness if the food, it was a veritable feast and it lightened the mood of the passengers as they began to talk and laugh and let their anxieties melt away.

One passenger, who had seemed rather better dressed than all the others at the beginning of the voyage, was looking rather worse for wear. His silver-grey hair was dishevelled and his coat was dirty and stained with vomit. The bottoms of his pants were discoloured from wading through the bilge and his fine shoes were now grey, wet and parting at the seams. He ate slowly at first. He too, like Henri seemed not particularly interested in talking to the other passengers. Perhaps he was used to travelling on ships and knew the dangers of fraternization. Or perhaps he was used to travelling in a bit more style. Henri was curious, but was not going to ask to find out.

'All passengers to remain on deck,' the captain shouted his command. He shouted some other instructions to the crew members and immediately they scurried about and some appeared from the cabin section with some wooden device attached to a canvas pipe. They disappeared down into the steerage section of the ship and, amidst shouts of orders and cursing of the stench, the knocking sound of the men pumping the bilge out through the latrine porthole gave an assuring pleasantness to the fine day on deck.

More of the crew emerged carrying wooden buckets which, by swinging them from ropes, filled them with sea water and placed them next to the rails. The passengers could use them for washing, for no fresh water was to be used for hygiene. In stages, all of the passengers stripped off their clothes completely and, using sponges and cloths supplied and, rubbing themselves with the course carbolic soap, managed to clean off much of the stench of confinement of the past few days and nights. Some attempted to wash their clothes, but although the effort succeeded in ridding the clothes of much of the debris, the salt water made the soap fatty and it left the garments little better if not worse looking.

Like the others, Henri took his turn to wash, taking off his clothes and boots and placing his under garments on top of his great coat. He placed them where he could see them at all times. Never did he allow himself to turn away from the pile of attire. The garments and what were in the pockets and lining were the only possessions with which he had come away from Yemara. But he didn't attempt to wash any of his clothes. He had avoided being sick and, although the clothes were rather smelly, they were dry and the contents of his pockets and the lining were safe for now at least. He hadn't boarded the ship with the intention of looking down and out, a man at the end of his fortune, a man returning from the desert mines with less money than when he had arrived. But the disguise he had adopted to escape from Drach had forced his hand, and despite knowing now that there were other people on the ship who knew that he carried something of value, he still didn't want to change his image. He needed as few people as possible to start wanting what he had got, instead of looking after what they had already. And he knew that, despite pretending to be poor, some of the passengers were carrying their fortunes gained from their time spent in Yemara. Not all would be returning penniless, for some would have found what they were looking for and would be returning home by this humble means because passenger ships seldom sailed to mining areas. Food and supplies was the cargo that made ship owners big money. Passengers seldom arrived in style, with lots of money, having decided to go to the gold rush areas to find their fortune, not spend it. And paying for a cabin on a cargo ship was a sure way of telling everyone you had made it.

Henri allowed himself one small concession. After a little fumbling in the pocket of his greatcoat, he took out a small but very sharp pocket knife, opened it up and, using the water from one of the buckets to swill his face, scraped off the growth of his beard that had accumulated over the past week or so. He took his time washing as did all the passengers, but once he had finished, and although the clothes he wore beneath his coat remained shabby, he no longer felt like a tramp.

The sun was rising when the passengers had emerged from their quarters and it was only an hour or so off setting when, after eating their fill of oatmeal bread, the captain ordered them back down into their section of the ship. When they descended into what had been a slopping sewer, they were all surprised and happy to see that the deck had been cleared of the stinking water, and had been swept clean and disinfected with chloride of lime, a chemical that burned the eyes and nostrils, but at least ended the stench for the time being. With the hatches open, the air had cleared and all the passengers settled down for the first good night's sleep that any of them had had in days. Henri was no exception. He too was tired and exhausted by the strife of the confinement during the previous storm days. He watched as many of the passengers gathered around the tables to play a game of cards by the light of a dim lantern that only began to shed any light when the sun had completely disappeared from the sky outside. The twinkling stars had taken its place in the space through which Henri had now got accustomed to gazing every night.

With his hands clenching the same things he had held every night of the voyage, he fell into a deep sleep long before the other passengers left the tables and retired to their beds. It was the best sleep he had had since boarding the ship and when awakened six hours or so later the lantern was still burning and passengers were still playing cards and chatting around the tables. They must have all been feeling the sheer sense of relief of being released from the rat-ridden prison and into the sun of a beautiful day. There was no better time to enjoy their liberation than the present. And many had dozed in the sun as their clothes dried and their first meal in days digested, so it was no surprise to Henri that there was a high degree of merriment that was continuing into the night.

But would it last? Henri doubted that very much.

❖

Chapter Five

THE SACRED SEAL

Captain Bartholomew, despite having been at sea for twenty years, was feeling a sense of relief as well. No doubt he had sailed his vessel through many storms over the years, but for some reason, he seemed particularly relieved when the storm of the last three days and nights had passed. He too seemed to be more jovial than ever before, and if that didn't convince Henri that the captain was feeling in a happy and generous mood, the fact that he suddenly permitted the passengers a limited amount of access to the upper deck during the fine weather made Henri realize that Bartholomew was as eager to get to the final port of destination as the rest of them.

Henri kept himself to himself during the following days, but although he didn't want to mingle with the rest of the passengers or the crew, he did spend some time on the upper deck, mainly early in the morning just as the sun was lifting out of the crimson sea, and when most of the crew and all of the other passengers were still sleeping. He would spend his time leaning on the rail near the bow of the ship, gazing out to see if there was any sign of land in sight. The crew ignored him totally, except for Jack. The wisp of a boy seemed out of place on a merchant ship or any other ship if it came to that. Henri couldn't make out just what it was about Jack, but he had the feeling that the lad had never been much of a sailor and wasn't really considered part of the crew. His meagre duties were to run about at the beck and call of the captain but he wasn't expected to man the yard or do any of the strenuous stuff that sailing a massive ship usually entailed, although he had, on occasion, seen Jack using the sextant.

'They're leaving you alone then?' asked Jack, as he wandered up behind Henri's still figure.

Henri turned to see Jack's pale features. 'You're allowed out!' he exclaimed. 'I thought you weren't allowed to talk to anyone!'

'No,' Jack responded. 'I'm not supposed to talk to you. Otherwise I can talk to whoever I like.'

'Right. So what is the problem with talking to a down and out like me?'

'That's just it, they know who you are.'

Henri thought for a moment and then said: 'They know who I am? So who is they and what is it they think they know?'

Jack smiled impishly. 'The captain knows that you carry the sacred seal.' He looked into Henri's eyes for a sign of recognition or denial.

Henri returned the smile. 'The sacred seal heh?'

Jack nodded.

'And just what is the sacred seal supposed to be?'

Jack shrugged and looked at the floor to avoid Henri's hard gaze.

'I suppose you are going to tell me you have no idea,' said Henri curiously.

'Oh I know what the seal is,' Jack replied confidently as he lifted his eyes back to look at Henri's face. 'The question is, do you?'

'So what is it?'

Jack smirked. 'Wouldn't you like to know? You really have no idea, do you?'

'You talk in riddles young man. I don't even know what you are talking about.' He raised his arms in a gesture of total ignorance. 'I lost everything in my possession when I fell into the sea.'

'Yes, that was rather entertaining,' Jack said with a low chuckle as he recalled what he had seen. 'What surprises me is that nobody came to your rescue. It was as if...'

'Except you. It was your hand that helped me over the rail.'

'Might have been. Might not. But the captain wasn't so busy watching the pandemonium going on at the quayside that he didn't see your little boat.' Jack paused for a long second. 'I'm sure they were seeing if what they had been told about the seal was true,' he went on.

'Well thanks for the hand,' Henri said, leaning back on the rail and turning to look back out to sea.

'They still think you have it. The captain knows why the soldiers were after you. He knows about the seal and now, seeing that you are alive and well, he is likely to believe everything he has been told about it. Drach offered him a substantial reward to recover it, but it is obvious from his reactions when they were calling the ship back to port, that he has different ideas.'

Henri turned to face Jack again. 'What seal? What are you talking about?'

Just then a voice sounded from the stern. It was the captain and even from the distance of the full length of the ship, he was looking particularly flushed.

'Got to go!' Jack said between clenched teeth, and turned away immediately. Before Henri could say another word, the young waif was running back towards the poop deck shouting: 'Coming Captain!'

Henri watched as Jack disappeared past Bartholomew catching a heavy blow on the back of the head from a fat but strong hand. He wondered if Jack would get a beating for talking to him. And anyway, what was the matter with talking to him? The conversation had left Henri with more questions than answers. After thinking for a good quarter of an hour, he pushed himself off the rail and walked towards the hatch.

The rest of the day he spent in his hammock, lying, hands behind his head, thinking. What was the seal? He dropped his left hand down to his pocket and felt the object that was deep inside it. So it was a seal? And a sacred one at that. But that made little sense to Henri.

Henri began to rue the day that he had met Hansenger. All gold rushes carry along a flood of prospectors. Some make a fortune. Most work eighteen hours a day every day in mud and cold and through all the pestilence that follows the search for a fortune for as long as it takes to lose everything they have got. At first he had thought Hansenger was one of the losers, but then the man spoke about his exploits in a land far, far away; a country overgrown by jungle, a country of a lost civilization. He was one of group of men on an expedition that discovered an ancient city by the side of a huge lake. He told Henri how he had found a golden cube glinting in the sunlight on the sandy shore.

But when he met Henri, he was destitute and desperately

short of money. As a last resort and in a desperate effort to return to his own country he traded the cube for enough gold coins to pay for his passage with enough left over to buy a horse and saddle when he arrived at his destination. After that, he promptly disappeared from Henri's life for ever. At first Henri presumed that Hansenger made it to his ship and departed in safety but he was soon to find out that, somehow, a man called Drach had discovered that Hansenger had the golden cube and had been hunting for him. Henri had heard of Drach. He owned whole towns in the gold fields. He had a private army and he had a reputation of being the law wherever he set his stall. Nobody went out of their way to upset him. But Henri discovered that Hansenger had possessed something Drach wanted; the golden cube. And it turned out that Drach was prepared to stop at nothing to get it. How he knew that Henri had traded a pouch of gold for the artefact, Henri never found out, but he soon heard that Drach was hunting for him and the cube. That sort of news travelled fast. Henri had to decide whether he wanted to keep the cube or whether he wanted to hand it over to Drach, but reasoning that the artefact must have had some special value, and having paid handsomely for it, he decided to leave the gold field and head for the coast and home.

But the nearer Henri got to the coast the more he heard how desperate Drach was to get his hands on the cube. 'If he knows you've got something he wants he will kill you for it,' a frightened prospector had said to Henri when he made some discrete enquiries. Clearly, Drach's reputation preceded him.

Despite not telling anyone of his plans, somehow, Drach must have found out that Henri was going to leave the country.

Drach's private army rode quickly to Yemara where Henri had already booked a passage. All they had to do in order to catch up with their quarry was to wait for *The Arinosta* to unload its cargo and take on its passengers before setting sail back to Europe.

❖

Chapter Six

IN THE DOLDRUMS

Six days of good weather and a steady following trade wind meant that *The Arinosta* made up the time it had lost during the storm with its sails stowed. But then the wind, always unpredictable, changed direction once again. Even in the midst of a vast ocean it soon became clear to see that the ship was making little headway. The captain gave the order to brace hard around so that the ship could sail closer to the wind. The crew worked hard, tugging at ropes, turning pulleys, adjusting the sails, some high up on the main, walking on the footropes or rats below it, some on deck, working with them as a well trained team. Their hard work paid off; the ship made reasonable headway once again. But the progress wasn't to last. Suddenly the wind changed again, but not its direction. This time it dropped from the sky and disappeared into a flat mirror sea. At one moment the crew were working hard with the myriad of ropes that led down from the yard to the belaying pins. Then the wind disappeared and they just stopped what they were doing and waited. Some were on the footropes high above, some were on deck. Nobody moved. They were all listening for the whisper of the wind to return. But the air remained as still as a dead man's breath.

Captain Bartholomew burst from his cabin and stood at the rail on the poop deck. He looked about, firstly up at the yard and the lifeless dangling canvas and then at the men balanced on the ropes slung below it. Slowly he lowered his gaze and looked along the deck, at the few passengers that were scattered about. Henri was one of them. He could tell that the captain was angry. Bartholomew's double chin and cheeks were flushed red. His lips were apart and his teeth were clenched.

'Are we ever going to see the end of this damned voyage?' he expostulated.

Henri looked at Jack, the cabin boy. He had appeared on the poop and was walking past the captain and down the steps onto the main deck. He saw Henri looking at him and just shrugged.

'Apparently he is retiring after this trip,' Jack explained as he walked past Henri and over to the hatch that led to the galley.

'Apparently?' Henri wondered if there was any doubt as to the veracity of the statement, but the cabin boy had already moved away, and if he did hear he didn't acknowledge what Henri had said.

'All the passengers to their quarters,' the captain shouted angrily, without any particular purpose other than that he had to take his temper out on somebody. Without waiting to see his command carried out, Bartholomew stormed off back along the poop and into his cabin, slamming the door behind him.

Every sail was set ready to catch the slightest breeze as, day after day in the intense heat of the doldrums, the ship stood stranded in the featureless, endless plain of water. Some passengers ventured up on the main deck during the day, but it was too hot to stay there for any length of time, and Henri found the heat so overpowering that unless he was prepared to shed his great coat, he had to stay down below, between decks where it was cooler during the day. But still the air was stifling and was filled with fumes from the chloride of lime that was slung into the latrine. As before, he ventured up on deck in the early hours of the morning to breathe the fresh air and to see the sun pushing itself up into the sky, as it gazed down at its twin in the glassy sea.

The other passengers still gathered in their cliques and chatted and played various games at the tables, and once or twice Blackwell tried to build up a conversation with Henri but failed miserably when he tried to ask him questions. To some extent Blackwell was as closed to enquiry as Henri, for apart from stating the obvious that he was travelling to the port of destiny, he would not be drawn on where he was heading after that or from where he had come in the first place. Despite that, he seemed determined to break through the barrier that Henri had erected about himself. His intention seemed resolute to find out where Henri was travelling, and by what means and with what resources.

Henri wasn't worried about Blackwell's attempt to be friendly. He had set out to look poor and maintained that his poverty was self imposed by his own failure and inexperience as a prospector in the gold fields. He was young and had much to learn, but he insisted that he had only made enough money to pay his fare back to London where his family, of some means, apparently, were now living, having fled from their own country during the French Revolution. Content with that,

Blackwell left Henri to sulk about his misfortune by himself in his own corner and went about pestering the other passengers.

What really worried Henri, however, was the possibility that there were other passengers who had suffered the same fate as he had. Had the thieves, whoever they were, searched all the other passengers? None had said, as indeed Henri had forgone any public complaint. Perhaps they slept too soundly to have noticed even if their belongings had been searched. None seemed to have any issues about missing items or money. Perhaps the thieves had only been on a reconnaissance mission, waiting till later in the voyage when they could return to take the spoils. He didn't know and he didn't ask.

Something else worried him. Jack had said that there were people on the ship who knew his secret. The only secret he thought he was keeping was that he was in possession of an artefact that was now alleged to have some kind of mystical or magical power. But he knew nothing of those powers because, during his flight from Abraham Drach, he had had little chance to stop and examine the article that seemed now to be burning deeply into the palm of his left hand. And there were not many places on board the vessel where he had enough light to examine the cube-shaped article that Jack called a seal, without being watched or noticed by either the other passengers if he was down between decks, or by the sailors up on the yard arm when he was on the upper deck.

With the ship still standing magnificently in the becalmed waters of the glassy sea, Henri took the opportunity, early on the morning of the fifth day of the calm, to go up on deck and find a place where there was a little privacy and plenty of light to examine the seal. He eased himself out of his hammock and quietly strode towards the steps. As his head cleared the deck, he could see none of the crew up on the rigging. They seemed to have long given up waiting for the wind to rise and were probably all still fast asleep, restoring their energy ready for the tough job that lay ahead of them when the wind finally did fill the sails. Slowly he made his way to the spot where he had first arrived on the ship, and hunkered down between the rail and the capstan. It was perhaps as good a time as any to inspect the seal properly. With no movement of the ship, there was little chance of dropping it or losing it overboard.

The seal seemed to weigh heavy as he lifted it out of the pocket of his great coat. At first glance, it looked just like a solid cube of gold bullion. But he knew it wasn't just like that. He had held it in his hands for so many hours that he knew it was slightly hollow on two of its opposing sides. He held it in front of his face and peered at it with his keen eyes. Sometimes, as he concentrated on it, staring intently, he got the impression it was not smooth on the surface, but to his touch it felt smooth. Other than that, he could see nothing else that would give him any clue as to what it did, what it could do or how one would make it do anything other than look like a two inch square block of gold. He was just about to put it back in his pocket when he noticed that there was a faint crack in its side. Taking the cube with the hollow sides in both palms, he pulled at it. Nothing happened. Then he twisted it. Still nothing happened, until, as he was releasing the pressure, the cube split along the crack and a section, perhaps one fifth of the thickness of the length of the cube, came away in his hand.

He waited to see if anything happened. After all, it was supposed to have some magical power. But nothing did happen and, retaining the small part in his right hand, he twisted the larger portion once more. Again, nothing happened until he began to release the pressure, and then, as before, another section, equal in size to the first came away in his hand. Quickly, he repeated the operation and each time the cube split down, until eventually it formed five equal parts in his hands.

He was just about to see how the parts of the seal fitted back together, when he heard a voice behind him.

'Is that it?' It was jack's voice and it was coming closer.

Quickly, Henri clasped the parts of the seal in his left hand, and turning to his right as he stood up, he thrust them into his left hand pocket.

'Is that it?' Jack asked again, nodding in the direction of the hand that was still deep inside his great coat.

It took Henri a long minute to steady his nerves. Eventually, firming his jaw, he spoke. 'Tell me what you know,' he ordered.

Now it was Jack's turn to be silent while he thought. When he spoke it was with a lighter voice than Henri had heard him speak before. 'I'm not what I seem,' Jack said quietly.

'No, I don't think you are.' Henri took hold of Jack's chin and moved his head so that he could examine his face. 'So what are you exactly? You're certainly not like any cabin boy I have seen before.'

Again, Jack was silent for a moment while he decided what he should tell Henri. Then he gave a deep sigh. 'Oh, what the heck! I'm a spy!' he blurted.

Henri looked shocked. 'A spy? I… I thought you were going to say that…'

'That what?'

'Oh, well perhaps I was expecting you to say something

else, that's all.'

'Like I've been watching you or something like that?'

'Er. Not exactly.'

Henri moved on. 'What do you know that I should know?'

Jack shrugged. 'I don't know what you know.'

'You first then,' Henri insisted. 'What is the seal?'

'Ah, the seal. Well it's not really a seal, although it could be mistaken for one I suppose.'

'Then what is it?'

'It… it's a kind of machine.' Jack seemed to be struggling with what to say. 'It does things.'

Henri laughed. 'Yeah, right. Like the gold sovereign in my hem. It buys things.'

'No, seriously, it's small but that doesn't mean it's not a machine.'

'And how would you know. Who told you about it?'

'Oh I've known about it for yea… a long, long time.'

'Since Hansenger found it? Or when he brought it back to his country, you mean?'

Jack frowned deeply. 'It's existed for a long time,' he stated with a shake of his head. 'I can't explain at the moment, but it will cost you your life if you aren't careful.'

'Huh, that's what I discovered when Hansenger sold it to me. I ended up on the run from some maniac with a private army.'

'Yes.' Jack scowled before saying, 'For people who have greed in their heart, there is no boundary to what they are prepared to do to get their hands on what you possess.'

'So you knew Hansenger?'

'I met him briefly.'

'And Drach?'

Jack nodded but averted his eyes. 'I know of him,' he said quietly.

'Did Hansenger manage to get to his ship?'

Jack shook his head. 'I don't know. Maybe he did, maybe he didn't. I had to follow you when he handed you the seal.'

'Follow me!' Henri exclaimed. 'You were on the ship before me! How could that be construed as following anyone?'

'I knew where you were heading.'

'Yes, but you didn't know I'd make it onto the ship.'

'Didn't I?' Jack smirked as if he knew more than he was letting on. 'Perhaps I had a hunch.'

'And perhaps I'm a mermaid and swam on board.'

'Something like that,' Jack said with a pleasant, unassuming smile, and then turned around and walked away.

'Wait,' Henri implored after him. 'Who are you? What do you want? If you want it why haven't you just got some of your fellow crewmen to take it?'

'Oh, believe me, they will try.' He swung his head around to look Henri in the eye. 'But it won't be to help me.'

Henri gave a little shiver as Jack turned to leave again. The lad raised more questions than he answered. And his parting words were a definite warning. On a ship at sea, there was nowhere to run and there was certainly nowhere to hide.

❖

Chapter Seven

MURDER IN THE SHADOWS

One minute the sea was flat and the sails hung limp and lifeless like washing hanging on a line in a warm summer evening. The next minute the sails took on a life of their own. Shaking themselves from their sleep as if they had rested long enough, and almost with a mind of their own, they filled out into the beautiful curved domes that they become as part of a majestic sailing vessel, and moved the ship along for the first time in days. At the same time, the glassy surface of the sea began to stir, rippled a thousand times by the movement of the vessel, and stroked gently by the welcome breeze. Shouts from the captain sent his second mate into action, scurrying down to the quarters where all but two of the fifteen man crew were resting out of the heat of the bludgeoning sun.

It was late in the evening of the sixth day of the becalmed passage when the weather changed and the ship began to slowly move forward. The whole crew were on deck within minutes, pulling at ropes, trimming the sails, doing what sailors do high up on the yard arm, generally enthusing about their renewed duties.

Slowly but surely the ship gathered speed as the cooling wind picked up and pushed the vessel towards its port and home.

Henri guessed that they still had six or seven days' good

sailing ahead of them before they would reach land. But at least the end of this ordeal was in sight. Now he could relax in anticipation of seeing solid ground again. He hated the sea. He disliked most of the people that sailed on it. He disliked the total power that captains had over the crew and the passengers, and he disliked travelling on an open, vast expanse of water that contained more pirates than the dry land held highwaymen. There was no place on earth like the high seas where a person could feel totally useless and impotent against the power of nature. Even the new idea of putting huge spinning paddles on the side of some ships did not protect them from the great and unforeseen danger of fog, storms or pirates, and not least the threat from other passengers or crew. The nearer Henri got to home, the safer he began to feel.

But it wasn't to last.

That very same night, as the ship rolled on a steady sea, and Henri lay in his hammock, staring up at the stars through the hatch, he heard what sounded like a struggle going on down in the dark fore end of the hold. It was hard to determine just what the sound was, but by the meagre light afforded by the stars, he could just make out two obscure figures moving about down in the distant shadows. Having lain awake for hours, his eyes were as accustomed to the darkness as they would ever be, and he knew that his earlier relief was premature. The robbers were back. Whoever they were, they had waited until the ship was on the move again so that their movements could be disguised to some degree by the natural sound of the sailing ship; the wind whistling in the sails, the sea rushing past the bow, the creaking of the masts. It was a background noise to which everyone became accustomed, but which had been noticeably absent during the calm.

Without raising his head he watched and waited. Were they coming back to him, he wondered? Had Jack told them that he was most certainly carrying the precious seal somewhere on his person? His left hand clasped the pieces of the seal that lay at the bottom of his pocket. He had had no opportunity in the daylight to try and put it back together. And in his right hand, once again he held his small derringer, cocked and ready to fire.

There was more shuffling in the blackness and suppressed whispers, so faint that he could not tell if it were the wind whispering to the masts, but then one of the shadowy figures moved nearer to the place where Henri lay. He could feel the sweat on his forehead and on his hands. The fist in his pocket was clenched so tightly that the pieces of the seal were biting into his flesh. The pearl handled derringer felt slippery in his other hand as he checked the hammer and levelled it across his chest to point towards whoever it was who was approaching him.

The figure moved slowly and silently, step by step, towards him. Suddenly, he could make out the arm of the man who was now only inches away from his hammock. As the figure stooped beside him, Henri tried to make out whose face it was, but alas, there was not enough starlight. A thin wispy cloud had veiled the star spangled sky. The intruder took a long slow and quiet breath and then took the last step towards Henri. Outside, the thin layer of cloud began to disperse. The light suddenly became sufficient to see the man raise his arm. Slowly Henri turned the tiny pistol to point at the face of the shadow. The faint light from a prominent star twinkled upon the blade of a long thin knife as the weapon was brought up level with Henri's face. He guessed that it was the same hand holding the same knife that had pressed against his throat that night that now seemed so long ago. His finger began to squeeze the trigger of his derringer. But the knife seemed to hover next to Henri's shoulder, neither pointing at him nor edging towards his throat. Tensed and ready to fire his pistol, Henri held his breath and waited to see if the man was going to search him again.

He had decided what he was going to do. He would press the barrel against the forehead of the man and silently indicate that the end result of any attack or intrusion on his person would be a small bullet in the man's brain. He began to raise his arm slowly, a fraction of an inch at a time as the seconds seemed to drag out for minutes. But then, he realized that the figure was not trying to search him nor was he pressing the knife against his throat as had happened before. If a blow came from the knife, would he have time to kill the man before the fatal blow killed him? He still held his breath but the man made no sudden moves. Henri doubted if his visitor had realized he was awake as, slowly and deliberately, the man's hand raised the flap of Henri's coat that was hanging over the edge of the hammock. Henri doubted he could hold his breath much longer. What was the man up to?

Slowly and deliberately, the hand placed the knife against Henri's side and withdrew again, letting the coat flap lay gently back where it had been before. The man breathed out as quietly as the breath of a ghost and then, slowly and silently, backed away as Henri started to breath again.

The shadow tiptoed back into the darkest part of the hold. There was a short spell of whispering, once again so faint that, had Henri not been listening, it would only have been attributed to the sounds of the ship. And then, he saw the fore end hatch open, and one of the shadows ascended out of the compartment, closing the end of the 'tween decks in total darkness once more.

So one is a passenger and one is a sailor, Henri thought as he watched the hatch close. There were two people involved but only one went back to the main deck. But what were they doing? Now knowing he was alone, he put the derringer back into his right hand pocket and reached across his chest to lift the tail of his coat. He folded it over to his right side and then reached down with his left hand. Icy shivers ran up his spine as his fingers touched the cold steel hilt of the knife. Gently, he ran his fingers along it to find the blade. It felt sticky as he lifted his hand and rubbed together his fingers and thumb. It felt like blood.

He knew now what had been taking place. Someone had been murdered this dark night and he was left holding the murder weapon. He didn't need long to work out that he was going to get the blame. Someone had awakened and that's what the scuffling sound had been. The villains had killed him as sure as they would have killed Henri the night that they had been searching his coat while he still wore it. The knife was the murder weapon and in Henri's possession of it would see him hanged before they reached port. He had to be the one to get the blame. After all, who would not suspect the man who had avoided talking to everybody? The scapegoat was set up. They would soon return under some pretext and search the entire deck, and then Henri would stand accused.

His mind racing, he knew he had little time to act, but one thing in his favour, was that, perhaps, the killers had not realized he was awake. Perhaps they would wait a while before descending back into the hold. But he wasn't prepared to wait and see. He cast his eyes about, trying to see a solution to his problem. It would soon be light and he had no answer to the dilemma. He took several deep breaths to steady his mind. He had to think logically and think fast. Panic would see him hanged as surely as if he were guilty. He had to get rid of the knife. But there would be blood on his coat, so going to the latrine and discarding it into the sea was not an option. The knife had to be found on another suspect.

The outline of a face he had seen close to him had seemed familiar, but he had looked at all the passengers and the crew over the last few weeks. It could have been any one of them. Somehow he had to work out who the accomplice 'tween decks was. Who was the most likely suspect? He cast his mind back to all the passengers whom he had seen and those to whom he had talked.

He considered the two men that had spent hours gambling at the table? They had been playing for farthings. No, they didn't seem likely suspects. What of Garside, the well-off looking man with the frill shirt and a gold hunter watch that he checked almost every hour and then placed it back into a silver braided waistcoat? He couldn't possibly be a cold blooded killer, but it could well be he who had been killed. The sounds came from his side of the hold. No, of all of the passengers, only one person seemed to fit the character that was likely to be in cahoots with the sailor. When the one sailor had ascended to the upper deck, where did the other shadow go? Henri racked his brain. For minutes he struggled to recall, and then he remembered. There had been a sound of someone getting into one of the six bunks. It had to be Blackwell. He was nosy and persistent at trying to discover what everybody was carrying with them. And he knew his way about the ship as well as any of the crew. Henri recalled how, during the storm, Blackwell, not only showed no sign of sea sickness, but walked straight to the lavatory to close the porthole, striding straight past Henri's bunk in a closed and blackened hold. And tonight, just the same, the figure had known his way around in the blackness.

It had to be Blackwell.

The light was beginning to increase as the sun began to break through into the morning. If Henri was going to do anything he had to do it now. There was no more time to think. As silently as he could, he lifted one knee and slowly and silently took off his right boot. Then he lifted his left knee and removed the other boot, carefully letting them down onto the wooden floor behind the low-slung hammock. Then he eased himself out of his hammock and let his feet feel for the floor. Slowly and carefully he removed his great coat for the first time on the voyage. He couldn't afford to make even the slightest rustling sound with his clothes. He placed the coat in the bottom of the hammock, picked up the knife and, with the derringer still in his right hand, he tiptoed around the tables and over to Blackwell's bunk. Heart pounding wildly, Henri watched as Blackwell stirred in the hard wooden bed. His back was to the bay, yet he would probably still be awake. But Henri had to act fast. He couldn't afford for anyone to see him with the knife in his hand and with every stride the light from the hatch seemed to be gaining strength.

Quickly, he made his way to Blackwell's side. The man's arm was resting peacefully on the canvas blanket. It was going to be impossible to lift the arm and place the knife beneath it. Blackwell stirred again and, realizing he was running out of time, and taking his only chance, Henri slipped the knife on the blanket beneath Blackwell's arm. As the arm relaxed, the knife rested less than a hair's breadth from his elbow.

Henri didn't wait to see if Blackwell was going to move again or if he was going to feel the hard knife against his arm. Without a second glance, he turned on his heel and glided back to his hammock. But he stopped when he saw the blood. As he passed the second bunk down from Blackwell, in the increasing light, he couldn't help but see the body of the elderly gentleman called Garside. His eyes stared blindly up at the ceiling. His throat had been cut from ear to ear. There was blood everywhere; on his fine clothes, on the walls, on the ceiling, on the floor. Henri stood there paralyzed with the thought that it could have so easily been him. And what had Garside been killed for? Henri looked quickly at the blood soaked clothes. His precious golden hunter chain was no longer slung in the waistcoat pocket. The murderers had taken it. Henri was in no doubt they would have searched all his pockets before leaving him there dying.

Now, it was becoming light with every beat of his heart. He wished he could do something for the man, but he knew he was far beyond help. Dragging his eyes from the corpse, he jerked himself into action and strode across to his bed. He reached under his hammock and slipped on his boots, took his coat out of the hammock, slung it around his shoulders and slid into the sling.

❖

Chapter Eight

THE FIRST SECTOR

The dim light of the hold seemed to spread rapidly to every corner as the hatch at the fore end of the ship was opened. Hardly half an hour had passed since the shadow in the night had placed the knife at Henri's side. Now, with full daylight outside and a sun so low in the sky that its light shone at an angle through the hatch and into the hold, the fateful moment had arrived.

Henri glanced around. There was still nobody stirring. Even Blackwell kept his back to the light and seemingly slept on. Perhaps he had detected the movement behind him when Henri planted the knife on his bunk. Perhaps he had not. Perhaps he was now soundly asleep, and perhaps he was pretending, waiting for his partner in crime to come and find the corpse. The corpse? Henri couldn't get the picture of what he had seen out of his mind. And even now, before anyone had begun to descend the steps into the hold, his worries were just beginning. Even without the knife to incriminate him, he had blood on his coat from the knife. And what's more, it was likely that the sailor who had been at the scene of the crime was going to be the first to descend into the passengers' quarters. Knowing where his accomplice had put the knife, he would make sure Henri was searched first. And if they didn't find the knife then they would insist on searching Henri.

He looked around. He could see nowhere to hide. But if they were allowed to search him then they would surely find the seal and then all his efforts to keep what he possessed would have been in vain. Quickly, he plunged his hand into his pocket and grasped all the pieces of the golden cube. He had to decide how to hide them. He took two between his fingers and placed them in a small crack in the top side of the beam that ran along the side of the hull. It was tight, but they would not be seen unless the people searching were feeling for them. There was no room for the other three pieces.

Voices from the upper deck seemed to sound alarmed. Henri had no time to think. Quickly, he walked over to the lavatory, stepped inside and closed the door behind him. He ran his fingers along the back of the beam that ran across the top of the door. There was a gap there. He placed a further two of the pieces of the seal up there, but as luck would have it, he couldn't manage to conceal the last one. With one final piece left in his hand, he eased the door open and looked out into the hold. Legs were appearing on the stairs as he ran over to his hammock. The man who first appeared in the hold was the first mate, a thin looking sailor called Roscar, who he had seen talking to some of the passengers a week or so ago, just before the ship was becalmed. He seemed to be the most senior person on the ship next to the captain. Although he wasn't called the sailing master, his duties included navigation and generally looking after the ship's instruments and maps. Henri had seen him handing the sextant to Jack who had subsequently taken it to the side of the ship and taken a reading. Henri watched as the man lifted a lantern and looked around. In the dim orange light it was clear to see that Blackwell hadn't stirred.

Two more men followed Roscar.

'Looks alright to me,' Roscar stated as he glanced around in the gloom.

'There was definitely some kind of disturbance,' said an elderly yet well built man. He had been nicknamed Stocky by everyone in the crew, most of whom were gaunt and thin but strong through years of climbing masts and loading cargo.

Henri steadied his breathing and casually walked over to the tables at a leisurely pace. 'Some disturbance,' he murmured to himself. 'They were like shadows in the night.' Even he had had difficulty hearing anything and he was down in the hold. He swung his leg over one of the benches and sat down, leaning his elbows on the table. He could feel the sweat on his back, trickling down his spine beneath his clothes. All he could do now was play it cool; no sudden movements, no guilty looks. He closed his eyes for a second to compose himself. His heart was still booming in his chest.

Stocky pointed to Henri's bunk. 'Take a look in there, Conwright,' he ordered the second sailor. A dark skinned man, with his frizzy hair tied in a pony tale, did as he was told. As Henri had suspected, he was homing straight in on his next victim, the man he was to accuse of killing Garside.

'Nobody here,' Conwright explained as he reached Henri's hammock.

'What!' Stocky looked visibly shocked. 'Look in the latrine,' he snapped.

The man jumped at his order and ran to the open lavatory door. The latrine was empty. He turned to Stocky and shook his head. Stocky was still milling about by Henri's hammock. 'This man did it, I'm sure,' he declared. He was hurriedly searching the canvas blanket. Wide eyed, and with a look of anger that would have subdued a clap of thunder, he cast his eyes wildly about the hold. 'He must have done it,' he declared once more, 'otherwise why would he have gone?'

What a stupid man, Henri thought, watching Stocky who was obviously so enraged and so preoccupied with finding the knife that he couldn't see what was straight in front of him.

Roscar looked at Stocky's face and frowned curiously. He went over to him and looked at the hammock. He shook his head. 'Did what?' he asked impatiently.

Stocky thought for a moment, his eyes flashing from one place to another while he squared what he wanted to say.

'Caused a disturbance of course,' he blurted.

'Doesn't look like there's been any trouble,' Roscar stated as he walked around the side of the hold where the bunks were constructed.

'I knew he was a trouble maker when I first clapped eyes on him,' Stocky still persisted.

Roscar shook his head. About to give up the task of answering Stocky's call, he walked past the tables and headed towards Blackwell's bunk. But then he suddenly stopped. He looked down at the floor. Even in the dingy light, he could tell he had stepped in some blood. He lifted his foot to see a thick sticky substance dripping from the sole. He followed the flow of the liquid with his eyes and they settled on Garside. He looked at the corpse for a long while, neither stooping to look any closer nor moving his head. Eventually he turned on his heel and looked around the floor.

'Search the deck,' he barked. 'Find the weapon that did this and find the man who held it.'

By this time, Blackwell was turning to see what all the commotion was about. He sat up and swung his legs over the side of his bunk. 'What's going on?' he asked in a dry, half-awake voice.

Henri was beginning to feel like he was in the middle of some kind of theatre play. Stocky had walked past him a couple of times and never even glanced at him. And there was something about Blackwell that suddenly made Henri feel like he had perhaps made a mistake.

'A man's been murdered,' Roscar said, turning to Blackwell. 'What do you know about it?'

Blackwell shook his head. 'Nothing,' he protested.

'Then who's is that knife?'

Roscar had seen the weapon lodged by the side of the board that held the horsehair mattress in place.

'No idea,' Blackwell stated, totally unfazed.

'Stand up,' Roscar shouted.

Blackwell did as he was told, tightening his belt as he did so.

Roscar looked at the rest of Blackwell's canvas sheets, examining them closely. 'You see who put the knife there?' he demanded.

Blackwell shook his head, his face suddenly registering the shock that had deserted him when he first awoke.

'Whoever did this,' Roscar said pointing back to Garside, 'will be covered in blood. It has gushed everywhere. It's quite obvious that the knife was dropped in your bunk as the murderer left.'

'Sorry,' Blackwell said. 'I was fast asleep till you came

down here.'

'Huh,' Roscar cursed. 'So who heard the disturbance?'

No one volunteered to say they had seen or heard anything.

Still everyone seemed to be ignoring Henri. Nobody even looked in his direction. Ever since he had boarded the ship he had tried to be inconspicuous, but this took the ship's biscuit.

Stocky was still milling about by Henri's hammock. 'This man did it, I'm sure,' he persisted.

Roscar went back over to him and looked at the hammock. He shook his head. 'No blood there,' he said, looking around. 'Where is the guy anyway?'

Henri suddenly felt safer. The second mate was obviously a clever and very astute man. Pushing himself up from the table he waved at Roscar. 'I'm here,' he declared. His voice sounded hollow in his head as if he were calling down a long tunnel.

Roscar just ignored him and carried on looking around. 'Check all the passengers,' he said, lifting the lantern above his head. 'Get them all out of their beds. See if any of them have had a blood bath,' he ordered. He waited as all the passengers were made to stand up. Slowly, he went from one to the other, first checking their clothes and their faces for any signs of blood splatter, and then lifting their blankets and coats off their beds and dropping them on the floor to see if any carried the necessary evidence.

A bead of sweat popped out on Henri's temple. Something was happening and he didn't know what. Why were they all looking for him when he was standing there in front of them? He had even spoken to them but they had just carried on as if he had never said a word. Somehow, the whole thing was starting to take on the proportions of a pantomime. *Where is he? There, behind you! Oh no he isn't. Oh yes he is!*

There he was standing at the tables, and despite the gloomy light he was no less visible than any of the other people who had stood up when the sailors entered the hold.

When Roscar had seen all remaining twenty two passengers, he stopped and looked around again. Still Henri just stood there watching, waiting for Roscar to come over to him and examine him as closely has he had examined the others, but as before, he totally ignored him and then turned and walked towards the rear hatch. 'I'll see if he's up on deck,' he stated, taking the steps two at a time.

Henri felt weak. He had to sit down. Things were not going right. The First Mate was obviously clever enough to not be fooled by any plot to incriminate an innocent passenger, but he must suspect Henri if, as they all seemed to be implying, Henri had disappeared. But why were they doing that? Was it an elaborate conspiracy, one in which everybody was involved except Henri? Were they all trying to implicate him by the mere fact that he had fled the scene of the crime? But he hadn't fled the scene. He was there for all to see and even talk to if they wished. Had his weeks of introverted self seclusion set them all against him?

He waited to see how the whole nightmare was going to play out. Eventually Stocky went to Henri's bunk and snatched up the canvas blanket that lay crumpled next to it on the floor. He walked over to Garside's bed and shook out the blanket on the floor a little away from the bed in order to avoid setting it down in the rapidly thickening pool of blood. He ordered his companion to get hold of Garside's legs. He grabbed the dead man by the armpits and together they lifted him out of his bed and lay him on the blanket. The thin man rolled the blanket around the corpse, in a manner that indicated he had done the same thing before, and then together the two sailors hoisted Garside on to their shoulders and carried him out of the hold.

Still Henri sat there in a daze. He was having serious trouble coming to terms with, not only the fact that he was now the chief suspect in a murder that he had not committed, but that he was a suspect because he had disappeared. He got up from the table and walked over to Blackwell. Blackwell was sitting on the side of his bed frowning, deep in thought. Henri stopped right in front of him, expecting him to look up. He didn't, so Henri spoke.

'Did you kill him?' he asked, and waited for Blackwell to respond.

Blackwell just sat there. He brushed his ear with his fingers, as if seeing off a mosquito and continued to sit there thinking and frowning.

Henri turned away and walked unsteadily past the tables, resting one hand on them for support as he went by them.

Was he dead? He wondered. Had the robbers succeeded in killing him and he was seeing everything as a ghost? He looked down at his great coat. It was as it always was, long, thick, a little grimy now. Then he remembered. He plunged his hand into his pocket. There! It fell upon the plate, the one section of the seal he had concealed on his body. It felt solid to him. It didn't pass through his fingers as he tried to grip it. It was solid and real, and so was his hand. Feeling a little more reassured, he stood up straight, pushed back his shoulders and walked confidently over to the latrine. He opened the door and stepped inside. Feeling behind the beam, he could feel the other sections of the seal that he had left there for safety. He let them remain there. If anything were to happen to him, then they would not find the rest of the precious cube.

For most of the morning, Henri wandered about the hold, watching as two more sailors arrived with a pair of buckets and a mop and began to clean up the mess by Garside's bed. Then he wandered up onto the upper deck and went past several sailors who were discussing whether the tramp, as they knew Henri, had thrown himself overboard to prevent being hanged. He stopped right in front of them and listed to them for several minutes, nodding his head and shaking it as if joining in their discussion. He even spoke to them, but as before when he had spoken, his voice seemed hollow as if it was coming not from his throat but from a tunnel beside him. The sailors stopped talking for a second or two, suddenly instilling some hope into Henri's dejected mood, but then, after looking around as if seeking some pestering insect or the like, they resumed their conversation more expeditiously than before.

From there, Henri paced along the deck and up to the landing in front of Bartholomew's cabin. He went up to the captain's door and opened it without knocking.

'Now look here,' Henri began, but the captain simply looked at the door curiously and got up from his desk where he was writing something in the ship's log and went over to the door and closed it. While he was doing that, Henri took a look at what he had been writing. There were the usual things about the ship's heading and the estimated time of arrival at London, England. Seven days maximum, he had predicted. Then Henri's eyes fell on the last two lines of the captain's neat handwriting.

Passenger Garside died at the hands of the murderer Dubois. Dubois nowhere on board. Committed suicide apparently.

❖

Chapter Nine

IGNORING HENRI

Henri thought there was little point in trying to talk the captain round. He, like the others neither seemed to see him nor hear him. Gradually, after some time inspecting the captain's cabin while the captain carried on writing in his log, Henri opened the door again and went out onto the poop deck, leaving the door open as he went. He heard a curse from the captain and his voice boomed out. 'Jackson!'

A faint voice of the ship's carpenter tinkled from down at the bow of the ship. 'Sir?'

'Get this damned door fixed!'

'Yes sir.' And with that the sailor ran off to a cabin and fetched some work tools.

Henri sighed. He had somehow become invisible and inaudible. Well, he thought, what better time than now to examine the sections of his seal. He wandered down into the hold and went to the Latrine. The door was ajar and, thankful that it was empty, he walked inside and reached behind the beam where he had hidden two of the sections of the seal. Standing on the wooden bench, he prized the leaves of the seal out of their hiding place, placed them in the pocket with his derringer and stepped down to the door. It was then he heard a voice.

'Where the hell have you been.' It was a passenger called Hallowell. 'They've bin lookin' for you mi boy. They's thinks y've killed old Garside!' He said it as if he didn't believe that Henri was a murderer.

Henri sighed. 'So I hear,' he said with as confident a smile as he could muster.

'So where've you bin hidin'?'

'Oh, here and there. Didn't know they'd been looking for me.' He shoved past the inquisitor and went over to his hammock. Why could Hallowell see him? he wondered. Then he realized that several other passengers were watching him. He knew from the way they were looking at him that it wouldn't be long before one of them reported his sudden reappearance to some of the crew.

So everyone could see him now. It wasn't just Hallowell. There had to be an explanation and it had to be something to do with the seal or the sections of the seal. Fidgeting with the two pieces he had in his right hand pocket, he decided he had to try and replicate his disappearance. He thought hard. When he carried the three sections together they somehow seemed to make him visible. When he only had the one that remained in his left hand pocket, he was no longer seen or heard by anybody. Or at least, that's how he reckoned it was working.

He looked behind him. There were voices approaching the hatch that led from the upper deck. They sounded urgent and definitely unfriendly. 'Where is he?' he heard the voice of Stocky. 'We'll have him now!'

Quickly, Henri ran back to the latrine. He bumped into Hallowell who was on his way out. He didn't stop to chat. Rushing through the doorway, he pulled the door closed behind him. He pushed himself up on the seat and, taking the two sections of the seal from his right hand pocket he thrust them back into their hiding place.

Hoping fervently that this was the solution to the mystery, he stepped back down, took a deep breath and opened the door. Stocky was three or four yards away, cudgel in hand, arm raised running at him. He was going to make sure Henri had no chance to plead his innocence. The club was heavy and Stocky wielded it with lethal force. Henri strode out of the doorway and got ready to parry the blow. As Stocky rushed forward, Henri sidestepped and reached to push the man forward so that with his own momentum, Stocky would be carried on through to the back of the latrine, giving Henri time to close the door and block it with his shoulder. But Stocky was already reeling sideways as if his shoulder had hit the door or its jamb, except that in the centre of the doorway there was absolutely nothing there to bump into.

Henri watched as Stocky was thrown completely off balance and decided then that he would fight him there rather than put off the inevitable. Stocky put his raised arm out to break his fall. His chest hit the bench with a thud as his arm went into the gap beneath it. His hand and cudgel disappeared into a pool of soft excrement. Winded for a moment, Stocky lay against the bench cursing. Then, when he had regained his strength, he cursed some more and, placing one soggy hand on the seat, pushed himself up, first onto his knees and then to a standing position. Henri was waiting for the cudgel to swing at him, but the blow never came. He looked Stocky straight in the eyes, but his opponent's eyes just gazed straight through him. They just flitted from one corner of the makeshift cabin to another, looking for something but finding nothing.

'Where is he?' he demanded. 'You said he was here.'

'He was,' a voice rang up from further down the hold.

'Well he ain't 'ere now,' Stocky yelled angrily He cursed and flung the cudgel scuttering across the wooden floor. He looked at his hand. It was dripping with filthy excrement. He screwed up his face in disgust and, carrying his hand extended out in front of him as if he were about to shake hands with somebody, he stormed off to the upper deck.

Henri felt elated. Never before had he felt so in control of events. He ran up behind Stocky and shouted in his ear but the man was cursing so loudly he didn't even notice the buzzing sound at his ear. Henri ran around him and stood in front of him. He extended his hand as if to shake hands and then withdrew it mockingly. He laughed out aloud at the thought of somebody meeting Stocky and taking the outstretched hand as a sign of greeting. 'That's right,' he shouted in the face of his assailant, 'there's plenty of water overboard for you to wash in.' He knew what he was doing. He wanted to shout. He wanted to see if anybody could hear him. But bellow as loud as he could, his hollow sounding voice seemed to be locked inside a barrel with him, for nobody seemed to be able to hear anything other than the tiniest reverberation of the beat of the wings of a fly.

He stood his ground, waiting for Stocky to bump into him, but the man's whole body seemed to be pushed aside as if he had hit some kind of invisible bubble. Fighting to maintain his balance, he simply flipped past Henri as if slipping against a huge bar of soap. Even then he didn't seem to notice what had happened. Maintaining his balance like any good seafarer on a moving ship, he carried on towards the steps, as if being moved bodily around the obstacle was as normal as breathing.

Henri's sense of achievement soared. He was invisible. No one could see him, but neither could anyone touch him even by accident for they would be deflected by some invisible breath of nature. Triumphantly he held out his arms and spun around. The world, or at least the ship for the time being, was his oyster. He ran down the steps into the hold and danced up to the tables. Stepping on a bench, he sprang onto the table top and jubilantly turned around, arms out, calling to everyone and no one, laughing and dancing. Never in his life had he heard of such a gift being bestowed on anybody. Never had he thought in his wildest and most outrageous dreams that such a power existed. And the power lay in the palm of his hand, the tiny segment, a section of the golden cube for which he had traded a pouch of gold sovereigns.

Eventually his excitement waned and he stepped down off the table. He felt no regret of being unable to talk to anybody else. He had kept himself to himself the whole trip. Another week of solitude would be no hardship. But he knew that he had to survive that week. From now on Henri was going to have to travel unseen. There was no other alternative. Already he was being accused of murdering Garside, and with every minute that passed where he was not found, and had not made himself available to answer the obvious questions, his guilt would be compounded.

How easy it is to reflect upon what one should have done when it's too late, he thought. He considered how events had turned round. He hadn't chosen to become invisible the first time it happened; he was rather thrown into it by accident. He didn't know that the seal had some kind of magical powers. In fact, he would have strongly denied even accepting that there was such a thing as magic before this day. Perhaps it wasn't magic. Perhaps it was some form of advanced science, perhaps it *was* a machine as Jack had suggested. He didn't know, and for the time being there was no real point in deliberating about it. What was done was done so he shrugged his shoulders and, now a little more sobered by his thoughts, he decided to just go along with it.

The first thing Henri did was to go up on the main deck and go down into the galley. Since food was neither provided in a satisfactory quality nor a satisfactory quantity, by this time, having used up an inordinate amount of nervous energy, he was feeling almost desperate with the pangs of hunger that squeezed at his stomach. The ship's cook wasn't there but Henri would have gone into the galley even if he had been. He helped himself to some salty biscuits and realized that, although he seemed incapable of coming into contact with any other person, he could grasp things, eat them and generally go about his life as normal except for not being seen. As he munched on the dry ration, he wondered if the biscuit disappeared as soon as he grabbed it, or when it was in his mouth, or when he had eaten it.

He stood and ate for a long time but, as he felt some energy charging back into his body, his inquisitiveness began to get the best of him. Deciding to find out just what were the boundaries to his new found gift, he grabbed a handful of biscuits and almost danced a jig up the steps onto the upper deck. Captain Bartholomew was standing with his back to him, hands on the rail, looking out to sea at the starboard side of the ship.

'Are you lost?' Henri chided, but of course, the captain heard nothing but the rush of the wind and the splashing of the sea as it rushed along the keel of the ship. He went alongside him and stood there for a moment looking to see what the captain was watching. The sea seemed completely empty of anything but endless miles of rolling water.

'You want a biscuit?' Henri asked, holding it out in front of the captain's face. Bartholomew seemed to notice nothing, continuing to watch the waves and looking into the distance.

He put a biscuit on the rail between the captain's hands and let it slip from his fingers. At first the captain did nothing; he was still looking out to sea. But then, glancing down, he noticed the biscuit and frowned. He regarded it for several seconds and then, with a sweep of his hand, brushed it off the rail as if it were not fit for the likes of him to eat. He watched it as it fell into the sea and stared for endless seconds at the place it had disappeared into the rushing water. Then, looking up again, he continued to look out at the horizon.

It was then that Henri noticed just what had grabbed Bartholomew's attention. The vast expanse of water was not entirely empty. Far away on the very tip of the horizon, the masts of another vessel in full sail could be seen. It was still a tiny speck on the line that connected the grey-green water to the grey-blue sky, but the muscles in the captain's face were tensed, his lips, pale thin lines.

Henri looked at the horizon and then back at Bartholomew's face. If he had felt as if he was floating on top of the world with his new found tricks, the concern he was seeing in the face of the captain beat him back down to the reality of what was happening now, as the search for him continued on the ship's deck.

❖

Chapter Ten

THE WITCH

But Henri was determined not to be distracted. For the first time since his flight from Yemara, he felt safe. After weeks of trying to avoid being noticed both on land and on the ship, now he couldn't get noticed even when he tried. For the first time in more than a month he was actually relaxing.

A good half hour or so must have slipped by while he leaned on the rail next to the captain and gazed out at the distant horizon. The tiny speck of a ship still looked no bigger than when Henri had first seen Bartholomew watching it, and he wondered just what the fascination of it was. Perhaps, like every one of the passengers, the captain became bored witless with the endless hours of confinement on his ship, living his life on a tiny speck on an endless ocean. Of course, for the captain the journeys were much more comfortable, but the days and nights of endless rolling waves when the crew did their job without instruction must have been a little hard to endure. Unlike the passengers, Bartholomew wasn't just making a single journey. He spent his whole life looking out at the vast expanse of water, enduring the boredom and risking his life when nature threw up unseen challenges.

Henri was not cut out to be a sailor like Bartholomew.

He felt that life had much more to offer. Gradually, he lost interest in watching the grey-green water and wandered away from the rail. Turning towards the stern, he had other things on his mind. He knew he wasn't entirely safe. Eventually he would have to retrieve the other pieces of the seal and then, if things happened the same way as they had before, he would become as visible and as solid as everybody else on the ship. Gazing down at the oak planks that ran along the deck, he wandered towards the steps that led to the poop deck, walked up them, turned around and sat at the top of them. From there he could see a few crew that were on deck, going about their task of searching every nook and cranny; others went about their duties, no rush, no urgency; just maintaining the heading for home, the port and their loved ones or whoever they had waiting for them.

Henri didn't see Jack at first. His eyes were set on a sailor way up in the crows nest. He too was looking out to the far horizon, watching the ship in the distance.

'You've managed to avoid being hung, then?' Jack's voice made him start. Henri's head swung around and there was the cabin boy, sitting on the step next to him. A sudden rush of panic ran through his whole body. Somehow his invisibility had worn off.

'Don't worry,' Jack said in a delicate and reassuring voice, '*they* can't see you.'

Henri's eyes were wide. His whole body had tensed ready for flight. His throat was dry. He tried to speak but no sound came out of his mouth.

'It's all right,' Jack said again. He put his hand on Henri's arm to reassure him.

Instantly Henri pulled back. How could Jack see him? How could he touch him?

'I told you before, I'm not what I seem,' the cabin boy stated. 'I know why the rest of the people on board cannot see you. I know about the seal.'

'What… Who exactly are you?' Henri asked, his throat rasping as he tried to cough some moisture into his mouth.

'As I told you before,' Jack said with a definite glint of mischief in his eye, 'I'm a spy.'

'And you can see me but nobody else can, is that right?'

Jack nodded.

'So what are you doing on board this ship? You're not a cabin boy.'

Jack clapped his hands. 'Well done! It only took you five weeks to work that out.'

'So why has the captain put up with you for all this time?'

'Oh, don't make the mistake that everybody can see me as I am, any more than they can see you as you are.'

'You talk in riddles young man. You…'

Henri paused. He was thinking about what the young lad had just said, and about what he had thought when he had first talked to him. 'You're not a cabin boy; you never have been, have you? How come they think you are?'

'You're right. I'm not a cabin boy. The real cabin boy got… Well let's say he missed the boat!'

'And you just took his place huh? No questions asked; no search for the real one?'

'Since you had never seen the real one, you wouldn't know what he looked like, would you?'

Henri shook his head and shrugged. 'No, you're right, but

that doesn't explain how you just came along in his place.'

'Because I look like him.'

'Yeah, and I look like old Bartholomew,' Henri chided.

Jack sighed. 'Look, it's hard to explain, but let me just say that just as I can see you now, you could see something of the real me when you first saw me. You suspected something then and you still do, don't you?' He looked Henri straight in the eye.

Henri didn't want to say. There had always been something about this cabin boy but his mind would not accept what he was thinking. 'I thought you were…'

'Go on, say it!'

'I thought you were… girlish,' He said, hoping that he wasn't going to upset the only friend he seemed to have on this ship. 'There, I've said it now!'

Jack chuckled. 'Girlish! I like that,' he said with a pleasant smile. 'I haven't been called that for a long while.' He shifted on his seat. 'You aren't wrong though. I am not a boy.'

Henri looked at Jack, wide eyed. 'You are a girl then! I thought you were!'

Jack shook his head. 'No, I'm not a girl.'

Henri just looked at this stranger and waited for an explanation. It was a while coming.

'I'm older than you,' the stranger said eventually. 'My name is Winifred. My friends call me Win.'

'Pah! You can't be much more than fifteen or sixteen. You're not a woman yet.'

'I'm not a girl, Henri. I mean it. I'm much older than that.'

Henri still waited for an explanation for he knew one was imminent.

'But I'm not really a woman either, well not in the strict sense of the word.'

'You are talking in riddles again,' said Henri, shaking his head.

'I'm a witch, Henri. I…'

'Don't talk rot!' Henri said, shaking his head and now believing he was seriously being mocked. 'There's no such thing as witches. It's a word made up by sinister religious people so that they can kill people who have got different talents to themselves, people they think are a threat to their very power base.'

'You have strong views on that then?'

'No, I just happen to know that in the past people have been killed and for no other reason than that they upset somebody.'

'No change there then,' Win stated. 'People have always been killed because they upset somebody.'

'I'm being more specific than that,' Henri insisted. 'My great grandmother was burned as a witch. My family have always told me that.'

'It's true.'

'What's true?'

'Your great grandmother was a witch.'

'That does it!' Henri said, standing up. 'You go back to being a cabin boy and I'll get on with surviving this horrendous trip.'

'*What?*' Win said holding out her arms from her sides disarmingly. 'I was only confirming what you have just told me.'

Henri looked down at Win's face. He couldn't understand how anybody could have mistaken her for a boy. She was far too… too feminine. Perhaps people want to believe what they are told. He had wanted to believe she was a cabin boy called Jack. After all, he couldn't just go around accusing young, prepubescent youths of being girlish; especially on a ship.

'I've just told you something I have never told anyone in my life,' Henri said, calming a little. 'How would you know anything about it?'

Win patted the step next to her. He took the message and, taking a deep breath to calm his anger, he sat down beside her again.

'Because I knew her.'

Henri sighed. 'Look, Jack, Win, whatever your real name is, I don't particularly like being messed about. You're a nice sort of fellow and I have to admit, you have something about you that makes you different to anybody else I have ever met, but…'

'Like I can see you when nobody else can?' Win interrupted.

'Like… Well, yes, that and…' He stopped himself saying any more. Win could see him; that was true. She definitely had some kind of gift that ordinary people didn't have. But saying she was a witch! And declaring she knew his great grandmother? That was… well that was just impossible. *Wasn't it?*

'Witches live for hundreds of years,' Win said confidently. 'We don't age like ordinary mortals.'

'Ordinary mortals? Are you saying that you are immortal?'

'Immortal? Oh no. Far from it!' Win exclaimed. 'We are just as easily killed as the next person. Your great grandmother was killed, remember?'

'Yes, but she wasn't a witch.'

'Oh yes she was.'

Henri looked hard into the girlish eyes that seemed to be brighter than any he had ever seen before, sparkling with life, glinting with a sense of mischief or adventure, he wasn't sure which.

'And you say you knew her?' he said with a disbelieving shake of his head.

'She was my father's second cousin,' Win stated matter of factly.

Henri was finding this a little too hard to comprehend. 'But you didn't really know her, did you?'

Win just nodded.

'You *did* know her?'

Win nodded again.

Henri looked around at the decks and the huge sails that were hoisted high above their heads. The man in the crows nest was still looking out to the horizon. This was real; the ship; the sea; the crew; the wind billowing out the sails; the water rushing past the keel. But Win? And his invisibility? He looked back at his side fully expecting Win to have disappeared and to discover that he was having some kind of mental aberration brought on by fatigue or some tropical disease. Win just sat there, as before, watching him, her bright eyes smiling at him; waiting for him to grasp the whole seriousness of the matter.

'The world is full of strange things,' Win explained. 'The seal, for instance. It's a machine that was invented thousands of years ago.'

'*Thousands* of years ago?'

Win nodded.

'But how? Who by?'

'I can't tell you that at the moment,' Win said, shaking her head and unlocking her gaze. 'You have enough to think about with what you have discovered in the last few hours. But you will find out, believe me.'

She stood up and looked down towards the main deck. Captain Bartholomew was striding towards them. He glared at his cabin boy. 'Get to the mate's cabin,' he barked, walking up the steps. 'Get him in my cabin immediately.'

❖

Chapter Eleven

THE PIRATE SHIP

Win, as Henri now knew her, ran off quickly to find the first mate. Henri just edged over to one side as the captain marched brusquely up the steps onto the poop deck. He walked over to where a hefty sailor stood with the ships wheel in his huge fists.

'Solomon, steer a course due east,' Bartholomew ordered.

'Ey, ey captain,' Solomon replied and, unhooking a loop that secured the wheel, spun it hard to starboard.

The ship began to alter course just as the first mate came running up to the deck. He took a long look at his captain and, seeing Bartholomew's face, he quickly realized there was a problem. Bartholomew didn't speak. The first mate had already seen the man up in the crows nest and had looked to starboard to see what he was looking at. The ship on the horizon was still only a speck, but the man in the crows nest was watching it through a thick, leather bound telescope.

'What do you see?' the first mate called.

'Unmarked ship, sir,' the sailor replied. 'Heading north by north west. Reckon it's trying to head us off.'

'Just what I thought,' Bartholomew said gravely. 'Just what I thought.'

'Trim the sails. Fill them with as much wind as you can,'

the first mate called to a row of three sailors who were heading towards him.

Bartholomew turned and headed to his cabin. 'Make sure every man is on deck and working to get this ship to the nearest port. Double their wages if we make it!' With that he strode away.

Henri looked at the ship that had gripped Bartholomew's attention for so long. It was hardly any nearer. He reckoned it could take two to three days to catch them if they were sailing directly away. But they weren't. They were still going to be on a course that gave the ship chance to cut them off. Bartholomew must know where the nearest port was, and he was heading for it. Unfortunately that meant not sailing directly away from the pursuing ship, but at an intercepting angle of about sixty degrees, once the other ship adjusted course to cut them off. He watched as the crew climbed the ropes and adjusted the sails. He wondered if there couldn't have been something he could have done to help, but decided that his invisibility could mean the difference between life and death once again, this time from the crew of the ship that was determined to chase them down.

Feeling rather helpless, he decided to follow the captain and see what preparations he was making. The door to the cabin was closed but when he tried the handle, it gave easily. The door moved ajar and he stepped inside, closing the door behind him, but remarkably, the captain was nowhere to be seen. Henri was sure he had seen Bartholomew go into the cabin, so where was he? He cast his eyes around. To the left was the large desk beneath a side window. On it were several papers and the ship's log book in which Bartholomew had been writing earlier. Ahead was a row of shelves which had glazed doors. Through them Henri could see several piles of books and a collection of small boxes. To the right was a solid oak door with heavy strapped hinges and an escutcheon that covered an enormous keyhole. A large silver coloured key was still in the lock. He walked over to the door and pulled it gently with his finger tips. It was heavy and moved only an inch or so.

Peering around the edge of the door, Henri took a firm grip and eased it open. It creaked. A lit lantern swung gently to and fro from a hook in the ceiling of an enclosed room. By the light emanating from it, Henri could see Bartholomew was bending down away from the door, but he rose and turned as the door opened. He saw no one there.

Henri half closed the door to try and make it appear to be moving with the movement of the ship, but Bartholomew scowled and turned and walked quickly over to it. He pushed the door open and looked around it. Confident that there was nobody outside, he reached down to the lock and pulled out the key. Henri was suddenly afraid that the captain was going to leave the room with him locked inside, but his fears soon subsided when Bartholomew pulled on a heavy loop handle and slammed the door closed from the inside. He pushed the key into the lock and turned it.

Bartholomew looked desperate. Hastily he went back over to the far end of the room where a large rack held three or four dozen or so strange looking muskets. They were all secured to the rack by a thick oak shelf that was fixed at one end by a cast iron hinge and at the other by a heavy padlock. Bartholomew didn't move to the padlock. Instead, he bent down and pulled at a long box that lay along the front of the rack. It slid forward surprisingly easily. Behind it there was something covered by a canvas sheet, which, as he pulled at it, slid to the floor revealing a domed, brass-banded travelling chest. With both hands, Bartholomew grabbed one of the hanging brass handles that adorned either side of the chest and pulled hard. When it was clear of the gun rack he pulled a small key from his waistcoat pocket and pushed it into the lock. The key turned and a lever sprang up. Quickly now, he lifted the lid and stared down at the contents.

Henri had moved closer to his shoulder. His curiosity was growing with every second that passed. Bartholomew was gazing into the chest. It was split into two sections. One side was almost full to the brim with small pouches and heaps of golden coins. In the other side were more boxes, all stacked neatly so that they fit into the chest wasting very little space. He lifted out the top most box and turned to the centre of the room. Beneath the lantern he opened the lid and peered inside.

Henri hadn't been prepared for the shock. The first thing he saw was the gold hunter pocket watch that had been Garside's prized possession. So Bartholomew was responsible for Garside's death. Of course he wouldn't have done the killing, but he was certainly involved. He had the man's possessions and they had been taken at the time of his murder, not after he had been discovered. It occurred to Henri that the chest was probably stuffed full of the possessions that had once belonged to other passengers who had failed to reach their destiny alive. Some would have died natural deaths, for that was the risk taken by all travellers on the high seas, encountering famine and suffering from disease spread by the rats and the sewage; but some would have inevitably been murdered. He wondered if his own death had been planned, or was he to hang for killing Garside once they reached port? Henri recalled the apt, old saying to kill two birds with one stone. He nodded to himself. Bartholomew would have had Henri's possessions then. Jack, or Win as Henri had to get used to calling her now, had said somebody knew about the seal. It had to be Bartholomew. So what did he want with the magical artefact?

Bartholomew considered the watch for a good long minute before closing the lid and turning and placing it on top of the long box. Then he went back to the chest and rooted through several other small boxes until he found what he was looking for. As his hand fell on a small leather pouch, he gave out a little gasp of pleasure. Eagerly he brought it over to the lamp light and pulled the strings that held it closed. As the pouch opened, his eyes widened, reflecting the yellow light of the lantern in the dark pools that were his irises. He upturned the pouch and emptied the contents into the palm of his hand.

Henri was stunned. There, in the palm of this ordinary looking sea captain's hand was another seal, identical to the one that Henri had brought on board. At first Henri thought that the captain had found the parts of his own seal and had put them together and stowed it away. But then, squeezing the one sector between his fingers, he realized that could not be the case. The seal in Bartholomew's palm was a twin, an exact same seal as that which Henri possessed.

Bartholomew gave the seal a caressing squeeze and put it down the side of his wide topped leather boot. Then, quickly, he put everything else back in its place, finally pushing the dark oak box back against the base of the gun rack. He went to the door, turned the key in the lock and opened it. He turned back to the lantern to extinguish the flame, giving Henri just enough time to exit before him, and then Henri stood while Bartholomew came out of the armoury, closed and locked the door and went to his desk. He sat in a large oak bow chair and flipped open the ship's log.

The light of the cabin, though subdued, seemed bright in comparison with the dim yellow light of the lantern in the dark room. It seemed to take a while for Bartholomew to adjust his vision to the open ship's log, which he pulled closer to him and turned back a page. As he read it, so did Henri, and, peering over his shoulder once again, he looked at the last few lines.

Dubois seems to have gone overboard with all his possessions. No sign of him after a thorough search. Expect it was he who murdered Garside. No further action deemed necessary.

Obviously Bartholomew hadn't discovered the magic properties of the seal or he would have known Henri was still on board.

Bartholomew turned the next page to read the latest entries. Henri's eyes scanned to the end and read on.

4th October. Ship seen eight miles or so to starboard. No markings. Suspected to be pirates. Crew will go to arms when the vessel draws near. God help us all.

Bartholomew sighed and turned the leaf, pressing down hard on the spine to make sure the log stayed open at a new and clean page. 'Damn damn, damn,' he cursed. 'Why now? One more week was all I needed!' he was pushing himself up from his chair when a knock sounded against the cabin door. As Win entered in a rush, she glanced at Henri and then flicked her eyes away as quickly as they had glanced at him to continue looking directly at the captain.

'The first mate says that it will take about thirty six hours for the pirates to catch us up, captain. He says they might not catch us at all if we sail directly away from them, sir.'

'No point, we'd be sailing out into open sea. Tell the man to maintain our course. Our only hope is to reach land before they get within cannon range. Do you understand?'

Win nodded dutifully. 'Yes sir,' she said and, with that last word and a quick glance at Henri, she withdrew as quickly as she had entered.

❖

Chapter Twelve

CALL TO ARMS

Henri counted every hour as the suspected pirate ship closed on them. The first mate's calculation was well out because that ship, too, had adjusted its course. Only thirteen hours had passed before its white sails could clearly be seen, even in the night, off starboard side, less than a mile away. All crew were on full alert. None of the passengers were called up onto the deck. Bartholomew went down into their hold. Henri followed and listened as the captain explained what was happening. The ship had still not identified itself, sailing without lights and showing no flag that could be seen from *The Arinosta*.

The Arinosta, however, sailed on with lanterns ablaze. Henri suspected that the captain had encountered pirates before, for he seemed to be dealing with the situation extremely calmly. In their arms, three of the crew carried some of the modern-looking muskets that Henri had seen in the gun rack, down into the hold. For the time being, all the passengers' lanterns were lit so as to throw as much light on what was happening as possible. Bartholomew stood in front of the passengers and calmly explained that the ship was under siege. He then suggested that all the men who knew how to use a gun take one up and be prepared to fight for their lives. Not one refused, though most were rather doubtful that the new fangled muskets would be of any use.

'They are Dreyse needle guns,' Bartholomew explained. 'Courtesy of some acquaintances I made from Prussia,' he added proudly. 'They have sealed cartridges, rifled barrels and are loaded at the breach.' He quickly demonstrated, pouring out several boxes of sealed rounds of ammunition onto one of the tables. He suggested that all those more at home with cap-fire, muzzle loading muskets, and who were unfamiliar with this modern firearm, should practice loading them, for their lives might just depend on being able to handle them with ease.

Leaving the passengers gathered together in the centre of the steerage deck, and with strict instructions not to show themselves, he went to check on his crew. They had already been issued with their rifles, and as Henri followed the captain around, he could see that they had placed their weapons near by but out of sight so that the inevitable marauding telescopes of the enemy could not see that they were armed and ready to fight.

The next two hours passed slowly, every wave seemed to wash against the flow of the ship whilst the pirate ship seemed to be skipping over the surface of the water like a skimming stone. Then, suddenly the following ship stopped closing on them. The captain of that vessel was biding his time. He was waiting until daylight.

Before dawn, Bartholomew, once more, visited the passengers in their quarters. 'The pirates will try and take the ship intact,' he explained to all. 'They want what we are carrying. They are robbers first, murderers second. They will not turn their cannons on our ship if they think we are going to capitulate. Most likely they will try to make us surrender by hoisting their pennant. Their flag is designed to put fear into their victims.'

'Are we going to capitulate?' one of the passengers asked, nervously.

'They will think so. We are a cargo ship. Cargo ships don't carry canon nor do they usually carry much in the way of small arms. And usually, cargo ships carry few passengers. But we have a good compliment of passengers. They may not anticipate that. Whatever they expected, however, they will not want to risk damaging our cargo, or sinking the ship, if they can get the spoils without damaging or risking losing them.' His face looked as sombre as a grave. 'They are unlikely to leave anybody alive once they have got what they want,' he added. 'They will scuttle the ship and leave no witnesses to what happened. We will become just another casualty of the sea.'

Then his mood lightened for a moment. 'So anybody who has a mind to embarrass me and surrender, speak up now so that you can be shot!'

A low chuckle could be heard from some of the crew who were hovering near the hatches to hear their captain speak. The passengers glanced at each other and then resumed their loading practice.

It takes a robber to know a robber, Henri thought, as he tried to suppress the memory of Garside's blood soaked body. Somehow, he couldn't reconcile the fact that this seemingly able captain was capable of killing and robbing his own passengers. But the evidence pointed to that fact plainer than a written confession. Garside's valuables were locked away in Bartholomew's chest and they had gone missing before the captain was supposed to have been informed of the murder.

He wondered if the pirates would be as well equipped as the captain of this ship. Bartholomew seemed sure they wouldn't be. Henri had to admit to himself that he had never come across these modern needle guns and he had travelled more widely than most people; and neither had he ever come across a cargo ship so well supplied with small arms.

He watched as, by the light of half a dozen lanterns or so, the passengers enthusiastically played with their new toys. They seemed quite eager to meet the invaders head on. Henri went up on deck and looked around for Win, but she was nowhere to be seen. He wasn't sure what a cabin boy would be expected to be doing at a time like this, but it certainly wasn't anything to do with sailing the ship. The crew were still pushing the ship as hard as they could, but it was now a forlorn hope that they would get within reach of any port or any other ship.

For some reason, his mind kept turning to his new friend. He wondered if she had seen the rifles. They were in the locked armoury above Bartholomew's secret chest. But even if she had seen them, he doubted very much if she had been shown how to use them. He wandered up towards the captain's cabin to see where she was, and looking back down at the main deck, by the growing light of dawn, he could make out Bartholomew talking to his second mate. There seemed to be some tension between them but at that distance and in the poor light, Henri couldn't be sure. Perhaps his mind was playing tricks on him. From his first impression of the second mate and how he handled the murder in the hold, Henri was convinced that he was not a party to the horrendous crimes being committed on the ship. He hoped that the man was of a better character and perhaps that was causing some friction between himself and his captain. Or perhaps it was all wishful thinking on Henri's part.

Henri turned back to the captain's quarters. The door was slightly ajar and he pushed it open and walked inside. Win was not there. He glanced around the cabin and at the heavy door of the arms room. That door, once again, was open, though barely noticeable from the cabin door. The huge key was in the lock, half turned as if waiting for someone to turn it back to engage the deadlock. He went over to the door, pulled it open and looked inside. The long trunk beneath the arms rack had been pulled aside and Win was there, bent over, busily looking in the heavy dome-topped chest.

Sensing a presence, she spun around. 'Oh, it's you,' she exclaimed, slightly breathless. 'I thought for a moment it was Bartholomew.' She blew out her cheeks and turned back to the task in hand. 'Keep an eye open for him will you. He left the key on his desk when they took out the guns.'

'You looking for anything in particular?' asked Henri, convinced he knew exactly what she was searching for.

'Just being nosey,' she replied without turning around again.

Henri wanted to tell her that she was wasting her time looking for the other seal, but decided against it. He went to the door and peered around it. 'You'll have to explain what you are doing in here if he comes into his cabin.'

'Do you think I don't know that?'

'So what are you going to tell him?'

'I'll think of something. I'm a witch, remember.' She continued going through each pouch and box.

'So what? Does that mean that you can make him believe anything you say? He isn't going to like you any more, if he ever liked you in the first place.'

'He sees what I make him see,' she said confidently.

'It's that easy is it?' Henri chuckled. This young slip of a girl was confident but she was also delusional.

'He sees his cabin boy when he looks at me.'

'Yes, so you've told me,' Henri said, still sceptical.

'It takes all my energy to do that so, as a last resort, I'd have to release him from that spell to do something else.'

'Real magic then?' Henri jested, shaking his head. Apart from being able to see Henri when nobody else on the ship could, and having the youthful looks to look like a young lad, she had shown no real aptitude to do anything out of the ordinary. He did wonder what she knew about the seals, however. Why was she looking for them? What was her real mission on this voyage? There was so much mystery about her that he was tempted to believe her.

'Real magic,' she stated bluntly before he could demesne her talents any further. She put the last box back in its place and pulled the lid of the chest closed. Pressing hard against the clasp, she locked it, then, seemingly, without too much effort, she pushed it under the empty gun rack. She pulled the long box back in front of it and said, 'Well that's that.'

'That's what?'

She stood up straight and turned to face Henri. 'Let's get out of here.' She waited for Henri to step out of the doorway.

'You still haven't told me why you are on this ship,' Henri asserted.

'Besides the fact that you don't believe a word I say, is there any good reason that I could give you?' She looked him directly in the eyes, her jaw squared, her temperament definitely showing a degree of impatience. 'If we get caught in here, we won't survive the journey, pirates or no pirates.'

Henri stood aside and let her pass. 'So why take the risk?' He followed her out and watched as she pushed the heavy door closed. She turned the huge key in the lock and withdrew it, walked over to the large desk and, seemingly thinking hard about it, with great care placed it at an angle on top of the ship's log.

'What are you up to?' a voice sounded behind them.

Henri spun around. The captain was standing at the door of the cabin with Stocky. They hadn't seen Henri, but neither had Henri or Win seen them. Neither Henri nor Win could know for sure how long the captain and his accomplice had been standing there, but it couldn't have been long. Had he seen her placing the key on the desk though? Henri wasn't sure. He had been too occupied watching Win, seeing how she walked, stepping across the floor as lightly as a breeze on a warm spring morning. There was so much about her that intrigued him that it was distracting him from concentrating on the task he had set himself, watching for Bartholomew.

Win didn't turn around. 'Just looking for a gun,' she said, her voice a little less wispy than it had seemed when she had been talking to Henri. 'Can I have one?' she asked bluntly.

'You're being a nosy little dog,' Bartholomew hissed. 'Get out on the deck and let me know when that ship starts to close in.'

Win didn't need telling twice. Even getting caught looking at the key to the armoury had upset Bartholomew. Henri was thankful she had finished her search and closed the door before he had returned. She rushed past the captain, tripping slightly as she went by and steadied herself by pressing her hand against his side. Bartholomew growled and swung his hand around to slap his cabin boy on the head, but Win ducked and scuttled out of the door before the fist could make contact.

'Damned brat of a lad,' he shouted after her. Then, as if suddenly remembering something, he pressed his fingers against the pocket of his waistcoat. 'Ah,' he whispered to himself, so faintly that even Stocky didn't hear, 'the little dog has put it back!'

Henri had no doubt that he was referring to the key to the chest. Win had obviously stolen it and, realizing it was missing, the captain had come back to the cabin in search of the thief.

'It would be nice if that worm didn't survive the attack,' he said to Stocky. 'There's something I don't like about him and he's too nosy by far.' He turned and grabbed the key to the armoury door. 'I'm going to check up,' he declared. 'I doubt if he's stolen anything, but he will no doubt have seen things I didn't want him to see.'

'He's just a strap of a lad, sir,' Stocky stated to Henri's surprise. 'Perhaps he didn't get as far as going into the room.'

'At the expense of being facetious, sailor, we are all in the same boat' Bartholomew snapped, turning on his accomplice. 'Getting a bit squeamish?' He curled his upper lip in disgust. 'Then just make sure that the little dog gets in the way of the enemy, if that salves your conscience.'

Stocky didn't reply. He watched as his captain placed the silver coloured key in the lock.

'What are you waiting for?' Bartholomew growled. 'Go and keep a look out for that blasted ship. Make sure you let me know when anything starts to happen.'

With that, Stocky turned and left the cabin. Henri waited

until he had closed the door behind him and then, when the captain had gone into his back room, he silently opened the cabin door and went out into the cool morning air.

Stocky was standing, looking down at the main deck. Win was nervously looking around. She knew Stocky was watching her and she might have even guessed that Bartholomew knew she had borrowed the key to his chest. He might even have left the Armoury door key on his desk for her to use as a test of her loyalty. For the first time on the voyage she looked less confident, less sure of herself, but when she spotted Henri at Stocky's shoulder, her eyes lit up. She suppressed a smile, but Stocky must have seen the look in her eyes. He sighed. Perhaps it was that look that had made him reluctant to kill the cabin boy. Perhaps he too could detect what Henri had suspected right from the start. But from now on, Henri wasn't going to let her out of his sight.

Chapter Thirteen

THE BATTLE

The first thing Henri did was check his invisibility. He stepped around Stocky and stood looking directly into the dark, bloodshot eyes of this cold blooded killer. If there was any mercy in this man's soul, there was certainly no sign of it in those eyes. They were dark bottomless pits. Henri gave out an involuntary shiver. This man would probably have cut his throat without a second thought, and Henri was sure that if they hadn't needed a scapegoat, or if they had found what they had been searching for, he would already have been feeding the fish at the bottom of the ocean. In the increasing daylight, Henri could study his enemy close up for the first time. This thick set man, with a salt tanned face and sweaty, salt stained clothes had been given his orders. Just what Henri was going to do about them, he knew not at the present time.

'I'll kill you if you touch her,' Henri said, only inches from the sailor's face.

Stocky tilted his head and touched his right ear. No doubt he could hear something, but it wasn't Henri's true voice. Stocky looked around as if seeking a pestering wasp or bluebottle. There were plenty of flying insects on a ship like this. They laid their eggs on the salted meat and on the biscuits. Their maggots were a constant strain on the stomachs of all but the most hardened seafarers, who had to pick them out of their food as they ate. The true seadogs just ate biscuit, maggots and all.

Tiring of the impotence of his confrontation, Henri turned and descended the steps onto the main deck. He had things to do and the daylight was increasing with every second that passed. First, he went down into the steerage to see how the other passengers were getting on. They were all sitting around the three tables discussing what they should do and how they should do it. Blackwell seemed to have appointed himself their leader. He seemed to be informing them that they must take their orders from the captain or in his absence from himself. There was no mention of taking orders from any other member of the crew if the captain fell in battle.

Henri needed to see what happened when he picked up a weapon. Up till now, when he picked up food from the table or from in front of the captain, nobody seemed to notice it hovering in mid air suspended by an invisible hand. As far as Henri could determine, as soon as something was in his grasp, it became part of him, masked by the invisible cloak. But that was food. He had no idea what would happen if he picked up one of the new fangled rifles. Slowly, he placed his hand on one that was laying on one of the tables in front of several of the passengers including Blackwell. Pressing his fingers beneath it, he grasped it in his fist. Still nobody seemed to see anything. Gradually, he lifted it off the table where no one could fail to see it rising in front of their eyes. Nothing. The conversation just carried on as before. So Henri was right. He could handle anything without it or him being seen. He put the rifle back down on the table and released it. Blackwell scowled, as if noticing it there, but obviously, in his eyes it must have been there all the time. He just hadn't been paying attention.

Henri decided he didn't need a gun for the time being. He could hardly take part in a gun battle without somebody noticing something strange. But he knew he would have to take part in the fight at some stage, if only to stand between Stocky and Win. And besides, he had his derringer. That was always a back-up. He could always help himself to a gun and cartridges at any time. Instead, he resolved to collect a suitable knife, much like the one that had killed Garside, sharpened to a razor edge, ten or twelve inches long and pointed so finely it could have stabbed a bluebottle without cutting it in half.

The sound of the captain shouting to his crew spun everybody's head in the direction of the open stern hatch.

Henri ran up the steps and up onto the open deck. The rogue ship had begun to close on them. Its pennant had been raised and, sure enough, the tell-tale insignia of the white skull on a black background had been hoisted for all to see. It was still a good eight hundred yards or so away but now, Bartholomew had slowed *The Arinosta*. The men up on the masts were busily stowing the main sail.

Bartholomew was looking out from the poop deck through a thick, leather-bound telescope. '*The Black Sword,*' he shouted so that all knew the name of their enemy's ship. 'They have six big canon but only pistols and swords.' He dropped the telescope from his eye and turned to address the crew. 'We must let them board,' he ordered. 'If we show any sign of aggression then they will use their canon; and if they do that, there's no saying who will be killed and what will be damaged.

We must let them think we are ready to capitulate. Only when the main of their crew are on board, are we safe from their big guns. Do you understand?'

'Ey, Captain,' came the united voices of his meagre crew. Henri realized then just how outnumbered the crew of *The Arinosta* was. Not only did the ship have no canon, it had a small crew of around thirty able bodied seamen including one infinitely inexperienced cabin boy who stood fearlessly at the starboard side of the ship, her hand tucked inside her smart blue jacket, firmly latched onto the hilt of a knife. *The Black Sword*, on the other hand seemed to be brimming with men, all tough-looking, all brandishing pistols and swords. At a rough count, Henri put their crew at more than one hundred and sixty, possibly nearer two hundred. Even including the passengers, the defending compliment of *The Arinosta* was vastly outnumbered.

'Spread out, hide your guns and stand beside them,' ordered Bartholomew to his crew. 'You,' he shouted, turning to look down the hatch into the passenger quarters, 'be ready to come out fighting when I give the order. Understand?'

There was a combined 'Ey' from the men below, and he disappeared from their sight, marching over to the starboard side of the ship to "welcome" the visitors on board.

Henri watched, intrigued by the man's calmness. Bartholomew might have been a murdering thug, but he had a nerve of steel running through the whole length of his body.

'Ahoy there!' Bartholomew shouted as *The Black Sword* drew slowly but surely alongside, edging closer and closer with every heartbeat. He was behaving like a man receiving a visit from royalty, but Henri knew the captain was prepared to die for what he had on his ship.

'Stand ready to be boarded!' a distant voice called from *The Black Sword*.

Bartholomew gave a submissive wave of his hand to acknowledge he had received the order and understood what was about to happen.

Henri made his way towards Win. She was standing at the rail of the ship, watching events unfold with as much interest as Henri. Solomon stood behind the entrance to the hatch, waiting to pass on any instructions given out by Bartholomew. But, only ten feet behind Win, Stocky was standing watching her more than seeing what was happening with the ship alongside. Henri decided he would not warn her of the imminent danger to her life just yet. She needed to watch the pirates for, taking into account what Bartholomew had said about the pirates leaving no witnesses, they were likely to be the biggest danger, and she didn't need another distraction at the moment. Henri didn't want either Stocky or Bartholomew to get any hint of her suspecting their intent to kill her. They both had too much to lose by letting her live, but they were going to be careful going about taking her life. The last thing he wanted was to panic them into acting hastily.

The full-rigged pirate ship was enormous. It was almost half as big again as *The Arinosta*. The hollow barrels of six massive twenty four pound bronze canon looked out of its side like huge empty eyes of the skeleton depicted on the pennant. At least three ranks of bearded, rough-looking sailors thronged the rail, watching silently, looking down from their elevated position, waiting for the signal to board. *The Arinosta* had practically come to a standstill now as *The Black Sword*, with expert and well practised manoeuvring, inched nearer and nearer. It all looked so peaceful; not a word was being said by anybody on either ship, but the air was weighed down with anticipation, hope, fear; all those feelings and emotions that precede a battle.

Henri noticed that a couple of the crew on his vessel were already inching closer to their weapons, but still nobody made a move. Bartholomew stood proudly at the rail, almost inviting the aggressors to board. When it came, the sound of the pirate captain bellowing to his men sent shivers down Henri's spine.

'Prepare to board!' he shouted into the chilled morning air.

Grappling hooks were thrown over the side rail of *The Arinosta*. Rapidly the end of the ropes were wrapped around capstans and within seconds, they were wound taut and drawing the ships together. The pirate crew were all gabbling noisily now. They were no longer waiting in anticipation. They were acting out a well rehearsed procedure.

The first file of pirates reached up to ropes that were dangling from the rigging. Once again it struck Henri just how organised the invading party were. Each man had a rope. Almost as if taking direct orders, they lifted themselves onto their own side rail, without so much as a whisper from their captain. Each one was either carrying a sheathed sword or pistol. Some carried knives between their teeth. He watched as, together, they began to push off their ship rail and swing down to *The Arinosta*.

'Now,' bellowed Bartholomew. He drew out a pistol and the first shot rang out, bringing one of the pirates down into the black water between the ships. The two vessels were too close now for the canon to be used. At this range, they would have cut off masts, but were far too high up to do any damage to the body of *The Arinosta*; and falling masts could have damaged the pirate ship. The revolving capstans were still drawing the ships together, and soon the two vessels would be touching, secured by ropes, their fates bound even if only for a short time.

With the first shot, the crew of *The Arinosta* picked up their arms and started firing. Solomon shouted down to the passengers, ordering them to come out fighting as he bent down for his rifle. Henri watched as he aimed it above Win's head and shot an airborne sailor. The man hit the side rail across his belly, and bounced off into the narrowing gulley, already dead.

Blackwell led the passengers out of the hatch at the stern. He took two shots with his rifle in rapid succession, reloading, each time, quickly and expertly hitting his mark both times. It made Henri realize that this man was not unaccustomed to fighting or to the new weaponry.

More passengers emerged at the forward hatch. Some got their first shot away while others still filed out onto the deck. It looked as if everything was going Bartholomew's way. Pirates were dying in mid air; guns were firing and being reloaded in a matter of seconds. Those pirates that did manage to get their feet onboard *The Arinosta* were quickly dispatched. Bartholomew had retrieved a rifle from somewhere and had taken cover behind the open hatch cover, firing repeatedly at the mass of bodies swinging on board. But nothing seemed to stop them. The endless hoards kept coming, and now angered by the trickery of the wily captain, they were almost frenzied in their eagerness to board the ship. Wave after wave took up the ropes and followed those that went before them. Pistol shots rang out from on board *The Black Sword*. Roscar was one of the first to fall. Then two other sailors dropped their guns and slumped onto the deck. Two or three of the passengers fell in rapid succession. The pirates were shooting back now but they only had single shot muzzle loading pistols. Once spent, the weapons were discarded and swords were drawn. More of their men landed safely on *The Arinosta*, swinging and scything with their weapons at any man who stood in their way. The noise was worse than any Henri had ever heard in his life. Pirates were giving out blood curdling calls; gun fire echoed off the ships hulls, the smoke-filled stench of burnt black powder muddied the still air so that it was almost impossible for anyone to see three feet in front of them.

Henri picked up a sword that had scuttled across the deck from a falling pirate. He looked for Win. In the dense smoke he could not see her. He had been so taken up with the heat of the battle, he almost forgot that Bartholomew had planned to kill her. He was still standing behind Stocky and Bartholomew, and decided the only way to see what was happening at the starboard side of the ship was to make his way through the smoke. Still rifles and pistols fired; still the yelling continued; still the sound of swords colliding rattled in his ears. Blackwell was now at the side of the ship, swinging a sword at anything that moved. Still Henri could not find Win. He looked around the deck, but didn't see her standing or lying there. Would there ever be an end to the numbers of invaders entering the ship?

Two pirates confronted Blackwell now. They both swung their swords together. Blackwell blocked one but was unable to block the other. Henri couldn't reach the man with his own sword but, as the pirate raised his weapon to strike, Henri's derringer sent a bullet into the forehead of Blackwell's would-be assailant. The sound of his tiny gun going off rang in his ears like the clanger in a church bell, but the target dropped down dead before his sword had chance to scythe through Blackwell's shoulder. Blackwell turned around to see who had fired the shot. He must have heard it. It was so loud inside the seemingly impenetrable force field that surrounded Henri, that it must have been audible outside to some extent. What he didn't know is that it sounded like a chestnut exploding on a hot griddle; a soft bang, completely unlike any gunshot.

Then he heard the cry. It had to be Win. Her light voice had cut through the fog like a piercing arrow. Henri spun towards the sound and, cutting down two invading sailors with an invisible weapon, he pushed past two of the passengers who had been unable to reload their guns fast enough to retaliate against the mob. One went down with a sword through his chest. The other, a wiry looking man called McGill, put up an arm to defend himself against a sword that would surely have cut through limb and body alike, but Henri's invisible sword deflected the blow. The pirate looked stunned. He had no idea what was happening and had no time to find out. Henri's sword sliced through his neck and the man fell in a heap at the feet of another pirate. This one had a hold of Win by her jacket and was trying to stab her with a vicious looking dagger. She had bitten one of his fingers clean off, and was in the throws of kicking the man with every ounce of strength she could muster. But against a life long, sea-hardened sailor, she had little chance of competing. Henri pushed hard past a throng of fighting bodies to reach her.

Suddenly, her whole shape altered. From a slight waif like girl she suddenly looked bigger and then darker and then, in the flash of an eye, the razor sharp teeth of a huge black cat ripped at the pirate's throat, while savage claws pulled him down onto the deck. It was over so quickly that Henri didn't realize it had actually happened. In less than a second something had taken place that he could not properly understand. It was a mirage, something you see in a dream or in a hot desert when the brain is starved of life-sustaining moisture. All he saw now was a dead pirate and an unconscious girl lying motionless beside him. Dropping his sword, he stooped down to pick her up in his arms but before his hands could reach her, Stocky appeared above her. He evaded a blow from another pirate who was knocked off balance and then he lifted his sword ready to swing it down at the motionless body of the cabin boy who, for some reason, now no longer looked like the cabin boy in his eyes, but looked more like a young woman in oversized, canvas clothes. One quick slice with his sword was all that was needed.

Henri had no time to pick up his sword and deflect the blow. Neither could he reach across Win's prostrate and limp form to push him aside. All he could do was to throw himself between Win and the descending sword. As the sword came down, Henri waited for the cold, bloodied metal to cut through his body. He heard Win moan as he landed on top of her. She was coming round. But it was too late, the sword was falling and he knew he would never see her again.

'What in hell's name!' Stocky exclaimed as his sword suddenly glanced off into open air. Somehow the weapon had been deflected, but by what, he could not see. Henri was on top of Win, lying on his left side, watching what was happening. Of course! His invisible shield was still working. In his panic he had forgotten that things from outside glanced off him like dried peas off a jelly. Stocky's sword couldn't hurt him. And as long as he blocked the man's way, neither could he harm Win.

Stocky hadn't time to find out if another blow would kill the cabin boy. The second pirate had already regained his balance and had lifted his sword and run it through Win's persecutor before he could defend himself. Henri thought that if Stocky hadn't been so intent on carrying out Bartholomew's orders, he would have had time to take on the pirate. But really, it had been the slightest hesitation when the surprise of his sword not hitting its target filled his mind that, with a hefty thrusting blow, the pirate had gained an advantage.

There were no more gunshots now; only the sound of swords colliding and men cursing and others dying. Henri picked up a sword and, using it to push himself up off the deck, he stooped down again and, this time, picked up the young girl and swung her over his shoulder. Nobody seemed to be able to see her now as he carried her off to the captain's cabin.

Bartholomew was already there before them, but Henri knew he couldn't see them. The captain was sweating profusely. With the effort of the battle, no man would be cool at this moment of time. The frilled cuffs of his shirt were dripping with the blood of men he had just killed defending his ship. Henri couldn't help feeling a little surge of admiration for this quite valiant captain and leader of men. But although this man seemed fearless, he was agitated as well. He knew that the pirates had gained the upper hand. Despite all his courage and his planning, their numbers had been too great to withstand. He took up a brace of pistols, shoved them in his belt and pulled his blood soaked coat closed around him. Steadily, and taking several deep breaths, he walked to the cabin door. He walked outside and shouted above the din.

'Hold up your arms!' he bellowed in a voice that seemed to gain momentum as it vented from his lungs. 'We will surrender.'

The clanking of swords slowly died to deathly silence. The gun smoke had already dissipated in the still morning air. All the rifles and pistols had been either dropped or spent, giving the smoke chance to clear without being further bolstered by more gunfire. The last few minutes had been a hacking swarming mass of bodies in close combat only.

Henri still had Win over his shoulder. She seemed so light that he hardly felt her presence. He walked out of the cabin and stepped up behind the captain to see what the final outcome of the battle was going to be; final until their execution, that is; for what Bartholomew had said was probably the truth of the matter. Pirates don't leave witnesses.

A tall muscular man stepped from among the standing, sword in his hand, hanging it casually by his side. He looked around to make sure that all Bartholomew's men had capitulated and dropped their weapons. They looked up at their captain and did as they had been ordered. Slowly the tall pirate pushed his sword down behind a thick leather belt and began to clap his hands.

'Bravo!' he cheered. 'A man worth his salt, I declare!' He walked carefully towards the poop deck, stepping over and around the dead and dying. 'You have managed to kill half my men!'

'I believe you have done much the same to mine,' Bartholomew shouted down to him.

Henri looked around. They were both right. There were probably twenty or so people, crew and passengers left alive and standing on the deck. As for the pirates, if most of them were on board *The Arinosta* then there were probably sixty to eighty of them still fit to fight.

'Can we strike a deal?' Bartholomew shouted. 'You have lost men. We can replace them.'

'What makes you think we want to have the likes of you on our ship?' One of the pirates growled loudly.

'Not so fast,' the pirate leader said, holding up his hand to stay the protest. 'The man may well have something to offer.'

'We are a mere cargo ship,' Bartholomew continued. We have nothing of value to you. But we have expertise. We are hardened sailors. All know how to rig a ship and as you can see, to your cost, all know how to fight.'

The pirate leader looked down at the deck. He picked up one of the needle-fire rifles. 'You have remarkable weaponry to say that yours is just a cargo ship, captain.'

'Look in the hold if you don't believe me,' Bartholomew retorted.

'Oh, I will. Believe me, there isn't an inch if this ship that I will not explore. It's my business, after all. We are into salvage in a big way!'

Bartholomew continued to stare straight into the man's eyes. The rest of the pirates cheered and chanted 'Salvage!' They began to laugh and chatter amongst themselves. Bartholomew knew full well that for a ship to be taken as salvage, there had to be no one in possession at the time. It was a stark reminder of the fate that was about to befall all the people who were still alive on his ship.

Their captain held up his hand. There was instant silence. 'I suppose we could use some of you,' the pirate captain stated.

'You can read charts and use instruments, I suppose?'

'Some of us can,' Bartholomew stated, beginning to walk towards the steps that led down to the main deck. Still his eyes never left those of the tall pirate.

Henri didn't like the sound of this deal. He realized that he couldn't carry Win about forever. If he put her down, then eventually Bartholomew would resort to his former plan, whatever ship he was on. He would kill her to keep his secret safe. But for now, she would be safe. Quickly, he went back into the cabin, laid her behind the desk and stood up. She was beginning to come round. 'Where are you going?' she asked, her voice shaky and weak. 'Is it all over?'

'It's over for the time being,' Henri replied. 'The problem is, we are the losers.'

Win groaned. 'Huh. Well I suppose it was inevitable.'

'Look,' Henri said quickly. Bartholomew instructed Stocky to kill you. He knows you are a spy or something. He knows you stole his key. He…'

'I know,' she cut in. 'It was only to be expected. He would have to kill me eventually.'

'How do you mean?'

She looked at him and sighed. 'We just don't have time to discuss it right now. We have to make sure that if they scuttle this ship, we are not on it!'

'Stay there,' Henri ordered. 'I'll see if Bartholomew manages to make a deal with them.'

'He won't,' Win countered.

'But he already has.'

'Not one that he will keep.'

Henri turned and paced over to the door. There was one of

the needle fire rifles on the top of the desk. He picked it up and checked to see if it was loaded. It was.

'There's some ammunition here,' Win said, pulling open a cupboard at the side of the desk. 'What are you going to do?

'I'm going to frighten the beggars,' he chuckled and stepped out onto the poop. 'Keep out of sight.'

He stood at the top of the steps and watched Bartholomew gesturing to the pirate captain.

'I have only a few pieces of gold in my pouch,' Bartholomew was stating. He had obviously not given up on saving his treasure. He put his hand inside his coat as if to reach for a purse.

The pirate captain just smirked and waited. He knew there would be more than a purse full of money on the ship. Most captains of cargo ships were very well off. All he had to do was dig it out. But before he realized what was happening, Bartholomew had pulled out a pistol and shot him in the forehead. As the man was dropping in a heap at his feet, he drew out the other pistol from his belt and pointed it at the head of the nearest man.

'I have one shot left. Which of you dogs wants it?' He was clearly insane or ready to die. The heat of the battle had totally turned his mind. He licked his dry lips and then clenched his teeth.

There was a moment of hesitation while the pirate crew considered their options. None were afraid to die in battle when the adrenaline was coursing through their veins, but choosing to take the bullet for the sake of the rest of their crew members was an entirely different matter. One of the pirates at the far side of the deck, one who thought he couldn't be seen by Bartholomew, picked up one of the pin fire rifles and was fiddling with it, seeing if it had a round of ammunition in it. It didn't take him long to work out how to use it. Carefully and unseen by Bartholomew, he lifted the gun to his shoulder. A shot rang out that sounded like a chestnut popping on an open fire. A trickle of blood ran out of the pirate's ear as a hole appeared in his forehead. He slumped, lifeless onto the deck. All the people on the deck swung around to see what was happening. Another pirate bent down to pick up the fallen weapon. He too, slumped forward, lifeless, blood oozing from his chest.

Bartholomew kept his pistol pointed at the nearest man. He was watching what was happening through the corner of his eye. No doubt he was as confused as the rest of the people down on the deck, but he kept his nerve. 'Anybody else want to die?' he still pressed.

The man whose head was in his sights backed away slowly. Another pirate lifted his arm in the air. His fist held a long flat-bladed knife. He began to throw it, but as his arm formed the arc, he too fell to the floor at the sound of a chestnut popping. The knife flew from his fist at an oblique angle, ricocheted off the side rail of the ship and disappeared into the sea.

All eyes were looking around, seeking the source of these mysterious and silent missiles that were dropping the pirates where they stood. Henri was seriously wishing he had put some gun cotton in his ears. The sound of the rifle firing was making his ears ring and his vision hazy. Each shot was like a blow on the head. How long he could keep this up, he didn't know, but he knew he had to do something other than fire the gun. He turned and stood it by the side of the cabin door.

'Here, you have a go!' he said to Win, shaking his head to try and clear his ears. 'I'm off out there.'

Quickly, he went out of the door and down the steps. He was watching one man in particular. The other pirates had been looking at him as if waiting for him to give them instructions. He wasn't the man facing Bartholomew; he stood well to one side, hardly distinguishable except for a dark tattoo on his shaven head. Usually, pirates elect their captains. When one dies, there are plenty of other men ready and waiting to take up the chain of command. Obviously Baldy was now somewhere near the head of that chain. As Henri walked up to him, he picked up a sword and gripped the handle tightly. He pushed through the crowd and stood by his side. Nobody seemed to notice how they wobbled to one side as Henri pressed past them; or if they did, they didn't understand the significance of it. No one had bothered to answer Bartholomew until Baldy spoke.

'He only has one shot. What are you waiting for?' With that, he lifted his sword and began to move forward. Bartholomew calmly curved his aim towards Baldy, but he didn't have time to fire. The man dropped to the floor behind a wall of comrades, cut down from behind. The crowd began to dissipate, moving away from the bleeding, fallen body. No one seemed interested in Bartholomew any more. They looked towards another man, this one, at the other side of the deck, was thin and lithe with eyes that would have suited a snake more than a human being. Bartholomew instinctively turned his aim on him. He was looking more confident each time a man fell. He didn't know what was happening, but he had expected to be dead by now anyway, so in his opinion he was doing all right.

But this man decided there was nothing for it but to get

the captain of *The Arinosta*. He put his head down, growled a defiant curse and sped towards Bartholomew. Henri couldn't get close to him. Bartholomew's pistol fired. This man, too, dropped mortally wounded to the deck.

Knowing Bartholomew had no more weapons, the crowd began to lift their sword and knives and move forward. Bartholomew didn't back away. His time was up. He stood there and waited. At least he had given them all a very bad day!

A rifle shot rang out. The man at the front of the crowd dropped onto his knees. A second shot rang out. The man beside him, a huge sailor, with long hair and a curly black beard fell forward, his face hitting the deck so hard that Bartholomew felt it shudder. The crowd looked up at the poop deck. The cabin boy was killing them coldly and methodically.

Henri realized what would happen next. Before the pirates could gather their wits, he ran towards the steps and barred their way before they could rush at the young soldier. The leaders fell, sliced and bleeding. Several of Bartholomew's crew had regained their weapons and were striking out at the passing pirates. Amongst a total mêlée of panic, one of the remaining leaders of the pirates shouted out.

'Withdraw! D'ye hear me? Withdraw!' And with that, the pirates, even though they outnumbered the men who were left on *The Arinosta*, began to back off towards the starboard side rail.

'Don't let them get back onto their ship!' Bartholomew shouted. 'Don't let them go.' He waited until he was sure that all his men had heard. 'We've lost too many of our crew today. If they get away they will blow us all clean out of the water!'

Henri realized that Bartholomew was right. *The Black Sword*, a huge, full-rigged ship, magnificent as it stood with high masts and neatly stowed, huge, white canvas sails, was armed with deadly, heavy canon. But what could anybody do? They were still outnumbered four to one. Many pirates were still fighting a rear guard battle to secure their retreat. Others were already slashing the ropes that bound the two vessels together and the bows of the ships were edging apart.

Quickly, Henri ran towards the rail, and seeing a space between two sabre swinging pirates, he jumped up on it. With a swipe of his sword, he knocked the two pirates completely off balance and, causing them to fall between the ships into the water below; he bounded onto the deck of *The Black Sword*. Swinging wildly with his sword, he cut down the pirates that were slashing the tie ropes.

To the onlookers, including Bartholomew, the men were somehow being slain by an eddy of wind that seemed to be passing amongst them. None knew how to defend themselves as they too realized they were being cut down by some form of witchcraft. Only six or so ropes remained. If they could cut them then the ships would be freed and *The Arinosta* could be dealt with from a distance of half a mile. But Henri realized that if they succeeded, then all would be lost; *The Arinosta*; Win; everybody. Wildly he swung his sword to the left and then to the right, he lost count of how many of the pirate crew he had slain, but he managed to protect the last four ties until, gradually, some of Bartholomew's men made it onto the deck of *The Black Sword*. Now the pirates were in retreat. Win's rifle still rang out, dropping pirates where they stood. More rifles had been recovered along with their rounds and more shots were fired at pirates as they tried to climb the ropes to let down the sails.

Eventually, unable to comprehend what force was scattering them on their own deck, what ghost was reeking retribution for all the lives they has squandered on the high seas, and realizing that the tables had been turned on them completely, defeated but not prepared to surrender, they began to run to the rail and jump into the sea. Knowing that the meagre crew on *The Arinosta* had no means to take and hold prisoners, one by one, the pirates disappeared over the rail rather than face the sword.

Bartholomew ordered the firing to continue. None of the pirates that stayed on the deck to fight were spared as *The Black Sword* came under Bartholomew's control.

Henri was a little saddened by the fact that he had saved the life of the man he most wished dead. But at the moment, out in the middle of an ocean on which perhaps Bartholomew was the only person left alive to safely navigate, saving the captain was saving the lives of all the people that remained on *The Arinosta*.

❖

Chapter Fourteen

THE PRIZE

Bartholomew knew there had been something not unlike witchcraft going on during the battle on the two ships. He had seen how an invisible force had gone amongst the pirates like a whirlwind, casting them aside and robbing them of their courage. But he seemed not too worried. His ship was safe, and on top of that, he had another ship which he lost no time in declaring as his own prize on the high seas.

His first action was to order the eleven wounded of his own crew and passengers to be taken down into the passenger hold, where they could be seen to; some would die, but he would save most of them. The ship's cook was also the ships surgeon and remarkably he had survived without so much as a scratch. He had turned out to be a first class swordsman.

Next, Bartholomew ordered that the dead pirates be thrown overboard. There were far too many of them to give them a decent burial at sea. The murdering thugs could go to their watery graves without a prayer, very much as they would have sent him and his crew had their piracy succeeded. But at least he gave the members of his own crew and the eleven passengers that had died a decent send off, wrapping each in a canvas shroud and saying a few prayers before committing their bodies to the sea.

The next stage was to wash all the decks down, including that of the captured pirate ship. While wooden pails on ropes were swung over the rails and into the sea and then hoisted up and sloshed over the deck, he walked the boards of *The Black Sword*, brow creased; obviously trying to work out just how so many pirates had died, in front of his very own eyes, by being hacked to pieces by something or someone invisible to the human eye. But as the decking became its normal dark brown hue and sailors and passengers alike, swilled water over the boards and mopped the blood off them, he seemed to forget his curiosity and went on his next task. He had many things to do, the next most important being to make an inventory of everything on *The Black Sword*, including the ship itself, its sails, masts and its huge bronze canon.

It took the whole of that day and the next to list and document everything he had salvaged. Of his crew, the only surviving member that could write, beside himself, was his cabin boy. But there was something about the lad that disturbed him deeply. The youngster no longer cowered away from him ready to dodge his sweeping fist when he rebuked him. Instead, there was a look in the cabin boy's eyes that defied the captain to lay a single finger on him. Bartholomew knew that the lad had played a significant part in the recovery from defeat that faced him on the deck that day. He knew that, without any training, the boy had sniped at the pirates accurately with rapid reactions and complete composure. The boy was dangerous indeed, and not just because of what he had discovered about the captain. He was a killer. He wasn't the Jack he knew.

Since he knew that Jack had seen his own chest of treasure,

his singular retirement fund which he had been looking forward to enjoying when he had finished this voyage, he wasted no time going through casks of gold coins and other valuables on *The Black Sword* that had obviously been taken off poor innocent travellers by the murdering pirates. He simply had all the casks and chests that were on the pirate ship transferred onto *The Arinosta* and into his own cabin and, as night drew in on the second day, he ordered three of his best remaining men to board *The Black Sword*, with instructions to steer the ship in shifts and to follow him home to England. He ordered a long thick rope be slung from the stern of *The Arinosta* to the bow of *The Black Sword* and, leaving the sails on the larger ship stowed in their yards, he cut the tie ropes that slung the ships together and set sail with the pirate ship in tow.

That left a meagre able-bodied crew of twelve, including passengers, plus invisible Henri and the cabin boy, who were to take *The Arinosta* steadily on its way.

Henri realized that he had no choice but to travel with Bartholomew, although his instincts told him to jump ship and sail on the huge white sailed *Black Sword*. There was no way he could leave Win alone with Bartholomew. He realized as well, during the day of the inventory, that the remainder of his own most valuable possession was still hidden away in the lower deck of *The Arinosta*. There was no way he could collect the other sections of his seal before the ship docked, without revealing himself.

'I told you I wanted a gun,' Win said to Bartholomew when she was busy, dutifully tidying up the captains cabin.

'You did well, young lad,' he responded, his eyes perhaps showing a softness that Henri had not seen before. For a while at least, the cabin boy had earned the captain's respect. But Henri was left in no doubt that Bartholomew could not leave her alive if the seal that the captain now carried in his boot was to remain his own secret. What was even more imperative now was that Bartholomew should never discover what had happened to Henri and his seal.

There was too much Henri did not know about the curiously shaped golden cubes. He would attempt to find out more before he set foot on firm land again. What's more, he understood little about Win. She knew about the seals. She said she was a spy. But most curious of all was the fact that, despite being invisible to anyone else, he was clearly visible to her. I'm a witch she had said to him. But that couldn't possibly be true. There was no such thing. It was just so unbelievable to even think that there were people who could perform magic. There were perhaps gifted people, people who could possibly see what others could not see; people who could bend other people's minds to make them believe what they saw was what they wanted to see. He had read something in a French newspaper about a man called Anton Mesmer who, nearly a hundred years before Henri's time seemed to have had an ability to control a person's mind. The word mesmerism was now a word used to explain just that sort of ability. He reflected on what happened when Win was about to be killed on the ship's deck. He, himself, had been mesmerised for a brief moment, he was sure of it.

And what about his mysterious seal, for that is what Win called it? What exactly was it? What sort of machine was it that when dismantled could place an impenetrable force field around a person so that nothing can harm them and nobody can see them, but when it was assembled, was just a hollow sided cube of something that looked like gold. Henri suddenly recalled Hansenger telling him that the cube did not conform to the properties of that metal? What was it Hansenger had told him? When he found the cube, it was lying in some sun baked sand on a golden beach. The sand was too hot to put his hand into, but the cube was as cool as the sea water that lapped against his feet. And when he had hit it with a wooden mallet, it neither marked the mallet nor was it marked itself. Later, he explained, he had hit it with a blacksmith's iron hammer and the result had been exactly the same. Neither cube not hammer was marked. Henri would have to wait to see what he could discover.

Bartholomew seemed to be making sure that his cabin boy didn't speak to anybody. Every moment of the day Win was busy doing the chores set by the captain. In effect, a cabin boy was simply a butler or servant that ran about fetching and serving and carrying things, polishing boots, brushing down coats, and generally giving the captain a real life of luxury.

'Why on earth have you reverted to being his cabin boy again!' Henri asked Win as she climbed the steps of the galley taking the captain's food to him on a tray.

'What would you have me do? Kill him?' she retorted.

'You could tell him to fetch his own food and clean his own boots,' Henri argued, angry at the thought that this talented young woman was reverting to being a poorly paid servant.

'And then what? He already knows that I am more dangerous than he had originally thought. He doesn't dare slap me about the head like he used to. I think we have an understanding,' she stated with a peculiar smile. 'And besides, as far as I know, he's the only sailor left that knows how to navigate this ship. We need him to get us back to the safety of land. Our lives depend on him.'

'I must admit, I felt like killing him when he ordered that thick set sailor to kill you before the fight commenced.'

'Yet the captain realizes now that, had Stocky succeeded, he would no longer be alive now.'

'Well he has turned out to be a surprisingly good captain,' Henri conceded.

'A good general, Mr Dubois. He's a good leader of men in a battle. That does not make him a good captain. A good captain does not have a gang of murderers killing passengers for what they are carrying. At least one of those passengers sails on the ship on every trip with Bartholomew. They are sailors disguised as passengers, and they work for the captain.'

'Huh. I suppose that's true,' Henri accepted. 'But why didn't he have me killed? Why did he pick on Garside?'

'Poor old Garside died because he had, what Bartholomew thought was, the one and only seal.'

'So how come, two unique and identical seals like mine turn up on the same ship at the same time? That sounds very strange to me.'

'You have to understand what the seals are, to understand that,' Win explained none too clearly.

'And I suppose you do understand them then?'

'Not entirely. We have read The Golden Book. We spent…'

'We? Who's we?'

'That would be me and some of my kin,' Win answered

evasively.

'You and your kin?'

'Yes.'

'And they would be…?'

'They would be…' She paused for a moment before continuing.

Henri just waited. He hadn't asked the question before, but he was determined to get the answer. It had been on his mind since he had decided for sure that Win was a young woman.

'They would be, er… witches,' she said, flicking her eyes away and looking out over the ship's rail at the rolling sea.

Henri sighed deeply. 'Here we go again. Witches and magic! What else are you going to try and tell me? That you fly on broomsticks and keep black cats?'

'They aren't really broomsticks,' Win answered innocently. They're…'

Henri waved his hand dismissively. 'Oh no you don't! I'm not getting hooked on your fantastic stories. You almost had me fooled before. But I've recovered from my momentary lapse into believing childish stories. I'm grown up now, or hadn't you noticed?'

'So am I, though I know you haven't noticed that yet.'

'Huh!'

'And as for black cats, well that is…'

'I'm not listening to any more of this!' Henri said loudly as he stood up and began to walk away.

Win just shrugged.

Win's quarters were a small room at the side of the captain's cabin. Since Henri had established that Win was a female, he had been reluctant to enter her private quarters. For some reason, Bartholomew never ventured into her small room either. When he needed his cabin boy, he would simply bellow his name and out he would come, bowing and scraping in a servile and befitting manner. But not now; not since Win had shown her skill with what he thought was a revolutionary new weapon; and not since Win had begun to look the captain straight in the eye. It was a belligerent stare; a look of utter self confidence; a look of defiance.

'You did well, young man,' he stated quietly one evening as he compiled his daily log by the light of a single lantern. Win could hear him as well as if the door were open. No doubt he was writing down a version of what happened on the day of the incursion.

'Despite your telling Stocky to kill me,' Win responded, making him raise his eyes and look towards her door.

Bartholomew grunted quietly. 'Who told you that story?

'Let's say I have it on very good authority,' Win said chirpily. 'You told him to kill me and make it look like I'd died in the battle.'

'Should I deny this?' Bartholomew queried casually, not lifting his eyes from the log.

'No point. What I know, I know.'

'Ah, well then, I must admit, I was a little angry.'

'Afraid I'd tell what I'd found out, you mean.' It was a statement not a question.

'You don't understand the importance of it,' he said bluntly. 'You just can't conceive…'

'Oh yes I can. I know just how important it is.'

'And who told you? Don't tell me; it was your friend!'

Win was silent for a moment. 'My friend?'

Now Bartholomew was quiet. He sat and gazed at the page he had written that evening. He knew Win was still listening. Eventually he spoke. 'I can't possibly mention it all in the log. Not everything that happened. I can't mention the golden cube,' he stated with a rather sad sigh. 'And I can't mention your friend. You see, I can't afford to let anybody know the truth.'

'You keep talking about my friend. I don't have any friends; not on this ship, anyway.'

'Perhaps I mean your associate then. The one who has mastered the art?'

'What art? You talk in riddles.'

'Oh that I wish I did,' Bartholomew said gravely. 'Oh that I wish I did.'

Win didn't reply. She remained silent after that. But by talking about it, he had given out a clear warning. He couldn't afford to let anyone know the truth.

Eventually, the captain returned to his writing, penned a final paragraph in the log, extinguished his light and then retired to his bunk. He was deeply troubled; Henri could tell.

Henri determined not to leave the captain's cabin when Win was in her room. Quietly, he sat down beneath the window, and watched the captain. There, and used to sleeping on bare ground and rocky desert floors, Henri would catch a few hours sleep, sitting on the hard oak floor and leaning against the side of the ship when he knew that Bartholomew was soundly asleep.

❖

Chapter Fifteen

WIN COMES CLEAN

So Bartholomew had worked it out. He knew that, somehow, Henri, or somebody if it wasn't Henri, had been helping during the battle. And he knew from Jack's whole demeanour that the young cabin boy was no longer afraid of him. Could whoever it was who had turned the tide of the battle to save the ship still be on board? Or was it a ghost that haunted *The Black Sword*? Perhaps it was something that had travelled with the pirates on board their vessel. But in his heart of hearts he knew that the answer did not lie in ghost stories. Men were frightened by ghosts; they were not slain by them. For the last few nights he had slept little and fitfully. There was a danger in uncertainty, a danger that could threaten everything he had worked for. With no solution to hand, he decided that he had no choice but to go in search of the mysterious invisible warrior.

First of all, he had to prepare a trap so that he could capture the being. Then he had to lure *The Thing* to him. His immediate problem was that he didn't know if *The Thing* was already in his cabin, so setting a trap to capture it in the cabin might seem pretty pointless. And then when he knew it was in the cabin, what was to stop it from doing to him exactly what it did to the pirates?

Nothing. But he did know that it had meant him no harm up to this moment in time. In fact it had saved his life several times out on the deck when he, himself, had already given up any chance of living to see his wealthy retirement.

So perhaps *The Thing* was on his side and not Jack's as the cabin boy was seemingly implying by his confident attitude. But there were too many uncertainties. Jack was too cocky for a start, and that was what really unsettled Bartholomew. And he was cocky because of what? Because he helped save the ship? Or was it because he was being helped by *The Thing*? There was only one way to find out.

'Jack!' Bartholomew called as a thin morning light forced its way in through the cabin window. He lay on his hard horsehair mattress in his bunk and waited for the cabin boy to respond, and when he heard some shuffling from behind the thin door that separated the cabin boy's quarters from his cabin, he called again.

'Jack, wake up boy!'

'Coming!' Win called lazily. She too had not been sleeping very well. But her problem wasn't wondering what *The Thing* was. Her problem was wondering how she had become so reliant on a person she'd had no intention of befriending other than for the purpose of taking from him what she had been sent to collect.

'Damn it boy, you get lazier by the day, I swear.'

'Moaning old goat,' Win whispered under her breath.

'What! What was that you said?' Bartholomew yelled, blood rising into his cheeks.

'Just putting on my coat,' Win lied, as she pulled on a boot and hopped to the door. She burst through it, hopping a few steps as, still pulling at the lugs, she pushed her foot into her boot.

'Huh. Suppose you feel I can't touch you now.'

'What do you mean Captain?' She looked at him with a curious gaze. 'Can't touch me?' She shook her head. 'You feeling all right, Captain?'

'Damn and blast, boy; you know very well what I'm getting at.'

'I'm afraid I have no idea sir,' Win said with as serious a look on her face as she could muster at this hour of the morning.

'Haven't you indeed! Well let's summarise, shall we? Let's just go over a few of the fundamental facts shall we. That way we might just clear the air. What about that then?'

'As you please.'

'As I plea…!' Bartholomew shouted exasperatedly but cut himself short. He gave a muffled groan and sat forward on the edge of his bunk. 'Look young lad, it's about time we put our cards on the table, don't you think?'

'Cards, Sir. You want a game of cards at this time of the morning? What about taking your readings? I'll get your sextant.' She turned to go over to the cupboard that formed one side of the huge desk.

'No you won't! Stand still boy while I talk to you!'

Win dutifully obeyed, her eyes smiling but her lips compressed to prevent the smile from spreading over her whole face. She didn't speak, content to wait for the captain to say what he wanted to get off his chest. She was pretty sure he didn't want her to fetch him something. She had been expecting him to talk to her, the only person who seemed confident about the whole situation. She knew he wanted her to throw at least a little plume of light on the whole cockeyed state of affairs.

'Who are you?'

The question was so direct that it took Win a few seconds to compose herself. Could Bartholomew see through her magic? 'What do you mean?' she asked as cheerily as she could. The less she said at this stage the better.

'Well you aren't Jack; that I know now.'

'Not Jack?'

'Stop messing about boy! I'm in no mood for silly games. We talked frankly yesterday. For goodness sake, talk frankly now. Tell me who you are. I know you are not the Jack I took on board six months ago. He was so frightened of guns he pissed himself if he had to handle one. You on the other hand, well you handled the weapon like a seasoned sniper. You didn't even have any difficulty loading the thing.'

'I watch and learn, Captain.'

Bartholomew stood up and plunged his hands deep in his trouser pockets. 'I'm waiting for you to tell me just who you are and what you want.' He gave Win a fierce look. 'I have all day.'

Win looked around the cabin. Henri was nowhere to be seen. Just when she needed him to back her up in the event that things turned nasty, he had felt it necessary to leave her unguarded.

Henri sat against the outside wall of the cabin, listening. He hadn't been able to sleep with the noise of Bartholomew's snoring, but besides that, he was beginning to feel rather unwell. Being in his invisible form seemed to be draining him somehow. He had needed to throw off the invisible cloaking device, even if it was only for a few short hours. During the blackness of the starless night, he had crept out of the cabin while the captain slept, and placed the section of the seal that, up to now he had kept safely stored in his pocket, in a small hollow on the poop deck where a sword had gouged out a chunk of wood. He sat, several feet away, out of sight, behind a coil of rope, the end of a long halyard. There, wrapped in his great coat to protect him against the chill of the cool night air, he breathed in and out as if he were in a different world; a wide open world free of the constrains; a world free of the protective invisible bubble.

He must have dozed off because it was Bartholomew's voice that stirred him back to consciousness. Quickly, he leaned over to the hollow in the deck and retrieved the small metal sector. Instantly he knew he was inside the force field again. His nausea seemed to have abated a little, but as soon as he picked up the sector of cube, he felt the weight of its power pressing against every fibre of his body once more.

He leaned against the cabin wall and pressed his ear against it. Bartholomew had worked out that there was something different about his cabin boy. Was Win losing her gift of mesmerising the captain and his crew?

'I don't know what you want, Captain,' Win was saying, rather defensively, it sounded.

'What or who is protecting you?' It was a direct question. Bartholomew was waiting for a response but none came other than a slight shrug of his cabin boy's shoulders. 'Well let's start at the beginning shall we,' Bartholomew began again, not unlike a lawyer presenting his case against the accused. 'First of all, and discounting that you have suddenly acquired an affinity for weapons, you'll recall that when you fired on the pirates, they began to rush up the steps towards you.' He waited for a sign of acknowledgement.

Win nodded. 'Yes, they did,' she said plainly.

'And they were suddenly halted?'

'Yes.' Again her answer was quiet and considered.

'And they were not only halted, but they fell all about bleeding and dying? To such an extent, that the ones behind them couldn't climb over the fallen!'

Win nodded.

'So are you capable of doing such things entirely on your own?' He paused and then added, 'I don't think so. I have seen all sorts of things in my lifetime. I've travelled the world but I've come across nothing like this kind of witchcraft.'

Win just stared at him, neither responding physically nor with words, but Bartholomew returned the stare. With lips compressed to merest slivers of white on a dark tanned seafarer's face, he waited and then waited some more. Eventually Win spoke.

'Witchcraft? If I were a witch then you should be afraid of me, of my powers.'

Bartholomew chuckled. 'And just why should that be young lad, heh? You saved my life by firing on the pirates. But somebody or something else saved your life by felling them in their stride, not just on the steps but on the deck of *The Black Sword*. No, you were simply carrying out my orders. You were on my side then. Why would I want to be afraid of you now?'

'We were all fighting for our lives then,' Win said, now not so conciliatorily. 'But the pirates have gone. The threat is completely different now. You don't need me any more and I certainly don't need you.'

'So on that basis I should be afraid of you?' He shook his head. 'I don't believe that for one moment.'

'You should be afraid of what I know.'

'Just what do you know?' Bartholomew snapped angrily. 'How could you use it against me? You can't. I am the master of this ship. Say one word against me and you would be the mutineer.'

'Perhaps I meant you should be careful,' Win said, knowing that a confrontation could cost them all their lives. 'You are a brilliant leader of men, and not a bad captain to your crew either, but you are a murderer. That would put you on any side other than mine.'

'A murderer!'

'Garside, remember?'

'Well, that was an unfortunate occurrence. Stocky went well beyond his orders. He was merely ordered to find and retrieve something. He wasn't supposed to kill anybody.'

'Oh, and I suppose he wasn't supposed to kill me on your orders either!'

'There you go again! Accusations! You don't know what I said to him,' Bartholomew shouted angrily.

'But I do, Captain Bartholomew. I do know what you said. And I don't believe that Garside was the first person you ever murdered. I have seen the chest stuffed full of things that you have looted off your passengers.'

Bartholomew composed himself. He suddenly became the same cool, calm captain that had walked out on the deck to face the pirates. 'When you travel the seas as long as I have, you realize that, with the risk of death on every wave of every voyage you take, other peoples lives are not so precious as they might be, any more than they are to those self enriching mill owners that don't give a damn about the welfare of their eight and ten year old workers. I look after my men... and my cabin boy. The worst you have had is a clip around the head with my fist!'

'And a sentence of death!'

'Pah!' he said, waving his heavy hand dismissively. 'It was all said in the heat of the moment. Remember what they said about Thomas the Becket?'

There was a long silence for well over a minute and then he recaptured his theme. 'So how are you going to explain what happened? How did the sailor with the knife suddenly lose his life when he tried to throw it at me? How were those men swept aside when they were trying to cut *The Black Sword* free? I know it wasn't you. A man died right in front of me. He had a bullet the size of a pea in his brain. The weapon that killed him sounded nothing like a large pin fire rifle and the hole it made in his forehead was a fraction of the size that a rifle would have made.'

'I have no answers for you Captain,' Win said firmly. Without Henri there beside her, she was determined not to give Bartholomew the explanations that he sought.

'There is somebody else on this ship, somebody who appears to be able to do magic. I don't deny, some magic has taken place on these ships, and everyone on board knows it, but was it yours? Was it you who controlled it? No,' he said, answering his own question, 'I believe it was under the control of someone else?' His eyes drilled into Win's.

'You really have no idea what you have got yourself into, have you,' Win said, suddenly losing her cool. 'You have killed somebody for something that you really have not the slightest inkling about, and for somebody who you should have avoided like the plague. You have killed a man for an ancient artefact but you have no idea why the person who offered to pay you for it, was prepared to pay so much for it. You…'

'Oh, and you do understand then!'

'I understand that you are carrying something that will eventually end in your being killed for it, just as you killed Garside for what he was carrying. I understand that Drach has probably had a ship dispatched which is already ahead of you and which has, on board, your assassin.'

'Drach? What do you know about Drach?' A few beads of perspiration began to grow on the captain's nose.

'More than you, obviously. It might well be that the pirates were in his pay as well. But they are uncouth and unsophisticated. Your assassin will be one person, man or woman who will seem to be your friend but who will, eventually, take from you what Drach has paid so much to retrieve.'

It was the captain's turn to be silent for a long while. 'I see,' he said eventually. 'You know about Drach, you know about the artefact. What do you know that I should know?'

Win was quick to respond to that question. 'You'll have to tell me what you know about Drach for me to be able to answer that,' she stated, hoping that Bartholomew would realize that he wasn't going to get answers without some of his own input to the discussion.

Bartholomew remained quiet while he thought. Eventually he sighed. 'So you think Drach will have already overtaken us? How you would know that, I have no idea, but if it is true then it is rather unfortunate. Towing that big pirate ship has slowed us considerably; and it took two days to evaluate what we had won before we took it in tow. Then we lost three days stowing the sails during the storm and a week or so in full sail and moving not a single inch, while we stalled in the doldrums. No, it is most unfortunate.' He shook his head.

Win waited while he seemed to be doing some mental calculations

'Yes,' he continued after a while, 'you are right, he might well be in London, already docked in the Thames.' His brow creased, he sighed again. 'I have my fortune; I didn't really need Drach's money. I was going to sell my ship and retire when we reached our destination. In fact I have already taken a promissory note as down payment on *The Arinosta*. Damn and blast this last voyage!'

'I can help you.' It was a clear statement of fact. No emotion, no pleading. Win stood with her hand on the captain's desk. She seemed to be trying to recover her energy after a strenuous run.

Bartholomew looked at the person he had seen as a cabin boy. For some reason he looked different now; more mature, perhaps even a little taller. 'So this is who you really are!' he said in a quiet whisper. 'So you have been performing some form of magic!'

'Kind of,' Win conceded. She sighed and then decided that the truth, although hard to believe, might be the best tool for extricating Bartholomew from her problems. 'I'm a witch.'

'A wit... A witch, you say? You're a witch?' Bartholomew scowled as he tried to work out what Win had just said. 'Did I hear you right?' His face showed total disbelief. The young waif of a girl that now stood before him seemed less than adequate for such business, if indeed witchcraft was any kind of profession.

Win nodded. Bartholomew was already beginning to see a feminine side to the lad who had slept in a small cupboard next to his cabin.

'By Gad, I must have been bewitched! How could I not have seen this?'

'It's called magic,' Win stated matter of factly. 'Witches are renowned for it!'

Bartholomew blew out his cheeks. 'Witchcraft; magic!' He slumped back onto his bunk, shook his head and then cradled his face in his big hands. Win just watched as the whole idea that there was another dimension to the captain's world, formulated in Bartholomew's mind. When he lifted his face again, he said, 'I knew there was something going on that was beyond the realms of my own reality. It was remarkable, though I say it myself. That battle! I have seen many things in my lifetime. I have travelled the world. I've heard about magic. But on my ship?' He compressed his lips and shook his head. 'On my ship!' he said again as if trying to come to terms with it.

'Well,' Win said to lessen the impact of her revelation, 'magic takes many forms. But it only uses the inert abilities that many humans possess.'

'Like the ability to wield an invisible sword!' he stated sarcastically.

'Well, not that, exactly.' She paused to consider how to explain. 'There are things that humans have yet to discover,' she went on, 'things they knew about many thousands of years ago, and have forgotten in the dark depths of time.'

'So what was that if it wasn't magic?'

'It was a kind of magic, but it wasn't my magic.'

Bartholomew gave a faint smile. Now, despite acknowledging that Win had somehow mesmerised him for weeks, he knew that he was getting nearer to the truth. He could feel it. 'No, I know it wasn't yours.'

Win nodded. 'I have a friend,' she began, not sure why she was referring to Henri as a friend. He was simply the person who had been the carrier of one of the seals, a seal that she was under instructions to recover at all costs. 'He can do much the same as I can, make you believe you are seeing one thing when, you are really seeing another.'

'He's a witch as well then?'

'A very powerful one,' she confirmed. It seemed an easy explanation, and if she implied that Henri had unknown powers then he might be safe from any plot to kill him if he revealed himself. 'He can make it impossible for people to see him.'

'He's invisible then?' In Bartholomew's mind that explained what happened on the ships decks. It didn't explain anything about how Henri did it.

Win thought carefully about what she was going to say next. 'Well yes. But nobody can hurt him either. You saw how the swinging swords of the pirates simply glided about in mid air, not connecting with anything solid.'

'He isn't solid!' Bartholomew gasped. 'You mean…?'

'I mean that whether he chooses to be seen or not, nobody can harm him.'

Henri was listening to all this. Win could definitely spin a good yarn when she felt like it. Perhaps the captain would believe it. Perhaps he could reveal himself now, especially since Bartholomew had confessed that Henri was not the person who killed Garside. So the captain could no longer use him as a scapegoat. Perhaps Win also knew that the protective force around Henri would gradually drain his life out of him. He was already starting to feel the effects of the sector of the seal in his hand, draining him again. He made his decision. Placing the small sector under the coil of rope, he stood up and walked away towards the cabin door.

Almost immediately he felt his strength returning as he became visible like a ghostly apparition appearing from out of nowhere on the poop deck. Henri was so intent on joining the two people in the captain's quarters that he had forgotten that the crew and most of the remaining passengers were likely to be on the deck. He turned around and looked down onto the main deck, but nobody seemed to be watching. Then he glanced up in the rigging. Blackwell was there, looking down at Henri. His face neither showed surprise nor rancour. Henri gave him a cursory wave and Blackwell, who was hanging onto the rigging with both hands, acknowledged with a nod as Henri turned back to the cabin door again. He tried to imagine what his own reaction would have been if he had seen somebody who had seemingly disappeared overboard days ago suddenly appeared out of thin air. A polite nod wouldn't have cut it. He took a deep breath and tried to concentrate on what he was doing.

As the cabin door opened and Win saw Henri standing there, her eyes showed a light that had not been there before. It was a radiance that lit up her whole face. It was as if she couldn't help herself as the smile broke across her lips.

'Captain,' she said, turning to address Bartholomew who was looking at Henri quizzically, 'meet my friend and colleague, Henri Dubois.' Obviously, Win could distinguish between the real Henri and the one which only she could see when he was inside his invisible bubble, for she knew that Bartholomew could see him plainly now.

Bartholomew looked less surprised than Henri had expected.

In fact, he looked to have no doubts whatsoever. 'So you are the person who saved our lives! Come in!' His gratitude seemed genuine as he waved Henri in. 'I've been longing to talk to you.'

Henri closed the cabin door behind him. He just stood there, waiting for someone to speak.

'The captain and I have been discussing our magic,' Win said by way of explanation. She hadn't known that Henri had been hanging on every word of the conversation that had been taking place within the captain's quarters.

'Have you?' Henri said guardedly.

'Indeed she has!' Bartholomew ventured. 'Indeed she has.' He pointed to the heavy captain's chair. 'Please be seated,' he said jovially, waving his chunky hand in the air once again. He sounded relieved. Suddenly, despite the outrageousness of the facts, he had answers to the troublesome questions that had plagued him since the pirate attack was repelled.

Henri's face remained solemn. 'Has she explained to you that you will not survive the journey if you try to harm her?'

'My good man,' Bartholomew said with a smile that seemed to only work on his lips. His eyes showed definite signs of wariness. 'I have no intention of harming anybody! My whole purpose is to get my ship, its cargo and my crew and passengers, what remain of them, thanks mainly to you, I believe, safely to London.'

'And the artefact?'

Bartholomew's face lost any sign of pleasure that it had just tried to portray. 'The artefact?'

'The golden cube?'

'W… what about it?' He seemed a little ruffled

'It doesn't belong to you,' Henri stated. 'You killed a man

for it.'

Bartholomew's eyes looked around shiftily while he thought how to respond. 'He was killed by a member of my crew who is now dead. I simply took charge of his possessions until we reach port.'

'He was relieved of his possessions before you were informed of his murder.'

'And you'd know this because…?'

'Because all the passengers saw his body. His watch, the one he was proud of and showed to everybody; it had gone before your men came down into the hold.'

'That proves nothing.'

'Whatever,' Henri said exasperated. Bartholomew still had the upper hand. There was nobody who could testify that the captain actually killed anybody or even robbed them. 'You are still going to relinquish the cube. You are going to hand it over to someone who knows how to deal with it.'

'And why should I do that?' His eyes flitted from Henri to Win and back again.

'A man called Drach is determined to kill anybody who has what he wants.'

'So I am informed. But I made no deal with that man' He paused to think. 'Perhaps there is a price we can discuss for my co-operation?'

Henri sighed. He was positive that Drach was the person who had offered to pay Bartholomew to get the seal. 'The price, dear captain is your life. The question is: are you tired of living?' His eyes bored into those of the captain.

'And how am I to tell if this isn't just a way of robbing me? I can't tell if possessing the cube will kill me.'

'We aren't trying to rob you. You still have your chest in the secure room.'

'When you land in London, Drach will kill you for it,' Win confirmed. 'Let me have it and, I assure you, no harm will come to you.'

Henri glanced sharply at Win, but restrained himself from asking why Win should be the holder of the second seal. He looked at Bartholomew. He was a brave, fighting man but, in his whole lifetime, the captain had never come so close to witchcraft before, and he certainly didn't take the warnings lightly.

'I'll consider my position,' Bartholomew said eventually. 'After all, we have three more days' sailing before we sight land, and that will not be the English coastline. That, we will not see for a further two days more.'

Henri nodded. 'You are a brave and slightly insanely courageous man, captain. Remember, I watched you on that deck out there. I doubt if I could have done what you did. But we need to settle this matter now. Either you are with us or against us.'

'Do I take that as a threat? You must know by now, how I respond to coercion.'

'Take it any way you want, Captain. You know what I am capable of doing.'

'Don't let a small artefact be the thing that makes Henri set against you,' Win put in. 'He saved you and he saved your ship.'

Bartholomew pondered a moment longer. 'Will you give me your word that you will not say anything to the authorities about… about my collection?'

Henri thought about the chest of gold and gems that the captain had acquired, probably over a lifetime of crime on the high sea. Bartholomew was no better than a pirate himself, and for that reason, Henri wanted to see Bartholomew hang for his crimes. But on board this ship only Win and Bartholomew knew that Henri hadn't killed Garside. Counter accusations could turn out to be rather more difficult to deal with if the passengers and crew backed the captain.

'We'll say nothing,' Henri said eventually, 'provided you do two things. First you hand over the artefact. That way you can deny you ever had it.

'And second?'

'And second, since we saved the two ships, then you share your prize, *The Black Sword*, Captain. When it is sold as salvage, the remaining passengers and crew can have their share. Their friends and colleagues died defending *The Arinosta* and every single one of the survivors fought hard to save it. The least you can do is repay them.'

'That is normally the case with salvage,' Bartholomew insisted. 'And you,' he went on, 'what do you want?'

Henri was about to say that as an explorer and prospector, he'd take his share, but he stopped short. Bartholomew thought he was some kind of witch and Henri doubted very much if people who had magic in their fingertips spent their lives scrabbling about with them in river beds feeling for nuggets of gold or pushing them into clay in search of buried diamonds. He had a plan of course, but he didn't say anything about it. 'I'll be happy just to get off this ship and onto firm soil again. You have no idea how much I hate the sea.'

Bartholomew chuckled. 'Well, I used to be in love with

it! Not now, though. Not any more. I've grown tired of being cooped up like a chicken. I have had no room and little chance to spread my wings. That's going to change.' He went silent and seemed to fall into a deep chasm of thought. Henri wondered if he hadn't fallen asleep, but eventually he lifted his head, slipped off his boots and spoke again. 'Here,' he said and threw his right boot at Henri. 'It's in there. Enjoy!'

Chapter Sixteen

THE SHIP'S COOK

Why Bartholomew thought that Henri should look after the golden seal, Henri couldn't guess, but Win had a look like thunder on her face as Henri drew the seal out of the boot. He gripped it between his finger and thumb and held it up to see it better with the light from the window. It looked exactly like the one he had disassembled and he wondered if it had the same minute markings and the magical properties as his own.

Eventually, and after being watched silently for several minutes, he tossed the empty boot back to its owner and tossed the seal to Win. Her look of surprise was obvious, but she overcame the shock and gave him a cursory smile before placing it in her trouser pocket.

'I suppose you are resigning as my cabin boy,' the captain sighed, as he pulled on his boots.

'You'll survive Mr. Bartholomew,' Win said conciliatorily. 'Only a few more days to go and you are home free. But,' she added, 'you will need us to back you up if anybody starts to question you. You mustn't tell anybody you found it. If you do, then they will want to know who has it now, and once you have told them that, then your usefulness will be at an end. Understand what I'm saying?'

The captain frowned solemnly. 'I do,' he said with a nod. 'I certainly do.'

With that, Henri went to the door. He had some small, golden segments of the seal to retrieve and he didn't want to waste any time doing it. Blackwell had seen him appear out of nowhere and he might be looking around outside the cabin to see what was there, whether it be some kind of hole in the air through which Henri stepped from another dimension or otherwise.

With a sigh of relief, Henri discovered that Blackwell had remained on watch. But Henri didn't want to retrieve the small section of the seal with him watching. Again, the man was looking down at Henri, as if he had never disappeared in the first place, and Henri knew he would disappear again if he picked up the small golden segment of the cube, and that might raise the suspicions of even the totally unmoved and uncurious Blackwell. So Henri just smiled and walked down the steps and towards the hatch that led to the lower deck.

It took less than three minutes to retrieve the other sections of his seal and, placing them in his great coat pocket once more he walked back up to the poop deck, lifted the coil of rope and retrieved the final part of the cube.

When he straightened back up, Win was standing there in the doorway of the cabin. 'I see you've got the other one then,' she observed.

'I need to go somewhere to try and put it back together,' he said, looking to her for a suggestion.

'No, don't.' She seemed agitated. 'Keep that last sector separate in your right hand pocket. If you need to become invisible again then you can drop the other pieces and walk away from them.'

'I have no intention of doing it again,' Henri insisted. 'The thing makes me feel quite unwell.'

'Only because you've used it for too long at one time. In a day or two, it won't affect you at all if you want to use it. Just take your time to recover. But keep it handy. Bartholomew might not be as compliable as you think. He knows who we are and what we have. He may not have given up on it yet or on that reward.'

'You don't trust him then?'

'About as much as I would have trusted the pirates.'

'That's good enough for me,' Henri said as she walked away through the door of the cabin. He watched her confidently returning to her new self appointed task of keeping an eye on Bartholomew. She walked as lightly as a sprite. A wisp of hair fell from beneath her cap. He hadn't seen her without it on. It was a soft cap with a neb at the front, and she must have always worn it to keep back some longer tresses that she had been reluctant to cut off in her act to become a cabin boy. As the door closed behind her, he placed four of the separate segments of the seal in his handkerchief, tied a knot in it to make sure the four pieces could not be accidentally lost and then placed it in his left hand pocket. The other part of the seal he placed in the pocket on the opposite side of his greatcoat.

Henri was prepared to take orders from the captain to help sail *The Arinosta* safely home. He hated ships now more than he had ever done on his travels before. He hated the food, he hated the way both passengers and crew had to live, he hated the helplessness of being washed up and down on huge waves like a cork in a bathtub and he hated being on what was, in reality, a floating prison; a prison without walls but instead just a wide expanse of murderous water waiting to kill him if he tried to escape.

He felt nervous mingling in with the rest of the made-up crew. He would have to spend an inordinate amount of time avoiding questions from all but a few of the people on board as to where he had been, especially the passenger McGill who he had managed to save during the battle. But eventually, after shrugging and making every effort to appear like he had never disappeared in the first place, he made his way back down to the main deck.

Some of the people who had been passengers, gathered, huddled together with odd members of the crew, whispering and looking out from the clique with furtive glances towards him. Obviously, Bartholomew hadn't enlightened them as to his innocence in the matter of Garside's death, and some were obviously still very wary of him. However, it seemed that the necessity of getting safely home overrode any fears, and nobody outwardly challenged Henri or made any accusations. Calmly, Henri walked up to the bow of the ship where the ship's cook was busy giving orders.

Blackwell was up on the main mast, carrying out a shift as lookout. Surprisingly, he seemed as friendly and outgoing as he ever had been in the dark stinking and dreary days of their confinement to the passenger hold. He would have to watch him, Henri thought. He was sure Blackwell was the sailor who Bartholomew used as an insider amongst the passengers to wheedle out any information about potential wealth or belongings. Stocky had had an accomplice and now, despite Stocky being gone, Bartholomew still had a dedicated and loyal insider.

It wasn't more than a few seconds, however, before Bartholomew emerged from his quarters carrying a large cone-like megaphone. He went to the rail of the poop deck and lifted the amplifying device to his lips. Calling at the top of his voice, he called instructions across the divide to the meagre crew of *The Black Sword* to hoist the two main sails so as to reduce the drag on *The Arinosta*. He had obviously taken very seriously the warning about Drach overtaking him. That worried Henri. Win knew much more than she had let on. The question was; how would she know that Drach had taken another ship if she was already on board *The Arinosta* and sailing away from land and any means of giving or receiving messages? And why did Bartholomew, who was as astute as any man Henri had ever met, accept her statement as being the whole truth? But whatever the reason for it, Bartholomew wanted to make better time getting to London and he pushed all the men he had to hand, including Win, who was no longer working her mesmeric powers to the full. Now, every time Henri saw her, she looked even more mature as a young woman and less and less like a pre-pubescent cabin boy. She was already wearing some better fitting and considerably better quality grey silk breeches and blue cotton coat borrowed from one of the chests that were retrieved from the pirate ship and which now languished alongside Bartholomew's treasure chest in the armoury. She too was drawing comments from the men on board, but then, boys mature into young men and nobody, as far as Henri knew, had been told that Jack was a witch. Rather, they probably presumed Jack was training in the art of navigation and chart plotting as, at noon each day by the marine chronometer, she had been taking the sextant out of its case, pointing it towards the sun and taking a sight to check the ship's latitude.

Bartholomew went to the ship's cook, the person who seemed now to have assumed the position of his second in command, and chatted to him away from the rest of the men, pointing and gesticulating, obviously giving instructions as to what orders were to be given to the crew to get *The Arinosta* to its destiny without any further loss of time. Hardly a couple of minutes had passed while Henri watched the two largest sails of the salvaged pirate ship being skilfully hauled, when Blackwell, who was still up in the crows nest, shouted, 'Land Ahoy!'

The air was suddenly awash with choruses of cheers and shouting. It heralded the end of this dreadful journey and none on board wished it to last a moment longer than it had to. If Blackwell had sighted the French coast, then Britain was not so many days travel beyond it. The French coastline was so far away on the horizon that it would be several hours later that the rest of the people on deck could actually see it, but the celebrations began.

Henri watched from a distance. He still had to face the problem of mingling with the rest of the men now that he was no longer invisible, and the fact that he was obviously still branded a murderer, made him cautious enough to stand back while the celebrations got under way.

The relief amongst the men was obvious. Even Captain Bartholomew's mood lightened instantly. Standing next to him, he loudly called for the ship's cook to break out a couple of bottles of rum and ordered that every man, able bodied and wounded alike, should be issued with a double measure.

Dutifully the sailor disappeared down into the galley and it wasn't long before he emerged carrying a large wooden tray filled with glasses, each of which already contained a full measure of dark brown liquid. An empty bottle stood on the tray beside them. Henri watched as the cook passed amongst the men, handing out the drinks and, eventually, when all seemed to have a glass in their hand, he turned to look for Henri. He gave Henri a broad smile.

'Ah, my friend!' he said in his strong French accent. 'You shall not be left out!' He placed the now empty tray on the deck. He took a glass from one pocket and from the other he pulled out another bottle. Pulling the cork out with his teeth, he poured the glass full as he walked over to Henri. 'You've returned just in time,' he said as if Henri had been a missing friend. 'Come, celebrate with us!'

Henri took the glass that was handed to him, reluctant to object that he had a definite dislike of sailors' rum. Had the cook offered him a jug of ale then he would have been much happier, but he took the proffered drink and held it up as a salute to the rest of the men who were gathered chatting and laughing around the captain who was, by now, using his amplifying device to call to the ship in tow and for the skeleton crew to take the same measure of rum to celebrate. As all watched him, Henri turned and, carrying his drink with him, silently went down to the hold where the wounded lay.

The hold was still gloomy and smelled of sickness, but there were several hanging lanterns giving out a flickering light for the men who were down there.

'See you're back then,' a fairly young man called Pringle stated. He had a wispy beard and his face was pale grey. He was the most seriously injured of the surviving wounded. He had received a severe wound to his side from a pistol shot. The surgeon had removed the ball, but Pringle was feverish and looked like he might die before anybody could get him to a hospital. Not that hospitals, in those days, were anything like they are today. Surgeons still advocated bleeding people to lessen their fever. What that did, in fact, was weaken the patient enough to stop him complaining and usually, after three or four treatments he would die from lack of blood. So being on board the ship possibly gave him the better chance of survival.

Henri felt that, for Pringle, any relief from his ague would be welcome. The drinks had not yet arrived down in the makeshift hospital, but explaining to the rest of the men that they were on their way, he handed Pringle the glass and turned away saying, 'I was never away really.'

'Some magic that!' Pringle said, swallowing some rum with a cough and a slight chuckle.

'You knew it was me then?' Henri said, turning back to him and taking the glass back in his own hand.

Pringle gave a grunt of disappointment. 'Said the wrong thing, have I?'

'No, no, not at all. It just took me a bit by surprise, that's all. I didn't think anybody knew.'

'Everybody did,' the wounded man replied. 'We all knew it was you.'

'And just how did you know that?' Henri asked, now suddenly welded to the spot. He was on the verge of some revelation or other.

'Oh, it was just a rumour that was going round. Somebody had said that you ain't gone overboard. They said you had just disappeared into thin air; became invisible, like.'

Now Henri was beginning to understand why the survivors of the battle were treating him with rather less bewilderment than he thought might have been the case. But who could possibly have said anything? The only person that knew he was invisible and still on the ship was Win.

'I don't suppose you know who told you that I was invisible, do you?'

'So you ain't denying it was you then, cutting 'em down like stalks o' barley!'

'Doesn't seem like there's any point,' Henri said, frowning while his mind raced through all the possibilities. 'I don't suppose it was the cabin boy that told you, was it?'

'Jack? Hell no! Jack said that the rumour was ridiculous. He said that people that believe in that kind of rubbish are soon deceived.'

'That kind of rubbish?'

'Magic and all that,' Pringle said, taking the glass from Henri's hand and drinking a good portion of the rum down in one gulp.

'He called it magic then?'

'Not Jack, no. As I said…'

'No, the man who told you I had become invisible.'

'Oh him! Hell no. He just swore at you. Cursed you all the time, he did. Called you a murdering dog. He…'

'Who said I was a murdering dog, Pringle? Who said they knew I was invisible?' Henri was losing patience.

'That hefty sailor, you know, the one built like a brick latrine.'

'You mean Stocky?'

'Yeah, that's the one. He said you'd made yourself invisible so that you didn't get hung for killing old Garside.'

'Is that right?' Henri said pensively. 'And you believed that, did you? You believe that it's possible for somebody to be standing right next to you but you cannot see them no matter which way you look at them?

Pringle shook his head. 'Never believed a word of it.' He frowned and thought for a second before adding, 'Not until we all saw it for ourselves. Pirates that just died on the deck; the dozen or so that fell dead on the steps to the captain's cabin; then the battle on *The Black Sword* when none of the pirates could cut the ties. Then we believed it all right. Inspired us it did!'

'Glad to hear it,' Henri said almost in a whisper. His mind was racing. 'So Stocky reckoned he knew,' he said, recapping on how it all happened. 'Worked it out, I suppose. He probably knew I wasn't the sort to jump into the sea.'

Pringle scowled. 'Well no, he said something. Now what was it? He said...' Pringle thought deeply for a moment or so while Henri just waited patiently. Then his eyes brightened. 'That's it! He said that you'd had something of theirs, something that they'd bin looking for, and they knew it made you invisible.'

'They? Who's they, Pringle. Think will you!'

'Well I reckoned it was his friend.'

'His friend?' Henri stayed Pringle's hand as he lifted the glass of rum to his lips again. 'Do you want the rest of this?'

Pringle nodded. 'Wouldn't mind.' He smiled. 'You're waiting for me to tell you who his friend is, ain't you?'

Henri nodded and then, releasing the man's hand, waited while Pringle's lifted it to his lips. 'It would help me,' Henri said as Pringle sipped at the rum.

'Mundulay,' said Pringle as the rum went smoothly down his throat.

'Mundulay?'

'The cook; the surgeon. His name's Mundulay'.

Henri nodded. 'Mundulay,' he repeated.

'You trying to make sure you don't forget his name?' Pringle asked inquisitively.

'Don't worry my young friend, I won't forget it!' He patted Pringle on the shoulder. 'You get well, do you hear?'

Pringle nodded. 'I'm not too well. Think I might not even reach land. Thanks for the rum though. That was really good on yer,' he said, holding his stomach and suddenly bursting into a bout of coughing.

Henri nodded and turned to leave, and as he did so, he spotted Win's feet on the steps that led out of the hold. The rest of her was above the beam that supported that section of the deck. The feet were backing up the stairs. Then her feet turned and they ran up the remaining steps and onto the upper deck.

Henri started to run after her, but suddenly he halted when he heard a gasping sound behind him. He spun on his heel. Pringle had sat up in his bunk and, with his septic wound bleeding through his fingers with every spasm, he was convulsing and shaking. Sweat beaded on his brow and his eyes stared blankly past Henri. He gasped again, as he clutched at his throat. Henri took two steps towards him but by the time he got to his side, Pringle was dead and falling back against the hard wooden bunk. Foam was beginning to come from the dead man's mouth.

Henri knew what had happened. The signs were clear to see; the rum had been poisoned. Henri began to sweat now. Had he taken a sip when he saluted the ship's crew? He couldn't remember. Then he remembered that Win had been watching from the steps.

He ran towards them, taking the steps two at a time and emerged onto the deck only to see Win running up onto the poop deck and disappearing into the captain's cabin.

❖

Chapter Seventeen

A STEP IN TIME

Henri couldn't think. His head was spinning. Win must have heard what Pringle had said. He'd said everybody knew Henri was invisible! Well, Mundulay had told Stocky and Stocky had told Pringle; that much was certain, but who had told Mundulay? And who had told that person? Everything suddenly seemed jumbled and confused. He was still sweating. Mundulay the cook and Stocky must have been the ones who had been looking for the seal when he felt them searching him in the blackness of the passenger hold, that dark night that now seemed long, long ago. But Henri could have sworn one of the murderers was a passenger. But then they had found a seal. Did they know there were two seals?

And Win? She knew about both seals. Both the golden cubes were on board *The Arinosta*. What sort of coincidence is that? And why did they try to frame him for Garside's murder if they didn't know that Henri had the other seal?

And why did Win run when Henri was turning towards her? Didn't she want him to see her? Had she seen what was happening to Pringle? Had she been waiting for it to happen to him?

Watched by several of the men on the deck, he walked up

the steps, slowing a little now with every stride. The men were saying something to him but it sounded all distorted, rather like he was listening through a thick door. As he reached it, the top step seemed higher than the others. It was an effort to lift his legs. He took a few deep breaths as he reached level decking and then walked along the poop deck towards the door of the captain's cabin. He knocked politely and, not waiting for the invitation to enter, he walked straight in.

Bartholomew was sitting at his desk. It looked as if he was reading through some pages of the ship's log, but Henri wasn't really taking too much notice. The captain lifted his head and smiled. It was a strange looking smile, more like a grin; or was it a sneer? Henri couldn't tell. Things were a bit distorted. Bartholomew's grin seemed to be fixed like the face of a wax puppet, just looking and watching; never changing. What was he looking at Bartholomew for anyway? He was searching for Win. He needed answers but wasn't sure now what the questions were. They had been clear in his mind as he set off to find her, but now his mind was wandering back to when he had first arrived on the ship; when he had lain there on the deck and the only hand that had helped him was Win's. He was thinking of the time when he had thrown himself on top of her prostrate body to prevent Stocky's sword from slicing her in two. He wondered if he would ever know what the seal and Win and the murders were all about.

All the murders? His murder? He knew now he had sipped the rum before taking the glass down to the passenger hold. It was one thing that he could remember now better than any other recollection. The bottle that Mundulay had taken from his pocket had been laced with a very strong poison. Pringle died quickly. He drank most of the rum in the glass. Henri would die more slowly but he knew he was dying. There was a flash of light at the back of his eyes.

Win was coming towards the door as if to answer the knock. 'Hello Henri,' she said deliberately slowly. 'Come quickly.' It was an order. Her face was as grave as a death mask.

Henri nodded. 'Yesh, I was wondering if you'd be kind'nuff to allow me to conshult you on a shmall matter.' His words were slurred. It was hard to breathe. His head was beginning to spin. As his eyes began to pan the room, he saw Bartholomew still looking up at him with the same insane grin pasted across his face.

'We'll take a walk, shall we?' Win said as she stepped straight to the door.

'I want you to perform shome of your magic,' Henri stated. 'Jush so I can be shoooor you're really a witch!' He was beginning to fall asleep.

'Stand up!' Win ordered.

Henri blinked awake and stood to attention.

'Now walk!' Win shouted, at the top of her voice. She must have known he was being deafened by a sledge hammer battering against a wooden door somewhere. Every heartbeat sent a thundering blast of noise clamouring through his whole body, shaking him from the very tips of his hair roots to his toe nails.

'Walk you stupid man!' she shouted again, this time grabbing his arm and pulling him forward with all her strength. Her cap fell off and tumbled to the floor as she pinned herself under Henri's armpit.

Things were becoming a lot clearer now. The banging was

getting quieter. The sledge hammer was still hitting its target, but it didn't seem to matter any more. There were more urgent things to consider; better things. Serenity was beginning to take over. He imagined he could see everything in the world all at one time; anything he wanted. At this moment he wanted to see his witch. He bent his head forward and looked down at the face by his shoulder. He noticed just how good looking she was, this slip of a girl, a young woman, with dark brown eyes and her dark brown, almost black hair now falling in ringlets down her cheeks as she struggled to keep him upright. Her body felt soft against the side of his rib cage. He supposed it was a good way to pass from this world.

Win must have been able to read his thoughts. 'You're going into another world,' she explained.

'I know!' Henri said in a faint whisper, surprised that she would even bother explaining that he was dying. They seemed to be walking forward, but he couldn't feel his legs moving. Perhaps she was carrying him. Perhaps he was floating. Did it matter?

The air felt chilled. It was suddenly misty. Strange, Henri thought. The mist was inside the cabin. He turned his head and looked around but could only see the mist. Win wasn't under his arm any more. She was looking down at him as if he were lying down and she were standing over him. Six more faces peered down at him, forming a circle around him. Their mouths were moving but the words didn't make sense. He tried to listen to each one separately but what the lips were saying didn't sound like any language Henri had ever heard. The faces began to become clearer. They were all women, all very similar in appearance, some reasonably young; some looked a little older and more mature. They all seemed to be dressed in black. Their pale faces, beautiful, with complexions like soft, fresh cream, looked to be concentrating; urging Henri to do something.

Suddenly he took in a sharp breath. He hadn't realized he had stopped breathing. He must have been holding his breath. But however long he had been holding it, the air felt good again in his lungs. The faces began to smile, first one and then another until all six strangers were all beaming. Win's face was still there, but her face wasn't smiling. Hers looked grey compared with the others. Her brow was creased and her eyes looked a little watery. She lifted her face away from him, as did all the others. Then they all backed away into the mist which seemed to be thinning. He heard Win say something, again in some foreign tongue and then she emerged from the mist and continued looking down at him as the hazy vapour thickened once again.

When it cleared, Henri realized he had been dreaming. He was lying on the captain's horsehair mattress, staring up at the ceiling of the cabin. The whole place was quiet. He moved his eyes from side to side. Win was nowhere to be seen. As he lifted his head, he spotted her sitting on the end of the bunk, her pale face relaxed and her eyes staring as if she were in a daze. He looked over at the desk. Bartholomew was still sitting there, his face still pasted with an insane grin. He looked as if he hadn't moved. Henri listened. There was no sound, not even the sound of the wind in the sails or the sea washing past the hull. It was so quiet that he could hear his own shallow breathing. Win was breathing too. Her breath was even fainter. She still seemed to be in some kind of trance. He looked at

Bartholomew again. He was sure that the captain was holding his breath. He was leaning forward at an awkward angle, in such a position that it would have been quite exhausting to maintain the pose. But he did maintain it and he seemed to be doing it effortlessly.

A moment later, Win took a deep breath as if waking up herself. She blinked, pushed a tiny tress of hair from in front of her forehead and looked at Henri. 'Oh, you're awake. Good!'

'I didn't realize I had fallen asleep,' Henri stated. 'Not until I woke up, that is.' He looked at her and pushed himself up on his elbows. 'What's with old Bartholomew?' he asked, nodding his head sideways in the direction of the captain. 'He seems to be frozen.'

'He is, sort of,' Win stated. She thought for a moment. 'I suppose you remember the mist?'

Henri nodded. 'And the faces?' he said after a moment's thought. 'Were there faces? Or was it all in a dream?'

Win smiled and then frowned. 'I'd like to tell you it was a dream,' she said, quietly. 'But they have told me to tell you the truth.'

'They?'

'The other six of us. The faces, remember?'

Henri nodded. 'They were real then?'

'Yes,' Win answered plainly, 'they were real, but they were in another dimension. They weren't on this ship. They weren't with us here.'

'So where were they? It was a dream then.'

'No, you went to them.'

Henri shook his head. He thought for a moment or two and then said, 'I'll try and get my head around that later. Just tell me now, what's up with Bartholomew?'

'He's frozen in time,' Win explained with a slight smile.

'Frozen in time,' Henri repeated to himself. 'Meaning just what exactly?'

'That his time has stopped for the time being,' Win chuckled. 'That sounds rather funny doesn't it? Time's stopped for the time being!'

'Very funny,' Henri said, shaking his head, not even remotely amused. He got up unsteadily and walked over to the door. It was still open from when he had stepped into the cabin. There was no movement to and fro as there usually was with the rolling movement of the ship. Surely they hadn't hit the doldrums again!

He stepped out onto the deck. Then the truth hit him. The ship was at a slight angle as if stayed on a reef or sandbank. The seas were still but not flat, as if in a giant seascape painting. A distant gull was suspended in the air as if hanging from an invisible chord. He looked down at the main deck. The men were still there, but they were all standing in different poses, frozen, as still as mannequins in an emporium window. At the rail on the starboard side, out of view of the other people on board, Mundulay was leaning forward, his arm outstretched, a bottle a few feet from his hand, in mid air, as if he had just pitched it over the side and had been caught in the act.

Henri walked back inside the cabin. His strength was coming back remarkably fast. Win was still sitting where he had left her. She smiled and said, 'Told you.'

Henri sat down beside her. 'So what happens now? How long does this go on?'

Win shrugged. 'Once the spell is cast, it can last for as long as we like.'

'We?'

'The witches.'

'The women I saw in the mist?'

'That's right.'

'And just how many of you are there?'

'Just seven of us left now' Win said sadly. 'But we're working on it.'

'And you can stop time?'

'It's not quite so simple. We can step out of this time or existence into another time to avoid its future. You see, where we are now, is one time or existence; but in the same place at the same time there are many other existences. They are called parallel universes. Experienced witches can step from one to another.'

'Right,' Henri said, shaking his head once again. 'So, we're in a different existence now, to that in which Bartholomew is sitting.

'Yes.'

And we've been avoiding Bartholomew's future by getting out of his existence, then?'

'Yes,' Win said smiling. 'And when we return to it, we will have altered it slightly.'

'In that?'

'In that you are alive and well. You had just been poisoned by Bartholomew and his cook. You do know that, don't you?'

Henri nodded.

'Well, that future must not exist.'

'And you can do that; alter the future?'

'Yes,' Win replied curtly. 'There are lots of different futures.

You'll find that out eventually.'

'I'll find that out?'

'You are linked to our future; the witches future. We can't permit anything to happen to you that isn't in it. In our future, witches survive. If we do not preserve that then witches will die out, become extinct like so many other creatures that have lived on this earth. We exist in no other future.' She paused and then added, 'And ordinary mortals will need us one day. One day very soon.'

Henri was silent. He could only imagine this was just a continuance of some fantastic dream. Was he really on this ship? Was the seal real? Was Win real? At this particular moment he was beginning to doubt if any of it existed at all, and if it did, on whose future was it so indelibly scratched? He sighed and looked Win straight in the eyes.

'This is real isn't it?'

'Yes it is.'

She watched Henri frown. 'Time is space really. Ordinary mortals don't understand it yet. We witches know about it and understand it already. I took you to my sisters to save you.'

Henri nodded again. He had been poisoned and now he was well. That much he did understand; but he didn't know what to say. It sounded totally impossible. It *was* totally impossible.

'And when you move from one place in space to another, one somewhere else, you move through time as well, even though it's only one step.'

Henri just smiled.

'And although we can see the time and place where we were, one step away; we are in an entirely different time or existence at the moment, so that the time we have left behind looks to be frozen. Any point in time, when you look back on it, is preserved. You remember it as it was. It's like a memory or a photograph. You've seen them haven't you?'

'Yes, they are becoming quite commonplace now,' Henri stated, glad at last to be able to relate to something he understood, if only a little.

'And that's how we can alter the future by seeing which one we want to choose.'

'So how long have witches been doing this then?'

'Our knowledge has been passed down for thousands of years but we are from your time. We are not from the past or the future.'

'Glad to hear it,' Henri said quietly. His brain was reeling. He had already given up trying to make sense of anything this rather small but attractive witch was saying.

'So, if we die without leaving any descendants, then witches will be no more. That's why it is so important to choose the right time in which we are to exist, because we share our future with ordinary mortals.'

'You keep talking about us as ordinary mortals. Aren't you an ordinary mortal?'

'I've told you before, that I am much older than you.'

'And I've told you, you hardly look seventeen!'

'Witches live for five or six hundred years. Only when we choose to be mortal do we shorten our lifespan. Your great grandmother was a witch. She married a mortal and when she did so she chose to be human. Outliving those you love by hundreds of years is sometimes too hard to bear. If she hadn't been killed and had lived her life out as a mortal, she would have only lived perhaps to the age of two hundred. It's a choice we make.'

'So she was a witch?'

'Yes, she was one of us. But because she had made the choice to be a mortal, she did not go on to develop the power to cast the spells that could have saved her life.'

Henri walked out to the rail and looked from the poop deck at the solid sea. Win followed behind him. 'So how long do we wait for their time to begin again?' he asked, nodding towards some of the crew.

'When I break the spell,' she said matter of factly. 'I shan't hold it much longer. All we have to do is step back into their time.'

'And where's that?'

'Beside the captain's desk. I took you through the time door as you came into the cabin.'

'Tell me something,' Henri suddenly asked. An idea was forming in his head. 'What would happen to these people if we didn't return to their time? Would they be frozen like this forever?'

Win laughed, 'Of course not. They are already carrying on with their lives in their future!'

'But aren't they stuck like that then,' Henri asked pointing at Bartholomew, still sitting with the insane grin on his face.

'No, no. That is just a moment in their time, the moment we left their future and entered another one, if only for a short time. When we return then we'll return at the same moment we left. As I have explained, it is just a photograph type of image that we can see. A single moment. But they are not affected by our other world any more than this one is affected by them.'

'Apart from the fact that we are no longer in their world.'

'Precisely! We have simply disappeared from that world. They are probably, at this very moment, wondering where we have both gone!'

'Like when I disappeared using the power of the golden seal?'

Win frowned. 'That is just what you did. You disappeared. Puff! Gone! But the seal didn't take you into another world like we've just done.' She put her hand on Henri's arm. 'I'm going to explain something to you, and I need you to understand,' she said. 'When you are not in someone's future, that is, if you are not in their existence, then you have no influence on anything that happens in their world as they see it, live it, breathe it.'

'That's obvious,' Henri agreed.

'But as soon as they can see you, then their whole future is changed. You don't have to even do anything. Just being able to see you is sufficient to affect both your existence and theirs. And it doesn't just apply to people. It applies to things as well.'

'So what about the seal? How is that different? When I was invisible, I could still see them carrying on in their lives, and I could affect those lives.'

'Well they weren't just a picture of a single moment in time. The seal did not take you into a different future, but it did come from a different future. The Seven Witches, those six you saw, plus myself, are trying to discover which future it came from so that it can be taken back there. You see, it cannot be destroyed. It is not gold.'

'I know,' Henri admitted. 'I was told something about it not being harder or softer than anything with which it comes into contact. And it does not absorb heat, so it cannot be melted down even at the highest temperatures.'

Win looked surprised. 'I didn't realize you had been told so much about it.'

'Only by the man who traded it for a purse of real gold,' Henri explained. 'He told me a few things about it which, at the time, I didn't believe. He said he had hit it with a hammer but it neither marked the hammer nor was marked by it. And he explained that he had found it on a hot, sunny, sandy beach, but when he went to pick it up it had absorbed none of the heat of the sand or the sun. It was cool on his fingers.'

'Did he? Well I can tell you, there are many more things that you don't know about it!'

'*Them* don't you mean?' Henri realized they were only talking about the one seal that he had carried onto the ship.

Win gave him a sympathetic smile. 'Yours is the only one. There are no others. I came on this ship to steal it from you. The Seven Witches made a very good copy so that I could exchange it without your knowing. But the copy was just a block of gold. It has no power to alter or change anything at all. The trouble was, you discovered that the real one came apart and that one section of it made you invisible if held on its own. I'd missed my chance. You would have known it had been swapped.'

'So what about Garside?'

'What about him?'

'How come he had the counterfeit seal?'

'He didn't.'

'But you told me…'

'I told you he had a seal.' Before Henri could ask why Bartholomew had a seal like his own along with Garside's watch, she held up her hand to stop him asking, and went on.

'He was killed by a passenger called Hepton. Hepton? You know, a gangly looking man with whiskers?'

Henri shook his head. Most of the passengers had whiskers in some form, either before they embarked on the trip, or grown due to lack of shaving facilities, during it.

'Hepton was killed by the pirates, so if you didn't know him before, then you won't get to know him now,' she went on.

'Really!'

Win just shrugged. Her humour wasn't working, that's for sure.

'So one of Bartholomew's accomplices is dead then?'

'Yes.'

'And what about Blackwell,' Henri added.

'Blackwell!' Win laughed. 'He wasn't working for Bartholomew! He's working for me!'

She watched Henri as his face showed complete and utter disbelief, even more than when she was explaining about parallel universes. 'He's worked with The Seven Witches for more than ten years,' she said, laughing.

It was the first time Henry had seen her so gleeful. His heart suddenly felt like it could burst. She looked so… He shook himself and brought his mind back down to earth, whichever earth it was he was on. She had saved his life and he was just feeling a bit appreciative. That was all. It couldn't be anything else.

'Anyway,' Win continued explaining, 'Hepton and his stubby little sailor friend killed Garside for the seal he carried. You know how it is when people are making friends and are, like on a ship, travelling quite intimately. Well, especially when boredom sets in, sometimes they let down their guard. Garside had let it slip that he had a seal when he was talking to Hepton. But his was actually a real gold seal, an article for putting wax seals on documents and envelopes. It wasn't shaped like a cube.'

'So who gave Bartholomew the counterfeit seal if it wasn't taken off Garside?' Henri had to ask.

'When those two murdering robbers had taken Garside's valuables,' Win explained, 'they wrapped them in a piece of canvas and left them on their captain's desk ready for him to stow away with the rest of his loot in the morning. I slipped the cube into the cloth before he rose. At the same time I removed the seal to which Garside had referred when he was bragging to Hepton.'

Henri creased his brow. 'But why?'

'Because I thought it would stop them searching for the real one, the one you had. Bartholomew presumed that they knew he had it, and I thought he would leave it at that, but his men, realizing they had made a mistake, continued looking for it. Most of the people on board had seen or heard about you fleeing from Drach and how you had somehow made it onto the ship. The captain had probably originally told them that you were the one most likely to have the seal, and they had simply been distracted by Garside. So they carried on looking; and, since someone had to be accountable for his murder, they tried to make it look like you had done it so that you would be searched.'

'So Garside died for nothing,' Henri said with a frown.

'It saved your life,' Win said confidently. 'They would have come to you if they hadn't been suddenly convinced that Garside had it.'

'They'd searched me once already.'

'And were probably told to go back and try again. It might have been too dark to do it properly when they carried out the first search. After that, most likely they were told to kill whoever had the seal. Bartholomew was determined and desperate to get it, and they would have killed you if Garside hadn't bragged about his.' She hesitated for a second before saying, 'And, not knowing that you were going to do your disappearing act, I couldn't risk them getting their hands on the real seal. It seemed like a good opportunity. Garside was dead, so he was the perfect person for me to point their fingers at.'

'Bartholomew looked pretty convinced that his seal was real.'

'Oh, the trick worked all right; although it wasn't supposed to fool everybody for ever. It was only to buy me more time. The problem was, you went and started making yourself invisible before I could steal the real one off you. I hadn't expected that you would discover any of its powers. Nobody else had ever been able to do it.'

'Any of its powers?'

'Yes,' Win said quite impatiently, at being interrupted. 'I'll explain later.' She went on, 'But you did discover one of its powers and so, when you did your vanishing act, and especially after the events during the battle with the pirates, rumours were bound to surface. It was too late to retrieve the fake seal from Bartholomew, so I decided to convince him that there were two seals. He was not so surprised when the rumour started that you had your own seal, a seal that made you invisible. He already suspected that the seal had special properties. Just thinking how he had overcome the pirates convinced him that his own seal had guided his good fortune.

Knowing what powers your seal could bestow, he would think his could do the same, and that would just increase its value.'

'You told him that I had a seal?'

'No; he wouldn't have believed anything I said. I told Mundulay, you know, our friendly cook, surgeon, master swordsman and poisoner extraordinaire. He was still looking for it. I suggested that you may have got your powers from it. He couldn't wait to tell the captain about his brilliant theory. Anyway,' Win said, her eyes lighting up a little more. 'I don't think they know yet that their seal is counterfeit and I don't think they know how it is supposed to work. They certainly don't know who you really are. Drach couldn't have known that, either, so he won't have told Bartholomew much. Drach knows about the real seal's powers, of course, because he's read the transcript of The Golden Book. But he will only know who you really are when he hears what has happened on this ship.'

'Who I *really* am? Just what do you mean by that?'

'You're the one who can make the seal work of course,' Win said rather impatiently. 'It's all laid down in The Golden Book.'

'And what precisely is The Golden Book?' Henri asked exasperatedly.

'Oh, it's just a book.'

'And who's got that may I ask?'

Win grinned. 'Me!'

'I suppose you stole it!'

'Well stealing's a bit strong isn't it? After all, Drach killed to get it in the first place.'

❖

Chapter Eighteen

BETRAYED AGAIN

'I've got a plan,' Henri said, as they went forward to step back into Bartholomew's time. 'What if we both disappeared with the seal and *The Black Sword?* What if we walked over that stiff looking sea and...'

Win shook her head. 'The sea is still sea in this time or any other. In that place, the sea is the sea. It looks like a solid three dimensional picture. It isn't. It is what it is. The men are men. The bird up there in the sky is a bird. The sea is the sea.'

'Huh,' Henri said with not a small degree of disappointment.

'And besides which, if we went over there, then we would still be in another time. We have to get back to our time. That is important. And that can only be done by stepping past our friend here,' she said, looking at Bartholomew.

'It was just an idea,' Henri said, rather sadly.

'And a good one. But we'll have to get onto *The Black Sword* another way.'

Henri raised his eyebrows. 'So you reckon we can get away without him going after us?' he asked as he looked for the opening into his time.

'We've got a bargaining chip, haven't we,' Win said, taking a firm hold on Henri's arm and dragging him forward.

'How can you tell where the opening is?' he asked as she led him.

'I can see it,' Win replied chirpily. 'The same as I can see your aura.'

'Aura?'

'Your energy field. The thing that is you, not just your body. You live in your body,' she explained, 'like a snail lives in a shell. There's more to you than just flesh and blood.'

They were about to step past the captain when Henri shouted, 'Stop!'

'What?' Win waited for him to explain.

'Can I reach Bartholomew's telescope without going back?' The large leather bound telescope lay on the desk next to the captain.

Win shrugged. 'Yes, why?'

'How?'

With Henri following in her footsteps, Win stepped back and walked around the edged of the cabin to the desk and picked up the telescope. Handing it to Henri, she said, 'Make it quick, whatever you want it for.'

Nodding, Henri took it from her hands and began to unscrew the brass collar that held the smallest section of the telescope into its sheath. Soon the section came free and he examined it before putting his hand in his pocket and bringing out the cloth pouch that contained four sections of the seal. From the other pocket he lifted the other segment. He placed them all on the desk then, careful to hold the makeshift microscope steady, he pointed it at them.

'What are you doing?' Win asked curiously.

'The small section of the telescope acts like a microscope if it is removed,' Henri explained. 'I used to look at insects eyes and things when I was a child, by taking my father's telescope to bits.'

'And what do you see?'

To steady his hands, Henri held his breath while he looked through the scope. When he breathed out he said, 'The seal is embossed with all sorts of weird characters,' he stated.

Win nodded.

'Their inner edges seem to be smooth yet something was holding them together.' He paused and then said, 'And the inner sections are hollow but there seems to be something inside them.'

'Yes.'

'You know all this?' Henri asked, peering hard through the makeshift microscope.

'Yes,' Win said, now a little agitated.

'But there seems to be some kind of tiny image inside the sections, something in the shape of…'

'We must hurry,' Win said, placing her hand on his. She prized the microscope from his fingers and Henri reluctantly let it go. Quickly, he put four of the seal segments back in the cloth and then placed it in his right pocket, placed the single segment in his left hand pocket while Win reassembled the telescope. He waited while she replaced the telescope where it had been on Bartholomew's desk, then, coming back around the desk she stood beside him and took his arm. The light around them seemed to flash lighter for a split second before returning to the dimmed light of the cabin as they stepped across two or three oak floor boards. It seemed a feeble step but in reality the single stride took them back to their time. It was impossible to even notice that there was a barrier of any kind there. Henri couldn't see it and he couldn't feel it as they past through it. He would have asked more questions but Bartholomew was still grinning at him. The captain still thought Henri was going to die. He was waiting for him to wobble some more, just as he had done coming through the cabin door. 'Hello Henri,' Win was saying slowly. 'Come quickly.'

Bartholomew chuckled. 'You're too late! He's a dying man, magic or no magic! You thought you could force me into giving you something I have worked so hard to get? Well I'm not so easily swayed. When he and his magic exist no more then you,' he said, waving a heavy finger at Win, 'you will be of no more use to me.' He held out his hand palm upwards. 'I'll have my golden seal back now if you don't mind.'

Now with unglazed eyes and a smile on his face, Henri turned and faced the captain. 'Just what's your problem?' he asked. 'Have you been drinking?' He smiled at Bartholomew. 'Oh, of course you have! We all have. Silly me!'

Bartholomew's grin gradually began to melt away. Like wax running off a candle, the grin changed to a leer and then an angry sneer. 'I saw you drink that rum!' He pointed his finger at Henri's eyes. 'You're going to close those eyes soon, never to wake again.'

'Not as soon as you'd like though,' Henri said, grabbing Bartholomew by the throat and hoisting him out of his chair. 'I perform magic, didn't anyone tell you?' He shook him. 'I ought to kill you here and now!'

'No,' Win said, placing her hand on Henri's arm. 'Let him be. Perhaps we can still make a bargain.'

'A bargain?' Henri asked, anger still rising in his chest. He tightened his grip on the man's throat. 'A bargain with this dung bag?'

'It would mean he takes his chances with Drach, but he was ready to do that a minute ago when he thought he was going to kill us both to get back the seal.'

Henri looked into Bartholomew's eyes. 'So you fancy your chances with Drach, do you?' He released the pressure on Bartholomew's throat so that he could respond.

'Yes I do,' Bartholomew choked. 'Now I know my enemy, I have nothing to fear. You've told me all I need to know.'

'I fancy he plans to take Drach's money and then kill him,' Win said, smiling.

'Well good luck to you then,' Henri said, pushing him back into his chair. 'Then perhaps we needn't kill you. We'll leave you to do that yourself since you seem to have a death wish.'

'The deal,' Win said, trying to pull Henri away from Bartholomew. She could tell he was tempted to kill the man who had tried to trick them, the man whose word was worthless, whose morals were absent, and whose mind only thought of riches and retirement. 'We know you are a fearless old seadog,' she continued. 'As you said, you risk your life every day travelling the high seas, weathering the storms, challenging the diseases that people bring on board. Why should you be afraid of anybody?'

Bartholomew smiled. 'Well done!' he said, his voice still rasping. 'You've summed me up perfectly. My life has been one big risk.'

'So, what we're going to do,' Win carried on, 'is make a deal with you where your only fear is certain death rather than a threat of it.' She waited for him to respond, but his eyes just flitted from one to the other.

'Get on with it!' he said eventually. His trap had worked but his poison hadn't. They wouldn't fall for making an agreement again without some form of insurance.

Win put her hand in her pocket and pulled out the seal that Bartholomew had tossed to Henri. 'Here,' she said, handing it to Bartholomew. 'Take it.'

Bartholomew scowled. The look of distrust on his face told all. Slowly, he put out his hand and took the seal between his finger and thumb. He turned it over a couple of times and then said, 'What's the price?'

Before Win could answer, Henri took over. '*The Black Sword*, and all that was on it when we took it.

'We?'

'It was my magic that won that ship. It's my prize to take as salvage. You'll get what you wanted; the golden cube and you still have all your own cache of looted treasure.'

'Or else?' He was still belligerent.

'No or else's,' Win stated. 'That's what we are going to do. Henri will become invisible again, and he will supervise your hauling *The Black Sword* in and transferring the goods back on board. He will kill anybody who stands in his way. You'll have no crew left to sail your ship. You'll be left all alone to reach land on your own.'

'Do you think I couldn't manage to do that? We are only eight miles from land.'

'But you want to sail your ship into the docks at London. You want to sell it. And you want to get off in one piece. That won't happen if you run up on the rocks around Brittany.'

Bartholomew thought for a moment, but it didn't take him

long to decide. With the seal in his hand, he had trebled his fortune already. He had his ship, his treasure and the massive reward for retrieving the golden cube. He grinned at the two novices in front of him. 'I might ask the same of you,' he stated cheerily. 'How do you intend sailing that massive full rigged vessel on your own? Now there's a challenge!' His eyes lit up with the thought of seeing them on the deck looking up at the massive rigging, helpless to sail or manoeuvre the ship.

'Since we can't trust any of your crew, then we'll take some of the passengers. They'll get by. As we said, it's only eight miles to France!'

'But not to port. It is still a hundred miles to Rouen.'

'We'll take our chances,' Henri grated. 'We are less at risk sailing *The Black Sword* than accompanying you to London.'

Bartholomew opened his hand. He looked at his golden cube, lying there, in the palm of his fist, and considered it for a moment. He sighed. 'Well you did save my ship,' he stated eventually. 'What the hell! Let's get on with it. I have a ship to man and a man to see! Let's get it sorted.'

With that, he pushed himself up and paced over to the door of the cabin.

Henri passed the small canvas pouch that he had placed in his pocket and slipped it into Win's hand. Instantly he felt the pressure of the force that the invisible bubble around him created. His ears began to throb. He hadn't recovered nearly enough to return to using the invisible cloaking device, but it was necessary now. He knew that with one small opportunity, Bartholomew would relent and try to kill them again. And a man like Bartholomew was no small enemy. He would succeed if he were given enough chances.

As Bartholomew opened his cabin door, he glanced around. He raised his eyebrows when he saw that Win was standing behind him all alone. 'Didn't waste much time, did he?' he said gruffly. 'Come on then,' he said despondently and, with his head held a little less confidently, he went to the rail that overlooked the main deck.

'Listen here,' he bawled at the top of his voice. 'Mundulay, get your crew to the capstan and haul *The Black Sword* to,' he ordered. He turned to Win. 'You, cabin boy, fetch my hailer.'

Win did as she was instructed, while Henri stood between them, determined that there would be no opportunity given to the captain to turn on her. She returned a moment or two later with the cone shaped megaphone and handed it to Bartholomew. He took it calmly and lifted it to his mouth.

'Listen here,' he shouted to the three men on board the pirate ship 'Stow your sails and prepare to come alongside.'

'Ey ey,' a distant voice came back to him over the steady breeze. Obediently the men climbed the rigging and began pulling on the ropes and folding the two big sails. They were good sailors. It took them less than fifteen minutes to do the job, while Henri and Win watched in awe of their skill. If only we had a couple of sailors like them to take with us, Henri thought. Still, he and the rest of the passengers had seen how most of the tasks and duties had been performed, so there was a good chance that the ship would make it to port.

While the men on *The Black Sword* performed their task, and some of the sailors on *The Arinosta* turned the huge capstan and tightened the ever shortening rope that bound the two ships together, Bartholomew supervised the stowing of the sails on his own ship so that the pressure on the rope soon began to slacken. Gradually the men on the other ship brought it alongside and grappling hooks were thrown to them. Quickly, the two ships were bound together and planks were lashed to the rails so that men could travel up to the higher deck of the attached ship.

Once the ships were lashed to each other, Bartholomew told all his men to step on board their own ship, then called to Win, and waited for her to speak.

'Blackwell, Sykes, Moody and Hellginsand,' she called confidently, 'If you wouldn't mind a detour to France, I would appreciate your help sailing *The Black Sword* to port.'

All the men on the deck looked at her. Some chuckled. Only Blackwell and Hellginsand stepped forward.

'The cabin boy's been promoted to captain, now, has he?' Mundulay called mockingly from the poop deck. He looked at his captain to see what his reaction was going to be to the declaration just made by this stripling, but Bartholomew said nothing. He just looked at his crew and smiled.

'The passengers who join *The Black Sword* will all take a share of the prize money,' Win declared.

There was a little chatter as they talked amongst themselves.

'What the heck! Sykes shouted. It'll be more than I made prospecting, that's for certain.'

'And me,' a voice from behind them shouted. It was one of the passengers who had been wounded. His name was Butler and he had seen what had happened to Pringle. He didn't trust any of the crew of *The Arinosta*. He hobbled forward on a crutch made out of a plank of wood.

'Welcome to a new life!' Win called back to him. She turned to Bartholomew. 'We'll take all the wounded,' she said plainly, 'and any passenger who wants to join us.'

There was a minute or two while the rest of the remaining passengers debated the offer. All but two had been prospecting for gold. Some were probably carrying their winnings with them, some were stony broke. They all volunteered for duty, including Dobbs, a man who had apparently been a consultant engineer, and Turbinson who nobody really knew anything about. But then, nobody knew much about Henri either. Like Henri, Turbinson had kept himself fairly well isolated from the rest of the passengers. Nobody had got to know him any better than they had got to know Henri. But he, like all the rest of the passengers had fought for his life, and he was entitled to a share of the salvage as much as anybody else.

'What about the crew of *The Arinosta*?' one of the sailors shouted. 'Aren't we to get a share?'

'Take that up with your captain,' Win shouted back. 'He holds your shares for you,' she said, not explaining further.

'And what if we don't want to let you take our ship?' a sailor called Bloom asked reticently. He stepped forward, hand on the hilt of his knife.

Bartholomew held up his hand. 'Stop where you are, sailor,' he ordered. 'You know full well the magic forces that wander the deck of this ship. There will be no objections, because we have no choice. Just as the pirates were slain at your feet, that same magic can do the same to you. I do not intend to lose any more of my men. I intend to reward all my crew. You have no need to worry. We are better rid of this lot.'

'I don't trust him,' Henri said, standing close to Win so that she could talk to him without looking distracted.

'He can't do anything once the ships are no longer lashed

together.'

'He can take his new fangled rifles and shoot everybody on the deck of *The Black Sword*,' Henry explained. He obviously wasn't taking any chances even with his own men when he took the powder for the canon on board *The Arinosta*, so when we're over there and he's over here, we would be unable to retaliate. He could kill you all. He might not be able to kill me, but he could leave me stranded in a ship which he knows I can't sail alone.'

'You think he'd do that?'

'I know you must not trust him. Look how many times he's broken his word up to now. He's a murderer, Win. He and his crew are no better than those pirates. He's bound to try something to get this ship back. It's money to him and he's a greedy man. And he's cunning with it.'

'But he's in a hurry, remember? He wants to get to London before Drach.'

'He's not afraid of Drach. I know, he ought to be, but he doesn't believe you; plain and simple. I'm not sure even I believe you! He's got the seal, or what he thinks is the seal and he thinks he's going to get a fortune for it from Drach.'

Win stood and watched for a minute and then Bartholomew bawled an order. 'Get a move on! Get them on board and push off!'

Without further ado, Win organised the transport of the wounded onto *The Black Sword*. Then she busily supervised the transfer of several chests, sacks, barrels and bundles.

Henri realized that Win seemed to have everything well organised as supplies were being put onto their ship and carried down into the hold. She looked around to see what

Bartholomew was doing. He was standing by his cabin door. Next to the captain stood Mundulay. Bartholomew gave Win a reassuring wave and threw her one of his manic smiles. 'I think you may be right,' she said eventually. 'He looks far too pleased with himself.'

'I'll be back,' Henri said and made his way up to the poop deck. Bartholomew was just standing with his thumbs in his waistcoat pockets, watching the movement on the decks as if it was a normal day's activity. But if Henri was hoping to learn anything by standing near to the captain and Mundulay, he was heading for a disappointment. Neither said a word to each other. The men just watched and smirked and occasionally Bartholomew would shout an order out to some of his men, but at no time were they going to give anything away. They knew Henri could be standing right next to them and they were not going let anyone know what was in their minds.

Despondently, Henri returned to the main deck where Win was still supervising the stowing of supplies. 'There's only one thing we can do,' Henri said, as he walked up to her.

'And that is?'

'Something that they haven't anticipated.'

Chapter Nineteen

THE LAST BARGAIN

Eventually Win told the makeshift crew to unfasten the ties, to push off and wait for the two ships to drift apart. Minutes later, she ordered that the braces be manned, pointing to Blackwell, Sykes, Turbinson and Moody. They all obeyed the tiny captain and set themselves to the task of dropping the sails.

Win watched as *The Arinosta* effortlessly set full sail and glided silently away into the distance.

Henri was still invisible. The pressure of the force field about him was beginning to tell on his energy again. His head ached and he was desperate to shed the cloak of invisibility as soon as Win was safe.

Win was not a captain and all except one of the men on board were civilians, not sailors. Blackwell was by far the most experienced. He had been a pirate when Win discovered that he had talents that would, if paid for, benefit the cause of The Seven Witches. She called him to the wheel and instructed him to take over the captaincy now that *The Arinosta* had left them. 'We have a task ahead and you'll do it best,' she said with a reassuring smile. She couldn't help feeling a rush of relief as her fears that Bartholomew might fire on them had come to nothing.

'Ahoy,' Moody shouted from one of the yards. He and Turbinson had been setting the sail.

Win turned her head and looked up at the mast. 'What is it?' she shouted.

'*The Arinosta* is turning. It's heading back towards us.'

Win sighed. She looked at Blackwell. 'Do your best to get this thing heading on a course for Rouen. If *The Arinosta* comes within eight hundred yards, get the men down into the hold and you go with them.'

'What about you, Miss? Surely you aren't staying up here on your own.' Then he added, 'We should have taken on gunpowder for the canon.'

'I know what I'm doing, Blackwell.' she replied, knowing that she could have never used the canon against *The Arinosta* even if they had anyone on board who knew how to use them. 'You concentrate on getting us home safe.' With that, she went to the port side of the ship and waited for the masts of *The Arinosta* to rise fully out of the horizon.

Bartholomew was clearly jubilant. As Henri had anticipated, he had ordered Mundulay to open the armoury and to issue the rifles to the crew. 'We have just seen a mutiny,' he explained to the crew. 'I was forced to capitulate because they had the force of magic with them on this ship. But now, they are on that ship and we cannot be reached by their magic unless they come alongside.' He gazed into the eyes of all his men, one at a time as he walked along the line they had formed against the rail. 'But mutiny can only end in a man being hanged. They know that. They will not allow themselves to be taken alive.' He smiled. 'I order you now to make sure there are none left to waste a rope on.'

'Ey, ey,' they all called obediently. Mundulay ordered three men to follow him and the rest of the men waited until they arrived back with arms full of weapons. As they passed along the line of men, each took a rifle. Finally, Bartholomew issued them with five rounds of ammunition each and then he emphasised that none of the makeshift crew on the other ship were to be spared.

As *The Black Sword* came within firing range, Bartholomew noticed that Win stood alone on the deck, looking out towards them. He used his leather bound telescope to see what was happening. Win's face came into view in the lens. She looked concerned. 'Where are the damned men?' Bartholomew asked, angrily. 'How do they expect to sail that thing if they don't man the yards! By Gad, they are insufferable!'

Suddenly, he saw Blackwell emerge from the hold and come up beside Win. She looked around and was clearly arguing with the man. He just kept shaking his head. Eventually, they stopped their quarrel and stood together at the side of the rail. Then more of the passenger-turned-sailors emerged from the hold and came and stood alongside their colleagues until all but the wounded stood there, giving Win their full support, almost welcoming the return of their mother ship.

'Prepare your weapons,' Bartholomew commanded.

Each man loaded a cartridge into his pin-fire rifle and stood to attention like well drilled soldiers.

'About turn,' came the next order.

All the crew turned to face the port side of *The Black Sword*.

'They're sitting ducks,' called Mundulay. 'We're going to have fun today!'

'Prepare to fire,' Bartholomew shouted. 'All kneel.'

One of the men checked again to make sure a round was in the chamber of his rifle. They all knelt at the side of the rail.

'Raise arms!'

The men lifted their weapons and rested them on the rail.

There was a long silence. Eventually, he spoke. 'Mundulay, do me the honour!'

'It will be my pleasure sir.' He took up his own rifle.

'Are you ready men?' he called, looking down the sights on the barrel. The rogue cabin boy was his first target. He would be the first to fall with a bullet in his chest.

'Ready!'

And then, he gasped. All the crew turned their heads to see what he was doing.

He was dying. A broad gash had appeared in his right shoulder, a gash that ran down to his beast bone.

Bartholomew cursed. 'You fiend!' he shouted. 'All turn and fire at will. One of you is bound to hit him!'

As ordered, the men turned and began to fire where they thought the invisible warrior would be standing. Henri hadn't expected this reaction. He was still standing behind Mundulay. At least six of the rifles pointed in his direction. They were all discharged and at least three were aimed at the right spot. He held his breath. Swords, he knew, bounced off the shield. But bullets?

The men fired and reloaded rapidly. As they lifted their guns for a second shot, they looked to see if anything had been hit.

Indeed their fusillade of bullets had gone straight at Henri. Until, that is, the missiles hit the invisible shield that surrounded him. He saw the bullets as they hit the force field. It was the only time he could see it. The point of impact glazed over as the missiles penetrated. Every one pushed through it a few inches, slowing down rapidly as they forced their way forward, finally coming to a halt at least twelve inched from their target. They rattled to the deck as the shield instantly restored itself to total transparency.

The sailors watched as their bullets dropped on the floor in front of them. They stopped raising their weapons and just gazed.

'Fire again you fools, Bartholomew yelled as he snatched up Mundulay's gun. It was already loaded. He intended to use it.

Henri just waited, his head throbbing but his adrenalin pumping.

'You are trapped on my ship,' Bartholomew growled at the spot where the bullets lay on the deck. 'You will never leave it alive!'

One of the men turned to take aim at the men on *The Black Sword*. He died before he could level the barrel. His body slumped forward against the rail.

'Fire your weapons you cowards,' Bartholomew shouted. Fire at the place he is standing.'

Again the sailors fired at the spot near the fallen sailor and again their bullets rattled onto the deck in front of them. Some spun off the shield at irregular angles and skimmed along the deck, whining as they ricocheted off into the sea. Henri hadn't moved. The effect of the dropping missiles on the crew was worse than seeing their colleagues cut down in front of them.

Then, suddenly, one of the sailors disappeared in front of their eyes. Henri had picked him up by his shirt and the man reappeared as Henri released him and he fell, yelling, into the sea.

The men began to stand up; backing away from where they thought the invisible man was standing. But Henri had moved around behind them and yet another sailor suddenly vanished and then appeared as he fell awkwardly into the water below. Then another and then another fell into the water until the men began to throw themselves overboard before the spectre could do it to them.

Soon Bartholomew was standing alone on the deck of his ship. 'You'll hang for this!' he growled at Henri. 'Mutiny! Piracy!'

'Murder?' came Henri's voice as he suddenly appeared in front of him. He had placed his sector of the seal under a coil of rope on the deck and walked away from it. Instantly his head began to clear. His sword in his hand, he walked towards the captain. Bartholomew raised his rifle, but Henri was too quick for him and his sword smashed against its barrel and swung it wildly out of control. Bartholomew's eyes widened. He expected to be killed. But Henri kept his cool and hit him. Taking him by his lapels, Henri hoisted Bartholomew up against the ships rail, snatched a key from his pocket and bundled him overboard.

Leaving his section of seal, he went to the starboard side of the ship where he knew there was a rowing boat stowed for taking the crew ashore if the ship had to anchor at sea. Lifting his sword, he slashed the ropes that held it to the side of the ship and watched as it plunged into the sea. It took on some water, but stayed afloat.

The ship was still in partial sail and was gliding away from the struggling sea men. He saw them swimming towards the boat, some strongly, some not so well. It would be their only chance to survive. He watched over the rail as two of the survivors reached the lifeboat and, after hauling themselves over into it, pulled its oars out of their stays and began to row towards the rest of their companions. Slowly but surely they disappeared into the distance as the ship moved away under its own sail.

Then he ran up to the captain's quarters, unlocked the armoury and picked up a keg of gunpowder.

There was a second small rowing boat stowed near the stern of the ship. He put the keg down on the deck, ran to the boat and dragged it to the side and, after tying a rope to it, to prevent it sailing too far away, with all his effort, he heaved it over the rail and sent it hurtling into the sea. It was his escape route to *The Black Sword* but the boat landed nose first in the water, steadied a little as it scooped in the sea and then sank as the weight of the water ballast dragged it under the waves. He grabbed the end of the rope and wrapped it around the rail, but before he could tie it off, the weight of the boat dragged the rope free and, despite all his efforts to hold onto it, it disappeared over the side of the ship, flopped into the water and followed the boat down to the sea bed. 'Damn!' he cursed. He knew there were no other boats on the ship. His plan to blow up *The Arinosta* would have to wait.

He sighed. All he could do now was leave the mainsails up and steer the ship if it came too close to land. The last thing he needed was for the men in the rowing boat to catch him up. But that fear soon dwindled as a greater one took its place. The land that had appeared on the horizon earlier in the day had disappeared again. Henri had no idea if he was sailing towards or away from it. He ran up and down the deck, peering over the ships rails to see if the ship had turned, but no land was in sight on any side of the ship, nor forward or aft. He ran to the captain's cabin and looked at the big brass compass. It wasn't good news. The wind had changed and now the ship was heading north by north west back out into the vast ocean. He went to the ship's wheel and turned it hard to starboard. Then he lashed it down so that the rudder would help to turn the ship onto the right course. As the ship turned the wind began catch the sails at a different angle and the huge vessel began to lean over on its side. Henri had to cling onto the rail to prevent himself from sliding off the deck and plunging overboard. He dragged himself slowly back to the wheel and fought to unlash it. It was tight against the leather loop that held it from turning. With all his strength he prized on the handles until the loop dropped off. Then, as he let go of the wheel, and before he could jump clear on the sloping deck, it began to spin wildly, hitting him on the side of his head. The pain was almost too much to bear. He felt dizzy and almost fell into unconsciousness but he shook his head to clear his vision and, as the ship righted itself, the wheel stopped spinning, reverting to a calm and almost mesmerising sway from side to side.

The next two and a half hours was spent trying to trim the sails. He had seen it done, and knew that if he could get the sails facing the right way then the ship would turn about. When he checked the compass again, his heart sank. The direction of the ship was still to the north. As far as he knew, there was no land in that direction until the cold arctic ice stopped all but the passing whale.

He was finding it hard to breath. At all costs he had to remain conscious. Fighting the desire to sit down and sleep, he kept going, and from the poop deck he released the ropes controlling the yards of the main and mizzen masts. Eventually he worked out how the winches and pulleys worked to raise and lower the yards and began to haul them one at a time up the masts. Then he climbed the rigging, pulled himself up onto the main yard.

The height made him feel dizzier than the blow on the head; the sea swirled far below him. One slip and he would fall to his death. There was no way home if he plunged into the icy waters of the Atlantic this far from land. He determined not to look down. Inch by inch he made his way along the rats that were slung below yard stopping every few feet to haul up a section of the sail. Then he would move on again. He lost count of how many times he had edged along the yard arm, but eventually, after traversing the cross beam seven or eight times, he managed to stow the first sail so that, what remained unfastened, flapped loosely in the wind. Then, exhausted, he climbed down and started the whole process again with the next sail.

Finally, with darkness closing in, and with all the sails stowed untidily but efficiently, he climbed once more to the poop deck, and turned the wheel. Without the wind behind it, the ship was turning. He would have to wait for wind to change before he set sail again. Even if it wasn't travelling, it was pointing in the right direction now.

As he went to find a place to sleep, he remembered his section of the seal that he had still retained. He went to where he had left it and felt on the dark deck with his hands. But the sector wasn't where he had left it. When the ship almost keeled over, it must have slid along the deck and into the sea. He blew out his cheeks and, now totally sapped of energy, he took the last weary steps up to the captain's cabin. Completely exhausted, he slumped into Bartholomew's bunk. He was asleep before his head touched the thin horsehair mattress.

❖

Chapter Twenty

THE LOST SECTOR

The noise that awakened him was sudden and so loud that it cut through him like an executioner's axe. His head shot off the bed as he tried to focus his eyes on the open cabin door. A black raven stood on the rail of the poop deck outside; its voice was harsh and sharper than its own flesh piercing beak. It squawked again, sending shivers down Henri's spine. Taking a deep breath, he pushed himself up and walked unsteadily over to the door. The bird screeched again, but seemed totally unfazed by Henri's advance.

'So, you thought I'd slept long enough,' Henri said to it as he looked up at the grey sky. The sun was trying to break through the cloud. Its angle indicated that it must have been at least six hours into the daytime. It was approaching noon.

The raven seemed to be intent on staying. Henri couldn't understand why this bird had come so far from land and why it had chosen to land on his ship. It screeched again, looking directly at Henri and bobbed about like a dancing marionette. It was as if it was trying to communicate. 'Going to keep me company, then?' he stated, holding a hand to his forehead. The blood from the blow had clotted over now, but the inside of his head still reverberated from a constant hammering inside his skull.

The big, black bird bobbed up and down again and then walked sideways along the rail so that it was right beside him as he approached the steps that led to the main deck. Henri could have reached out and touched it easily. He stood and thought about it. 'Are you hungry?' he asked, remembering that it was a long time since he had eaten anything. He went back into the captain's cabin and picked up some biscuits, biting on one as he returned to the door. 'Here,' he said, breaking one up and tossing it onto the deck in front of the raven. It could be that it had landed on his ship for a rest after a long flight across the sea. As it hopped down onto the boards to examine the food, and then lifted its head up to look at Henri, he noticed that it had odd coloured eyes. One was dark but the other was a vivid amber colour. Without touching the biscuit, it jumped back onto the rail of the poop deck, still doing a dance in front of its host.

'Are you trying to warn me?' Henri asked, still curious; its behaviour was so unlike that of any bird he had come across before.

The raven danced again only inches from his hand and then, with a single flap of its wings, hopped across to the starboard ship rail. Henri walked along the deck and looked over the side. About a mile away was a ship in full sail and heading straight towards him. His heart leapt. Win was searching for him. He hadn't been abandoned. He wondered if Win had been too far away to see what happened to the men on *The Arinosta*. Had she been close enough to see how Henri had tossed Bartholomew and his crew overboard? By the time Henri had jettisoned them, *The Arinosta* was almost a mile away and still travelling at full speed, while *The Black Sword* was still motionless in the water. Win and her inexperienced crew had taken a long time to get the ship travelling in pursuit of *The Arinosta* and even longer to get all *The Black Sword*'s sails down and secured. But they were coming for him now, and it wouldn't be long before he was amongst friends once again.

While he waited for *The Black Sword* to reach him, he went down to the main deck to see if he had indeed lost his sector of the seal for ever. The raven fluttered down onto the deck behind him. It seemed to know that he was looking for something and, lowering its head from looking up at Henri, it began walking up and down the deck like a chicken looking for worms.

Henri tried to remember just where he had left the little piece of the seal. He glanced at the raven. Just what was it doing here? Was it waiting for something tastier than biscuits or was it searching for the same thing for which he now looked? Convinced that he was letting his imagination run out of control, he took another biscuit out of his pocket and crumbled it up before scattering it in front of the bird. But, again, the raven ignored the food and carried on watching him not more than a few feet from where he was searching.

The rope coil that had been the protecting cover of the segment, had disappeared. It wasn't surprising, considering that the ship had almost capsized as it keeled over onto its side. Henri was convinced that had he not managed to free the wheel then he and the ship would have disappeared into the ocean forever. A shiver ran along his back as he thought of the watery death that had reached out at him and whose cold intention, although only just thwarted by his own quick reactions, had been brought on by his own stupidity.

His eyes swept from one side of the deck to the other. There was no sign of the rope or the sector of the seal. He sighed. Without that segment, examining the properties of the complete seal would now be impossible. He stood up and sighed, blowing out his cheeks to vent his exasperation. Still, he was alive, and the seal had saved him. He wondered if he would have been in this position in the first place if he hadn't traded a pouch of gold for it, but the answer didn't come to mind.

He went to the side rail and looked out at the white sailed ship as it gradually made its way towards him. But what he saw now made his heart sink. As the ship was coming plainly into view, he recognised not *The Black Sword*, but a French naval frigate.

So Win wasn't looking for him. That was no real surprise. In the main, the crew of *The Black Sword* were not any more experienced than Henri and their priority would be to make land safely. He looked at the frigate as it sailed gracefully towards him and wondered why he hadn't recognised it for what it was. Even at a distance it didn't look the same as Win's ship. But the wars with the French had ceased for the time being and there was a good chance they would help him. He spoke good French. He had been raised in England, but his mother was French and he himself had been born in Western France. As he stood at the rail watching and waiting, he pulled out his derringer and made sure that each barrel was loaded and the caps were in place. He didn't want any trouble but he had to be prepared for it. Though what use the tiny weapon would be, he had absolutely no idea. The armoury door was still open, as far as he could recall. But even then, he was totally outnumbered. Even if he could repel the men from boarding, the French ship had only to open fire with its canon to put an end to any belligerence.

Eventually, the sails of the frigate were trimmed and it gradually rested a hundred yards or so from *The Arinosta*. A rowing boat was lowered and then Henri realized that this wasn't a rescue. One of the men now climbing into the rowing boat wore a blue jacket. Henri hadn't seen him on the deck as the sailors looked out at him, but now, there was no mistake. It was Bartholomew. The French must have picked up their boat and Bartholomew would have lost no time in accusing Henri of piracy. Now would have been a good time to find the sector of the seal, but Henri knew it was lost. He had time to make another search, but he knew it was a forlorn hope. Even the friendly raven had flown off while he had been watching the approaching boat. He wondered if the seal which was now with Win had a sector that could have enable him to fly like that bird, but at the present time, he had no chance to escape. He just waited.

Bartholomew stood proudly at the front of the boat as the rest of the sailors rowed. Henri recognised at least six of them as crew of *The Arinosta*. The rest were French, all smart and trim in their uniforms, a legacy of Queen Victoria's fashion of dressing her princes in sailor suits; a fashion that spread throughout all of Europe. It would have been all very reassuring had it not been for the man standing proudly, watching the boat come nearer and nearer to his own ship. The captain looked quite magnificent, all clean and spruced after his dip in the ocean. His hands were tucked into his waistcoat and he smiled radiantly. He was about to regain his beloved craft.

As the boat drew alongside *The Arinosta*, Bartholomew looked up at Henri. He frowned. Perhaps he was puzzled as to why Henri was not making himself invisible. Instead, Henri just leaned on the side rail and waited for the inevitable. There was nothing more he could do. Then the real surprise came.

'Well done, Henri!' Bartholomew shouted up to him. 'Well done!'

Henri just looked back at him blankly.

'Stand ready to be boarded,' a sailor shouted in a strong French accent as he stood up and lifted his arm as a signal that he was waiting for Henri to throw down a rope.

Henri sighed and turned to look around. There were several coils of rope ladders wrapped and hanging on hooks around the ship's deck. He went to one, lifted it free and casually went back to the side of the ship. The men below watched and waited patiently as he returned and, after securing one end to the rails, let the rest of the ladder unfurl on its way down to his visitors. The sailor who had shouted to him caught the ladder and pulled their rowing boat tight to the side of the ship. One by one, all but two of the men below climbed aboard and minutes later, Henri was standing facing twelve sailors. Six of them were French, six were crew of *The Arinosta*, and the remaining one, still climbing up from the boat, was Captain Bartholomew. Henri had looked at each of the sailors closely. None of Bartholomew's men were armed; not as far as he could see at least. The French captain wore a sword and two of his sailors had pistols. Henri kept his hand in his pocket, firmly clenching his small two shot pocket pistol.

Bartholomew was the last to climb aboard. As one of the

sailors took his arm to help him onto the deck, the captain looked up at Henri and smiled. Almost imperceptibly, he tilted his head and considered the bloodied face in front of him for the briefest of moments before breaking from the thought. 'Let me introduce you to my good friend, Henri Dubois,' he stated jovially as he looked around the faces of the men beside him. 'Henri, meet Captain Bergamot.'

The leading man stepped forward and offered his hand. Still puzzled, Henri took it and shook it firmly. 'Mon plaisir,' Henri said in as friendly tone as he could.

The man looked at Henri with friendly eyes. 'You have been in the wars?' he said in quite good English. He pointed to Henri's head and then to his shoulder where blood still remained crusted on his coat. Henri hadn't taken too much notice of his injury; his need to survive had driven him past the pain. He realized, now, that he must have looked a total contrast to the smart sailors who now stood in front of him. He hadn't shaven for a day, his head was caked with blood, as were his clothes, and those clothes were the same ones in which he had set sail over a month ago. They were filthy and, even though he could not smell them, he knew the primly dressed men before him were politely averting their faces to prevent breathing too close to him.

'We'll get him cleaned up soon enough,' said Bartholomew, once again proffering his friendly smile. He turned to the captain of the frigate and took hold of his hand. 'I cannot thank you enough,' he said, shaking the man's arm vigorously. 'Thank you for restoring me to my ship.'

'It was a pleasure,' replied the Frenchman, glancing up at the untidy rigging. 'It is the duty of all men of the sea,' he stated plainly. Then he added, 'The rest of your men are already nearly here,' he said and nodded towards the second rowing boat that was coming alongside; and with that he signalled for his men to return to their rowing boat, turned and gave Henri one last friendly smile and then followed his men down the rope ladder.

All the men on the deck watched as what remained of Bartholomew's crew climbed the ladder onto the deck and the French sailors returned to their ship. Henri just stood with his hand in his pocket, firmly holding onto his tiny pistol. Things were happening and he had no idea what they were or why; but he knew all would be made clear soon enough.

'Make all sail,' the captain ordered his men. 'Set a course due east.' Straight away, and without a single word being spoken, they obeyed, and set about rigging the sails and getting the ship under way. Henri watched them for a minute or two, wondering at their agility and the way they went about their job effortlessly climbing to the mains and skipping along the rat lines. He would look at sailors in a completely different light from now on. If he survived.

Eventually, Bartholomew put his arm around Henri's shoulder and began to lead him up to the cabin. Once again, he gave Henri a friendly smile. 'I underestimated you,' he said, his voice conciliatory.

'What are you up to now?' Henri asked, still gripping his tiny pistol tightly in his hand. Bartholomew was a snake, and it was only a matter of time before he struck again.

'I don't blame you!' Bartholomew said, raising his voice apologetically. 'I don't blame you at all! We got off on the wrong foot.'

'That's what it was!'

'The wrong foot. Exactly!'

'So now we are on the right foot, are we?'

Bartholomew grinned. 'We certainly are Mr Dubois…Henri. We certainly are.'

'Perhaps you'd like to explain? We seem to have plenty of time.'

'Indeed we have.'

They were climbing the steps to the poop deck. He removed his arm from Henri's shoulder and stepped ahead of him to open the cabin door. He pushed it open and waited for Henri to enter.

'After you,' Henri said, politely. The last thing he wanted to do now was to turn his back on the captain.

Bartholomew nodded his head and entered first. 'But you will take a seat?' he asked as he pulled out a chair at the rear of his huge desk and sank into it.

Henri accepted the invitation and picked up a chair from the corner of the room. It had obviously fallen over when the ship listed onto its side. He placed it in front of Bartholomew's desk and, without a word, sat on it. He waited for the captain to speak.

'First of all,' Bartholomew began, 'let me thank you for not doing your disappearing act when I was boarding the ship with our good friends from France.' He smiled. 'You see, you are the only thing that stood between my losing the ship as salvage to the French navy, and my regaining it.'

'Really?'

Bartholomew nodded. 'Really! An unmanned ship is salvage, you know that. The Frenchies…' He hesitated. 'I mean nothing personal by that. But they wouldn't have been so cooperative had there been nobody on board. It would have cost me dearly, my friend, very dearly. I may have been obliged to pay them a large amount of money to retrieve it. I may not have got my ship back at all. So you see I am rather grateful you decided to stay with us, if you get my meaning.'

'So you told them what exactly? I threw all of you overboard in a friendly jousting competition and then the ship took off without you?'

Bartholomew suppressed a smile but his face radiated self congratulation. 'No, I just told them that the ship was hit by a freak wave and we were all washed overboard except for you who managed to hang on and release a life boat.' His smile eventually broke free. 'I was quite convincing really, though I doubt if they believed anybody was left onboard. I think perhaps they were hoping that there wasn't.'

Henri just nodded. 'So when does the friendly cooperation end?' He didn't expect a frank answer.

'Ah, well,' the captain said, taking a fist out of his pocket and placing both hands on the desk in front of him. 'I have had time to reflect on things a little while I was mourning the loss of both ships. For a brief moment I almost had a fleet!' he said with a chuckle. 'But then, sometimes you don't realize what you have got until you have lost it, don't you agree?'

Henri thought of the seal or at least the sector of it that he had lost overboard. But before he could reply, Bartholomew opened the fist of his right hand and placed the golden cube he had been given by Win in the centre of the desk. 'I believe you have one of these,' He stated plainly. 'I believe you know how they work.'

'What makes you think I have one of those things?' Henri

asked with a shrug.

'You are an ordinary man. You are not a wizard or a witch or whatever people call magicians now days. But,' he said with great emphasis, 'you have got an extraordinary power that you can only have got from a treasure such as this.' His face was serious now. The wide eyed affable look had been replaced with a keen eyed stare of sheer determination; a look not unlike that which Henri had seen on Bartholomew's face when he went out on the deck with the two pistols under his coat, determined to take as many pirates with him as he could if he were to die. He waved his hand at Henri. 'Oh, don't deny it, Mr Dubois, I know it is the power of the seal that gives you *your* powers. Why else would someone be prepared to pay me a fortune, twenty thousand guineas, for this simple little block of gold? Why would the man called Drach kill anybody who had it to get it? Why would he race across the world to be in London before me? There is only one reason. That golden cube is worth much more than its weight in gold. Am I right Henri Dubois?'

Henri nodded. 'It sounds like good reasoning. About Drach, I mean.' He shook his head. 'But what makes you think I have got one, I can't imagine.'

'Come along Henri,' Bartholomew said condescendingly. 'Please let's not play games any more. You can make yourself invisible. You are immune to attack by swords and bullets, and even poison, but you can still bleed,' he stated, waving a finger at Henri's head wound. So, what else could it be but an ordinary man using magic?'

'What else indeed!' He didn't know if the captain actually knew that the sector of the seal only protected him when he was invisible. He didn't know if the captain knew the seal came to pieces, and he didn't know if the one that Bartholomew had in his hand was an exact replica with separate sectors; but he didn't want to ask to inspect it for fear that the captain would infer that there was something worth examining more closely. What Henri did know for sure, was that Win would never have let Bartholomew have that seal if it had had the powers of the one that was now lost to him for ever.

They looked at each other for a while before Bartholomew spoke again.

'All I want in return for your safe passage home, is to know how to use the seal; my seal, not yours. I don't seek ownership of yours. And I'll tell you why.' He paused to make sure he had Henri's full attention. 'The buyer thinks there is only one of these golden cubes. He called it a seal, but it is absolutely no good for that purpose, believe me. Other than that, he didn't explain anything about it to me. But I know it has to be something powerful; something the man called Drach would want to use to fulfil his ambition to take over everything and everybody. I know of Drach and I know what he wants. He wants control, and to have that, he has got to have power. In the right hands, that cube, or seal if you want to call it that, is power.'

'And you are not prepared to let him have it?'

Bartholomew frowned. 'My friend, Drach is the last person in the world who should own this little artefact.'

Henri thought the same could well apply to Bartholomew.

'And what do you want to do with that power?'

'That, Mr Dubois, is a good question. Do I want to control the world? The answer to that is no; plainly and simply. But it will make me incredibly rich!'

'You are already a rich man, Captain. Your chest full of treasure is still safely stowed in the armoury. You still have your ship. Despite losing *The Black Sword* and its treasure, you don't need to work ever again. You don't need to risk storms and piracy any longer. You can buy a sizeable estate with that lot.'

'True,' Bartholomew answered frankly.' He sighed. 'But it's a sort of disease. Once you have riches, you seek more,' he said with a shrug. 'And since I have the seal, then what the hell, I might as well make use of it!'

'That's probably just what Drach said when he discovered it.'

Bartholomew shook his head. 'No, if I'm correct, Drach has always wanted to take over everything. First he wanted to take over his town. And he did that without the seal. Then he wanted to take over his country, but he had not the means to buy the army so he went about accumulating wealth with just that ambition in mind. I have heard about this man, and he will not stop there, mark my words. He will not stop until he has taken over the entire world.'

'That sounds all a bit of a fantastic fairy story,' Henri commented.

'Believe me, there are people like that. There have been in the past and there will be again in the future. That is what happens when one person begins to build an empire. And I know that for a fact; believe me. I have had plenty of time to read history books. And most of these people come from humble backgrounds. They are rarely born kings.'

'But you're not one of them? You don't want to build an

empire?'

Bartholomew smiled. For once, Henri thought he saw a little humanity in those dark eyes, eyes that seemed now to be in the head of a different person to the one he had fought against. 'Ambition can take many forms,' he said eventually. 'Take yourself, for instance. You have a seal and you don't have any ambitions like that of Drach, have you? Each man has his own aims and goals in life. Mine are pretty modest, possibly higher than yours, but modest when compared to those of a complete megalomaniac.'

Henri was in a quandary. He didn't want to tell Bartholomew that he had lost his sector of his seal. He didn't want to explain that the seal came apart or where the rest of his seal was. He didn't even know if it was his seal any more. He might never see Win again. That thought suddenly weighed heavy on his heart. And worst of all, the seal was incomplete. If it was the only real one, then Win would never be able to use it to do what she needed to do, with part of it lost at the bottom of the ocean.

'I'll make a deal with you, Captain,' Henri suggested. 'I'll tell you everything I know once I am safely on land. There's nothing much you can do with it, anyway, while you are on the ship. You need to be away from your crew and everybody else when we discuss it, come to that. You cannot experiment with these things in public,' he stated authoritatively, assuming that the seal, were it a genuine one, would have remarkable powers that he had not yet discovered himself. He had decided he would tell the captain all he knew. But that wasn't much, as Bartholomew would soon find out.

Bartholomew took up the seal and put it back in his pocket.

'I already think it has brought me good fortune. That will do for now,' he said and pushed himself up from his seat. 'We have a bargain on one condition.'

'Which is?'

'You don't do your disappearing act any more. I can't trust somebody I can't see. We'll make London in a few days. Then you can show me how you do it.'

Henri nodded. 'You've got a deal.'

❖

Chapter Twenty One

THE SURPRISE VISITOR

Henri knew that he would be foolish to trust the captain. But as things stood, Bartholomew seemed willing to make the best of what he had. Several times over the next few days he alluded to the fact that he would probably have been dead and lying in a watery grave by now if it hadn't been for Henri, and his gratitude seemed perfectly genuine. And Henri acknowledged that, despite his misgivings… no it went deeper than that; despite his inherent dislike of the man, it was Bartholomew's fearlessness and leadership that inspired everyone, that fateful day, to fight to save his ship. It was a strange feeling of mutual respect on the one hand and total distrust on the other. And they both had something that the other needed. Bartholomew wanted a way to increase his wealth and Henri needed to have some way of getting off this dreadful, endless sea. He carelessly swore to himself that he would never set foot on a boat or a ship again. He had no idea just how wishful those endless thoughts of retiring to his own estate were.

Bartholomew must have ordered his men not to bother Henri, for they just went about sailing the ship as if he were still invisible. Even when their eyes did meet with Henri's, they just nodded politely or stepped out of his way and then carried on with what they were doing. Perhaps they were a little afraid of him. Perhaps, like Bartholomew, they thought Henri was invincible even when he was plainly in view. Perhaps Bartholomew was right in thinking that the seal had a remarkable effect on a person's luck. If what Win had told Henri was true, Bartholomew only possessed a replica, but of course he didn't know that.

In fact, Henri had complete freedom of the ship. The captain remained friendly and even offered to let him share his cabin, but Henri preferred to sleep in a bunk down below. The steerage section of the ship was airy and fresh now without the other passengers and he was never fazed by solitude. It suited him well. He spent much of his time at nights lying awake, thinking about his motives for trading the seal and about his small fortune he had amassed over the years of roaming the globe. He thought about Win. He wondered where she was now and if she had tried to look for him. He wondered what she would do now that her ambition to use the seal had vanished with the loss of part of it. Sometimes he wondered if she missed him, but then he would shake himself and come to his senses. She was just another person with whom his path had crossed for a brief moment in time. Time. What was it she had said about time? They were in a different time, or there were different times and different presents and different futures. So there might be different pasts as well. He just couldn't get his head around all this science stuff.

Endless hour upon hour of bobbing about on ship didn't help. It was total boredom. There weren't any other passengers now whom he could watch and make probably totally incorrect assumptions and theories about. Most of the sailors did next to nothing when the ship was in full sail and on course, so there were only short periods of time when he could observe them with any interest. More and more he felt himself drawn to thinking about Win, the fascinating slip of a lass. If only he hadn't lost that important sector of the seal, then he could have gone looking for her; he could have taken it to her.

With that thought, he spent hours searching nooks and crannies where his section of the seal might have got jammed, but to no avail. As the ship sailed up the Thames estuary he realized that he would never have his seal again. He would never see Win and worse, he had to explain to Bartholomew that his knowledge about the seal was totally inadequate to enable the captain to use his own useless replica.

Bartholomew seemed fidgety as his men worked on sailing the ship into port. His orders were scant, but they seemed to work at their jobs with a speed and dexterity that underpinned the talent of all good seamen. The captain had picked himself a skilled team; a team for sailing. Henri hoped that the other part of the team, that skilled in deception and murder were all but eliminated, but he had no way of telling. One thing he did know for sure was that Bartholomew was a deep and devious man. Perhaps he was a little afraid of Henri, of his undisclosed powers, of his ability to disappear. But Henri was under no misapprehension. His allowing Henri to remain on board and unchallenged had been at a price, and now, as Henri impatiently paced the deck, looking out at the shores of the land he had taken for his home since the age of ten, he could feel that the time was near when the captain would want to exact it.

He tried to avoid Bartholomew's gaze, but he could feel his eyes upon him. Could he jump ship before it docked, Henri thought, but he was sure that the ever watchful crew were at hand to stop him. And even if he did manage to avoid being seen, he wouldn't get far in the murky waters of the Thames wearing his boots and a heavy great coat. And the gold sewn into the lining of that coat would weigh him down faster than a falling anchor. He had almost drowned once, trying to get onto the ship. He wasn't about to make the same mistake again attempting to get off it. There would be no friendly hand waiting to cast him a rope this time if he tried to escape unseen. So he waited and tried to be as casual as he could, like any passenger arriving home. He leaned on the portside rail and watched as the ship docked.

As the crew prepared to disembark, Bartholomew, a curious smile on his lips, walked up to Henri. 'Well, Mr Dubois, you have remained with us for the whole journey!'

'Didn't you expect me to?'

Bartholomew shrugged. 'Unlike me, you seem to be a man of your word,' he said, casually glancing around at the busy dockside. 'You really do seem to be a man of honour!'

'So you admit that you are a…'

Bartholomew cut in. 'I admit I am drawn to surviving in a world where death is commonplace and life is cheap,' he stated blandly. 'I put no greater value on my own life than I do any other person's. I just happen to have a vested interest in keeping mine going a little longer, that's all.'

Henri nodded but remained silent. He would have liked to have disagreed, but he knew that Bartholomew was right. Life was cheap. People died every day because of other people's dreams; because of their search for power; because of their hunger. He looked at this stout veteran of the sea and only wished that the man had never crossed his path.

'All right then,' Henri said eventually. 'Let's get it over with.' He held out his arm to indicate that Bartholomew should lead the way, but the captain smiled.

'Now is not a good time to turn my back on you, I think.'

Henri sighed. 'Come on then, we'll walk off the ship together.'

Bartholomew grinned. 'I see we are going to get on fine! I shall take you to my London home and there we will discuss our futures.'

'Our futures? You mean yours, don't you?'

Bartholomew continued smiling. 'Mr Dubois… Henri,' he said, turning to look at Henri as they walked side by side down the gangplank to the dockside. 'You have much to learn about life. For some of us life is laid out in front of us. For others, a path has to be trodden for them.'

It was something in Bartholomew's face as he said it that made Henri suddenly feel that Bartholomew had some kind of inkling about the things that Win explained to him. But that couldn't be. The man was just a captain of a ship. Everybody knows that the future depends on what happens in the present. Bartholomew couldn't possibly know that there were many different presents.

Henri shook his head. He couldn't believe that he had swallowed everything Win had said, and without a single doubt.

Bartholomew saw him shake his head but he had no idea what Henri was thinking. He just presumed it was a continuance of their conversation. 'Despite all your abilities, Henri,' he said in a friendly tone, 'you are still not in control of your own destiny.'

A shiver went down Henri's spine. 'Just what do you mean

by that?' he asked.

Bartholomew just smiled. As they reached the bottom of the gangplank, he took a hold of Henri's elbow. 'Come, we'll take a carriage.'

Henri saw that, already, some of Bartholomew's men were loading the big chest and several other small trunks and valises onto a large cart. The team of horses that were to pull it stood patiently beside a large horse drawn carriage which was apparently waiting for the captain. That again seemed strange. Henri had travelled on ships many times before and never did the people at the destination know exactly when a ship was to arrive in port. Travelling by sea was far too uncertain for that kind of prediction. Yet, here were people ready and waiting for Bartholomew. And what seemed strange now, was that for some reason, Bartholomew seemed totally unconcerned that the man called Drach might have reached London before him.

The captain walked over to one of his men, said a few words and then, as the man nodded, he turned back to Henri, lifted his arm and indicated that his carriage was waiting. The driver opened the door but didn't speak and Henri stepped up into the carriage, followed closely by the captain. It was then that Henri realized that he had been so intent on watching Bartholomew, that he hadn't noticed that there was someone already sitting in the carriage. The figure turned his face to Henri as he sat opposite him.

'Well done, you made it!' said Hansenger.

Bartholomew was already seated beside Hansenger and the door closed before Henri had come to his senses.

'You've already met,' Bartholomew said in an introductory tone.

Henri didn't speak. Casually he put his hand into his great coat pocket and, lightly with his fingers, pulled his derringer into the palm of his hand.

'I can see you have questions to ask,' said Hansenger, his face quite serious, his voice not unfriendly.

Henri didn't respond. Hansenger didn't look anywhere near as destitute as when Henri had exchanged a purse full of gold for the golden seal. Henri tightened his jaw and just stared. No doubt one of his companions would get to the point when they wanted to speak. Hansenger didn't wait long before continuing.

'I must apologise Mr Dubois,' he said to begin. 'You are probably wondering why I have turned up here when I left you in such dire straights.'

'You were the one in trouble, not me, as I recall.'

'No, that's what I mean,' Hansenger corrected. 'I was the one in a calamitous situation. You kindly helped me out.'

Henri just scowled and waited for him to continue.

'We have a good hour's drive to our destination,' Hansenger went on. 'Let me tell you a story.'

'Like you knew what the seal was when you sold it to me?' Henri said sarcastically.

'What I was going to say was that I found the golden cube on the sandy shore of a lake deep in the jungle of the South American continent.'

'You told me all that when you sold it to me,' Henri interrupted.

'Ah, yes, so I did. But I don't think I told you my story about the buried city and The Golden Book.'

Henri just looked him, and waited for him to continue.

'I discovered a golden book buried in an overgrown city. The book had gold plates as thin as a leaf of paper, each one embossed with strange characters. I had presumed that it described how men made gold. Even in our modern world the alchemists have failed to find the ancient formula for turning base metal into gold, but the gold from the ancient city was real and so, without any heed to discovering the secrets of the ancient civilization, the gold was plundered by the rest of the men on the expedition.

'There were twenty or so men involved in the end. They were survivors of a long and hazardous journey into the jungle. Our captain had died from a fever contracted within days of dropping anchor off the palm strewn coast. The water in the jungle streams was good, but there was an underlying danger that no one had suspected. Six more men died before the rest of the men realized that the illness was being contracted from contact with the skin by a jungle plant that, when we got to it, also surrounded the walls of an ancient city. The bosun was the last victim of the unknown sickness, but he had realized what had caused the illness, and he warned the men who had not touched the leaves of the plant to hack it down with their swords before passing through its thick, lush, leafy undergrowth.

'When we did finally get inside the walls of the buried city, the men soon forgot all the hardship they had gone through as they looked upon a palace that had remained untouched for thousands of years. It had been totally overgrown on the outside by an ever encroaching jungle, but inside had remained sealed. When we eventually broke through the massive walls, we discovered a palace as modern looking as any occupied by the kings and rulers of Europe today. Everywhere there was golden furniture and artefacts. Alas, it was all plundered; little remained in its original state. In order to carry the precious metal back through the jungle, it was melted down and made into blocks that could be packed into roughly made chests. Of those items that were not melted down, were the forty seven leaves of The Golden Book which I kept. I never revealed that I had found the golden cube but I wanted to find out what the writings on the leaves of the book said, for I firmly believed that they held a secret to unimaginable riches. I wanted to discover the secret recipe of the alchemists. I would no longer hunt for gold; I would endeavour to make it!'

'Don't tell me; it didn't work!' Henri sniped.

'Alas, I didn't get the chance to find out. My secret was not safe. When, eventually, our ship docked back in Portsmouth, I left the rest of the explorers and headed with my share of the fortune and the book and golden cube to my parent's farm in the county of Oxford. But some of the other sailors got drunk and bragged about their exploits, and eventually, there were fewer people that didn't know about the golden city than those who did. And what was worse, they told stories to an audience about The Golden Book and one man in that audience had been Abraham Drach.'

'I wondered when you'd get round to him.'

Hansenger continued unperturbed. Looking away from Henri and gazing out of the window with a glazed expression as he recalled the facts, he said, 'The Golden Book was the only thing the other sailors had mentioned to Drach for, as I have said, I never told a soul about the cube. But Drach tracked me down and one day he broke into the family farmstead, killed the old man who was living there and left with both The Golden Book and the golden cube. The loss of my father was great. It was almost a year before I decided to go in pursuit of the thief and even longer before my detectives tracked him down; five years in fact.

'Never once did I give up hope that one day I would regain my possessions and kill the man who had killed my father. Drach and I had never met, so when I eventually caught up with him, I took a job as a miner in one of Drach's gold excavations. I needed time to find out where my cube and my golden book were kept, and it took less time to discover that Drach was a very dangerous man indeed. He had a private army and controlled the town and all the people in it. But that didn't deter me from my goal to retrieve my property. I let it be known that I was well educated and that I could do clerical work and eventually, the information filtered back to Drach and he approached me and offered me employment in his office.'

He looked at Henri to make sure he was still listening and then continued. 'But the most intriguing part of my story is yet to come. While I worked for him, patiently collecting more and more information, over a period of time, I discovered that he had left the book with scholars back in London. I was in his office when he got news from those scholars. One had travelled all the way to the gold fields to seek him out, just to tell him personally what The Golden Book actually said. It was all about a magic golden cube. My cube! I couldn't believe my luck. If he hadn't stolen them I would probably never have discovered anything about the seal or how it actually worked. Drach spent a small fortune paying the scholars to interpret the ancient texts. It took him five years to discover that the book was not a book about alchemy.'

'Really?' Henri tried hard to be overwhelmed with that bit

of news but it was quite impossible.

'No, it was much more important than that!' Hansenger went on regardless. 'It was a text that outlined four different futures of the world, histories that had not yet happened and each one dependent on what happened to a golden cube, an ancient seal made up of five interlocking sections.'

Here we go again, Henri thought; more presents and futures. He would be glad to leave it all behind and just get on with his own life, his own present.

'And then I saw it!' Hansenger continued, totally enthused. 'I saw it. My seal. I watched as he went to his safe and retrieved it. Apparently he carried it with him wherever he travelled. He never let it out of his sight when it wasn't locked away in his vault. After he had read the transcript of The Golden Book, he spent day after day examining the seal, trying to get it to come apart. But he could never get it to do what the book said it did.

'Over a time he had come to trust me with his accounts and his money. It took a little longer for him to trust me with his precious seal. But when he did, he asked me to see if I could get it to work. But alas, I was no better than he was. It would take time to get the seal to reveal its secrets, and it was then that I decided to carry out the rest of my plan.'

'You had a plan?' Henri said, trying to feign surprise.

'My plan had always been to kill Drach and take back my property. The plan, however, was rather flawed, or should I say, it was not so good that it could not be thwarted by misfortune. A man called Stuckbridge who had been on that fateful expedition in the jungles of South America just happened to arrive in the little hotel where I was lodging. He had lost his share of the fortune and had come to the gold fields to find another. I tried to avoid the man, but inevitably, he recognised his old companion and came to greet me. The news soon got back to Drach, and always a curious sort, he began to ask questions as to where and when Stuckbridge had known me. If it got out that I was the man from whom Drach had stolen The Golden Book, then I knew that Drach would, without hesitation, kill me.'

Henri glanced at Bartholomew. The captain was sitting with his head turned to Hansenger, enthralled by the story.

'Quickly, I prepared to leave. I broke into Drach's quarters and retrieved the seal and the written interpretation of the book from the vault. But when I fled back to my room at the hotel to collect my things, I realized that I was too late. Stuckbridge was lying dead in the alley that ran between the small hotel and the casino. He must have told Drach everything and paid for the information with his life. Drach's men were watching the hotel doors and I knew that if I entered the building now, I would suffer the same fate as Stuckbridge. I had missed my opportunity to kill him, and now I was the fugitive. With little more preparation and the company of a stubborn mule, I set off across the country towards Yemara.

'But luck still wasn't with me. Drach and his men travelled fast on horseback. I knew they would be waiting for me at the next town. That's when I traded the cube for a pouch of gold. I needed to get away.'

Henri was still trying to work out just where all this was leading. Hansenger, the down and out man who needed to trade his last and valuable possession in order to flee the country had now turned up, quite clearly better off than he had appeared before.

'I needed help,' Hansenger stated. 'I tell you no lies about that rogue. He killed my only living relative and stole some things that belonged to me and I followed him to the ends of the earth to kill him and recover them. But I had in my hands the interpretation of the book and in order to benefit from what I had learned about my sacred seal, I had to remain alive! I had to get out of the country and get out fast. But I had left all my money in the hotel. I was seriously broke. So you see, I had to trade my seal just to escape.'

'So you admit that the seal was rightfully mine, bought and paid for with hard cash?'

'I saw it more of a loan, with the seal handed over as security.' He paused and then added, 'And I couldn't just trade it with anybody. I had to loan it to someone who was travelling back to London.'

'You didn't think to mention that at the time. How remarkably forgetful!'

'Ah, but I had also to divert Drach from his course. By letting you carry the seal, I was able to escape.'

Henri thought about the private army that Drach commanded, and how he, on coming into possession of the seal, had become the hare hounded by the pack. He understood well why Hansenger had been afraid for his life. 'You could have escaped the way I did,' Henri suggested.

Hansenger shook his head. 'I don't think so. I am far too old for that kind of thing.' He looked Henri straight in the eye. 'And besides, I had other things to do. You were a diversion as well as a welcome agent. I couldn't have paid anyone to do what you did for me. You paid me for the privilege!'

'You talk as if you still own the seal.'

Hansenger beamed, his face radiant with pleasure. 'I do. It

is *my* seal. You carried it for me.'

'Your seal!' Henri expostulated. He calmed himself before going on. 'It was your seal, but it isn't any more.'

Hansenger just shook his head. 'You stood a far better chance of getting away than I did. And once Drach knew you had it, it left me free to go back to Britain to retrieve my golden book. True, I knew now what it said, but I had to have my treasure back and I needed a diversion. You were it.'

Henri grunted. 'So you got The Golden Book back when you arrived back in London did you?' he half asked, half stated.

Again Hansenger shook his head. 'No, it had been stolen from the university. But I know where it is now and who has got it. I will get it back when I want it,' he said confidently.

Henri was sure that Win had said that the Seven Witches had got The Golden Book, so what made Hansenger so sure he could regain it? How did the witches get their hands on it? But he didn't ask.

'But you still have my seal, I believe,' Hansenger went on. 'I would like to offer to buy it back.'

'I'm afraid he… we have discovered a few things about it since then,' Bartholomew cut in. 'He not only knows what it is, he knows how it works.'

Hansenger scowled and his face became grave. He thought for a moment and then, shaking his head, said, 'You mean he can use it?'

Bartholomew nodded.

'You cannot possibly know. I've spent…' Hansenger stopped and thought for a moment. 'No, it cannot possibly be you.' He contemplated for a minute or so and then went on. 'If you know how to use it then, perhaps you can tell me what it does and how it does it?' he said eventually.

'Ask your friend here,' Henri suggested, waving his free hand at Bartholomew. 'You obviously know him better than you know me.'

'I met Hansenger on a previous trip to Yemara,' Bartholomew explained. 'Saw him again when we docked in Yemara this last time, a couple of days before you arrived and booked your passage.'

'Purely business,' Hansenger was quick to put in.

'Well perhaps he can explain how his seal works,' Henri fired back.

'His seal?' Hansenger's face went stiff. 'You've let him have the seal!'

Bartholomew shot a glance at Henri and then steadied his gaze back on Hansenger. But he didn't speak.

'So what have you two cooked up between you?' Hansenger asked suspiciously. His eyes flitted from Henri to Bartholomew. Bartholomew shuffled a little uncomfortably.

Henri just stared hard back into Hansenger's face. He had had enough of the whole business. He couldn't work out if it was Hansenger or Drach who had paid Bartholomew to retrieve the seal. Either way, they could sort it out between themselves. The inside of the carriage was quiet for a while. The rolling of the steel wheel rims on the cobbled street and the clip-clopping of the horse's steel shoes seemed to amplify into the void. Eventually, he leaned forward and put his face to the open window.

'Driver, let me out here,' he ordered angrily. His hand tightened on his derringer.

'Now let's not be too hasty,' Hansenger said, his voice mellowing a little.

'Unless what you told me was yet another lie,' Henri spat, drilling his eyes into Hansenger's face, 'you know all there is to know about the seal. So you can explain to the captain here, just how to use it and how it works.' As the carriage pulled to a halt at the side of the busy street, Henri reached for the handle of the door. 'I hope you'll both be happy together when Drach finds you.'

'Wait!' Bartholomew's face went a ruddy colour around his jowls. 'You mustn't go,' he said nervously. 'You have your future to consider. We all have our future to think about!'

'No, captain,' Henri replied firmly, recalling what Win had said about different futures. 'I am not in your future.' He started to lean forward and pressed the carriage door handle, but when he tried to move his legs, they didn't seem to respond as they should.

Hansenger's face had changed. His dark eyes were glaring at him, but at the same time they had a peculiar, dark, trance-like look about them.

Henri felt compelled to sit back down on his seat. In his mind he knew he wanted to get up and leave. In fact he intended to get up and leave. His body did nothing of the sort. He tried to lift his hand from his pocket, the one in which his pistol was tightly clasped, but his hand relaxed and it came out of his pocket empty. He felt as if a wave of warmth was flowing up from his feet and running up through his legs, past his waist, up through his chest and arms and finally, as the feeling flowed into his neck, he slumped back in his seat and remembered no more.

❖

PART TWO

The Manor

Chapter Twenty Two

ANOTHER WORLD

The sound of thunder overhead woke Henri. It shook the whole building. Then another loud crack almost as if it were in the room. He clung onto the hard bed beneath him and opened his eyes wide, not knowing what to expect. He was alone. His whole body ached, and the air felt cold around him as he realized he was lying face down on a massive, horsehair mattress. A thick sheet had been pulled over him but he still felt chilled to the bone. All he could see was a smooth, white wall until he rolled onto his side and lifted his head. As he looked around, he could see that he was at the far side of a large, bare room which had three high windows and a large metallic-looking door at the furthest end. Turning his head, he looked at his body. He was wearing only his shirt and trousers, but then he noticed that his boots and some other items of clothing were stacked neatly at the foot of the bed. But there was no great coat. He rubbed his chin and felt at his beard; it felt soft and longer than he remembered. As he pushed himself up from a lying position his stomach suddenly became racked with painful cramps. He didn't know how long he had been there, but he was seriously in need of food. He climbed out of the bed and began to put on some more clothes, none of which had ever belonged to him. But they were warm and he was thankful for that. Finally, he sat on the end of the bed, pulled on his boots and looked around.

There was no way to tell what time it was, nor even what day it was. The light from the windows was dull grey, and he couldn't even tell if it came from a murky sky or from some other source, because the windows were set so high.

As he stood up between the bed and the wall, another crack of thunder sounded above the room, rattling the huge, empty bed with tremendous shuddering sound waves that sledge hammered at the air. His whole body vibrated from the inside. He felt faint and steadied himself by bracing his arm against the cold wall. Unsteadily he walked around the edge of the room until he reached the huge door, and then gripped the handle. It turned. He pulled the door gently, not expecting it to move, but to his surprise, it slid not towards him but sideways into the wall, until a sliver of light showed along its edge. Cautiously he put his eye to the gap and peeped through.

At first he thought the room at the other side was empty, but then, suddenly and quite unexpectedly, a man in a white laboratory coat walked hurriedly past. Gently, Henri eased the door open a little further until his whole face filled the gap. What he saw seemed utterly bizarre. There were rows of large tables and above each was an array of unusual, brightly lit lamps. Some tables were empty, others had a collection of some kind of scientific equipment on them, and apparatus the kind of which Henri had never seen before in his life. There were at least a dozen men that he could see, scurrying about. Some were working at and around one of the tables, and several were coming and going in and out of view from other parts of the vast room. All seemed to be working with a great sense of urgency.

'Quickly,' one man shouted, holding hard onto something in front of him on the bench. 'We must stop it! Bring the magnets closer.'

Several other men pulled a heavy piece of equipment forward and one of them positioned part of it over the place where the man was struggling. Another man threw a large switch and, as all the lights dimmed, the arm of the machine seemed to radiate a greenish glow. Seconds passed and then the thunder sounded again, only, this time, in the very far distance.

'That's enough,' the man said, bending up from the table. He took a handkerchief from his white overall pocket and wiped the sweat from his brow. 'God only knows where that one will end up,' he said as he stuffed his handkerchief back in his pocket.

As Henri stepped into the room, one of the men happened to glance in his direction. The man put down whatever he was holding in his hands, gently on the worktable, and turned away, walking with a definite purpose towards a large door that, as he approached it, just seemed to appear from nowhere at the side of the enormous room.

Henri continued to look around, but no one else seemed to take any notice of him. Eventually the man, who Henri had seen depart, returned with Hansenger. Hansenger seemed to be in control. He nodded to the worker and the man veered away and went back to his task. Hansenger carried on walking towards Henri.

'You've come round then?' he said, a slightly puzzled look flitting across his eyes. 'You've been out for nearly two days. I didn't know if I'd killed you.'

'Obviously not,' Henri croaked.' His throat was dry. His

belly still felt like it was sticking to his backbone.

Hansenger looked truly concerned. 'It would have been very unfortunate if I had. Sometimes I can't control it.'

'It?'

'Anger my friend. Sometimes when I am angry, I go a little too far.'

'Anger! That's what it was! Well, it's a relief to know that whatever you did to me wasn't intentional.'

'Oh, I wouldn't say that I didn't intend to stop you leaving. I just sometimes don't know my own strength.'

'Your nursing care was exceptional,' Henri sniped.

'Ah, well that may be something you don't yet understand. What I did to bring you back to consciousness didn't depend on bed sheets and doctors.' He looked at Henri with deep dark eyes. 'Total isolation is the only cure. Believe me.'

'In a cold empty room?'

'In a cold empty room, yes.'

'You wouldn't like to explain would you,' Henri said, gasping as another pang of hunger sent a pain through his abdomen. He leaned heavily against one of the laboratory tables.

Hansenger sighed. 'Perhaps I should explain a little.' He held out his hand to offer to help Henri, but Henri pushed himself upright and, seeing Hansenger turn to lead the way, followed without another word.

'You need some food and a hot drink. Come with me.'

Hansenger led Henri through another sliding door that appeared in the wall as they walked towards it, and along a long straight passageway that had high, smooth walls that shimmered like smoky glass. The ceiling of the passageway was the same, only it emanated a steady white light. The whole place looked like a tunnel cut through a huge block of ice. He felt at the wall. It wasn't cold, it wasn't ice. It was glass.

'You've seen my research centre,' Hansenger stated as he led Henri through another door into a warm interior of what was, apparently, the dining room for all the workers. A dozen round tables were set out randomly across the floor that led to a hatch in the wall. A man approached the hatch from the other side. He was wearing a long white overall and a strange looking white cap that reminded Henri of a tea cosy, only this hat appeared to be made from a white, cotton sheet that had been shredded in some strange way.

'A full meal for our guest,' he said to the man, 'and a coffee for me,' he added, picking up a bright metal tray.

'Water for me,' said Henri.

The man placed a large plate on the tray, opened up a container and dished out some boiled potatoes. Henri stood and watched, his stomach rumbling at the sight of food. His mouth began to water. He swallowed and his body seemed to suddenly begin to feel normal again as more containers were opened and more food was dished out. Eventually, with a full plate and two metal mugs, one of water and one of coffee, Hansenger carried the tray to the nearest table and sat down. Henri followed suit, sitting opposite the man, his eyes still watching him suspiciously. Hansenger lifted the plate and placed it in front of Henri, and then watched as his guest took up a fork and began to shovel food into his mouth. Henri took a long drink of water, emptying the mug. The man brought a glass jug of water and placed it on the table, and without a word, silently went back to whatever he did behind the hatch.

'How much do you know about the seal?' Hansenger asked,

after sipping most of his coffee.

Henri didn't reply. He carried on eating and washing the food down with gulps of water.

'Perhaps I should tell you,' Hansenger went on. 'You have discovered that the seal has several secret sections.' He looked at Henri to get confirmation, but Henri just carried on eating as if Hansenger wasn't there.

'And you have discovered that each section has its own individual influence on the universe?'

Still Henri just carried on eating, but he couldn't help thinking that Hansenger had gone a little over the top with his description of the powers of the seal.

'And one of the segments can make a man invisible. That much you have found out.'

Henri raised an eyebrow and slowed in his mission to fill his belly.

'What about the other sections?' asked Hansenger. 'What have you discovered about them?'

Henri put down his fork and wiped his mouth on his sleeve. 'You've got the seal now, so why are you asking me?'

'I have the seal? Good heavens, no! It wasn't in your coat. We searched every thread.'

'Bartholomew had it, I remember telling you that.'

'Ah, not so. The captain only had a replica. True, it was a good copy. It came to pieces, but not like the real seal. The real seal has its own locking system. It takes a special hand to undo the segments. You had that special hand, Henri. But the seal Bartholomew had could be opened by anybody who knew it was made up of segments. A simple twist and it fell to pieces.'

'That's just what happened when I had it,' Henri confirmed.

'Ah, but not everybody can open the real seal. You did, but I could never get it apart.'

'So how did you know it came apart then?'

'From The Golden Book of course. It is all explained in there.'

'And what else did it explain?'

Hansenger looked a little uncomfortable. He cleared his throat and looked over Henri's shoulder as he spoke. 'The other segments, as with the one you used, work both independently when they are not with or in close proximity to the other segments, but also work together in many different combinations. There are five segments in all. That makes twenty nine combinations if we include the seal as a whole as being one combination. Whoever designed this article must have had access to technology that is many hundreds of years more advanced than our present knowledge.'

'So you're saying that there has been a more advanced civilization on earth then?'

Hansenger scowled. 'Well, no, not exactly. It seems that there are a number of different presents, pasts and futures. The seal crosses these boundaries where no one, or no other article can.'

'So why are you telling me all this? I haven't got another seal. The one Bartholomew had is the one I had.'

Hansenger shook his head. 'Not true. The original seal has been switched. I hadn't expected that. I was sure you would keep a hold of it.'

Henri lifted his eyebrows questioningly.

'He has told me that you were friendly with a young cabin boy, or should I say girl? She took the original seal, and that is why you didn't do your disappearing act again. Am I right?'

'Well you are right in that respect. I did become invisible because I split the seal, or at least I took off the section that did whatever it did to make me invisible. That bit of the seal was lost overboard.'

Hansenger's face changed suddenly. No longer was there a look of friendly acquaintance in his eyes. Now they became dark and angry pools of murky quicksand. 'Tell me that isn't true,' he said in a deep growl.

Henri could feel some power emanating from Hansenger, the same power he had felt when he had been overcome in the coach. But suddenly the feeling of being drained of energy by an overpowering force subsided. Hansenger leaned back in his seat looking weary. Henri watched him as he looked somewhere beyond Henri, contemplating his options.

'Bartholomew thought you still had it,' he said quietly. 'But I know when a man is telling me the truth.'

'So where is your friend?' Henri asked. 'I presume he didn't know that his seal was not the real one.'

'He had no idea. He thought he had one of two seals.' Hansenger looked at Henri with his dark eyes. Henri felt as if the eyes were reading his mind. 'Only one has ever existed. The Golden Book tells me so. The owner… no the maker of the seal would not want anyone else to have the same power, trust me.'

'The same power?'

'Incredible power.' He shook his head in dismay.

'So Bartholomew isn't as rich a man as he thought after all,' Henri said, smiling.

'Bartholomew,' Hansenger said slowly, 'will no doubt

muddle through.' Then he added, 'If he doesn't try to sell his counterfeit seal to Drach. I have warned him! That man has no morals. He'd already agreed to retrieve it for me.' He paused for a moment and then said, 'The sector of the seal. How did you lose it?'

'I was aboard a ship and on my own.'

Henri looked at Hansenger to see if he required an explanation. Hansenger just nodded. Bartholomew must have told him what happened. 'I tried to turn the ship around so that I wasn't being carried further out into an endless ocean and the ship almost capsized,' Henri continued. 'The part of the seal must have slid off the deck.' Now it was Henri's turn to sigh. Once again his thoughts turned to Win. As far as he knew, she still had the rest of the seal. What she could use it for, however, he had no idea. 'So what are you going to do now?' he asked.

'Well, as it happens, even though I do not now have The Golden Book, I have the transcript of the text. It explains how the seal was constructed. But in the years I had it, I could never get it to come apart, something that I'd never have expected you, a simple explorer, to be able to accomplish with, it seems, little effort whatsoever.'

'So why am I here?' Henri glanced around. 'Wherever here is.'

'Let me explain. You and Bartholomew were never part of my permanent plans. But everything changed when he mentioned you'd been able to use the seal. When he'd seen me put you to sleep, he was quite willing to tell me everything that had happened.'

'I'm sure he was. How did you do that sleeping thing, anyway?' Henri asked, now curious as to just who this man was.

'For the time being, just let's say that I have a gift. Many people can use their minds to affect other people; some to a greater or lesser degree. I just happen to be one of the former.'

Henri thought about how Win could do the same thing. 'So you are a witch as well then?' he asked frankly.

'Not to the same degree as that little cabin boy, I'm afraid. She's… well let's not go into that at the moment. We have far more important things to discuss.

'I have…' He paused. 'Well let's say I have discovered this place. I have been working on certain experiments for years now. It's surprising what you can do when you have a fortune at your disposal. I was an explorer like you once, but when I became rich beyond my wildest dreams, I turned my attention to exploration of another kind. I began to explore science.'

'Yes, I saw your laboratory.'

Hansenger nodded. 'However, I only went in search of my seal when I heard that the scholars had interpreted the text of The Golden Book. You see, when you are rich, you can buy people's co-operation. You can pay them to tell you about secret assignments and all that sort of thing.'

'And you obviously discovered what Drach was up to.'

'Quite, and I realized that the seal was far more important than I had originally thought. I discovered what it really did.'

'And this tells me what exactly?'

'Well what I am trying to explain, Henri, is that, in the years that I didn't possess my seal or my book, I set upon the task of experimenting with time.'

'Oh, here we go again!' Henri shook his head. He was rapidly losing interest.

'Strangely enough, he who controls time controls the

universe. You'll come to understand that before long.'

'I had intended just getting on with my own life and taking my own time over it,' Henri commented.

'Ah, that was before you discovered you could operate the seal,' Hansenger said, emphasizing the words to indicate the importance of the little artefact. 'That's why I brought you here of course.' He paused to consider what he was about to say. 'You see,' he continued tentatively, 'we are already in a different time.'

'You surprise me.' Henri wasn't impressed.

'Our laboratories have been working with a technology that I discovered. You see, I still carried on exploring, in a way. But instead of discovering a far and distant land I discovered a near and distant land!'

Henri could at least see the humour in what Hansenger had just said. He chuckled and shook his head. Hansenger looked so pan-faced.

'Ah, I see you think I am joking. But I have to tell you Henri, I have never been more serious. We are in a land, another world really, that is only a stride away from our own. The key is to find the opening from one to the other.'

'So you found this door. What did you find at the other side?'

'Technology. Advanced technology. We are in a world that uses electricity. Electric lights, electric carriages. It uses an ergametron to generate immense power. It transports that energy by using some form of light waves. No wires, no coils.'

'You've lost me now,' Henri admitted. 'You say that electricity runs the lights? Not gas?'

'The lights and everything else.'

'And all this is in a different world?'

'In this world. Not our own world.'

'And you brought me here for what?'

'I have worked for years now on creating a device for travelling from one place to another using magnetism. This is the only place we can obtain unlimited energy. It is ideal for running electro magnets. But so far, even though we are near to discovering the secret, every experiment has failed. With time, we would have been able to complete the job. But we have run out of time. Every attempt to test a prototype creates an energy field which seems to eat into the atmosphere. The experiments seem to have affected not just this world but our own.'

Henri frowned. 'This world? Our own world? What do you mean?'

Hansenger ignored the questions. 'The result of our trials has begun a chain affect which is destroying this and our own world. Our only hope of stopping what we have started is to get what remains of the original seal and get you to make it work.' He looked directly at Henri again. 'You can help us.'

'I can help you?'

'Your friend the cabin boy, she has four remaining sectors as far as I can see. And as far as I know, she has now got The Golden Book. There's still a good chance we can get the seal to work.'

Henri shook his head. 'I have no idea where she is or how I would persuade her to hand it over. I'm sorry, but I can't see how I can help.'

Hansenger smiled.

'Ah, but I do!'

❖

Chapter Twenty Three

THE CITY OF DARKNESS

It soon became apparent to Henri that he was more a prisoner than a guest. Quite clearly, he was not going to be allowed to leave, and although his host was cordial enough, there was an underlying atmosphere of menace.

The place where he was being detained turned out not to be just a building with a laboratory, for only a few hours later, he was allowed to accompany Hansenger on a trip. They left the building through one of a pair of huge doors that would not have looked out of place on the front of a cathedral, and which stood at least thirty feet high. Hansenger saw the look on Henri's face but seemed unmoved by his curiosity. As Henri looked back at the laboratory building his first impression was that the whole thing had been built like a gigantic prison. The two huge doors were square at the top, and there was no opening in either of them to allow anyone to pass through what he had always known as a Judas gate. Anyone wishing to enter or leave had to wait for the huge pulley system to smoothly drag one or both of the doors open and shut. They were constructed not from planks of wood, but from actual wooden beams about nine inches thick.

On the outside of the building, the sky had a peculiar greyish-green tinge to it. It was unlike any sky Henri had seen at any time in his life, in any of the near and distant lands to which he had travelled. Once again, Hansenger watched his reaction, but made no attempt to explain.

'Where is this place,' Henri asked, looking across a street that could have taken twenty carriages side by side. All the buildings were of similar gigantic proportions, lining a street that was so straight that the far end, in whichever direction he looked, vanished to a point in a haze that seemed invisible close up but which got more opaque the farther one looked. And there were no carriages, no people even. The only men in sight were Hansenger and Henri. And that was another thing Henri had noticed, all the people back at the laboratory were men. Not a single woman worked there, even in the huge office that Hansenger used to lay out his plans and diagrams on large square wooden tables.

'It is where I work', came back a simple and totally inadequate reply.

'But I know of no city like it,' Henri pressed on as they walked past the end of another wide street that crossed at right angles. That street, also, was twenty carriages wide and disappeared into a haze at each far distant end. Hansenger remained silent and in deep thought. Henri began to wonder how far they were going to walk to get to where they were going but no more than fifteen minutes had passed when suddenly the sky darkened. In a matter of two or three seconds it changed from a greenish-grey day to a dark purple night. Urgently, Hansenger took a hold of Henri's arm and led him up some big steps fronting a nearby building. He looked about, his face grave, his body tense. A bolt of lightning suddenly streaked across the sky, only, it seemed, a few feet above their heads, turning the purple sky black for an instant as the crack of thunder that accompanied it ripped at the air about them like a thousand canons. Hansenger ran up the remaining steps and approached another large door like the one they had left behind. Henri expected Hansenger to have some means of rapping on the huge solid beams, but he simply touched the door at what seemed to be no place in particular and it smoothly glided open, and flooded the step with light. Another crack like canons exploding, accompanying as big a streak of electrical flame as before, rattled the door on its massive hinges.

'Please enter,' he said. 'Quickly now!'

Henri knew it wasn't a request. He had thought of making a run for it, but where could he go, and who would help him if he needed to hide? He was confident he could overpower Hansenger so long as this strange man wasn't using his mind to do whatever magic he did to control him. At the moment Hansenger seemed totally distracted.

'Damn, damn, damn!' he exclaimed, but gave no explanations. If Henri was going to escape, now would have been as good a time as any, but without anywhere to go, the whole idea seemed pointless. So, obediently, he entered the building. He felt the swish of air as the door closed silently behind him and began to follow Hansenger when the earth trembled again. The lights flickered and the whole building visibly shook.

'Idiots!' Hansenger exploded. 'Idiots!'

Henri looked at him for answers, but still none came.

Three men turned a nearby corner in the passage and came towards them. 'They've called to say they're setting the magnets now,' one of the men informed his leader.

They've called? Henri hadn't seen or heard anybody.

Hansenger nodded. 'Every time they do this, the earth gets weaker,' he growled.

The lights flickered, but this time without the lightning or thunder. The men at the laboratory must have thrown the massive switch again. Whatever the magnets did, it certainly drove the storm away. Soon, another peel of thunder could be heard, but now far, far away. Hansenger exhaled heavily, seemingly breathing a sigh of relief.

Henri just watched him and the other three men as they talked together in a huddle. Then they all turned towards him.

'There is only one way in and out of this city,' Hansenger stated, almost apologetically. 'So long as you neither know where that entrance is or how to use it, then go where you may, you'll not return to… to your world.' He waved a hand at the three men. 'These men are my most trusted servants. They will see that you are not harmed. You will be safer here than in our laboratory. The electromagnetic devices used to control the weather are very dangerous.'

'Why are you keeping me in this dreadful place,' Henri demanded. 'What use am I to you?'

'You will be the bait that brings the owner of the seal, or what is left of it, here to what the witches call The City of Darkness.' He gave out a clumsy laugh. 'What do they know?' he sneered, shrugging his shoulders and turning to leave. 'Your little witch will be coming to find you, and when she does, she'll have to use the seal to enter.'

Those were Hansenger's final words before walking back to the door which seemed to close on its own behind him.

His Little Witch. What a strange thing to say, thought

Henri. Why on earth, or wherever this forsaken place might be, would anyone want to come here to save Henri Dubois? And why Win? She had probably forgotten about him already, and was getting on with whatever witches do.

What do witches do? he asked himself. 'Huh,' he grunted. 'It looks like I'm in for a long break,' he said to one of the men. He gave out a resigned sigh and then added, 'Well, it can't be anywhere as bad as riding in those rat-ridden, bilge-stinking, disease-swimming buckets, they call ships!'

'I think you are trying to convince yourself', the man replied. 'I'm McFadden,' he said cordially. Everybody calls me Mac.' He pointed at the other two men. 'Johnny - that's short for Jonathan, and Charlie. That's short for…'

'Mac's a bit stupid,' Charlie broke in shaking his head and pulling a face which could have won competitions. 'Basically, we were all brought here before the experiments began. We were employed to resize the laboratories and some of the doors. The engineers that built the electro magnetic stuff still work over there along with the scientists, but we have done what we were brought here to do, so we live in relative comfort doing very little.'

'And you haven't returned home? Why?'

Mac sighed. 'We are as much prisoners as you are. You've heard the saying: *"If I tell you, then I'll have to kill you,"* haven't you?'

'No.'

'Well, we know about The City of Darkness. In order to not be killed, we *volunteered* to stay here.'

'It's that important to him, is it?' Henri asked.

'Well, if you consider that Ivan the Terrible killed all the people who built his St Basil's Palace to stop them from building one for somebody else, then you might say that Hansenger has put a high degree of importance on this place.'

'Well thanks for that, Mac,' Henri said jadedly. 'At least I don't feel like I am completely alone here now.'

'Oh, there are lots more like us,' Charlie said, pulling another face. Henri wondered if they all hadn't gone a little insane with it all.

They took him through to another large room. Once again the proportions of the building were immense. Towering high walls enclosed rooms as big as a football field, with high up windows that now let in no light from the purple sky of night outside. Some kind of sealed artificial lights, which were inserted into hollows in the ceiling, gave off a better clear light. Henri looked at them. They were identical to the lights in the laboratory building. He had never seen anything illuminated like that before arriving in this city.

'They're run by electricity.' Johnny said with a wry smile.

'And what about these storms?' Henri enquired.

'They are caused by the experiments that Hansenger is carrying out.' He frowned. 'And, apparently, every storm they create here causes massive disruption to the weather in our world, the one we left behind. One of the scientists has said that the storms are causing earthquakes and volcanic eruptions in some places over there, which in turn causes more storms. He told us that unless they get this experiment right, then it's the end of the world as we know it.'

'And what is he trying to make?'

'That's just it; he isn't trying to make anything. It already exists, but he's become obsessed with finding out exactly how it works. He doesn't understand it and never will if you ask me.'

The three strangers all seemed resigned to staying in Hansenger's City of Darkness, but Henri wasn't so sure he could adapt that well. The whole idea of being kept in this oppressive, grey, sunless place drained him. Through a window he could see that the sky had turned from grey-green to purple. Eventually, he asked them where he could sleep and Johnny showed him to a room on the ground floor. It was no exception to the rule of size. The ceiling was at least twenty feet high and, like the room in which he had first regained consciousness in the laboratory block, the windows were near the ceiling, and there, now, the troubled sky remained a menacing dark purple.

At the far end of the room was a large bed, one big enough to sleep six men side by side and long enough for another row.

'Will that do for you?' Johnny asked with a smile. 'We each have our own small little box room like yours!'

'Huh.' Henri was working out that The City of Darkness was also a city of secrets; dark secrets. If the houses were built for men then they were not men like himself. From the height of the windows and the size of the bed, Henri reckoned that the people who lived in this place were at least twelve feet tall. As Johnny turned to leave, Henri spoke again. 'Do any of the original inhabitants still live here?' he asked.

Johnny's face turned a shade of grey that matched the dull colour of the sky coming through the windows that Henri had first seen back at the laboratory. He nodded. 'There are some people here that I can't fathom,' he said in a whisper. 'I don't like them.'

'Are they…?

'Big?' Johnny's face returned to normal. He knew what Henri was thinking. He, and no doubt all the others, had thought the same when they first set eyes on the size of the buildings and the rooms inside them. He smiled. 'Gosh no. They're smaller than us. In fact, I'd say they are as much strangers here in this awful place as we are.'

With that Johnny turned to leave. 'Oh, by the way, you turn the lights down by thinking about them,' he said with a grin. 'See you in the morning. Breakfast is up the corridor, three rooms to the left. Any time. We have all day!' With that, he went out, and the door swished shut, all but for the rush of air, silently behind him.

Henri wandered about the huge room, examining the walls and the floor. At the side of the room was another large door. It had no frame and seemed to be set into the wall but as he walked towards it, it moved forward towards him, and slid silently to one side. Beyond it was an all white ceramic walled room with ceramic furniture unlike anything he had seen before. On one wall there was a wash basin that was about his shoulder height, and big enough for him to sit in, with gold coloured levers at the back. There was something similar but lower down, and that, too, had two similar levers about the length of his forearm. It was free standing and when he turned one of the levers, water flowed into its basin from underneath a rim. The water was warm. He turned the tap off and looked at what was clearly a huge bath. Its sides came up to the middle of his chest. And finally there was a huge ceramic lavatory, big enough to seat a horse. It was all very futuristic, with no towels but warm air blowers that looked like gold, grill-fronted boxes that dried hands and body alike. Soap was dispensed by a jet that squirted a fine spray on his hands when he put them in front of it. It was strange but he soon got used to the place and spent a long hour in the huge bath before climbing out of the water onto the broad rim, dropping down to the floor at the other side and getting blow dried beside it.

Other than the bed, there was no other furniture in the room. The base of the bed was about two and a half feet off the ground, the bed head was elaborately carved out of one solid piece of wood, as was the foot of the bed. The carving seemed strange. There was a scrolling pattern down the sides of huge panels, but along the top was an angular cut pattern and in the centre of the panels were rows and rows of carved shapes which could have been a complicated pattern, but he thought that perhaps it was more likely that they were some form of characters, some form of writing. He wondered where he had seen such characters before, but his brain seemed to want to switch into sleep mode. He would think about it some more in the morning.

Wearily, he slipped into his underwear, and thinking about what Johnny had said, looked up at the lights in the ceiling. Expecting Johnny to have been joking with him, he thought about the white, inset panels, willing them to dim down to emit a merest shimmer of light. He was smiling inwardly, almost chuckling at just how gullible he was becoming, when, hardly had the thought crossed his mind than, to his utter surprise, the lights seemingly obeyed by slowly losing their power until they remained barely on; dim and only giving off enough light to enable him to see the bed.

He wondered if the three men were watching him from some secret place, waiting for him to look up at the lights. Rebelliously he thought about them getting brighter again. He was nobody's fool. But once again to his surprise, the lights responded, gaining in brightness until the room was, once again, fully illuminated. He rubbed his hands through his hair and thought about what was happening. Was it some kind of fantastic dream, some illusion created, perhaps, by a drug? But no answer came to mind. He shook his head and, now feeling drained of all his energy, he thought once more about the lights as he crawled onto the giant bed, and once again, the lights dimmed to darkness, leaving him only to pull the thin sheet over him before he fell soundly asleep.

But after a while, he didn't sleep at all well. The first time he woke up, he sat up abruptly, breathing heavily and in a cold sweat. He had been dreaming that he was in a prison cell on a ship which had a barred window that looked out over the sea, a sea with a green and purple sky. But his fatigue gained on him and, once more, he dropped back against the hard mattress and fell into sleep. The second time he woke was when he heard a voice he knew. It was Win's voice talking to him, first from somewhere in the distance, and then much closer. She seemed to know he was a prisoner.

'I'm sorry I can't help you,' her voice said, as clearly as if he had been standing beside her. 'The Seven Witches need to keep the seal to survive.'

He woke up sweating again, sitting up abruptly amid a knot of sheets that had formed wet coils around his. But this time it wasn't a cold sweat. He was hot. His heart was beating rapidly and his breathing was erratic. He brushed his hand through his hair and steadied his breathing. No, if he was going to get out of this place, he knew he could only rely on himself.

❖

Chapter Twenty Four

THE FIVE MAROX

A dim light emanated into the room from the high windows. Henri woke and realized that he had slept well, after his second dream; but he had no idea what the time was. His watch had not been returned with his clothes, so he had no way of telling if it was morning or late in the day. He had, at one time, been able to tell the time reasonably well by the position of the sun, but that wasn't going to be possible now. In The City of Darkness, there was no sun; just the grey-green light of day and the dark purple night with ominous black sky in between, whenever Hansenger created one of his home-made magnetic storms.

He sighed and looked around. The room seemed the same as when he came into it except that the sheets, which were made from some kind of silky cotton, were all twisted, coiled and shuffled into an untidy pile.

He took a deep breath to try and prepare himself for the next day. He sat up, threw his legs out of bed, and leaned forward to pick up his pants. It was then that he noticed something he hadn't seen when the night before. As his head bent forward, his eyes caught a glimpse of something under the bed. At first it seemed like a dark shadow, but he couldn't make out just exactly what it was. He glanced around, and then, remembering what he had done the previous night, he looked up at the lights and willed them to brighten as much as they could. Almost as soon as he began forming the thought in his mind, the lights gradually brightened. But they didn't stop brightening when they reached the light level they had been the night before. They continued to get brighter and brighter until the light they gave off was so intense it was almost blinding him. Shielding his eyes with his arm, quickly, he moderated his thought command so that they would provide sufficient light without being as bright as looking straight at the sun, and immediately, the light level began to drop until it became comfortable on the eye.

But it took several minutes for his eyes to adjust. As the white spots inside his eyes faded, he dropped his head down below his knees again and looked under the bed. Now, plain to see, was a large, square, shiny metallic box. He had to crawl on his knees to reach it, but then found there were no handles on it with which to pull it out, and the box was too wide to get his arms around it. He pushed himself from under the bed and stood up. Bracing himself, he put his hands on the underside of the edge of the bed and heaved, but it was too heavy to move. It didn't budge even a fraction of an inch. He thought for a moment and then, sliding under the bed feet first, he held onto the bed side support with both hands and pushed the box with is feet. It moved surprisingly easily on the smooth floor and, as he repositioned himself a couple of times to get the best leverage, eventually it slid out at the opposite side of the bed.

Pulling himself back out, he pushed himself upright and walked around the bed to see exactly what he had struggled so hard to reveal. He stared at it for a moment, almost entranced. He had seen this box before, though not exactly this size. He pulled it away from the bed and walked around it. It had two slightly hollow sides and was covered in strange characters. There was no doubt in his mind that it was a giant copy of the golden cube that seemed to have come to be known by everyone as *The Seal*.

He studied it for some time, running his hands around its edges. Each face had different forms of tiny characters moulded or carved onto it in relief. The Seal had been like that. His brief inspection of it with the top section of Bartholomew's telescope had shown him enough to recognise the similarity. He knelt down and looked closely to see if he could see any connecting lines, lines to indicate that it was segmented like The Seal, but the sides showed no lines that he could see. Not convinced, however, he put his arms around the top of the box and twisted as hard as he could. Nothing happened until he began to ease off the pressure. Then, effortlessly, the top of the box turned and, where no lines had existed before, now the box top split away from the rest.

As he lifted the top section of the box away, it was so light he could have sworn it was made out of thin paper. But whatever it was, it remained strong and totally incapable of being bent out of shape. Even in its large scale, it didn't have any visible means of connecting it to the rest.

He was about to place it to one side when something dropped lightly out from its underside onto the floor between his feet. His eyes followed it for a moment and then, suddenly, it seemed to take on an animal form, landing as skilfully as a cat, but changing shape all the time as it sprung back off all fours and stood up erect. Careful not to step on whatever it was, Henri straightened his back, stood up, placed the top of the box on the bed, and rubbed his eyes. In front of him stood a creature the likes of which, in all his travels, he had never seen before. It stood there, facing him, like a tiny man, but nothing like a human being really, other than holding its upright form with legs and arms, and with hands which rested on its hips as if it were patiently waiting for Henri to say something. Its face seemed familiar in some way; to some extent resembling that of a chameleon, a lizard that Henri had seen in one of the jungles he had explored. Except that, unlike a lizard, this creature had eyebrows. The little creature was very similar in size and colour, a green that varied in shades over its whole body. But then, just like a chameleon, it changed its colour, turning a light brown. Still, it watched Henri, seemingly waiting for a reaction.

Eventually, Henri spoke. 'So what exactly are you, then little creature?' he said, as if talking to a pet dog or cat.

Suddenly, the creature began to get bigger until it had changed from being the size of a small lizard to the size of an average cat.

Henri stepped back, not knowing if this creature was going to be friendly.

Still it stood on its hind legs. Still it had its hands on its hips. Of its odd eyes, one seemed so dark that it didn't seem to have any pupil; the other had a black pupil but its iris was vivid amber. The two eyes examined Henri closely, moving independently and flitting over him, scanning his every feature. Henry wondered where he's seen those eyes before, but had no time to work it out before the creature spoke.

'So you are Henri!' it said suddenly, taking Henri totally

by surprise and making him jump. He hadn't expected it to speak, although having regard to all the other magic that had been happening around him lately, he didn't know why it had been such a shock that, not only could the creature talk, but it spoke his language too. He just looked at it, his mouth open in surprise.

'I am Solitan,' the creature stated, its eyebrows, each rising and falling in a peculiar way as it spoke. It regarded Henri for a few more moments before saying: 'You mustn't trust those men.'

Gathering his senses, Henri spoke. 'I gather that they don't have magical boxes under their beds?'

'We came during your night,' Solitan replied.

'During my night? We?'

'There is one of us for each section of The Seal.'

'The Seal?'

'Der! Yes, The Seal.' Solitan tilted its head towards the box. 'Don't you recognise it? When it's assembled we can travel in it.' He spoke as if Henri should have already known what he was talking about.

'That's The Seal?' Henri was trying hard to get his head round all this.

Solitan nodded and gave a patient smile; one that a nurse would give to a rather slow witted child.

'And who's we?'

Solitan pointed to the rest of the box. 'Quickly, turn the rest of the segments,' it ordered.

Without waiting for any further explanation, Henri obeyed, twisting hard and then easing off the pressure, turning the top of the box and each time, peeling off another section, the same way as The Seal had come apart back on *The Arinosta*. And each time he lifted the section onto his bed, out dropped another creature like Solitan.

There were five sections in all and five creatures eventually stood in a row in front of him.

'Quickly, put The Seal back together.' Solitan seemed to be totally in command now. Henri just did as he was told, replacing each section and turning it to lock it into place. When he had replaced the final section on the box, he turned that also. Then, suddenly, the box began to vibrate, only very slightly, and abruptly, it began to shrink. Only a few seconds passed before it became the size of the seal he had possessed once before.

'I thought there was only one seal,' Henri stated.

Solitan, the first of the five creatures nodded. 'There is. This is it.'

'But I lost part of the original seal.'

'Your loss, our gain,' the creature said with a chuckle. 'It was never lost.'

'It wasn't?'

'No, we collected it for safe keeping.'

Henri thought back to the time he had been on the ship all alone. The bird had odd eyes, one of them a vivid amber colour. 'The raven. It found the top segment?'

Solitan nodded. 'Hence my presence here,' the creature said, bowing and smiling as it did so.

'And The Seal changes size!' Henri said, almost to himself.

'Only when we need to be transported with it.'

'So you travel in it?'

'Only when we have to reach our master.'

'You have a master?

Again the creature nodded. 'Yes, we have a master.' It smiled patiently again.

'And your master is here, in this god-forsaken city?'

'He most certainly is.'

'Hm. So I suppose I will be getting to meet him, shall I?'

The creature shook its head and a frown creased its little forehead. It looked at the others who simply shrugged back at it. 'What are we to do with him?' it said tilting its head at Henri. 'Seems like he's going to be hard work, don't you think?'

The other four chuckled. All had high pitched little voices.

'We are the five Marox. There are only five of us. We belong with The Seal.' The creature waited for Henri to respond, but Henry just listened and waited for Solitan to continue. It shrugged and then said, 'As I said, I am called Solitan.' It paused again and then added, 'We gave ourselves names since we created ourselves!'

Henri nodded. 'Go on,' he instructed, not knowing what to say. He noticed that the Marox all looked individual. The one who had done all the talking was slightly smaller than the others. It had a wispy beard like a young boy gets before he starts to shave properly, whereas the others seemed to have smooth faces. Its one vivid amber eye seemed to follow Henri's movements meticulously, quite independently of its other eye. Its eyebrows still kept moving expressively with each syllable of speech.

'We have no gender as you know it,' Solitan continued, 'though I like to be thought of as male. 'Raelmin, Rasa, Olmar, and Gorang are more your female types. Knowing that, might be useful if you are talking to us. But you must never talk about us, not to anybody.'

'As if I would,' Henri said with a look of utter disbelief on his face. 'I would probably get locked away in an asylum.'

'Well then, we'd get you out in that case,' Olmar said, speaking for the first time. She had a squeaky, high pitched voice, whereas Solitan's voice sounded deeper. But she spoke slowly and deliberately as if making sure that what she said was understood.

'Would you? Well that's good of you.' Henri thought for a second or two and then went on. 'I don't suppose you've come to get me out of this place by any chance have you?'

'Indeed we have, the Marox called Raelmin said, her voice slightly softer than Olmar's. Her eyes were black, her face slightly pointed, whereas Olmar's face, like Solitan's was round, making her black eyes more pronounced. Like Solitan's, their little eyebrows moved expressively as they spoke. Henri smiled, but restrained a chuckle.

'You'll get used to us,' the fourth Marox, Gorang, said, her voice softer and deeper as she rattled out the words rapidly. 'Our last master did.' Her eyes were also black but her face was squarer than the others.

'Your last… Oh, I see! You seem to think that I'm your master?'

'Think it, know it, couldn't be more sure of it,' the last of the five said in a humourous and light hearted tone. 'They all find us hard to believe in, at first.' Henri recalled that her name was Rasa. She had a slightly more creased face than the others. Her eyes were both vivid green. Her eyebrows were no less expressive, but they moved sideways as well as up and down.

Then he began to see that what he had thought of as being

their skin. It was, in fact, a smooth, very close fitting garment through which their heads and hands protruded and it fitted tightly to their wrists and necks. He looked more closely at their feet, and they too seemed to be covered in the same close fitting silky fabric. Apart from their faces, which could never have been recognised as human, the creatures certainly had the look of being miniature people.

'You *will* get used to us,' Olmar repeated bluntly, her eyebrows continuing to move up and down separately with each syllable of speech. 'But you'll have plenty of time for that. For now, you had better go and have something to eat with those men you have met. You're going to need all your strength in the next few days. And we can't guarantee your getting much else to eat until you are out of here.'

'But don't say anything about us,' said Raelmin. 'And don't tell them anything about yourself. They are spies for Hansenger. They cannot be trusted.'

That surprised Henri. He thought the three men had been very friendly and easy going. But then, he recalled that they were huddled in a whisper with Hansenger when he brought Henri to meet them.

'They are instructed to find out anything you know about The Seal. After they have found out everything you know, then you will be in serious danger.'

'I'd rather go now then,' Henri said, seriously doubting his own ability to deceive the deceivers.

'You must talk to them once more,' Raelmin persisted. 'They will tell you what you want to know. They think you are never going to leave here.' He paused and then added, 'They know very little.'

'And just what do I want to know?' Henri asked bluntly.

'Well, the way out of here of course. We can't take you out in The Seal can we?'

'And they're bound to tell me that I suppose,' Henri said sarcastically.

'Of course not,' squeaked Olmar. 'They'll tell you where your food comes in!'

❖

Chapter Twenty Five

THE GRAFTIANS

As instructed the night before, Henri went to the third door to the left along the corridor, opened it and walked into yet another huge room. This room was little different to any of the others. It had the same high ceilings with the same sunken lights, the same high windows, the same square layout. Over in the middle of the room was a large table whose legs, it appeared, had been sawn off before the taper to make it the right height from which to eat, and the thick, heavy, spindle legs of the wooden chairs had suffered the same fate.

At first, Henri thought that he was alone in the room, but suddenly a voice called to him from the furthest corner. 'Hello my friend!' came Charlie's voice.

Henri looked over towards him and saw that the three men had entered the room by an open door in the corner, a door he hadn't noticed when entering. As the door closed behind them, Henri realized why it had not been so obvious. When closed, like the door he had seen in the laboratory, it became part of the wall. There was hardly a seam to be seen where the aperture had been.

All three men were carrying a tray, each tray piled high with food. They walked over to the table and placed the trays down.

'Please, take a seat,' Charlie said, waving his hand towards one of the massive chairs. Its seat was big enough to hold the bottoms of at least two adults. It made Henri feel like a little child at a grown up's birthday party as he sat with his feet hardly touching the floor. The three men sat along the same side of the table as Henri.

Henri thought it quite a coincidence that they arrived immediately after he had entered the room. He didn't ask why. 'It looks like there's a good supply of food,' he commented, seeing the potatoes and cabbage on one tray and fruit on another, 'despite the bleak and inhospitable landscape outside.'

'It's brought in from outside the city,' Mac stated.

Charlie threw Mac a hostile look but didn't say anything. But Henri definitely detected an atmosphere. There was evidently some disagreement between them as to what exactly they should tell Henri.

'So there are fields and vineyards nearby?' Henri pressed.

'Well, not so near,' Mac said defensively. 'It is transported a long way.'

'What sort of transport is there?' Henri asked. 'I haven't seen any horses or wagons.'

Nobody seemed eager to answer.

'Here,' Johnny said, trying to make Henri feel comfortable. He handed him some bread and a knife. But despite all the efforts of the men beside him, Henri didn't think they could ever make him feel at home.

'I know!' Henri said suddenly, after chewing a mouthful of food, 'You can take me on a sightseeing tour! If you are not too busy, that is.'

Having admitted to Henri the night before that they had

all the time in the world, whatever world they were in, Johnny capitulated. 'Okay. We'll show you around. Better get a good meal in you though. It could take all day.'

'In that case, I'll take a little extra with me,' Henri said affably as he scooped some bread and some cheese into his handkerchief. 'You could do the same,' he suggested. 'It'll give us chance not to miss anything.'

There was a grunt of agreement from the others and from then on, they ate quietly, only their eyes exchanging words between them. Henri watched them, amused that they were so uncomfortable with their task.

Eventually the meal ended and the men began to clear away the trays. They kept glancing at each other as the table was cleared. Henri watched and waited until they headed with trays towards the undetectable door. It opened automatically as they walked nearer to it. Charlie looked over his shoulder. 'We'll be back in a…'

But Henri was beside him before he could finish. 'Might as well have a good look around if I'm going to be staying,' he said light heartedly. But his heart couldn't have been heavier. These three men were clearly not going to easily render up their most protected secret - the way from and to The City of Darkness.

The passageway they entered seemed smaller in proportion to the massive door that led to it. He followed them as they led the way, still silently carrying their trays. Eventually, they turned down another passage and approached a more normal sized door that was only about seven feet tall, and after knocking on it, Mac opened it and led the way.

The inside of the room was a complete contrast to everything

Henri had seen anywhere in The City of Darkness. Everything had either been made or altered so that it looked normal size. But in contrast to that, the dozen or so people working there seemed small compared with the men he was following. When the people turned to see who had entered the room it became apparent that they were not a race with which Henri was familiar. The tallest of them was no more that four feet tall. They were all light skinned but had broad faces, broad noses and sloping foreheads. Although they all looked different, there was an obvious genetic link between them.

Slowly, yet methodically they carried on loading something that looked like a small railway wagon. The difference was, there were no rails on which it could run and it had wheels that were neither made of, nor clad in steel. At one end of the vehicle there was a small cabin that had an upholstered, leather-covered seat bench big enough for three people to sit on side by side, and facing the seat were dials and gadgets which looked totally unfamiliar. It stood alongside one of the walls of the room and was already half full of empty crates.

'The Graftians,' Mac explained, 'and there aren't many of them,' he added, 'are a race of people who have been working as labourers in the City of Darkness for centuries. They know all about its vast streets and they also know where the farm produce comes from.'

'And they are going to take me to the countryside?' Henri asked.

'Gosh, no!' Mac exclaimed as he handed his tray to a passing Graftian. The other trays were offered forward and then Mac continued. 'None of us are allowed to go anywhere with them. But this is where your food comes from. This is the depot where all the goods necessary for your survival and comfortable living enter The City, and this is where all the empty containers are shipped back out.'

'The containers. Do they go back to be refilled or are they sent to be dumped?' asked Henri, trying to seem interested solely in the economies of the matter.

'Oh, nothing is wasted here. The Graftians are more skilled than anybody at reusing waste. They got their training from the Vasitterites.'

'Vasitterites?'

'The people that inhabited this gigantic heartless city.' Mac turned to point to the Graftian who had come close, pushing a cart full of laundry that looked like laboratory coats. That cart too had strange soft wheels. 'They survived but their masters didn't. It seems ironic really; such huge people being weaker than these puny beings.'

It was said quite clearly with the intention of being heard by the Graftian, but there was no visible response by the being. He couldn't tell if they could speak or understand the language that Mac was using. Neither was he sure if this Graftian was a man or a woman. Walking taller than the others, it had long, smooth, black hair, combed back and held down by a gold brooch slide. Its face was smooth with no sign of a beard whereas some of the other workers did have beards, but they also had long bushy hair, some letting it frizz out loosely, others tying it back in a pony tail; and yet others had almost shaven heads.

'So what happened to these Vasitterites then?' Henri enquired, as he examined the strange being and the cart that was going by. The Graftian stopped and nodded to him. Henri acknowledged with a nod of his own and then the Graftian resumed its chores.

'Is that a man or a woman?' Henri whispered when he thought that the Graftian was well out of earshot.

'I'm a woman, you foolish man,' the Graftian said, turning her head and looking at Henri with eyes that seemed different, somehow, to what they had been a moment or two ago.

'That's quite enough of…' Mac began to reprehend her, but was stopped short by a firm grip on his arm by Johnny.

'You know our instructions,' he said, giving Mac a harsh glare. Just what those instructions were, Henri wasn't going to be told, obviously, but Johnny commented further. 'She is new to this job. I've not seen her here before. She'll learn.'

'So they are under your control?' Henri pressed.

'They're under Hansenger's control,' Mac emphasised. Then he added, 'Much like us really. Only we are senior to them, if you like. Not that that says much,' he said with a rather desultory smirk.

'So where did the tall people go?' Henri asked, still watching and thinking about the bold Graftian who was now rather busy talking to a group of her colleagues.

'Nobody knows. They just disappeared, according to what these folk say. Left them high and dry! But they left everything running though. The lights and all the other mechanical stuff still run to this day. All kept going by these little fellows.' Mac seemed to have gained some respect for the noble workers. He turned to Henri. 'So there you have it!' he said as if that explained everything. Which it didn't, but Henri decided not to push the subject any further.

He would have liked to have spent more time watching and

talking to the Graftians. For people who looked so unrefined, they spoke well. Or at least the female one that had rebuked him did. And then another Graftian seemed keen to talk to him. He had been listening to what the female one had had to say and when he saw that the men and Henri were going to stay and watch them, he came over and introduced himself.

'I am Yukla,' he said in a surprisingly deep voice. 'I couldn't help noticing that you seem to be new to our sunless world.'

Mac tried to cut in. 'But we mustn't stop you working,' he said politely.

'No trouble, I assure you,' Yukla said, giving Mac a hard stare. Workers or not, whoever were the rulers now, the Graftians were quite obviously not fazed by the presence of their visitors. This part of The City was definitely their domain.

'I am new here,' Henri said, nodding and smiling affably. 'Just a short visit, I think, though.'

Yukla smiled and glanced at the other three men. The look on their faces seemed strained. Some of the other Graftians had stopped working and were watching from a distance, obviously waiting to see how the scene played out.

'Perhaps we can talk some more,' Henri said cordially. He sensed that there was a conflict somewhere, and that Hansenger's men were there by force, rather than at the bequest of the Graftians.

'That would be interesting,' Yukla said with a furtive smile, and turned to carry on with his tasks. 'That would be very interesting.'

Henri watched him as he pushed his cart towards another doorway and left, followed by three of the other Graftians, and then he turned to Mac and said, 'Well, what else is there to see?'

'This way,' Mac said, seemingly relieved to be getting out of that place. Without another word, Henri and the other two followed him from the workplace, many eyes watching them as they passed through the first of several doors that led to more passageways which led eventually out into the grey-green daylight of the vast empty street.

'Can we walk the streets a bit? Henri asked. 'I have become a little claustrophobic these last few weeks, what with being holed up on a stinking ship and then shut away in these huge empty buildings.'

'Perfect!' Mac proclaimed, enthusiastically. He seemed much relieved that Henri wasn't pursuing his earlier line of conversation. 'Let's go window shopping!'

With that, he led the way down several passages that cut through the endless terraces of buildings, traversed several wide boulevards and eventually emerged on a street that had buildings that actually resembled shops.

The windows all looked dirty and unwashed on the outside. There was a distinct look of neglect about all the wide streets. But neglected as it seemed, there was no vegetation beginning to invade the cracks and crevices. In fact it was remarkable that The City of Darkness had no vegetation whatsoever; no trees, no grass, no flowers; not even invading aerial borne spores of moss had found their way into the city. He looked up at the plain glass windows. They were huge, made of single panes of glass, something unseen in the towns and cities that Henri had visited on his wide travels. Henri rubbed his sleeve against one of the windows and realized just how smooth the glass was; far smoother than the glass that manufacturers in England or France could make. In the world that Henri knew, the shop windows there were made up of small panes of quite uneven glass in criss-crossed frames. As he peered through the window, he noticed that the shops were still full of goods. This one had dozens of rails full of all kinds of different clothes, all long enough to make two garments for each window shopper. And over to one side were two metal staircases, side by side, with huge slatted steps like nothing he had seen before.

Mac and the others just watched him, content to let Henri explore the city to his heart's content. They had obviously become accustomed to what things were like here. The next shop had boots and shoes in the window, all completely useless to anyone with normal feet. But the styles were very interesting. 'I suppose they are all made of leather,' Henri suggested.

'Finest leather you could buy anywhere,' Johnny said, as if he was proud of the standard of workmanship, despite the fact that there wasn't a single item that could be used by anybody.

'Thought so,' Henri said, smiling as if he had cleverly worked it out all by himself. He looked down at his own scuffed and dusty shoes and then chuckled. 'Not my size,' he said, lifting his head and marching on. The guided tour must continue while he thought about what he was seeing. What he had worked out for sure was that there must have been a supply of cattle or other hide bearing creatures somewhere in this world or there must have been a way to get to such materials in another. He suspected that it was the latter and it boosted his morale a little to realize that there had to be a way through to his own country, his own world, again. All he had to do was find it. And so the day went on and he let Johnny, Mac and Charlie entertain him and show him places that they wanted him to see. It appeared that, at times, they were attempting to steer Henri in a direction other than that which he might have wandered had he had more freedom; but he didn't mind. To an explorer and adventurer, the whole trip out was a fantastic experience.

Yet not once during the whole day did he see anybody or anything else moving on the streets. And however far they walked down a street, it still disappeared in a straight line and to a point far away in the hazy distance.

It was as well that he had somebody to guide him back to his quarters. He had lost all sense of direction and at one time feared that the men would never actually return to the same building from which they started their journey. But it was a pointless fear. Eventually they came to a door which didn't seem any more familiar than many of the others they had passed that day, but it turned out to be in the building where Henri had left his room and his small friends. They all went to the dining room and had another meal, all the time now, Mac asking questions about The Seal and how it was made and how Henri had used it, but Henri parried the questions skilfully by replying to them with questions of his own.

'How did you discover how to use The Seal?' Mac had asked.

'It just seemed to do things, a bit like your lights. When you think about them, then they respond,' he said and then asked, 'Where is the device that powers the lights? Is it close by? Can we visit it sometime?'

Of course he had no intention of hanging about long enough to find out, but to some extent, the three men, or spies as Henri now thought of them, were put at ease with the innuendo put into place by his questions. So long as they thought they had plenty of time to question him, they were not going to be too assertive. Not today, anyway. But tomorrow was another day, and Henri had already decided he would be long gone before that day began.

❖

Chapter Twenty Six

RETURN TO THE MAROX

The five Marox were nowhere in sight when he entered his quarters for the night. The lights were dim, but lit well enough to see around the room. The bed was as he had left it, unmade; and when he checked under his pillow, The Seal was still there. Solitan had promised to keep it safe and so he had. But the little creatures were not with The Seal.

Henri checked that the doors were all firmly closed and then called out softly. 'Solitan. Olmar. Raelmin. Gorang. Rasa.' He had made a special effort to remember their names. Although he never seemed to have any difficulty remembering things, he particularly wanted his small friends to know he appreciated their being there with him. Calling each by name was just his way of showing his gratitude. At first, none of them responded, but after a while, during which Henri went casually around the bed, lifting up all the loose sheets, and looking beneath them, suddenly he heard a soft chuckling sound coming from near the bed head. As he prodded the bedding, one of the pillow cases gave a soft grunt of acknowledgement that he had found them.

Why these unknown little creatures should lift his heart so, was something of a surprise to him. Not only had he looked forward to seeing them again, but when he did, he picked them all up in his arms and danced around the room, laughing and talking to them like long lost friends. And they swung off his shoulders and arms like small acrobats, rejoicing with him.

But eventually, as their high spirits subsided, they all came to rest on the edge of the enormous bed. 'We shall leave in the morning,' Henri proclaimed, leaning back and putting his hands behind his head. 'I haven't worked out just how to do it, but I intend following some people out of this place and I'm never coming back.'

Henri didn't sleep at all well. The Marox lay at the bottom of the bed, seemingly not needing to sleep. Not once, when Henri woke and looked at them in the subdued light did he see them with their eyes closed. He thought that perhaps, like him, they were too wound up to relax. He had brought some bread and cheese back for them in his pocket but they hadn't even nibbled at the food. They smiled at him whenever he looked their way. It was still middle of the dark purple night when he eventually sat up and spoke to them.

'We'll set off now,' he stated, determined to bring his ordeal to an end. He had thought of using The Seal's power to make him invisible, but had turned down the idea when, on consideration, that if he were to use the single segment that made him invisible, the remainder of The Seal would have to be left behind. He would never leave without carrying the Marox with him.

'You can use it as a last resort,' said Olmar, seeing Henri look at The Seal and reading his thoughts. 'But you have not yet discovered all the powers of The Seal. Each segment controls its own power base and, likewise, because each of us belong to a separate segment, then so do we.'

Henri thought for a minute, pondering on just what these little creatures could do. He had already seen them appear from The Seal, and had seen them change size. 'So, are you going to tell me just what we have got here?'

Olmar was the first to reply. 'We and The Seal are one,' she said. 'We are each segment and each segment is one of us. We cannot change which segment we are part of, and we have stayed inside each of our segments now for many thousands of your years.'

Henri frowned. He was getting used to the magic of a world which he thought he knew well, but nothing the Marox were saying seemed to make any sense. He thought it better to just hear them out.

Solitan took over. 'We use The Seal, to travel between different times. You saw your friend do it when you were on *The Arinosta*. But she can only do it for a very brief time. We can do it any time we like and for as long as we like. We are destined to help The Seven Witches. We have known it for centuries, but we had to wait for you.'

'Me? What have I got to do with anything? What have I got to do with witches?'

'You'll find out soon enough; but for now, you have to know who you are and who we are.' He looked at Henri inquisitively. 'Oh yes, you think you know who you are, but I can assure you that you've not got the faintest idea. When Hansenger handed you The Seal to deliver to England, it was because he thought he would be caught by a man called Drach. He had no idea that you were the one actually destined to get The Seal.

'Hansenger is a warlock. That is, he's a male witch. I shall refer to them as warlocks from now on because the only true witches that exist are The Seven. Warlocks do not have the same powers as females. Neither do they live as long as true witches. They are, in effect outcasts from the witch community because they took the secrets of the coven and tried to use them to gain control of not just the earth, but of their universe as they know it. But of course, a universe is not a single piece of space. They think that it is layered like a fancy cake. And that is where they have gone wrong. Where we stand now is not just a single parallel universe to your own. There are many of them. In a fancy cake you can reach no more than two other layers. But every parallel universe touches all the others.

'You can reach any universe from another so long as you can find or make an opening or window to it. But to do that you have to have a key. Hansenger discovered this universe, when he appeared in this time and place by accident. He managed to make a very rudimentary key with a thing called an electro magnet. He had no idea where he would end up, but now he has discovered it, he guards the gateway to this place fanatically. He lets no one out; not even his own men.

'Here, he discovered the particle transporters and the ergametron. But he also discovered the laboratories left behind by the previous occupants. Before Hansenger knew about the power of The Seal, he and his scientists, here, in The City of Darkness were trying to manufacture something that actually does the same as The Seal; and when Hansenger discovered from the transcript of The Golden Book that The Seal can skip freely to one and then another parallel universe without going back to any universe in particular, he was convinced that if he could get The Seal back, then he could dispense with his work here.

'Until he gets it back, however, he is concentrating on building The Seal from the description in The Golden Book. It cannot be done of course,' the tiny Marox said with a sense of pride that only comes from being unique.

'In years to come, the particle transporter will be discovered and experimented with but, even in its most basic form, it will not be mastered by mankind for another thousand years,' Solitan stated confidently. 'Hansenger has no idea how the technology works. All he is doing is trying to understand it and then make it work properly but every time an experiment fails, some of his men die, others are made invisible but cannot control it, and fade in and out of sight because they are between universes. They don't know where they are. They are lost to Hansenger and to anyone else. And worse, some of his men have been fused into inanimate objects; into the work benches, into the floor. He kills them of course. He puts them out of their misery; calls them martyrs to his cause.

'And every time an experiment fails, it causes disruption in all the other universes; creating earthquakes and storms that seem to spring from nowhere in your own time. That's because they don't originate in your time. They are made in another layer of the cake and then break through into yours. But if you destroy enough of one layer then you will inevitably damage any other layer that it touches, and, in this case, because all universes are connected, Hansenger is disrupting, and in some cases destroying, everything in each and every one of them.'

By this time, Henri's head was spinning. Perhaps a little sleep would not be a bad thing after all, he thought, now utterly exhausted. He'd had a long day and now this science stuff was really hard work. But Solitan continued, bolstered by Henri's silence.

'And that's why he wants The Seal. It negates the necessity of using gateways.'

'I suppose he's realizes he's destroying this world, then?' Henry asked.

'Yes he does, but he wants The Seal because it is a shortcut to getting where he wants, plain and simple; no more experimenting; no more wasted time; and since time is money, no more expense.'

'So just why does he want the seal?'

'The Seal gives whoever controls it absolute power to not only travel between the universes at will, without finding the opening. It conveys therefore, the power to enter different respective times, and to change that time, by changing what is happening in it.'

'And that's also why Win wanted The Seal?' Henri asked.

'Precisely. The Seven Witches need to change back their time. Hansenger's experiments have disrupted their time and they need to repair it in order that their kind will survive.'

'And what about Drach? Is he a warlock too?'

Solitan nodded. 'Oh yes, but although he has had The Golden Book and has found that there are different universes, he has never actually discovered one, because he could never find a gateway. Nor could he get The Seal to work. Only chosen people can do that. While Hansenger is here, experimenting, Drach is back in your time trying to catch up. But where Hansenger is just clumsily fumbling about searching for the knowledge, Drach has only one motive; total power.'

'So Hansenger is afraid of Drach?'

'Frightened witless! He knows he's safe here, in The City.

I don't think he knew just how dangerous Drach was until he went to steal back The Seal and The Golden Book. Before, he went chasing after Drach and his seal, he would come and go between his home in his own world and this place, where he was carrying out his experiments. Now, however, he rarely leaves The City of Darkness. It is his sanctuary.'

'Right,' Henri said pensively. 'So just how am I part of all this? And why me?'

Solitan thought for a moment before answering. He shuffled a little uncomfortably on the big bed and then, with his eyebrows dancing to every syllable, he said, 'Everybody has a destiny. Some people have only a small effect on the world, as they know it. Others have a greater effect.' He paused and then went on. 'And everyone is born, lives and dies for a reason. Every mortal soul is a stitch in the fabric that makes up their time. Think of your time as a big canvas sail. Destroy one stitch and perhaps the cloth will hold together. Perhaps the sail can withstand a hundred stitches destroyed, perhaps thousands, and still cope with its task. But destroy enough stitches in enough places, especially those that are close together, and the sail rips!'

'So I'm a stitch in time?' Henri asked.

'Where do you think the saying came from?' Olmar said smiling. 'A stitch in time saves nine.'

'But I thought that meant…'

'It does. It means both. It means a stitch saved in a cloth prevents it ripping later on. But it was originally a saying about every person being a stitch in the fabric of time. Trust me.'

'Hmm' Henri grunted. 'So we are stitching up more than just a sail cloth here then.' It was a statement, not a question.

He was beginning to understand at last.

Olmar danced on the bed, smiling and chuckling. 'I think you've cracked it this time, Solitan! I really think he understands!'

'Don't sound too surprised,' her little comrade said crossly. 'I've had thousands of years to come up with an explanation!'

'Well it sounds a pretty good one,' Henri agreed. 'But why am I such an important stitch?'

'Somebody's got to do it,' Olmar said with a shrug.

'Yes, somebody has to do it,' the other four Marox chimed in cheerfully.

'And besides,' Solitan added, 'you have other things to do. You are not just an important stitch in your fabric of time, a healer of time, you might say, you are…'

'That's quite enough of that!' Olmar shouted, louder than Henri had thought such a small creature could ever have lifted her voice. 'You know you can't do that.'

'I was only…'

'You were only what? You were only going to reveal the future to a mortal, that's what. For someone who has existed for so long, you certainly haven't developed much common sense.'

'Sorree!' Solitan said, shrugging while he looked at Henri. 'Just let's say, you ain't finished yet!'

'No,' Henri said with a sigh. 'I don't suppose I have.'

They were all quiet after that. Henri was thinking, digesting everything that Solitan had told him. The Marox, all sitting closely together, were content to shove each other with their elbows as if the bed were not big enough for all five of them. But eventually Henri spoke.

'I've got to do something about Hansenger before I leave,'

he said picking his words deliberately. 'I have to stop his experiments or they will carry on even after I get out of this place.'

The Marox all nodded. They remained quiet, looking at each other as if they knew what each was thinking. But they waited for Henri to continue. For the time being, they had helped him as much as they could. He had to work out his own destiny. He had to be the leader, not the led.

'Just escaping won't solve the problem,' he said more to himself than to his little friends. 'But what can I do?'

'Perhaps you should sleep on it,' Raelmin suggested. 'It's always a good way to get to the root of a problem, is that.'

'Indeed it is,' said Solitan.

They watched him, waiting for a decision.

'OK then,' Henri said wearily. 'Perhaps I could use a little more sleep.' And with that, he lay out on the huge bed, his head only inches away from the Marox, he closed his eyes and, remarkably, despite all that was on his mind, he fell into a deep sleep.

❖

Chapter Twenty Seven

YUKLA'S PROMISE

Henri didn't know how long he had slept. The dark purple sky outside the windows showed it was still the middle of the night. The five Marox sat where he had left them, five pairs of eyes still watching him, waiting for him to make the next move. The dim lights in the room were as he had left them when he dozed off. Despite their size, he felt remarkably safe with the Marox there beside him, watching over him. He wondered if they ever slept or if they ever ate anything. They hadn't touched the bread and cheese he had brought back for them.

'We work off light,' Olmar said as if reading his thoughts. 'Any light. Starlight, moonlight, sunlight, artificial light. Any light you can think of. We rest. We do a lot of that especially when we are in The Seal. But we don't sleep. Not as you know it, anyway.'

Henri took a deep breath and nodded. 'Right,' he said and threw his legs off the side of the bed. He dropped to the floor and went over to the closet and then washed his hands and face. He spent some time looking into a mirror, wondering what was so special about the person he saw reflected there.

'What do I have to do to become invisible again?' he asked on his return. 'I'm going to do a little spying of my own.'

'You just take me with you,' Solitan answered. 'That sector of The Seal and I are one and the same. We are activated the same. When we are separated from the rest of the Marox then whatever power we possess becomes dominant.

It didn't take Henri long to get ready to go. Reckoning that he had at least a couple of hours before the three spies realized he had gone, he made a small pouch out of one of the pillow cases, tied it around his waist and then placed Solitan in it. As he walked away from the other Marox he knew he had become invisible. Already he began to detect the feeling of nausea that came with using the power of The Seal, something he had not recognised when first he used it. Then, he had just believed that it was nausea from a combination of mild *mal de mer,* and being trapped in the stinking steerage section of the ship. But now, he knew that the slight throbbing in his temple was clear assurance that he was not visible to the human eye.

The Marox seemed to still be able to see him from the bed. Their eyes followed him as he looked back.

'Make sure you are well hidden,' he instructed.'

'Don't worry,' said Olmar. 'We've had centuries of experience at being unseen.'

With that last word, Henri and Solitan went to the door through which the three spies had taken him the previous day. Retracing his footstep exactly, he moved quickly through the passages and doorways until he came to the area where he had seen the Graftians at work. The area seemed deserted at first as he strode across the vast room, yet he couldn't help feeling that there was someone there, someone who knew he was there, watching him.

'Don't worry,' said Solitan, detecting Henri's every thought, 'you are quite safe.'

Henri didn't know just how Solitan could be so sure, but he trusted him as he chuckled away, his head poking out of the sling, his tiny hands on the edge of the material, pulling it down so that it wasn't uncomfortable under his chin. Henri carried on through to the opening where he had seen the Graftians take the strange carriage and was soon walking up a long wide passage. The overhead lights were glowing just as they did in his room, seemingly lit by some perpetual source of energy.

He passed the ends of several other corridors before coming to an abrupt halt at the corner of another one. He could hear the sound of several voices coming from down the corridor to the right. Quickly he followed the sounds until he came to another corner, and carefully eased his head around the bend to see who was there. Several Graftians were seated in a wide alcove, seemingly waiting for something or someone, but none appeared to notice Henri. There was a soft-wheeled cart to one side, and some long-handled brooms stood neatly against the nearest wall.

Confident now that he could not be seen, Henri moved around the corner and went closer to them. As he approached, he picked up one of the brooms and, standing on it, pulled the handle out of its head. The cart was half full of used containers and wrapping materials, so it was an easy task to get rid of the broom head without the talkative Graftians noticing anything unusual.

He thought it strange that they spoke his language. On his travels he had met many people and acquired rudimentary understanding of several languages, but here, in this foreign world, there seemed no hint of a foreign language. Even the

Graftians' accents were hardly different from his own.

'She'll be here soon,' the Graftian who Henri had met and knew as Yukla, stated.

'But is she going to make any difference?' another asked.

'We have nothing to lose,' Yukla responded.

Henri couldn't help feeling that he had not just arrived here by accident. He looked down at his little companion who smiled back up at him and shrugged disarmingly. The Graftians remained silent and waited some more. Henri just sat down on the floor beside them and waited. His plan was to follow them when they eventually decided to move on, but the plan was soon forgotten when he saw the young female Graftian, the same one that had rebuked him the previous day. She came up to the corridor from a closed door that had been hitherto almost invisible until it silently popped into the wall and then moved sideways. She walked with a confident stride, looking less like any of the other Graftians not just by her height and the way she walked, but by the way she addressed them.

'Hope you haven't been waiting long,' she said cheerily.

'We've been waiting for years,' said Yukla, who seemed to be the elected leader of the six Graftians. 'A few hours are unlikely to make us break down into fits of sobbing.'

'A few hours is all you will need to reverse the effect of the ergametron,' she replied, now looking quite serious.

'The Vasitterites destroyed our world and its atmosphere. What makes you, a complete stranger, think you can change things now?'

'I'm not a Graftian,' she stated abruptly as she glanced in Henri's direction.

Henri suddenly realized who this person was. She could

see him. Her eyes lit up as they looked at him, seeing every bit of his body. Only one person had ever been able to see him when he was using the power of The Seal to become invisible to human eyes. The Graftians were incapable of seeing him. But Win could see him. He would have known those eyes anywhere. They had seemed familiar when he had looked into them in the clearing depot. But he hadn't expected to ever see Win again so his mind had just blocked out any thought of the witch he loved. He loved! What made him start to think like that now of all things? He had forced himself not to think about her. She was on a mission. She had admitted it. Her job was to secure possession of The Seal. So what was she doing here in this world? Whatever the reason, it lifted his heart to see her.

Henri's face cracked into a broad grin as Win looked interestedly at the creature he had tied firmly to his side. She smiled and looked away, bringing her eyes back to Yukla and his friends.

'I am a witch,' she said, now watching their reaction closely. 'I have disguised myself as a Graftian because otherwise, Hansenger's spies would have arrested me and then where would we be?'

'Where?' asked Yukla.

'Not here for a start,' Win responded lightly. 'I can only help you if I am not seen as a threat to Hansenger.'

'Just being a Graftian, or looking like one will not make you any more capable of reversing the ergametron's energy fields than we have been able to do.'

'No, but I have a secret ability that nobody knows about,' she replied, glancing once more at Henri. 'I can get into the power station where you cannot.'

'We're wasting our time,' one of the other Graftians said angrily.' She isn't even worth half of one of us. How would she be able to do what our brothers and sisters and children died trying to do?'

'Oh, it won't be without risk,' Win stated. 'We still might die. But, whatever opportunities you have had in the past, we have a better chance now of righting the wrongs of the Vasitterites than you'll ever have again.'

Another Graftian stood up, and moving towards her, said, 'Do you think we don't know that you are a spy? What makes you think you can get out of here alive to tell those men that we are rebellious trouble makers?'

He raised his hand to grab Win's collar but just as his fingers touched the fabric of her coat his arm was suddenly thrust down to his waist by an invisible force. The look of surprise on his face didn't last long, as his other hand swung quickly around to grab her. But once again, his arm was parried by Henri's broom handle, like a solid block of air that moved independently of the rest of the atmosphere.

'I think you had better hear me out,' Win said, standing her ground.

Yukla nodded. 'Let her be,' he commanded. 'If she had wanted to report us, she could have done it already.' He looked at Win directly. 'Well, what is your plan?'

'Only I can get into the power station. Only I can destroy the ergametron.'

'But if you destroy the ergametron, then we will lose all the power of light and heat that it provides,' another Graftian came in.

'Maybe yes, maybe no. But look what it has done to your

world. Look at the sky. Your fathers and their fathers before them used to look out at a blue sky with red sunsets, and gaze upon fields covered in early morning dew. The ergametron destroyed all that. It even destroyed its creators. And how many of you are there left now? Two hundred, three?'

'There are more of us than that,' Yukla answered. 'But they are all hiding, all living like rats in a sewer. In fact many of them are in the sewers! There is no quality of life for them, but they choose that rather than be slaves to their new masters.'

'Then you should be ready to do what you can to save them from their fate. Even death is better than what you've got now.'

Yukla nodded, as did the other five Graftians beside him. They were clearly all at the end of their tether, out of options and clean out of patience to endure the life inflicted upon them.

'So what do you need from us?' another Graftian asked, now totally in support of the young witch. 'I'm ready to follow you and I'm ready to die if there is the slightest chance of regaining our lives.'

'I don't guarantee no one will be hurt. But if I can get into the power station then I am as sure as I can be that I can return your world to you,' Win lied. She had no idea what was going to happen when the Graftians' world was wrenched back to a medieval existence. 'You won't have perpetual light and heat and all the other luxuries you have shared with your rulers, but you will be free to start work on redeveloping your own lives, free from the Vasitterites and free from Hansenger and his men.'

The Graftians all looked one to the other, their eyes already telling their decision. 'We'll do what we can to help,' Yukla said gravely. 'What do you need?'

'I'll need to be shown the way to the building where all the power is generated.'

'That can be done, but the guards will kill us all.'

'Perhaps,' Win said, concentrating on her list of requirements. 'Then I'll need you to cause a diversion while I get into the place. I must not be seen, so I shall slip by when you have distracted the guards.'

Yukla laughed out loudly. 'The guards are not easily distracted. They are very well trained, and would never leave their posts all at the same time.'

'We'll see,' Win said and then stipulated her third and final requirement. 'I have a friend here who may need to be shown the gateway to his own world. It is the opening you use for receiving supplies.'

'You should know where it is,' Yukla said angrily. 'After all, you have come here!'

'Not through your gateway, though,' Win said firmly. 'I can appear in your world, but I cannot travel out the way I came in with anyone who was not with me when I entered.'

Henri recalled travelling to see the Seven Witches with Win when he had been poisoned and how he and Win had no choice but to return to their own time back on *The Arinosta*.

'All right, we'll go and get him,' Yukla said, enthusiastically. 'But I can't see how he can get out if the humans do not let us out. Hansenger's guards at the opening have instructions only to allow food through and to search all goods being sent back through it.'

'There will be no guards there,' Win stated, with no further explanation.

'I should explain,' continued Yukla. It is very far from here.

We do not travel through the opening ourselves. We send and receive things by way of a strange glass cart, one that Hansenger says he invented; but we know he didn't. We are never allowed to get into it. Only the guards load and unload it. But the problem,' Yukla said, waving a fat grizzly finger at the little witch, 'is that without the power of the ergametron, the carriage that transports us to and from the glass cart at the opening will be useless. Everything here uses power from that mysterious generating machine. Without power, everything will grind to a halt. When the Vasitterites were here, all their commerce and trade depended on it.'

'But yours doesn't,' Win explained. 'You could live happily, providing that your agricultural life could be returned to normal. A blue sky and sunshine and rain would change the fields back to being productive farm land again.'

'True,' said Yukla. 'And all those Graftians that are hiding could return to a normal life. We would be happy again. We were a truly peaceful nation before the Vasitterites came and enslaved us. I don't know where they came from or where they went, but they surely didn't do anything to benefit the Graftians.'

'Come on then,' one of the other Graftians said. 'What are we waiting for? Let's do it and get it over with.'

'We still haven't solved the problem of getting my friend out,' Win stated. 'Isn't there any way we can get him to the opening without the powered carriage?'

Yukla thought for a moment. He was trying to think of a solution to the problem when the keen Graftian spoke again. 'I can get him there,' he said, his eyes widening with a pride that had once thought to have been lost in the Graftian race. 'I can get him out before we destroy the ergametron!'

Win shook her head. 'Unfortunately, that is not an option. He must remain where he is until the job is done. I can't explain now, but he is an essential key to the plan.'

'And where is he now?'

'He'll be at the ergametron. He's the man you met yesterday.'

Yukla nodded. 'I thought it might be,' he said, pensively. 'Then we will walk to the gateway,' Yukla declared eventually. 'Where we can travel in a matter of minutes, it will take many weeks on foot, but with no hassle from those terrible men, then we should be able to take him to the opening to his world at our leisure. But I can't guarantee that the glass carriage at the gateway, which takes goods to and from this world, will still be working.'

'That's a risk we must take,' Win said gravely as they all set out down the wide corridor, and headed for the broad main street.

❖

Chapter Twenty Eight

THE ERGAMETRON

The dark purple night was slowly fading into grey as they all walked quickly across several streets to what looked like a huge railway station very similar to the train stations of London, only the whole place, the walls, the footways, were made of shiny metal and not smoke and oil-stained concrete, bricks and sandstone. There were no rails in the bottom of the deep shiny-bottomed roadway that ran along the side of the platform, and everything and everywhere was spotlessly clean.

Almost as soon as they arrived at the edge of the platform, a large silver blue pod glided alongside, silent except for the rush of air that flowed around its pointed nose. It didn't seem to touch the ground, but instead hovered mysteriously, relying on nothing but the air around it for support. A door not unlike the ones in the walls of the corridors, and just as big, popped inwards and opened to one side of the strange vehicle as silently as if it were moving in a dream. Following Yukla, they all stepped inside the strange elliptical pod and as soon as they had passed through it, the door slid silently closed.

On what the vehicle travelled, Henri could not tell for there were neither lines on the ground nor wheels on the vehicle to carry the thing. It simply travelled along a very large, shiny, metal, square-sectioned gulley which took it from one station to the next.

The group were totally alone. No passengers waited for the carriage to arrive and none got off it when it did. It seemed to be one long compartment with a hundred or so comfortable seats set in rows of four at each side of a central aisle. All were empty. Yukla led the way once the doors had closed, and they all took seats near to each other. Win sat alone and just looked out of the window as Henri sat nearby.

Some of the seats had a small panel set into the back of them. Yukla touched the panel with his finger, waited for something to appear on it, and, choosing one of the lines of strange writing that appeared on it, touched it again. The carriage moved away from the platform sideways at first and then it moved suddenly forward with such acceleration that it made Henri feel dizzy watching the scenery outside the windows suddenly turn to a blur. But he felt no other effect of the acceleration; no being thrust back against the seat, nothing to indicate that they were moving or gaining speed in any way. There was not even the sound of the wind outside as it travelled past buildings and bare open spaces faster than the speed of a bullet.

Using the Vasitterite carriage, their journey to the outskirts of the city took less than ten minutes. It stopped as abruptly as it had shot away from the place of departure, yet the passengers were not thrust forward as the vehicle braked.

As they got out of the pod and walked out of the vast opening of the station, the contrast was remarkable. Behind them, from where they had travelled, the entire skyline from left to right was filled with the huge dark metropolis of The City. Ahead, in the direction they were to travel, was a bare, open desert with not a tree, a plant nor even a blade of grass in the rock-hard barren ground. The only thing that broke up that desolate landscape was a huge and magnificent looking white ball, rising out of the ground, far away in the distance.

Although he had no timepiece, Henri calculated that it had taken a good hour and a half heading away on foot from the bleak, grey buildings to reach a huge distant dome. As they drew closer, it became apparent to Henri that it must be at least a thousand feet high, dwarfing the hills that surrounded it. It was way beyond the outskirts of The City of Darkness and stood out against the still, green-grey sky like a huge moon rising out of the desolate horizon. It was lighter now than it had been when they set out, but the sky over The City seemed to remain purple longer. Even in his short stay there, Henri had noticed that today the colour of the sky seemed darker than the day before. He wondered if, in days to come, the sky would remain permanently like night.

As before, Yukla led the way and Win was escorted on both sides and from behind by the eager group of insurgents. Henri had remained a few yards behind, following silently except for the constant chat of his little companion, who couldn't help himself when it came to giving guided tours. It would seem that he had already seen this world before, and he was most certainly well informed about the huge generator that was ensconced inside the giant globe. Apparently it was a form of technology that even humans in Henri's world were unlikely to discover for hundreds of centuries. But Henri listened patiently and only told Solitan to hush when they were within a half a mile or so of the high impenetrable wall.

Beyond a gate which lay ahead of them, the guards stationed

outside the dome had already spotted them when Yukla pointed to a huge arched entrance that led into the dome. From a small building by the side of the gateway, and dwarfed by the sheer size of the opening, four guards ran forward with spindly looking sticks which they brandished in the same way that soldiers would hold a musket, but the weapons, if that is what they were, bore no resemblance to even the advanced pin-fire rifles that Captain Bartholomew had carried on his ship. In fact they looked just like thin walking canes; but Henri knew better and so did the others.

Quickly, Henri walked forward and took a hold of Win by the hand and pulled her close against his body. Because she was now within his field of invisibility, she suddenly disappeared not just before the eyes of her guides, but in front of the guards as well. Suddenly unsettled, the guards lifted their weapons. It was a signal that Yukla and his gang took seriously. Without another word, and presuming that Win's disappearance was part of her plan, they turned on their heels and ran for their lives. But the guards were not going to let the prowlers escape so easily and, had the Graftians known just what danger they faced, Henri seriously doubted that they would have come so close to the fenced enclosure.

The leading guard lifted his wand-like weapon and aimed it at the backs of the fleeing visitors; but unexpectedly, jabbed by a broom handle, and with a sudden pain in his groin, he slumped to the floor onto his knees, only prevented from falling completely flat on his face by propping himself on his weapon. It made him look like an old man trying to stand up with the aid of a walking stick. As a support, the weapon was no help when it, too, was knocked from beneath his hand by

Henri's makeshift staff, leaving the guard to roll forward onto his shoulder. He was a fit young man and, recovering quickly, he pushed himself up from the ground, regained his balance on his knees and reached for the stick. But it had disappeared, and looking at it in total bewilderment, he saw a plain and ordinary broom handle. Henri had dropped it in front of the guard and picked up the guard's weapon instead. He definitely felt safer for it, although he had serious doubts as to how the stick weapon worked or what it did.

The other guards were running towards their comrade but, like their companion, tripped by a quick insertion of Henri's stick between their running legs, each in turn stumbled or tripped as they raised their weapons to point them at the fleeing Graftians. Then, suddenly, shots were fired as the stumbling guards gripped hard on their sticks. The first shot went into the air as the man's arm swung erratically in an attempt to regain his balance.

Henri watched the awesome power that the slim weapon possessed. The shot that went skyward looked simply like a very thin, disconnected light beam about a hundred feet long, disappearing into the now green-grey sky. Suddenly it evoked a mesh of forked lighting followed a second or two later with peels of rolling thunder; and the sky instantly turned black around the point of entry where the light beam had passed through it. Harmless enough if fired in the air, he thought until a second stumbling guard shot at the ground and blasted a six foot wide crater in the hard, solid concrete floor, showering everyone nearby with flying lumps of shrapnel. The only people not affected by the soaring debris were Henri, Win and Solitan, whose safety had been ensured by the force field that still rendered them all invisible. From that explosive impact, pieces of concrete the size of a man's head bounced harmlessly off the shield and into a mid-air trajectory before returning to earth as yet another lethal flying projectile, bigger and more forceful than a ship's cannon ball. As debris hit the one remaining guard a stray shot from his weapon hit his companion on the leg, evaporating his whole being as quickly as a drop of water on a red hot stove.

Henri looked at the stick weapon in his hand more closely. There was a tiny button near the handle that he hadn't noticed before. He pointed the stick at the heavy metal gate and squeezed the button with his thumb. It took little pressure to fire the weapon. With a thunderous crack, the shot opened up an eight foot hole in the entrance, cutting the edges of the gap as neatly as a knife cutting paper. Like the disappearing guard, the middle section of the gate had just evaporated like a mist in a breeze.

With an opening into the grounds of the giant globe, and still holding tightly onto Win's hand, Henri wasted no time in running forward and jumping through it. He couldn't have felt happier. Just having her near to him once again was creating a surge of energy through his whole body. So happy was he that, irrespective of the danger ahead, he almost danced on his toes across a vast yard, towards the huge arched entrance of the building.

Somehow, an alarm must have been raised, and more guards were being called out from inside. As the door opened to let them out, so Henri and Win, hand in hand, shoulder to shoulder, skipped lightly passed them and into the building. Red lights were flashing as the armed men came along the wide corridor, after emerging from doors that only appeared when part of the corridor wall popped backward and began to slide inside the wall.

Sheltering Win behind him, and with her arms around his waist, Henri remained close to the side of the corridor. Those guards that were coming towards him, and who were also close to the wall, were simply deflected, stumbling and bumping into some of their other running colleagues as they continued on their way. They recovered their balance and carried on as if nothing had happened. A siren suddenly began to wail outside, but it brought no more guards out into the corridor. Eventually, they took up their posts either outside the main door or just inside it. They quite clearly had instructions not to let anybody enter.

Without Solitan, neither Henri nor Win would have even got into the grounds, let alone deep inside where they were heading now. Seemingly, without anybody noticing, they left the main access corridors and entered a deserted ante room that appeared to be a place where row upon row of white overalls were hanging in plastic sheaths, overalls that would have easily covered three people with plenty left for wrap around.

Now walking, they approached another door, but, unlike the doors that appeared out of the wall when he stepped up to them, this door was set in a huge frame. It was not automatic and it did not open when they went towards it.

There was a set of makeshift steps and above them was some sort of small glass panel next to the door. Neither Win nor Henri knew what to do with it. Leaving go of each other's hands, together they climbed the steps and studied the contrivance which they worked out must be some kind of safety device to keep the door shut to all but the people who knew how to operate it.

'Wait until somebody comes out,' Solitan said, now clearly able to take control of the situation. And then, 'You'd better hold onto Henri's hand again,' he said, looking directly at Win. Henri noticed that she no longer maintained the disguise of a Graftian. She had reverted to being the slim girl-like figure looking just as he had remembered her as she sailed away on *The Black Sword*.

'I can do invisible,' she said, 'now that I don't have to use all my power to look like a Graftian.

'Better hold my hand,' said Henri. 'You might be able to see me when I am not seen by others, but I need to be able to see you. I don't have the gifts of a witch.'

Realizing Henri was right, Win did as Solitan had suggested. At first, she thought that Solitan was being over cautious, but within seconds of her gripping Henri's hand and, becoming enveloped in his magical shield, the door emitted a buzzing sound, it swung inwards and opened wide as Hansenger began to walk out towards them.

The black look on Hansenger's face told a tale of woe. He was clearly anguished, and by what, Henri and his companions were soon to discover. He and Win walked down the eight or so steps and watched as the man strode past them and went towards the opposite wall. Suddenly, as before, an unmarked door popped inwards as if from nowhere, and slid silently sideways into the wall, leaving the way clear for them to enter a long, bare room. Four men stood at the far end. They stopped talking when they saw Hansenger. Apart from a large blue glass tank and a strange time-keeping device on the wall, there was nothing else to see. The clock, for that was what Henri concluded it was, displayed the time in red numbers, clicking the seconds silently forward. It read 11.45:26.

'Damn the ergametron,' Hansenger cursed, shouting towards the men. Suddenly a strange contraption came into view in the centre of the room. It looked like a long, glass box and, if this was a device for travelling, it looked quite unsuitable for carrying passengers at speed to their desired location. Unlike the travelling pod at the station, this machine wasn't pointed; in fact neither did this machine, if indeed it was a machine, travel in a metallic gulley. It had an elliptical attachment on the base to stand on and it kept fading in and out of view like a vision in a restless dream. It had see-through sides, and now, as he got closer, Henri could see that it had rows of glass seats inside. 'You need to get back to the laboratory,' Hansenger shouted. 'We must stop the experiments until we have worked out how this generator works once and for all. Every time we fail, it increases its output. We have no way of regulating it, and until we do then it is endangering our entire project.'

'Doctor Fingle is working on it full time,' one of the men retorted. He was a heavily built muscular looking man with hands like shovels.

'That's not enough. We use the power from this contraption to run our experiments, but until we know how it works then we risk destroying the only thing that enables us to do our research. You three go back in the particle transporter and tell them to wind down all activity; and report back here within fifteen minutes,' he said pointing to all but one of the men. 'You come with me,' he commanded the fourth.

Henri thought that a remarkable feat, to go all the way back to somewhere in the centre of The City, perform their mission and return within a quarter of an hour. He would have liked to have accompanied them, but resisted the temptation to follow. Instead, he watched as the carriage thing appeared back into a solid form. The three men stepped inside it as if passing through the solid glass wall. They all took seats and then the thing faded out of sight once again, taking the three men with it. Henri was about to look away when suddenly the contraption appeared again, now completely empty of passengers. Hansenger nodded to himself and turned towards the space where the door had opened to let them in.

'Follow me Ruskin,' he instructed the burly character, and went out of the room the way he had come. Henri and Win were close on his heels as the door closed behind them. Hansenger walked across the wide corridor, up the makeshift steps and placed his hand on the glass screen that had puzzled Henri and his companions. The huge door, like the smaller ones, opened sideways to reveal another huge and circular room, this one with a domed ceiling as high as a ten ships masts. Yet this room was completely empty. It looked to be six hundred yards or more in diameter.

Hoping that they were heading in the right direction to find the generator, Henri and Win just followed Hansenger and Ruskin as they went around the inside of the curved edge of the dome. But then Hansenger and Ruskin suddenly stopped. They looked around as if waiting for someone and then, without any warning, a large circular section of the floor gave way.

Henri almost let go of Win as his stomach seemed to reach his mouth but soon the acceleration of the dropping floor evened out and the floor continued to flash past floor upon floor before stopping only slightly slower than it had dropped from beneath his feet in the first place. Hansenger and Ruskin appeared completely relaxed. They had obviously no fear of the mechanism that had seemingly carried them deep into the bowels of the earth. Henri and Win watched and waited, ready to move with Hansenger to avoid being left in the strange travelling device.

When the floor came to a complete standstill, Hansenger and Ruskin walked forward. They were now in a relatively confined space, and although it was large, it was nowhere as gigantic as the room they had left miles above their heads. The ceiling was about thirty feet high and the corridor, if it was a corridor curved slightly. They stepped away from the inside wall through one of the remarkable appearing doorways to come face to face with another curved wall that was giving off a dim blue light. It glowed eerily. As Henri and Win followed the two men along the side of this glowing wall he calculated that the diameter of the curve probably matched that of the gigantic domed room on the surface.

Eventually, they came to a wall that blocked the entire corridor. Hansenger placed his hand on the wall and, at once, a door appeared and slid to one side. Once again they followed, unsure if they would ever get out of the place without Hansenger to lead them. Henri had serious doubts that he could do anything to stop the contraption working. He had no idea where it was but presumed that the luminous wall was part of it. But without any other options, holding tight onto Win's hand, he just continued to follow the leader.

His reasoning seemed to be right, for inside the new room, there was what appeared to be some sort of control centre. It was obviously designed for giants. Steps, three feet high, led to several very high seats. Hansenger had obviously improvised by building a small gantry along the front of whatever it was that the seats were facing. On the platform stood another man; he wore spectacles and busily moved from one dial to another on a huge sloping table. Hansenger stepped up onto the platform and went alongside.

'Anything?' he asked the bespectacled man.

The man shook his head. 'Sorry. Even dismantling these dials seems to be impossible,' he stated as he tapped one of hundreds of small, square, glass windows in which numbers flashed miraculously from nowhere, and then changed to another number and then another continuously. 'See, the output is fluctuating wildly,' he continued. 'But the pressure on this wall is rising rapidly now with every hour that passes. There seems no way to control or regulate anything. The whole unit is sealed and goodness knows what will happen if we do manage to get into it.'

'That is not helping me, Fingle,' Hansenger snapped. 'Unless we can control it then we can't continue the experiments. We need to be able to moderate the output.'

Fingle shrugged. 'The technology is hundreds if not thousands of years beyond our time. It's as advanced to us as a train is to a parrot.' He looked directly into Hansenger's eyes, totally unperturbed by his ferocious glare. 'The process of reverse engineering something, has to start from a knowledge base that we already possess. For instance, in our own world, Gilbert discovered electricity and magnetism in the sixteen sixties but, working from that, as you have done, Ampere and Maxwell have only just discovered the connection between magnets and electricity. However, your experiments here, are a continuation of work left behind by the Vasitterites. If they hadn't left their laboratories intact then you wouldn't have been able to carry on trying to develop their technology.

'But what I find curious is that this generator and, even more so, the particle transporter seem to be more advanced than even the Vasitterites had reached in their civilization. Somehow they, like you, had inherited these things. This machine that makes perpetual energy is so much more advanced than anything else in this green and purple world that I can't imagine they just stumbled on the idea. We do not understand how the energy is transferred, yet it is the root of power for your electro magnets a hundred miles away. It even drives the trains from one place to another. It could even be the same power source used by the particle transporters. It's…'

'I know what it is. It powers everything by sending the energy through the air,' Hansenger growled. 'I brought you here, remember?'

'Indeed you did. But you've seen the transcript of The Golden Book and now think that the ergametron and the transporters are linked to The Seal. You think they work the same. The whole scope of your experiments is now based on that one assumption. But I don't think they do work the same. What looks like glass and liquid,' he said, pointing at the wall, 'is, in fact, nothing of the kind. You are still experimenting with metals and wires to construct your magnets. How far behind this world's technology do you reckon you are?'

'I have the best minds working on it,' Hansenger retorted.

'But not good enough. They don't know the science that has preceded these machines, so they cannot make anything like them.'

'The particle transporter is already made. We can work

from that.'

'But it only conveys you from one place to another in this world or from this world to another only if you leave it by the gap it makes through to that world. According to The Golden Book, The Seal conveys people between worlds, separate universes, different times, without using any space-gap window like the one we use to pass between our two worlds; and it does it without any other key. They are not the same.'

'That is your opinion, is it, Fingle?'

'Yes it is.'

Hansenger turned and looked at all the little square window dials on the console. He sighed and then, after a considerable length of thought, said, 'So why are our experiments disrupting all the other parallel worlds. Why are they affecting this machine?'

Fingle shrugged. 'I can only think that the ergametron *is* another world. What we are seeing here is possibly just a vision of something somewhere else.'

'What!' Hansenger seemed angrier than ever.

'It's hard to grasp, I know,' Fingle went on. 'But everything we see and touch is just a vision; one thing at one point in time. Nothing is really solid. Even you and I and the walls around us are just gasses, tiny particles bound together in some way.'

'Interesting that she knows that,' Solitan suddenly called from Henri's hip.

Henri glanced down at Solitan and frowned. 'Interesting that you think *he's* a woman,' he said with a shake of his head. For such an old and wise little being, sometimes, Solitan wasn't the brightest button.

Solitan shrugged. His eyebrows danced as he said, 'Woman?

Did I say that? I meant…'

Hansenger touched his ear. No doubt he had heard something but it would have been no more than the sound of a passing mosquito. The only problem was, this building, in fact the whole world above them, was so sterile there was no likelihood of any such creature getting into even the ground floor section. He scowled.

'Keep working on it,' he said, shaking his head but now speaking in a friendlier tone. 'I know you are doing your best and I know you *are* the best.' He patted Fingle on the shoulder and stepped down off the gantry.

Henri was about to follow him when Solitan spoke again.

'Stay master. We must stay.'

Hansenger rubbed his ear again and looked around. He regarded Fingle for a long moment while the scientist continued fiddling and poking at the console. 'Did you hear a sound just now?' Hansenger asked.

Fingle turned to face him. He regarded his master curiously for a moment and then shook his head. 'Sound? What kind of sound?' he asked.

Hansenger glared at him but then, after a while, and after watching Fingle meticulously return to his work, he turned to go.

'We need to be able to control it,' were his parting words. 'Ruskin, you stay and help him.'

'Yes sir,' Ruskin said obediently, and stepped up beside Fingle.

To Henri, Ruskin didn't seem the scientific type.

❖

Chapter Twenty Nine

BARMOUGH

Henri, Win and the Marox watched Hansenger depart. Despite the silence of the doors, somehow, Fingle knew when Hansenger had left. He turned and looked around and then, without seeming to have any difficulty, looked over his spectacles directly at Win and Henri.

'What are you looking at?' demanded Ruskin, seeing Fingle apparently concentrating on a block of air.

'Just thinking,' Fingle retorted. 'No need for you to stay. This is thinking work.'

'I have my orders,' Ruskin stated gruffly. 'Not that I understand them any better than you.'

'I understand them entirely,' Fingle replied, pushing his pair of square, gold rimmed spectacles onto his face. 'Yes, I understand them entirely.' He regarded Ruskin for a moment and then said, 'You can get me a drink if you like. Tea…'

'Not too strong,' Ruskin continued. 'I know, I can remember things you know.' He looked pleased that he could be of some service to the old scientist. It was obvious that he liked Fingle.

'Good man,' Fingle said, smiling. 'I'll have some bread as well, if you would. See you when you get back.'

Obediently, Ruskin headed off with his orders. Fingle

watched him depart and then, sure that he was not returning, turned to face Henri and Win.

'So, who are you and what do you want?' He was a direct speaker. 'You look surprised that I can see you.'

'A little,' Win replied.

'A lot,' Henri confirmed.

Fingle Smiled.

'Does Hansenger know you're a witch?' asked Win, candidly. 'A female witch at that.'

Fingle shook his head.

Henri regarded Win with sceptical eyes. Was she going mad or becoming paranoid?

But Fingle's face was serious now. 'So you understand,' he said.

Henri watched as Win studied Fingle. The scientist's face seemed to change each time he blinked.

'Barmough?' Win said, suddenly tilting her head to one side.

Henri watched as Fingle's features continued to slowly change. Gradually, the creased lines of his face smoothed out and the eyes became rounder and brighter. A few moments later, Fingle was no more. Before them stood an elderly woman with pale lips, round, dark brown eyes and a clear smooth complexion. She took the spectacles from her face and placed them on the console beside her.

'Surprise!' she said in a high pitched voice.

'But we thought you were dead!' Win gasped.

'There's still life in the old dog yet,' Barmough replied with a chilling chuckle. Henri didn't much care for her.

'So why are you here?' Win asked.

'Why do you think, silly witch? I'm here because I want to

discover just what it is that Hansenger is up to.'

'And have you?'

Barmough chuckled again. 'Oh yes!' Her smile was quite awful, Henri thought. Her teeth were slightly yellowed and she had a glint in her eye that didn't convey a feeling of trust. 'Gosh, it seems a long time,' she said, now leaning on the smooth topped console that was attached to the blue, liquid-filled wall of the ergametron.

'Only a hundred and five years,' said Win in a tone of voice that made Henri think that she didn't like the older witch either. It was strange that there were more witches than Win had originally said.

'A hundred and five years! Is that all?' Once again there was a heart chilling chuckle. 'A hundred and five years! You were only a sprout of a thing then,' she said, her voice rising on the last word. As she paused she bent forward towards Win who was standing a couple of steps below her on the gantry. 'You've changed,' she said quietly.

'You haven't, it seems,' Win replied. 'You are still the same old trouble maker.'

'Trouble maker! Just because I wanted to try out new things, new ideas!'

'You destroyed our world. You know that. It was your illegitimate work that changed our time. It was your spells that ended the reign of the witches. It was your spells that made them follow you. They never returned.'

'Puwee,' Barmough remarked snidely. 'Not all of them I see. And anyway, it was just a mistake, that's what it was; a simple mistake.'

'And now you are working with Hansenger,' Win continued.

'As if killing your own kind wasn't enough. Now you are set on killing the Graftians and anybody else whose world is affected by his experiments. Don't you realize that hundreds of different worlds, all separate parallel universes in their own times, are going to be wiped out if he continues?'

Barmough looked at her and smirked. 'I'll tell you something,' she grated bitterly. 'When the Seven vanquished me, they thought that by doing so they had killed me. Or at least they left me to die a long and lonely death. And they felt no remorse. At first I hated them. And it was revenge that fed my will to stay alive. But I have had over a hundred years to regret what I did. And since then I have had the time to try and find out what went wrong with my spells. The Seven didn't even want to know why I did what I did.'

'And what exactly did you do?' asked Henri, trying to piece together what Win had said about The Seal being the only way to save the race of witches.

'She invited powers into our world that she could not control,' Win said bitterly. 'She…'

'I tried to increase the powers we possessed,' Barmough cut in. 'We were in danger of being too clever for our own good. We were being persecuted, stoned and burned to death. Oh, there were a few of us who were clever enough to be able to escape by being extremely gifted. We could make ourselves invisible or change our appearance to look like somebody else. But the majority of younger witches had not developed their powers enough to do that. It takes a witch a hundred and fifty years to become totally proficient. We were being wiped out by religious persecutors. And on top of that, we were marrying ordinary humans because most of the male witches had left.

They had become power crazed. They had abandoned us.'

'So where did they go?' asked Henri.

'They went to follow a male witch called Drach.'

'Drach?' Henri exclaimed.

'You've heard of him, I see,' Barmough said with a smile. 'Well, he was the downfall of the witch society. And because witches had no men folk, they went with humans. And as soon as they do that, well, they just lose it!'

'Lose it?' asked Henri.

'They become human. They live an ordinary human life, perhaps a little longer, but they do not live for hundreds of years. So, since it takes well over a hundred and fifty years to become a proficient witch, they could never live long enough to become capable witches. And even though the young witches only had gifts of clairvoyance and of healing, they were different to the religious fanatics who envied and feared even the slightest ability that they might possess, and so they had to die. And die they did; in the hundreds and thousands. And I intended to do something about it.'

'You cast spells that affected our world forever.'

'Yes, that's true. I did. I thought we could use more power against these religion-crazed infidels. I thought Drach was going to be our salvation! I was wrong. And I realized it when female witches began to disappear. Thousands of us followed him but, their numbers dwindled so rapidly I could only assume he was killing them. And I was right, in a way. He was stripping them of their talents.' She paused to reflect on what she had been saying. 'He was making sure that the male and the female witches were dispersed to separate parts of the world,' she said eventually.

'And by doing so, they could not breed with their own kind

and produce more young witches who could possibly grow up to be a threat to him,' Win stated. 'But you survived,' she added bitterly.

Barmough frowned. 'Even now you accuse me. Even now you think I was one of his followers, seeking total power over his universe. But I was older than all the other witches. I was old enough and gifted enough to make him see me as a man. I became a spy. Male witches, however powerful, cannot see through the invisible cloak we females can put around ourselves. They never could, despite having other formidable powers. You know that. That's why, when you realized that I could see you, you knew I was not the man called Fingle. You knew I was a female witch.'

'That still doesn't explain why you are here. Why are you helping Hansenger? Don't you know he's destroying our universe?'

'I know that only too well,' the old witch snapped. 'Why do you think I am here?'

'I have no idea. The last time I saw you, you were dabbling with time. It looks just like the good old days!'

'Nonsense! All Hansenger wants, is to replicate The Seal. It was made once. He thinks it can be made again.' She looked at the wall of the ergametron. 'It's too late, though,' she said with a genuine sigh. 'Far too late.'

'You're wrong about that,' Solitan said in his squeaky voice. Henri thought that his eyebrows moved very deliberately as he spoke. 'Hansenger cannot make The Seal again. Nobody can.'

'Oh, and who might you be little creature?' Barmough asked, peering down at the head poking out of Henri's makeshift pouch. 'And what would you know about it anyway?'

'He knows everything about it,' Henri answered for his little friend. 'If he says it is impossible then he is right.'

'Since when have leprechauns been right about anything?' Barmough snapped. 'And why on earth are you carrying the little freak around on your belt?' She gave out a raucous chuckle. 'Oh you humans are so naive! You'll believe anything, anyone…' She paused and looked at Solitan again. 'You'll believe anything anyone or anything tells you. You are so superstitious!'

'I am not a leprechaun,' Solitan argued disdainfully. 'Leprechauns are many and they travel in their own world just as humans do in theirs. It just happens that, like yourself, some of them came upon and stumbled through a doorway to the world of humans on an island you call Ireland. Since then they have been made and born in the world of humans, just as all the other species of man. They just keep out of other men's way because they are likely to get killed!'

'And you'd know all that, would you?' Barmough retorted.

'Yes I would,' Solitan snapped. 'I happen to know all about witches as well. They came into and live in the world of humans the same way.'

'Well, little creature, I am five hundred and twelve years old and I don't recall any such thing.'

'You wouldn't,' Solitan replied. 'In every world the inhabitants either forget their past or destroy their history because they choose not to believe it. Or should I say they don't want anybody else to know or believe it.'

'And you know all this forgotten history do you?' Barmough said contemptuously. 'By some miracle you have been given the histories by *your* predecessors!'

'Not quite,' Solitan said, pausing to see if Barmough was

going to cut in.

She remained belligerent. 'Whatever you are, you have proved your own fallibility. Your history will have been altered or forgotten like all our own.'

'You may think you are old,' Solitan remarked. 'But let me tell you, I was around before this earth in your universe had anything but a few trilobites scrambling about in the murky, muddy seas.'

'Trilobites?'

'Forget it,' Solitan answered derisively. 'You obviously don't know as much as you think.'

'And are you going to enlighten me little one?'

'You tried to explain to Hansenger that we… everything is made up of particles so small that they are as wide apart as the stars are in a galaxy.'

'How interesting!' Barmough was still scornful. 'Quite a good analogy for a little… what are you by the way?'

Solitan ignored the question. 'So it shouldn't surprise you then if I can change size simply by increasing or decreasing the distance between those particles?'

'We witches can do all that sort of thing. We can change our appearance. Didn't you see my impression of Doctor Fingle?' she asked proudly. She had a look of complete satisfaction on her face.

Solitan climbed out of the pouch and balanced on the edge of it, holding onto Henri's sleeve to keep his balance. Suddenly he disappeared. A tiny voice called out. 'Can you see me? I'm a speck of dust on his sleeve?'

Henri lifted his arm to see for himself. Win just watched in silence. It was impressive magic.

Barmough moved quickly. She grabbed the speck between her finger and thumb. 'You are stupid. I could crush you in a second if I wished,' she sniped jovially. 'You put yourself in great danger doing that.'

Henri was about to grab her wrist when, suddenly, her hand was thrown back against her body. In the blink of an eye Solitan had grown bigger again, but not to the size he had been. He was now resting on Henri's arm with one hand, and his feet had reached the floor. Barmough's body was squashed up against the console.

'Finding it hard to breath?' asked Solitan, his voice now much deeper. 'Ribs being squeezed a little heh?'

Barmough gasped a faint breath and then grinned. She wasn't beaten yet. Her whole body flattened out as thin as a sword blade and then she slipped to one side before re-forming as herself. 'As I said, I can do all that.' She regarded Solitan for a few seconds and then said, 'I'm impressed though, I have to admit.'

'And I respect your magic, too,' said Solitan, also returning to his former size. 'But don't attack me again. Do you understand?'

Barmough's eyes narrowed. 'Just testing!' she muttered, and then, 'So what are you trying to prove?'

'You've just proved it yourself,' Solitan chuckled. 'Size has nothing to do with anything. I am what I want to be. I am not like you. I don't eat and I don't sleep. I will live forever and I have lived from the time I was made.'

'And just when was that?'

'As I said, before real life developed on the planet you know as Earth. I was brought here from another universe. One more advanced than yours by many hundreds of millions of years.

The one that first brought all but rudimentary life to your past.'

'You've been reading that new book by what's his name, I bet,' said Barmough scathingly.

'You mean Darwin? No, he's got some of it right,' Solitan responded, taking up the challenge once again, 'but his idea that everything developed from a common ancestor on one earth in one time is flawed. Hundreds of different species came to your earth in your universe from other universes. Through doors if you like. Just as you and the Leprechauns entered that world. What happened after that, Darwin may have got near right. They changed and developed. But then new species were introduced again and again at later periods, like after the giant reptiles were wiped out.'

'Giant reptiles?' asked Henri, fascinated. 'Wiped out?'

'I'll tell you later,' Solitan said reassuringly as if talking to an inquisitive child. 'In the meantime, just take it from me that I have been around for a very long time.'

'I will,' said Henri with a nod, quite impressed.

'I know *you* will. It's *her* I'm trying to convince,' said Solitan, nodding towards Barmough.

'So why try to convince me, little one?' Barmough asked, now a little more agreeable.

'Because you hit on the answer when you were talking to Hansenger.' He paused for thought and then continued. 'And because you must know that The Seal cannot be replicated. It is so far advanced beyond the technology with which Hansenger is dabbling now.' He paused and then added, 'Like this ergametron.'

Barmough looked a little dejected. 'What you say about an advanced civilization is probably true,' she said nodding slowly towards the blue, liquid-filled wall. 'All this is impossible to work out because it isn't mechanical. It is some sort of fluid with the ability to produce energy perpetually. It can send that energy to any place that requires it. It is sent through the air. Unseen. Unstoppable. It powers everything, from the lights to the train-like machines on which Hansenger's men and the Graftians travel inside the city. But it doesn't power the particle transporters. Not directly, at least. Those things are powered by their own energy force, I believe; blue tank like things, which Hansenger is trying to replicate with wires!'

'They are called mag-plas drives,' Solitan put in. 'And you are right, they are independent of the ergametron. You are also right in thinking that the Vasitterites inherited them from another civilization. But not so the ergametron.' He looked at Barmough and studied her reaction. She looked interested to hear more, as her eyes studied him and the way his eyebrows moved as he spoke. 'They made the ergametron. They were trying to copy or convert one of the mag-plas drives in order to create a bigger machine that would supply their huge city with energy. They didn't realize, however, that in the case of mag-plas drives size did actually matter. In their present form, they are perfectly safe.'

'Glad to hear it,' Henri put in.

Solitan ignored him and carried on. 'But once mag-plas drives reach a particular and crucial size, or critical mass, then they become unstable. It's like stacking a pile of bricks,' he explained. 'A stack of five or six stand firm; a dozen or so can still stand upright. But the higher the stack, then the nearer you get to the point where they all eventually topple over.'

Barmough scowled at the little Marox. The creature could

well be right, but she couldn't imagine how he could know all this. 'Anyway,' she forged on, 'it is a particle transporter that, as you know, Hansenger uses to travel back to his own time. He discovered them here when he broke through to this world using his own crude apparatus, and he's used them ever since. But it is the power to travel freely between parallel universes without returning back to this dying world that Hansenger wants to develop and to copy. He has read what The Seal can do and he wants to do the same.

'But only The Seal makes that kind of travel possible. The particle transporters can only travel from this universe and back, wherever they are going. They cannot go somewhere and then travel onwards from there, because their source of power does not seem to travel with them. Once the transporter is out of this world and moves away from the gateway it has created, then the gap closes and it is shut off from its power source for ever.'

'So why are you telling us all this?' Win said, still reluctant to accept any offering from the older witch. 'Solitan, here, could have told you all that.'

'I'm trying to explain why I'm here and how I am trying to put things right.'

Win just shook her head. 'You went over to Drach's side,' she said bitterly.

'Drach never suspected me until the day I left,' Barmough said, totally unfazed.

'You discovered the existence of The Seal and you went to research it for Drach.'

'No, you are wrong. I heard that he had discovered the existence of The Seal,' Barmough corrected, 'and so, naturally,

I wanted it. I followed him when he stole it from Hansenger and I learned that he had left The Golden Book at the university to be translated. I knew they were connected, and yet even then, I didn't know how; but once I'd seen the transcript - that wasn't difficult since I just made myself invisible and read it over his shoulder - I wanted to use The Seal myself to go back in our own time to change what happened. As the powers of the witches stood, we could only travel laterally. That is, from one existing time to another; but not backwards and forwards in time. It is very dangerous for us to even try to do that. It takes so much energy that we are unlikely to be able to return. That's if we can make it to where we are going in the first place.'

'You should have been able to do it. You are old enough,' Win argued.

'And if I didn't make it there, wherever I was going, then that would be the end of it. I couldn't take the risk of failing. I had to get back to a time when it was possible to destroy the ergametron, before it got out of control; and I was never completely sure just when that was. You, Winifred, could do it with the power of the coven behind you. I had no such help. I was on my own and I reckon I would only get one shot at it; and, because the ergametron would be draining my strength, I would probably be killed before I succeeded in my mission. That's where The Seal came in.'

'So you came to Hansenger instead?' asked Henri.

'Not exactly. I was *following* The Seal. I intended to steal it. It was the only way I could securely travel back in time and change what Drach had done. But when Hansenger stole it, I didn't realize he had given it away! I followed him back here but The Seal was with you.'

'I don't think he thought he was giving it away,' Henri stated. 'He was using me to get it back to London. His gateway to The City must be somewhere there.'

'That's how he brought you here, Henri,' Win stated.

'Hmm, so he knew he could not outrun Drach, not while he had The Seal and the transcript of The Golden Book,' Barmough went on as she pieced everything together in her own mind. 'From what you say, Hansenger was very clever at diverting Drach's search when he fled from Yemara empty handed. The search was on for another fugitive.'

Henri shook his head. How could he have been so gullible? 'I had The Seal, but, didn't you say you had The Golden Book?' he asked Win.

'One of The Seven liberated it from its vault in the university.' Win answered.

'If you are telling the truth,' Solitan asked, gripping Barmough with his gaze, 'then how come you were so hostile to us?'

'You have all come here looking for a solution. Well you won't find one. I've been here for weeks now and I know. The ergametron is growing in power. It is creating currents in the fabric of this universe that are transcending the boundaries between different worlds and different times and by doing so, it is, in turn, somehow giving more power to the ergametron. It is an ever increasing chain reaction. I do regret what I did, but it all would have happened anyway, whatever I had done a hundred years ago. Since then, Hansenger found The Seal. Since then, he found an opening into this dying world where he discovered the particle transporters, but he found the ergametron as well; and since then he has begun his experiments to discover the power source of the transporters, which has speeded up the rate at which the ergametron is growing. It would have all happened, anyway!

'But you still blame me!' Barmough growled. 'And because of that I resent your coming here and interfering. I have one chance of stopping all this and one chance only. If you mess it up for me then all will be lost. Get out while you still can. That is my one and only warning to you.'

'We're here to stop it as well,' Henri stated.

'You can't. You'll die and your lives will be wasted.'

'So you reckon that you are capable of stopping the ergametron, but no one else is?' Win asked, obviously a little irritated.

'When the ergametron is stopped, then all power to escape this city will be lost. It is likely that the drives for the particle transporters, whether they are independent of the ergametron or not, will be destroyed as well. They will cease to operate because everything in this world will simply cease to exist. Your friends here,' Barmough said, waving a hand at Henri and his small companion, 'must have entered by the door used by the particle transporter. Once the power ceases then the door will be closed for ever. You will be trapped and die a horrible death. This world will be destroyed.'

'And you?' Henri asked.

'I shall not survive. And I don't want to either. There's nothing for me if I succeed and there's nothing for me if I fail. You see? I have nothing to lose either way.'

'You can travel out with me,' Win said. 'I came in through our witches' door.' She turned to Henri. 'The same way as I took you to see the other surviving witches, Henri. So I can return the same way.'

'I did not come in that way,' Barmough corrected. 'I came in on a particle transporter. I stowed away. They couldn't see me. I wasn't to know that I would discover what I have, and, I'm afraid it is far too late to travel out by that transporter and come back another way. The ergametron must be stopped now. Every day, every hour, every minute, it continues to exist, the stronger it gets and the more difficult it will be to destroy it.'

'You are wrong,' Solitan suddenly broke in. All eyes turned to him.

'Wrong?' Barmough said angrily.

'You are wrong if you think you can destroy the ergametron,' Solitan stated. 'You can't destroy it for the same reason the Vasitterites could not destroy it once it got out of control; so they have been doing everything they can to contain it.

'You were right about the ergametron though' Solitan continued. 'It has become a different universe in its own right. It just exists *inside* this universe, *inside* this City of Darkness, instead of beside it. That is why it has sucked the life out of this place. It has become a living organism like any universe. We are all part of one large living being. Call it a planet, call it a galaxy, call it a universe of galaxies. This ergametron was created here to produce energy, and although it looks like it is providing this place with power, it is really just consuming the energy that existed here in this world in the first place. And by doing so it has become bigger itself. When it has finished eating up this world, it won't take it long to devour this universe. And then it will start on another.

'Hansenger has already given it doorways into other parallel universes. His failed experiments with electro magnetism are opening up more and more holes, and where those holes have been, then the fabric of the universe is exceptionally weak. Every failed experiment sends electrical storms and huge energy shifts not just through to our time but to many others. It will have no trouble travelling to each and every one that has been breeched. And you are absolutely right; time is of the utmost importance here. If we don't act now, all will be lost; your time, the Graftians' time, and many, many others.'

'Quite a little scientist, aren't you?' Barmough said, reasonably impressed.

'You wouldn't believe me if I told you,' said Solitan, now fully in control. 'But you must know that I am right.'

❖

Chapter Thirty

THE TRIP INTO THE ERGAMETRON

With time running out, Henri had to make a decision. Was he going to try and save himself or was he going to try and stop the ergametron from sucking the life out of, not just this world but the world he had left behind? Logically he worked out that there was little chance of making a run for it and surviving anyway. And if he left any of the rest of them behind and they failed to stop the ergametron, then his life would cease to exist.

'I'm going to stay and see this through,' he stated emphatically before anyone could make the decision for him. 'You say you can stop it,' he said to Barmough, 'so you might as well start explaining how you reckon this thing can be stopped.'

'She has no idea,' said Solitan.

Barmough spun towards him. 'And I suppose you have?' she said bitterly.

'I suppose I have,' Solitan said meekly. 'But it means you taking me back to the rest of the Marox,' he said turning his face up to Henri and winking with his right eye. He quite clearly did not want to mention The Seal.

'The Marox?' asked Barmough.

'There are more of us,' Solitan declared. 'We work as a team.'

'Intriguing!' Barmough jibed.

'But how are we going to get back out of here and return unseen?' asked Henri sceptically. 'It could take hours.'

'Not more than five minutes,' Solitan said in reply. 'If we use the particle transporter then we'll be there and back in the blink of an eye.'

'And you know how to use it?'

'You just think of the place to which you wish to travel, and it will take us there.'

'Huh,' said Henri, not quite sure what to believe. But up to now, Solitan had not let him down.

'Okay. Let's get on with it,' he stated, now nervous at going anywhere near the particle transporter. 'But what happens if the power fails?'

'Well for one thing, it won't,' replied his little companion. 'And secondly, if it did then you would end up like some of Hansenger's men after his experiments; all mixed up with the paintwork!'

'Very reassuring,' Henri mumbled.

'Hold onto each other tightly,' Solitan instructed, and then, 'If we leave you here,' he said turning to Barmough, 'will you resist doing anything until we return?'

'Just time to have my sandwich,' she said with a smirk, on hearing Ruskin's footsteps on the hard corridor floor. Instantly she turned back to being Fingle. 'See you in a bit then,' she said without any attempt to prevent Ruskin hearing her or seeing her lips moving. 'Or should I say see you in a bite?'

'Who are you talking to?' he asked as he placed the tray on the cold surface of the console.

'Why, you my dear man,' she said, now in the deeper voice

of a man. 'Call of nature.'

Invisible once more, Henri, Solitan and Win walked past Ruskin and made their way back around the curve of the room, to the door through which they had entered. As they approached, the door opened silently and they passed through unseen and unheard. They walked across the wide corridor and waited for the door opposite to open. When it did they were shocked to see that Hansenger was returning with an armed escort of four men. They had just come out of the particle transporter and each guard carried one of their deadly stick weapons. Their expressions were not reassuring. Hansenger's jaw was set, his eyes glared angrily straight ahead. The guards had obviously been briefed about something. The look on their faces was no less severe; it was one of force and hostility. He had obviously seen the mayhem Henri and Win had caused at the gates.

Henri gripped Win's hand hard and they stood and waited until Hansenger and his men had gone across the corridor and entered the door to the ergametron generator.

'Should we follow them?' asked Henri, very concerned for the safety of the old witch, despite his dislike of her.

Solitan thought for a moment and then shook his head. 'No,' he said emphatically. 'We must get to the other Marox and complete The Seal if we are to stop anything.'

'You seemed careful not to mention that inside there,' Henri said, curiously. 'Why mention it now?'

'Win knows about us,' he responded, turning quickly towards the particle transporter. 'She sent us here to find you.'

'She sent you…' Henri didn't want to say any more. Suddenly he felt deserted. The Marox had seemed to indicate that he was to be their new master. Clearly, Win had prior call on that arrangement.

'Yes,' Solitan said, glancing into Henri's eyes momentarily. 'You are both… well let's say that your destinies are linked for the time being.'

Henri looked at Win. She just shrugged and continued to walk towards the particle transporter without glancing back at him. She stepped inside it. It was like stepping into a vision that had been conjured up by his mind. The whole machine was just an optical illusion, flickering in and out of existence in front of his eyes. He didn't know how Win could be so confident, stepping into something that hardly seemed to be there. He fully expected her to miss her step and just fall clumsily forward, but instead, she stepped up into it, and sat on the flickering seat. Nervously, he followed her inside. The thing was surprisingly solid under his feet, but he was careful settling onto his seat, when he realized that there were no solid walls to the contraption.

'Think where you are going,' Solitan instructed Henri. As soon as he did, everything around them shimmered and changed. He had no chance to come to any conclusion about the thing. When he looked around, he noticed that they had already arrived in the huge bedroom where he had spent the last couple of nights. But the element of total bewilderment was quickly overcome. The whole room, despite its sparse furnishing, had been ransacked. Henri felt the heavy weight of despair drag on his insides.

Obviously, as well as knowing about the insurgency by the Graftians at the gate of the Ergametron generator dome, Hansenger had found out that Henri was missing. But it worried Henri little that Hansenger was looking for him. He knew Hansenger would have linked Henri's disappearance to the insurgents that had caused havoc outside the power plant, but what really concerned him was that the other four Marox were nowhere to be seen. He stepped away from the transporter and walked over to the bed. The sheets and pillows were strewn on the floor and the heavy mattress had been cast over the other side of the bed and slashed to pieces. He bent down and ruffled the torn pillow where the Marox had hidden before but there was nothing nor anyone there. He looked under the bed. Again, there was no sign of the other Marox. Henri began to panic but then, suddenly, Solitan squeaked. 'Ha-ha!' and looking towards the farthest corner of the room, he said, 'There they are.' He shouted it out again in a shrill voice as he danced across the floor.

In the very farthest corner was a small object which, as Henri followed Solitan closer, he could make it out to be The Seal, in full splendour, in its original pocket size.

'How did they miss that?' Henri asked, curiosity now overtaking his despair.

'The Seal has its own safety device,' Solitan answered. 'It blends into the surrounding area like a moth on a tree. It has a cryptic camouflage that can deceive even the cleverest of investigators. And failing that,' he added, 'it can reduce its size. As I explained to Barmough, The Seal, like everything else in this universe is made of particles so far apart that if we just lessen those distances by a half, the thing, be it The Seal or a massive sailing ship, will become so small, the human eye cannot perceive it.' He ran over to it, touched it, and instantly the sectors fell away from each other revealing his four little companions. As they stepped onto the floor, they immediately gained in size until they were the same height as Solitan. They danced a little jig together and then waited for Solitan to speak.

'Quickly,' he instructed. 'We must go immediately.' He ran ahead of them and jumped inside the transporter. Win and Henri lost no time. He picked up the empty sectors of The Seal that lay on the ground and ran behind them. Within seconds he had caught them up.'

'Here,' he said to Win. 'You hold these. You don't need them to make yourself invisible and I can't hold them all together if I want to disappear.'

Win nodded and put them in one of her pockets.

A moment later they were back at the same room in which they had first embarked on the illusionary particle transporter. There was nobody there waiting to greet them as Henri had feared. From looking at the strange clock, it seemed that they had arrived almost immediately after they had left.

Win ran to the door. It opened as she approached it and as it did, she realized that she had made a mistake. She had not made herself invisible nor had she invoked Henri's power to do so. In fact, because all the five Marox, were close together nobody was invisible. In the corridor, two guards stood with their weapons pointing towards her.

'You must come with us,' the guard nearest the door growled. He held out an arm to indicate that Henri and Win should follow him. Then he spotted the five small creatures that had, until now, been out of sight behind Henri. Suddenly they all disappeared. They had made themselves so small that neither the guards nor Henri or Win could see them. But to all appearances they had simply vanished.

As small as fleas and just as agile, the Marox split up, leaving Solitan to throw himself forward onto Henri's leg. Instantly Henri disappeared. The guard's reaction was one of sheer disbelief. As Solitan resumed his size and climbed back into the pouch on Henri's belt, the guard waved his stick around in an arc, trying to locate the young man who had just stood before him. But Henri had anticipated some reaction and stepped in front of Win.

Henri reached for the weapon that he had recovered from the guard by the gate but it wasn't in his belt. He must have dropped it when he was searching the bedroom for the Marox.

The second guard was going to take no chances on Win disappearing the same way. He raised his stick to fire at her. If she was going to vanish, it was going to be because he had sent every particle of her body into another dimension. He squeezed the button trigger. His shot was directed straight at Win's chest, but instead of vaporising her, she disappeared as Henri yanked her to one side. But the light ray touched the invisible shield, and Win and Henri had momentarily become visible again as the shield weakened.

Before the guard could recover from the shock of seeing Henri and the woman appear again in front of him, and then seeing part of the building evaporate with an almighty crack, as the light beam refracted off the shield, Henri kicked him hard in the stomach and once again in the head. As he faded back to invisibility, Henri grabbed the stick weapon and pushed it down his belt behind his back. The guard fell semi-conscious to the floor, but his comrade, thinking quickly, stepped to where he had seen Henri. He swung his weapon upwards, but, swerving to the side, Henri swung his fist at the man's arm and drove it downwards. Once again, the light ray passed through the edge of the invisible shield, making Henri and Win visible again as it weakened. But, the shot was deflected, this time, to the floor which was instantly parted at their feet by an almighty crack like thunder. A hole appeared that looked bottomless. It would seem that there were more floors even below the one to which they had travelled deep inside the earth.

The guard was still moving forward and, as the hole appeared, he tried to stop. Henri tried to catch him by his coat, but it was too late. The momentum of the guard's arm being forced down made him lose his balance and, still stumbling forward, and turning his head towards his attackers with a look of sheer bewilderment, he gave out an awkward scream and disappeared into the chasm.

The shield was definitely weakening. Henri looked down at Solitan. The little Marox didn't look well. The weapons were trying his strength to the limit. Goodness knows what a direct hit would have done.

'You Okay?' Henri asked, placing his hand on Solitan's tiny shoulder.

'Okay master,' came back the reply. 'Just keep going. We must get back to the ergametron.'

Henri cast his eyes around behind them. 'Where are the other Marox?' he said, fearing some of them had been hit by the force of the weapon.

'Here master,' one of them said as she appeared back to normal size and bounded towards Henri. The others followed, leaping towards him and clambering up his body with their tiny, claw-like hands until all were slung from his waist like pelts on a trapper's belt.

Now they headed through the opposite door, bolted along the corridor and through the last door into the vast generator room. Quickly they headed alongside the curved blue liquid filled wall towards Barmough and the console.

Hansenger was nowhere to be seen. Neither were his guards, nor Ruskin nor the old witch. The scaffolding next to the console was completely empty. They ran up onto the gantry and looked at the coloured glass squares which seemed to be some form of dials. There was blood on the console; fresh blood.

'They've taken your friend,' Henri said matter of factly.

'No friend of mine,' Win retorted, though she stood and stared at the blood for a long while. 'So what do we do now? she asked eventually. 'Hansenger must know we are here and why we have come.'

'That hardly matters now,' Henri said. 'We need to reassemble The Seal.' He held out his hand and Win took the sectors from her pocket and dropped them in the palm of his hand.

'That won't help,' Solitan stated. 'Remember, *we* are The Seal,' he said, waving his hand at his fellow Marox. 'The Seal is just our method of transportation. It is empty now so its powers are with us not the sectors.

'Right,' Henri said, still listening.

'But when it is assembled, with us incorporated into it, then it does give our master our powers, especially the power to transport himself between universes.'

'I wish I'd known that when I was on that stinking ship,' Henri protested.

Solitan looked up at him and shook his head. 'When will

you realize that everything happens for a purpose.'

'So what is my…?'

But Solitan cut in. 'We haven't time to discuss any of that now. What the Marox must do is return to The Seal. Then you can go inside the ergametron.'

'If I travel there, then maybe I'll be able to stop it?'

'When I give the command, you *must* stop it,' Solitan retorted. 'And I mean, make it cease to exist.'

Win's face paled but she stopped herself from speaking.

'And how do I do that?' Henri asked.

'That is up to you. If you succeed then this world will cease to exist as it is now, since it will return to a time before the ergametron was let into it. If you fail then you and the world you left behind will cease to exist along with many others.'

'No pressure there then,' Henri croaked. His mouth and throat were drier than an empty cooking pot on a hot griddle.

'None at all,' Solitan said wryly. 'You have no choice. If you don't go then the result will be the same as failing when you get there. So just be prepared to do your best.'

'But why me?'

'It had to be somebody. Why not you?'

Henri had no answer. As Solitan had said, *everything happens for a purpose*. Skipping something leads to an entirely different chain of consequences. Up to now the chain had led him here. If he were to fail then that's what he was meant to do. But he thought positively. If he were going to fail then why had he got this far? No, he was going to succeed.

Bolstered by that single thought, he held out the sectors of The Seal. Each of the Marox returned to their original size and to their respective segment, fitting snugly inside each. Then they waited patiently for Henri to turn each section of the golden cube back into place. As he did so, he wondered how come nobody else seemed to be able to dismantle the object. No doubt the Marox would explain.

If he lived long enough to find out.

Once The Seal was complete, Henri held it up in the palm of his hand. 'Now what?' he asked, looking at Win, who was watching him with wide eyes. 'Perhaps Solitan should have explained how this thing works!'

But Win didn't respond. It was as if she were frozen. Like a manikin in a shop window, she stood there in front of him, a picture caught in the blink of an eye.

'Don't worry,' he said, placing his hand on her arm. But his hand just passed through her. He took a sharp breath. Looking around, everything had stopped, the flashing lights on the console were now an array of brilliant coloured circles and squares. He remembered the time when Win had taken him out of the present world on board *The Arinosta*. Then, everything, everybody around them had done the same thing, frozen at a moment of their time. He hadn't realized that they were not solid. But why should they be? He wasn't in their time any more. It was just a picture, a vision.

Now he began to worry. The Seal had already begun to carry him into the ergametron and he was leaving Win behind. If he succeeded then he might save his own life, but Win might be trapped in that other place; the one Henri hated as much as being on a seaborne vessel: The City of Darkness. He sincerely hoped that she would leave now.

'Why can't life be normal?' he asked himself aloud as his eyes turned to scan the ergametron. But he had no time to contemplate further. He had been wondering how to get inside this thing; this other universe within a universe. How could he travel through this solid, see-through wall? But already, things were happening. He shook his head, thinking that he was hallucinating. 'Phew, for a moment I thought I was fading into the console!' he said to the figure that was still motionless beside him. He could see his own body fading in and out of the solid wall, one minute part of it, another moment, a separate and completely different object. As he turned his head, the consol seemed to turn. Now he could see the back of it. The wall was still see-through but the other side of it, where Win remained motionless, seemed to be getting further and further away.

Then, he caught a glimpse of Hansenger and three guards, in the distance, walking along the curved glass wall at the other side of the barrier, heading towards Win. Why were they moving and nobody else? The whole experience seemed like a silent dream. Win was still a statue but Hansenger and his men were moving. And then, as suddenly as they had appeared, they vanished, leaving Win, a tiny figure, alone as before. He had absolutely no idea what it could mean?

And then, as Win disappeared, shrinking to a mere speck in the far, far distance, he suddenly realized that he was at the other side of the immensely thick wall. Now all he could see through the thick glass-like barrier was a dark green-grey colour that had been the colour of the sky in The City of Darkness. He resisted the temptation to try and work out why he could now see the sky of a place that he had left buried miles below the surface of the ground. Instead, he turned and looked away from what was now definitely a point in his past.

He was in a place so unlike any he had seen before that it

took him some time to even take another breath.

The air seemed clear, but it seemed thicker somehow. There was no breeze. There were no clouds in the dense blue sky. As Henri breathed in, he felt like his lungs were full to bursting and his head began to spin. After steadying himself against something that resembled a cylindrical rock obelisk, he realized he didn't need to take another breath for a long time and when he did, he took in the air with slow short breaths.

He was standing on a blue-green mossy surface from which protruded a mat of strange, squat, spiky, green flowers. It all felt spongy under his feet, and strange disc-shaped creatures about the size of his hand wafted through the thick air from one bloom to another like butterflies in a cornfield. As far as the eye could see there were thousands, uncountable numbers, of cylindrical rock pillars about twice the girth of a good sized oak tree and about twice the height, poking up out of this flat, windless landscape. He rubbed the rock against which he was leaning with the tips of his fingers. It was perfectly smooth like polished granite, only it didn't look like it had been polished and it didn't look like any rock he had ever seen. It was dark blue, much darker than the still sky above. The rock reminded him of the strange non-mechanical magnets that were used to drive the particle transporters. He recalled Barmough explaining to Hansenger that although they looked like liquid filled tanks from a distance, the devices were in fact solid. Now, looking at the pillars he could well imagine the devices were made of this incredibly vivid blue substance. The pillars looked hard and unyielding, but there was something about them that defied solidness. They looked like you could push a stick or even your arm into them for no other purpose but to try and reach the other side. But when he pressed his fist against one, it resisted as would any normal rock.

He began to walk forward. As he took a step he felt buoyant like walking in the sea. How far, he walked, he wouldn't recall, because a moment later, he was struck from behind and, as everything began to fade to blackness, he felt a vice like grip around his torso and he was snatched up and carried above the spongy ground at an incredible speed.

❖

Chapter Thirty One

THE VASITTERITES

When he awoke, he was lying on a hard, bare floor. But this was not the same place where he had seen the dark blue of the pillars; it was almost black; nor was there a blue sky. There were no walls that he could make out. As far as he could tell, he was inside a huge silver dome. Everything seemed rounded like the inside of a huge but evenly shaped cave with a curved ceiling that glowed and gave off light enough to see that he was not alone. As in The City of Darkness, he looked up at the dome and, instantly, the light from it increased.

Henri had seen many creatures but none like the one that stood before him. From a distance he might have mistaken the being as man. Whatever it was had arms and legs like he had, but the head was enormous, spanning broad shoulders and on a thick wrinkled neck. It wore clothes, a one piece affair that was almost as metallic as the dome around him and on top of that the creature wore a similarly metallic looking cloak that was slung behind and wasn't noticeable until it turned slightly sideways. The face was light grey with eyes twice as big as they might have been in a human head, and the head itself was totally smooth and, apart from being slightly elliptical, was evenly rounded with no protruding ears or even a nose. Big eyelids dropped down occasionally in front of the black eyes in such a way that, when closed, the whole head could have been mistaken for a large smooth ostrich egg.

A gap opened, breaking the smooth exterior near the bottom of the head, like a long red and sore-looking knife wound.

'Explain yourself,' a surprisingly soft but firm voice said before the slit closed and became unnoticeable once again.

For a long moment Henri leaned back on his hands and just stared at the creature. As he pushed himself into a proper sitting position, he felt for the stick weapon that he had pushed down his belt when he had confronted Hansenger's guards. It had definitely gone. 'You speak my language!' he exclaimed. And then, 'I hadn't expected anything like that.'

The slit appeared again and the head leaned forward. He noticed tiny holes near the top of the head. They suddenly closed, once again leaving a smooth egg-like surface.

'Why are you here?' The holes opened again. It seemed that they remained open only when the creature awaited a response.

Henri didn't know exactly what to say. He was sure his mission was to stop this world from sucking the life out of so many others, but he wasn't so sure he should share that information with this being. 'I'm an explorer,' he replied meekly.

The listening devices closed again. 'How did you get here?'

Now that was an easier question.

'I thought about coming here, and somehow I just appeared in a place full of green ground and blue pillars.'

The big head nodded. Henri reckoned that the creature was no more than seven feet tall including the huge head. 'Now you are telling the truth,' the voice said, now a little more relaxed. 'But you might as well know that I can tell what you are thinking.'

Well then, you won't mind if I leave now, Henri thought as he struggled to stand up. He looked around for an exit. There wasn't one.

'You are looking for something?'

So much for telepathy, thought Henri. 'I was looking to see where I was,' he said while all the time thinking that he should perhaps use The Seal to think himself elsewhere.

'There is no way out of here,' the creature stated gruffly. It turned and lifted a large hand which had long webbed fingers. It waved to the blank wall and, bizarre as it seemed, an opening appeared in the side of the dome and a dozen or so similar creatures entered, before waving and closing the door behind them. Henri noticed that the back of the first creature's head had two more small holes, apertures which opened and closed slowly but constantly. It was possible that these were some kind of nostrils. He wasn't sure. Now that the creature had turned, what he had originally thought to be a cloak was, in fact, something more like a fish's dorsal fin, neatly folded against its back.

As the face turned back towards him, the other creatures arrived by its side. There were several clicking and whistling noises and then one of them said, 'You must tell us everything we need to know.'

'Who or what are you?' asked Henri.

'We are the Vasitterites,' the first one replied.

'They are much bigger than you are,' Henri replied a little too quickly.

The heads of the creatures turned to each other. More

clicking and whistling. 'What would you know about that?' the second creature demanded in a very different voice, a voice that if it were not designed to instil fear, certainly began to work that way on Henri.

'I have just explored their world,' Henri decided to answer truthfully. 'They must be at least twice as big as you are.'

'You met them then?' The second creature's big eyes suddenly glared at Henri.

'No, I didn't say that.'

'You travel between worlds?' the first one asked.

'I'm not exactly sure. I think I have done.'

'And you know how you did that?

Now Henri was going to test if they could really read his mind. 'There's some kind of contraption that transports people, that is, creatures like me, to what seem to be different worlds. It's called a particle transporter.'

'And you arrived in that?'

Henri nodded. 'Yes.'

'And where is it?'

'It stays where you arrive.'

The creature turned to the others, clicked a few times and three of them departed the way they had come. No doubt they were going to look for it.

Henri wondered how much time that would give him. He didn't know how long it had taken for them to bring him to this place. 'I need to know how you create your power. How do you light up this room? What drives the door mechanisms?'

'You are asking us? What gives you the right to ask questions?'

Henri decided he had nothing to lose. Either The Seal would work or it wouldn't when he needed it. 'I am trying to find out how your world takes energy from other worlds. It is destroying them.' He waited for their reply.

The creatures looked at each other and then all eyes turned back to Henri.

'We really are the Vasitterites,' the first one said. 'We understand what you are saying. Regarding our size, it is the atmosphere here that has made us smaller. The pressure is such that eventually you will become a third of your size. It takes years though. And if you came in a particle transporter then the bad news is that you will never be able to return to the place from whence you came.'

Henri tried to look suitably shocked. 'But I must return,' he said feebly. 'I…'

'You will remain here, like it or not.' The voice was harsh now. 'You have entered a world that has an atmospheric pressure many hundreds of times greater than it is in the place you left. If you ever try to leave, your blood will simply boil.'

'Oh that's great,' Henry said. He didn't have to pretend any more. Now he was seriously worried.

'But we have discussed you and you seem to be of little risk to us. We will of course interrogate you further.' The creature turned to go but then turned back to face him. 'What do you call yourself?'

'Henri. Henri Dubois.'

'Hmm.' The creature looked unimpressed.

'What do I call you?' Henri asked in as friendly a tone as he could.

'You would not understand our names,' the first creature responded. 'You can call me God!'

All the other creatures burst into a fit of clicking and wheezy whistles. The first creature waved his webby fingers and instantly they all fell silent.

'I am… we are masters of all the stars and galaxies in all the universes. We are taking the matter in them and creating perpetual energy.'

'Why?'

'Why!' Because we can, that's why. Because we have found the very source of all creation. And its core is only a few minutes walk from here,' the creature said proudly.

'And by here, you mean inside the ergametron?'

'So you know what it is called. Well, no matter. You say you are an explorer, then let me tell you this, Henry Dubois: your kind look up at their sky and see stars and galaxies. Within that space, there are many places eating up all the energy around them. They are so dense and heavy that you cannot see them. We call them sink holes. Your kind has never discovered them. So congratulations, you are the first. Unfortunately, as I have explained, you will never be able to return to tell the tale.

'However,' the creature went on, 'We have created our own, sink hole, not so dense that it is black, but very dense all the same. We have created it inside our own world so that it draws in energy that we can use perpetually.

'Why don't you just make your own energy,' Henri asked, unsure what he should say.

'Hmm. You are not very bright, are you?' The creature held out its webby hand and took a hold of Henri's shoulder. He began to steer him towards the exit. 'Energy exists,' the creature stated, revelling in his ability to strike awe into some smaller, lesser being. 'You don't make it. You just convert one form of energy into another. Unless you take energy from another source then you are limited to turning it around within your own world. We, on the other hand, are increasing our energy supply in this world, by taking it from elsewhere.'

With that last word, the holes for listening on the creature's egg-head closed for the last time and they marched Henri silently out of the dome and into a small, round, silver coloured room that was quite clearly going to be his cell. He didn't know how long they were going to keep him there. He hadn't eaten for a long time and he wondered if they were likely to consider feeding him. But he sat on the bare floor and waited until the door closed behind them. The door had a glass or at least a see-through panel in it.

After waiting for what he considered was a safe length of time, he stood up. He had to stand on tiptoe to see through the panel but when he did, the creature at the other side was not the same as the egg-heads. It looked like a true predator, a giant wolf like creature, five feet to the shoulder if it was an inch, and with a snout like a crocodile's, at least three feet long. It sat patiently outside the door, not moving much, apart from an occasional shuffle and a lick of its purple-pink lips. Standing on his very tiptoes, Henri could see that it had huge paws, splayed like the feet of a duck, webbed between all its toes. Its claws looked like they could rip a hole in the shiny metal door if it so much as flicked them at it. Henri swallowed and then backed away from the panel.

He couldn't remember what he had done with The Seal. He could remember holding it in his hand as he travelled through the barrier between the worlds, and he'd had it in his fist when whatever it was grabbed him and knocked the wind from his body. Had he dropped it? He felt in all his pockets.

There was no seal.

Feeling totally helpless, dejectedly, he slumped down on the floor. A small tear formed in the corner of his eye. The creature had told him he would never return to his own world and, for a brief moment, the thought was just too much to bear. But then he remembered that Egg-God had said they could read his mind, and he knew that was an outright lie, so they were probably lying about his having to remain there.

If there had been a corner in the cell, he would have curled up in it, but there was no sanctuary in this place. The domed room was austere and unyielding in every way. He had never felt so lonely in all his life. Even the Marox had deserted him.

But no sooner had he thought about his tiny friends than a gold speck on the jet black floor suddenly began to grow in size. It took less than two seconds for him to recognise it. It was his golden seal. He bent forward to pick it up but he hesitated as it kept growing in front of his eyes. A few moments later, when it had reached the dimensions of a good-sized trunk, it stopped growing and just stood there in front of him, as if waiting for him to do something. He jumped to his feet, grabbed a tight hold on the top of The Seal and twisted. Instantly it came away from the rest of the cube, and out dropped Solitan. Without a word, Henri turned the other sectors and, one by one, his small friends appeared before him.

'Aren't you a sight for sore eyes?' he said, grabbing them gently and lifting them up to his chest. 'If ever I thought you had deserted me, it was always going to be in a place worse than the one we just left.'

'It's worse, much worse,' Olmar chirped. 'The City of Darkness has nothing on this *World of Death*.'

Henri shivered. 'It's that bad is it?'

'Worse than you could ever imagine,' Solitan stated. 'Think of the worst thing that could happen and then double it a dozen times. It has drawn the life out of the world around, and including, The City of Darkness, and soon it will become so strong that it will devour the whole of this world. It is an insatiable creature into which people, cities, worlds will be sucked at an ever increasing speed and once they are within its grip, then there is no hope, no chance of stopping it from sucking them in; pulling them in and compressing them to the size of a pin head.'

'It often happens in universes and even within galaxies,' Olmar began to explain.

'Yes, the Vasitterites call them sink holes,' Henri stated.

'But not within another world, not within another place in time and space,' Solitan cut in. 'Yet now, the more matter or energy the ergametron draws in, the denser its core gets, and the heavier the mass becomes, the more gravitational pull it creates.'

'You can call it a world, but it is much more than that,' Olmar explained. 'There are three dimensions in your world, up, down and along. Then there is time which gives everything another dimension. The fifth dimension is the different times and places that exist alongside your own. But this is a sixth dimension; it is another existence, not one running alongside and outside our own. It is an organism, a parasite, *within* our own existence, eating up its host.'

'There is not enough energy to feed this parasitic world,' Solitan continued after pausing for Olmar's input. 'The energy field and its shield were not created and built to withstand the pressure of taking an ever increasing supply of power. Since they cannot stop it now that they have created the ergametron, however strong the shield is built, eventually the forces are going to be too great for it to withstand. When it gives way then the chain reaction will be unstoppable. It will suck in, not only a whole world, the one they left behind, as it feeds on all the energy and matter around it, but it will destroy many hundreds of different parallel existences. Huge blocks of alternative universes will simply disappear.'

'And the beings that live within this world?' Henri asked, thinking about the Eggheads.

'The beings that are here now are a few remnants of the race that brought all this upon themselves. They have worked for so many years trying to control the power they have unleashed, that they have become totally delusional. They think they *are* the power.'

'So who is running the show?'

'What really exists here is total power, unrelenting, undiminishing, intelligent energy. It is feeding on their universe, on our universe and all the others running alongside it. The remaining creatures in this place have very little time left. They have ensconced themselves in this dome-like creation, but it can't withstand the pressure any longer. Its gravitational pull is now doubling every hour. They can't see what they have done and they are carrying on as if it has all happened for their benefit.'

'So what do we do now?'

'We go and find a way to stop them. That's what you were born to do. Your fate, if you like. That's why you are here.'

'My fate?'

The future came first,' Olmar began to explain. 'History is written backwards.'

'What do you mean, history is written backwards? What are you talking about?'

'Have you never heard the saying God had a plan?'

Henri shrugged. He couldn't recall much about any religious education he might have stumbled through as a small child. 'I wouldn't have thought religion would have been one of your specialities,' he said sarcastically.

'It isn't,' replied Olmar. 'But the future, the past and the present co-exist. Time and space are not, as you may think, hands marching relentlessly around a dial. The three, past, present and future are just as individual as separate parallel universes.'

'So what are you saying here?'

'What we are saying is that you have to travel not to a different space or world in the same time, as we have just been doing, but you must travel to a different time in *this* space. You must go *back* in time to when the Vasitterites lost control of their experiments.'

Henri felt a terrible weight on his soul. If anyone was less well equipped to sort something out on so massive a scale, it was Henri Dubois; young, enthusiastic adventurer, explorer and fortune hunter, yes; but world saver? Or was it a time saver? He wasn't too sure. Whatever he was to try and save, it seemed massively out of range of any of his experience or capabilities. He looked at his five companions. They seemed so small and so reliant on him. But they had knowledge that spanned the ages. They travelled by way of their magic golden cube. They had magical powers, or at least one that Henri knew of, anyway. Couldn't they just do something magical and make it all just go away?

'Can't you stop all this from happening?'

'Not without your help.' Solitan assured.

'What can I do?' he asked, dejected by the enormity of the problem.

'You can stop it all happening,' Olmar said, confidently.

'Or die trying,' Solitan added authoritatively. For a moment Henri thought that Solitan was looking a little down at heart, but the tiny Marox rallied. 'We'll all die trying, all seven of us.'

Henri scratched his head. Solitan was losing it. So clever but he couldn't count! 'Six,' he corrected. 'There are six of us, unless there are more of you little fellas that I haven't spotted yet.'

'No, you are right,' Solitan said, his eyebrows knitted into a V.

'So what now?' Henri asked with a shrug. 'Can I wish myself out of this place?'

'You can travel anywhere you like,' Gorang suddenly spoke up. 'That's my function. I am the Marox that transports you between co-existing worlds or universes when we are all within The Seal. It is I who brought you here.'

'And when you are outside it?' Henri asked.

'Then you always have a shoulder to cry on,' she chuckled. 'A bit of a small shoulder, mind.'

Raelmin and Rasa chuckled with her.

'Take no notice of her,' Solitan said crossly. 'Her sense of humour is only an asset *sometimes*.'

'But not at the moment,' Olmar added.

'So to travel we need to keep you all together. You have to

be inside The Seal?' Henri asked.

'Correct,' said Gorang.

'Except for me,' Raelmin suddenly came in. 'I'm the only one that can remain outside The Seal and still travel because...'

'Because she is made to do that,' said Solitan, giving her a stern look. 'She is made to be able to...'

Suddenly there was a noise like a distant roll of thunder from outside the cell. The floor shook. Henri ran to the window in the door. The crocodile-wolf had disappeared.

'Quickly, a voice said from behind him. We haven't much time. An hour at the most.'

Henri spun around. There, with the five Marox stood Win.

'You get about a bit, don't you?' Henri said, trying to be as casual as he could, his heart suddenly lightened for a moment. 'How did you...?'

Win gave him a raised eyebrow look and held her hand down to touch each of the Marox. She looked a little paler than she had been when he had looked upon her wax figure face. 'I'm a witch. Remember?' She was wearing a long black cloak. Henri supposed that she looked more like a witch now than she had ever done, but she still looked young and beautiful. She pulled a sword out from beneath the cloak and handed it to him. 'You might need this,' she said, handing it forward.

Henri took it from her small hand and looked at it. It looked expensive with its golden hilt and a blade that shimmered even in the flat light of the cell. It was almost weightless. 'But you said you couldn't travel between worlds without...'

'Without returning to my own world first. Correct. I've been busy while you have been lazing about here.'

'Lazing!'

'Did you see any pillars on your journey? Thick blue rock-like pillars?'

Henri nodded. 'Yes, they are everywhere.'

'And a deep blue sky?'

He nodded again.

'That blue substance acts like a powerful magnet.

'So, is it those pillars that are drawing the energy out of the other worlds?'

'Not those pillars, no. They are repelling, holding in place a vast artificial sphere made on the inside to look like a natural world. It is all an illusion. You are deep below the ground. The pillars are holding back the crushing, overwhelming gravitational forces inside as the ergametron tries to suck in the world you left behind where Hansenger is doing all his experiments. But the ergametron will ultimately win. When the barrier between this artificial world and the core of the ergametron collapses, we will be crushed as the sphere disappears into a space the size of a cannon ball and it will drag in the other connecting worlds, firstly Hansenger's City of Darkness world and then shortly after that our own. And it is going to happen soon. We have to stop it.'

'Stop it? It's impossible!' Henri exclaimed.

'It might not be,' said Solitan. 'We have one chance.'

Both Win and Henri looked at the little Marox.

'I'm afraid my magic is too weak now to do anything to help,' Win said sadly. 'My strength is slowly ebbing away. I might just be able to help in some way, but I cannot stop it.'

'I wasn't thinking of you,' Solitan said, his voice kind and gentle. He looked at Henri. 'We must travel with you. We must travel inside The Seal. We must go to where the source of this vortex started. The trouble is…'

'And the trouble is, it's going to be guarded,' Henri said with a nod.

'And the trouble is,' Solitan said, knitting his little eyebrows in an impatient manner before letting them move freely again with every word, 'whoever gets there will never survive if they do succeed.'

Henri looked at his little friend. A cold chill went down his back. 'I don't suppose it's worth asking who that will be?' he said with a wry smile.

Win and the Marox all remained silent for a minute while Henri contemplated. Win had gone even paler.

'I don't suppose I could use your sector of The Seal to make myself invisible, could I?' he asked, frowning.

'You'll need all of us if you are going to succeed.'

'So we are all going there?'

Solitan looked at Win and then back at Henri. 'The Marox must be there,' he said eventually. 'And you. But not our kind witch here. She must survive.'

'Fortunately you don't control me,' Win said angrily. 'We are all in this together. You need me. I know the way around the control centre.' She paused before asking, 'Did you hear a loud sound like thunder a short while ago?'

'We did,' Henri replied with a nod.

'That was me. I created a diversion. There are no guards here because they were called to the control centre. I've been there.'

❖

Chapter Thirty Two

RAELMIN

'How long ago are we going back?' asked Henri.

'The Vasitterites only started this experiment a few years ago.' Raelmin was speaking now. 'I am the one who takes The Seal back in time and space as opposed to travelling laterally - in the same time, place to place - as we do when Gorang is in charge. We all have different functions, you see.

'The Vasitterites, with their experiments with the mag-plas drives, actually created what they called a sink hole.'

'Although, your world will call them something else when they discover them,' Solitan added.

'They were trying to use their super-sized mag-plas drive to generate power for their own use,' Raelmin carried on as if Solitan hadn't even spoken. 'And they built something that they thought would contain it. But they have not only dabbled beyond their capabilities and totally underestimated it, they have, in effect, unleashed something on their world that should have remained as they found. Once the mag-plas drive reached critical mass, it became a sink hole. Some sink holes have grown so big over the vast expanse of time, that they are now devouring entire galaxies.'

'So what happened to the Vasitterites?' Henri asked.

'The beings that you saw are the remnants of the Vasitterites,' said Solitan. 'The rest don't exist any more. They were wiped out by something they brought here.'

'By a simple virus,' Raelmin added. 'A disease,' she said to explain what a virus was.

'And because they used particle transporters to get here, they spread the virus back to their own City of Darkness and wiped out the rest of them.

'But the Graftians are still there,' Henri protested. 'How come they weren't eliminated by the disease as well?'

'Who knows for sure,' replied Raelmin. 'They possibly survived, though not in great numbers, because they had places they could hide for long periods of time. A little like they do now with Hansenger. Or possible they had natural immunities that the Vasitterites and their advanced civilization had lost through having things too sterile. If they were too clean then they could have fallen ill because their bodies never got the chance to build up any immunity.'

Henri took it all in, but then changed the subject. 'So we go back what, hundreds of years?'

'I calculate it as only seventeen years, and two hundred and one days, to the point before the Vasitterites began to lose control of their experiment.' Raelmin replied, her eyebrows dancing jerkily as if they were doing some sort of deep thinking calculation. 'That's when we'll be able to get to the core.' She looked at Henri with worried eyes. 'Remember, think time and place when you grip The Seal,' she instructed as she and the other Marox proceeded to go back to the large version of the cube. 'I'll do the same.'

'Quickly, now,' Solitan said as he climbed into his sector.

Put it together and concentrate, think of yourself in the time and the place. We cannot risk any mistakes.'

Henri did as he was told, helped by Win who's face was as white as snow now.

The Seal contracted to its hand held size and Henri picked it up. 'What are you to do?' he asked Win.

'I'll join you,' she said, as she disappeared like a fading cloud of steam dispersing into the air.

Now completely alone but for the golden cube in one hand and the razor sharp sword in the other, Henri thought of a time seventeen years and two hundred and one days ago at a point near the control centre of this ghastly place. He had no idea where it was, nor whether he would arrive at the right time of day or night to meet Win there. He just hoped he was doing it right and that Raelmin had the right time and space co-ordinates to take him where he wanted.

It happened so fast that he wasn't sure anything had happened. He was standing in a domed room, but one that was quite a bit larger than the one he had left. It was, like the cell in which he had been imprisoned, silver inside and the underside of the dome gave out light from no particular point. He looked around. Eggheads were all around, walking to and fro, going about their business. But these Eggheads were at least twenty feet tall. Henri had appeared in their world standing beside a large bank of dials that were on a panel at about his chin height. He knew he had arrived in the right place. The trouble was that at least six of the Vasitterites had seen him suddenly appear from nowhere.

There must have been some kind of alarm system in the dome, as he was suddenly aware that more and more of these giant beings were turning to see what was happening and at the same time they were beginning to head towards him. They weren't moving particularly fast. He reckoned that he had five or six seconds to decide what to do before they reached him. He looked at The Seal in the palm of his hand. He had to get Solitan out and quickly. Twisting the top of The Seal, he pulled it from the rest of the cube and tossed the larger section on the floor. As it rolled away from him he knew he had become invisible.

The Vasitterites cast their eyes about, seeking the illusionary man. But it was in vain. Henri stepped around their huge legs and walked in the direction from which the Vasitterites had approached. He looked back to see what they were doing. A group of them had walked over to the remainder of The Seal and were discussing it as it lay before them.

Henri couldn't go back to retrieve it. He knew that if he picked it up it would blow his cover. He just hoped that the stories he had heard about it were true, that it was indestructible.

'They are Okay,' Solitan's voice suddenly broke into his silence. He had emerged from his sector of The Seal. 'Win is on her way. We don't need a confrontation until we get to the core of the ergametron. Keep going!' he said as he grew to his normal size.

Henri stopped looking back and ran forward as quickly as he could. Suddenly they were going along a high, tubular corridor, as big as a railway tunnel; with no idea where they were except that they were either heading to the centre of the base or totally in the wrong direction. The only clue was that all the Vasitterites had appeared from the entrance to the tunnel system. What was that story about dropping breadcrumbs to find your way back? No chance to think of doing anything like that. No chance to get back anyway, if what Solitan and his fellow Marox had said was right.

Henri just kept running as fast as he could. Until, that is, the tunnel, one of several branches he had come upon and chosen, simply because it was the one that seemed to carry on in a straight line, suddenly came to a blank wall.

'What now?' Henri gasped.

Solitan was unusually silent. His eyes seemed glazed. But just as Henri was slowing to a stop he spoke. 'I can feel the power. Can you not feel it?'

Henri felt weak. The invisible capsule was drawing on his strength faster than it had ever done before. 'I… I think it is weakening our shield,' he gasped, trying to control his breathing. 'I think that the…'

As he dropped his sword, he looked down at Solitan. The Marox was slumped in the pouch, his little hands gripping the edges to prevent himself from falling right inside.

Unlike Henri with his seal, each time Win wanted to travel to a different place, if she could not walk there, then she had to return to her own time first and then travel a separate journey. She had never travelled back in time before. She had been to this place twice already; once to create a diversion which she did using the stick weapon Henri had taken from Hansenger's guard. The second time she had travelled back to her time and returned inside the cell.

It was at a moment like this that she wished that she could

bring an army of helpers. As it was, she returned to the coven once more and explained what Barmough had told her, that, with their combined powers, they could send her back in time; but the coven decided that, because this mission meant certain death to whoever undertook it, Win would embark on the task on her own.

Now she had travelled from her own time once more to the same place that Raelmin had taken Henri. Each time she travelled she became much weaker, and now, travelling back in time took an enormous toll on her energy. She appeared amongst a crowd of giant egg-headed Vasitterites, with little strength left in her body to make herself unseen.

The Vasitterites, who were milling about searching for something, instantly turned their eyes to the tiny woman in a black dress and cloak. A huge hand reached down to seize her about the waist. The Vasitterite vanished like a drop of water on a hot stove. She had fired the stick weapon only once before in order to create the diversion more than seventeen years in the future. Then a piece of machinery, where the shell-like egg-heads were hovering, had disappeared with an ear-cracking blast. But this time she had fired the stick weapon at the hand of the Vasitterite. As the massive fingers reached out to grasp her body, she stepped backwards to avoid it, lifted the stick, and with her thumb, she pressed the button that lay within the handle of the weapon. This time the effect was amazing.

'Phew,' she gasped, staggering away from the empty space it had created. 'Better than a wand,' she said tensely, realizing that if the hand had reached just another inch and touched her, then quite probably, she would have been vapourised as well.

All the other giants had halted in their tracks. They had

seen the weapon but they were all unarmed. 'What do you want here?' the closest demanded. The language was clear but stilted.

Win didn't bother answering. She backed away and used what remaining strength she had to make herself disappear. At first she thought she had succeeded. The Vasitterites cast around, their big feet coming perilously close as she wove in and out between them. Then, suddenly, she saw what they were really looking at. On the ground the four remaining sectors of The Seal were still bound together but were hardly visible. The Marox travelling machine, by changing its colour to look exactly like the floor, had become so cryptically camouflaged that she had stepped upon it. As she faded in and out of visibility, she swept it up in her free hand and ran.

The tunnels carried sound better than any telegraph system. The noise was coming from behind them, from the direction from which they had come. Since Henri had no other choice, he picked up his sword and ran back along the tunnels, listening all the time so that he followed the right passage back to the gigantic dome. He thought he would try going down a different tunnel, but as he got nearer to the dome, he realized that the commotion must have something to do with another intruder. He knew it had to be Win.

As he broke out into the open, he saw Win running for her life. She was not invisible nor seemed to be using anything to hide herself. She was just running.

'Over here,' Henri shouted, but then realized that over the

commotion of shouting and thundering footsteps, she had not heard him. He shouted again.

'She will not hear you,' Solitan said weakly. 'You must abandon me so that she can heed you. She looks weak and may not even be able to see you.'

'I can't leave you at the mercy of this lot,' Henri shouted. He was finding it hard to hear himself now. Win had spun around and disintegrated another pursuer. The noise and commotion was deafening. The giants were shouting and making clicking noises so loud that the dome became one huge auditorium.

But Henri had no choice. Without another word, Solitan had pulled his weak body from the pouch and had dropped to the floor. Instantly Henri emerged from his invisible bubble. 'Win!' he shouted. 'Over here.'

Still she could not hear him over the din. But with his sword in his hand, he ran towards her, waving his arms wildly. The Vasitterites saw him first. Huge legs and feet turned towards him.

Another two giants dispersed into the atmosphere as Win fired her weapon at them. There was more din; more outrage. The Vasitterites were desperate to stop these insurgents at any cost. They were laying down their lives to stop the two tiny intruders. Some had left the dome and were returning, as yet a long way away, riding on some kind of gigantic crocodile-jawed wolves. The riders seemed to be struggling to control the creatures beneath them, some losing their balance and a few falling off awkwardly onto the solid floor, their grunts of pain adding to the bedlam. Those that remained mounted travelled across the ground of the huge dome so fast that, from seeing them enter at the far side, Henri and Win had only just time to reach each other before the creatures were charging down upon them. At the same time, more and more of the creatures with their riders were appearing and eating up the ground between them and their quarry.

As they approached, snapping with jaws full of dagger-like teeth, Henri struck out with his sword, swiping at the neck of the nearest attacker. He had to jump quickly to one side as the Vasitterite, toppling off its slaughtered mount, plunged to the floor where Henri had been standing. It grabbed at him, desperately trying to be the one to stop the tiny intruder but Henri felled it with a single swipe of his sword that was so forceful he wondered if he hadn't suddenly gained some supernatural strength. The Vasitterite just crumbled before him.

Breathing heavily now, he struck out at another and another of the oncoming attackers, while Win sent others to oblivion with the stick weapon. Henri knew it was only a matter of time before one of them got past his swinging sword. Several fell slain, but he knew that one bite from the jaws of these creatures was all it would take to kill him. Henri dispatched one after another with his amazing weapon, but still they came on at the intruders relentlessly, jumping over the fallen and landing at their feet.

The sword seemed to be giving Henri strength, agility and speed, but the Vasitterites were now bounding over the fallen, four and five at a time. Henri knew that it would only be seconds before one of the attackers' mounts got to him with its lashing teeth before he could strike it down. Another came at him from the side, slain with another almighty swing of his sword; then another bounded over it as it fell slaughtered in front of him. It, too, died in mid air, but with the momentum and downward force of it surging towards him, it hit him square in his side with its head. He fell awkwardly to the floor and his sword was wrenched from his hand by yet another huge pair of snapping jaws.

Win was holding back those creatures and their riders that charged towards her, but there was little chance now of her saving Henri. If she took her eyes off her attackers for one second then they would be upon her.

Henry struggled to get to his feet, but another crocodile-jawed creature was already clearing the casualties with a powerful leap. Its fangs were frightful as its lips curled back against its gums. Henri glanced towards Win. 'Good luck,' he called out. There was no more he could do.

Then suddenly another diversion appeared, dragging the eyes of the giant predators away from Henri and Win. Somehow, his attacker had frozen in mid air and sailed helplessly over his shoulder. One after another of the creatures began to fall to the ground, rolling and tumbling forward and tipping off their riders as they lost their balance. Watching the events unfold, he looked on as the Vasitterites suddenly fell silent. They were milling about aimlessly, chaotically.

'Run! Do what you came here to do!' a piercing voice shouted. It was as grating a woman's voice as Henri had ever heard. But he had heard it before and knew it as well as if he'd known it forever. It was the old witch, Barmough, suspended in the air like a toy hanging in a child's bedroom. Somehow she had escaped from The City of Darkness, and had used her powers to arrive at the scene and contribute to the pandemonium. There was total mayhem as, somehow, waving a stick not unlike the weapon that Win was carrying, all the chasing giants were thrown by their mounts, and all those standing were suddenly putting their webbed hands up to the sides of their egg-heads and swaying dizzily.

'Come,' Henri shouted to Win as the din began to get louder again.

Without another word, and leaving Barmough skimming through the air and thrusting her wand forward at every approaching Vasitterite, they ran side by side back towards the tunnel system.

As Henri looked sideways at his favourite witch, he noticed that Solitan had grabbed a hold of her cloak and was clinging on with his long finger nails. Henri watched as Solitan reached out his hand to Win. 'The Seal!' Solitan called to her over the commotion of falling wolf reptiles and their riders. 'We must remain together now!'

As they ran, Win handed The Seal to Henri and then, grasping Solitan around his waist, passed him to her companion.

Barmough continued to create total chaos as she circled overhead on what looked like nothing other than yet another thin stick. There were now tens if not a hundred giants on their wolf-like reptiles, but all that got close to their quarry crashed dizzily to the floor. As Henri and Win disappeared into the tunnel one of the riders and his mount crashed to the floor at its entrance. Then another as it was about to jump clear over them. And yet another slid against them, and another until the light from the dome began to fade.

The tunnel had its own lighting system. Similar to that of the dome, light emanated from the curved surface above them. It wasn't as bright a light as in the dome, but it was adequate with which to see.

But then, suddenly the passageway behind them was cast in blackness. The lights faded and the whole domed tunnel seemed to implode behind them. Solid section after solid section slid across the tunnel in the same way as the doors in the domes slid aside. But these were not opening anything, they were closing off the tunnel; and as each solid section shot out of one tunnel wall and slammed up against the opposite one, it rapidly sealed the intruders in. The shutting down process rushed faster and faster towards them. Something or someone was sealing the tunnel. As the tunnel ahead branched, once again Henri tried to work out the most direct route to the ergametron control centre. One of the passages must have a door to the exterior.

But Solitan thought not. 'I suspect that all the tunnels have been sealed up ahead,' Solitan said shakily as he bounced up and down on Henri's hip. 'It is probably what they designed to contain the ergametron in the case of emergency.'

'So how do we get in?' Henri panted. The sealing process was rapidly catching them up from behind. The huge dome above and around them was becoming solid. The Vasitterites were ensuring that nothing got in or out.

'Perhaps we can't and shouldn't,' Win called from his side. They were still running fast. Henri swerved down a side tunnel. Win followed just in time as the tunnel they left behind continued to close up, the closure rushing past like an express train.

'So how do we stop this thing?' Henri shouted and then realized that there was a loud humming sound over which he was trying to hear and be heard.

'We were supposed to arrive before the Vasitterites started

the chain reactor,' Solitan called. 'The humming that we can hear sounds like we may have arrived at the wrong time.'

'No,' Win said, as they slowed to a jog. 'We are in time but we have no idea how to prevent it happening. And I can't think of anybody who can.'

They jogged on for several minutes until, suddenly, they stopped. Now they had come upon another dead end. They could not go back. It wouldn't be long before the last remaining tunnel began to seal itself up with them inside, crushing them like grapes under a wagon wheel. The buzzing seemed to be coming through the walls, not just the one ahead, but from those of the domed walls all around them.

'Put The Seal back together,' Solitan said, growing smaller with each word and each flick of his eyebrows. 'We are going to the other side of the wall.'

'We?'

'The Marox,' Solitan said with authority. 'Put The Seal together when I am inside. We will see if it is safe for humans to go there.'

Within seconds, Solitan had climbed onto Henri's hand and had diminished to the size of a common fly. As he was getting into The Seal, Henri heard a tinkling voice say, 'Back in a minute,' and then he disappeared inside. Henri began to reassemble it and no sooner had he clicked Solitan's sector in place than it disappeared right in front of his eyes. A second later it reappeared. Henri began to wonder if something had gone wrong. He stared at the cube in his palm.'

Open it,' Win said hurriedly. 'They are back.'

'I thought he said a minute,' Henri protested, still waiting for The Seal to disappear again.

'Not in our time. In their time,' Win explained. They travel through space and time, remember?'

'Right,' Henri said, meekly as he reached for the top of The Seal and began to twist. He never would get his head around all this. The top of The Seal parted immediately and out fell the miniature Solitan. He was back to his normal size, if he had one, in less than two seconds.

'We've had a good look around,' Solitan explained. The place is a smaller version of what we left behind in The City of Darkness. Huge consoles and lots of flashing lights. There is no blue wall, however. The consoles surround a single giant magnetic blue pillar. I suspect that is the very first one that was brought here.'

'Brought here?' asked Henri. 'What about all the ones I saw outside?'

'They aren't there yet. They were made later to stop the roof of the dome being sucked in. The one with the artificial sky, remember? Of course it didn't look like a dome any more than the sky on your earth. They were made in ever increasing numbers to resist the forces beyond it. A task at which the dome was about to fail.'

'I presume that you are talking about the future *was*?'

'Of course; the one from which we have all travelled. That future existed before or at least at the same time as this present. Remember what I told you?'

'I remember, but that doesn't mean I know what the heck you are talking about.'

Solitan shook his head. 'I said…'

'So am I going in there or what?' Henri cut in. He was getting impatient. He could already hear their last tunnel beginning to close. There was no time to carry on this conversation.

'The magnetic pillars are self replicating,' Solitan explained. 'The vibrations and the humming are the sound of it spawning the first clone.'

'Clone?'

'Never mind,' Solitan said irritably. 'What you need to know is that it is a living organism, not a rock as you know rock. They are dumb cells doing what they do best, multiplying whilst still repelling or attracting. But as they reproduce, so they are eating up all the energy around them. And as they eat up that energy, then they create a vacuum into which they must draw more matter, more energy. The tunnel system is the only route through the shield that the Vasitterites have built to retain the power of the ergametron cell. Until now they haven't realized that the ergametron will carry on increasing in size. It has been their fatal mistake and I suspect that the Vasitterites now know of their folly. And I suspect that it is why they have begun to seal the tunnels. They are trying to contain it.'

'So they really will cease to exist?' Henri questioned.

'That all depends,' said Solitan, 'They built this shell to withstand the weight and pressures of their single experiment. They had no idea that they were starting a chain reaction. We know of course that it will take less than eighteen years for the ergametron to become so strong that it takes over their whole world.'

'So where's Raelmin?' Henri asked, beginning to dissemble The Seal once more. 'She can take me through to that place.'

'No, she takes you through time. It's Gorang who takes you through walls and doors and to other places in the same world. When will you remember?' Solitan scolded angrily.

Was there much point in remembering now? Henri thought. In a minute or two he expected to be dead or well on the way there. 'What's the point in lecturing me?' he said crossly. He fumbled with The Seal and as it broke apart, the other four Marox tumbled onto his hand. Remarkably, as they all grew each to their pint size, he recognised every one of them. 'Right Gorang, my little magical friend,' he said, now quite resigned to his fate. 'How about a trip to the other side of this wall?'

'Not so fast,' Solitan shouted. 'I have not explained all yet.'

'So what now, for goodness sake!'

'Gorang can't take you there. It would mean leaving us behind. You can't do that.'

'I'll come back,' Henri said with a shrug.

'No good. When you destroy the ergametron, you will have to be already on your way out of this world. You can't travel back here to the outside of the shield because it will be destroyed. And you need all of The Seal to travel out of this world. Only the complete seal will take you through time, remember?'

Solitan was lecturing again. When would he realize that Henri had resigned himself to dying? When would he just let him get on with…

'Hang on a minute,' he said crossly. 'I thought you said we had no chance of getting out of here alive?'

'That was before the old hag came to our help,' Solitan said, grinning impertinently.

'Now look here,' Win broke in, 'I might have said I hate the old… the old witch, but she's come good. She's three times older than any other witch alive. That means she is three times more powerful. If she's trying to put things right then she deserves a little respect.'

'Oooh! Get a load of that!' he chanted uncharacteristically, shrugging and looking up at Henri. 'I think we've hit a nerve!' he said with dancing eyebrows that seemed to be deliberately mocking her. The power of the ergametron was even affecting Solitan's manner now. Henri noticed that he appeared to be losing the thread. He was more intent on arguing than setting his mind to a solution to the present predicament.

'Solitan,' Henri said crossly, 'just get on with whatever you want me to do will you? We're a team now.'

Solitan looked suitably admonished. 'Sorry young witch,' he said to Win. He looked back at Henri. Henri couldn't help noticing that Solitan was beginning to sway erratically. 'Right, here's what we have to do,' he chirped, as he corrected his balance by staggering backwards a few more steps.

Chapter Thirty Three

THE FINAL DECISION

If Henri held tight onto Win then in theory, just as she had become invisible by touching Henri, she would be able to travel through different barriers in this world without first returning to her own world. It was a gamble. All the Marox were losing strength rapidly. They could only put it down to the immense strength of the ergametron. But whatever the reason, it was a risk Solitan explained they had now to take. Win was too weak to travel back and forth any more. But if it worked then the downside of the plan was that Win might not be able to reconnect with her own world. She might be lost in time just the same as they hoped to lose the ergametron, lose it in the past so that the future remained unharmed. What was it Solitan had said? The future already existed. So how could they alter it now? Henri hadn't realized that he was thinking aloud.

'Because one future exists without the ergametron,' Win explained while they looked at the sectors of The Seal. They knew they had to reassemble it while everything seemed to be spinning around them. 'But we are something that happened in that future's past. Otherwise, if we weren't part of its past, then you are looking at a different future, one without you, without me, without The Seal, without the Marox, and possibly a future without human kind. Our future, our present depends on us being here at this time and place in our past. It's like taking a knitted jumper and running it back to the first stitch. If we drop a stitch at the beginning or even anywhere on the way to reconstructing it, then when we knit the final stitch the jumper will never be the same as it was before. It will be a different jumper made up of the same wool just as our future is made up of all the same ingredients as all the other possible futures. It just depends what stitches are dropped and which ones are caught.'

'You make it sound so plausible,' Henri said with a big sigh. 'Whatever happened to just having an ordinary life?'

'Your life would never have been ordinary, you know that. You have been designed, been fated, call it what you like, to fit into your and our future.'

By this time, Henri's head was thumping. He didn't know if was because he was trying to get his mind around everything he was being told and everything he was seeing and experiencing, or just that the ergametron was sapping his energy too. It was more likely to be the latter. He felt drained; drained of energy, drained of enthusiasm, drained of hope. 'There's no way we can do anything to stop this machine or whatever it is, growing up as it is in the future that we have just left,' he said dismally.

'Wrong,' snapped Solitan. 'That future was not yours. It is trying to be but it isn't going to be. You must trust me.'

'Oh, I do,' Henri said wearily. His head was pounding as the biggest bell in the whole of existence hammered its clanger inside his skull. He glanced at Win and noticed that she was no longer pale, she was white. He looked at all the Marox. They were listless; their limbs seemed weak and rubbery; their eyes were staring wildly. Even Solitan's eyes were wide, flitting about, looking but not really seeing anything as he struggled to keep his concentration. And what really worried Henri was that Solitan's eyebrows had stopped moving. They were knitted together, locked in a deep, deep, scowling frown. One eye suddenly closed. His amber eye remained wide open and stared straight ahead.

The walls around them began to vibrate. Henri had to shout to hear his own voice.

'We're not going anywhere together from here,' Henri suddenly announced. He waited for Solitan or even one of the other Marox to contradict him but they were all silent. 'Solitan, if I am your master then you must do as I wish.'

Solitan remained silent. He seemed to be straining every tiny fibre of his tiny body in a struggle to keep his concentration. Still he gazed with the one amber eye straight past Henri's shoulder.

'Win, you are the master of the Marox now. I command it. If you want your witch clan to survive then you must take the Marox, take The Seal and return to your own time. Do it now while you have the strength. I'll stop the ergametron, I promise. But I'll only do it if I know you have left here safely.'

The thick wall that separated the centre of the ergametron from the end of the tunnel began to shake. It seemed to craze like an old pot jug. The light in the tunnel began to fade. The tunnel was closing fast; section after section crashing across the opening; rushing up behind them.

As Henri thrust the segments of The Seal at Win, he snatched the stick weapon from her hand and tucked it into his belt. Win grabbed The Seal and held it in her hands, trembling as Henri assembled it with the Marox inside.

'Now!' he commanded. 'Go now!'

The wall began to darken as the crazing lines became thicker. It was going to give way. 'I command you to take her home,' Henri shouted at the top of his voice. The sound was deafening now. 'Go! Go and don't look back!'

The whole subway became dark as the last few yards of tunnel behind them finally sealed up. It was heading towards them as each section closed faster and faster. The light from the domed ceiling blinked out completely. The crazed wall still gave out a faint, eerie blue light around the ever-increasing cracks as the fractures rapidly merged together. Now, once again, the wall seemed blue. Only seconds remained before they would all be entombed as completely as a sealed cave beneath a mountain. He felt the force in the remaining space crushing him as the closing wall of the tunnel compressed the remaining air. As it pushed towards the crazed barrier, he could hardly breathe.

Then suddenly a splinter of bright light appeared in the centre of the bending blockade. The wall twisted inwards as it began to surrender to the immense gravitational, pulling force beyond.

Henri doubled up with the pain of the pressure in his ears. With his hands over the sides of his head, he fought to prevent himself sinking to the floor on his knees. With the intense pressure, the last few feet of tunnel were sealed by the huge sections as they were driven forward towards Henri. It was now upon him, hitting him like an express train and throwing him forward through the air as the wall ahead caved in and gave way. He fumbled with his fingers to free the stick weapon from his belt. He couldn't tell if Win had gone nor if she or The Seal had had the strength to take her and the Marox out of there, but he knew he had no time left. As he tumbled against the imploding wall, the pressure sucked him through it towards the centre of the ergametron. He could feel himself flying through the blackness towards the bright point of light; and then, suddenly, the faint, blue, glowing background beyond the brighter light began to get bigger; slowly at first. It seemed so far away.

And then he could see what was happening. As if falling to earth, something was sucking him towards a single, massive, blue pillar.

As he hurtled towards it, the pillar filled more and more space until all he could see was a solid blue wall getting bigger and bigger and bigger; the size of a city, and then a country; then a world. He hadn't expected that. It was bigger than anything he could have imagined. Still he careered towards it, a tiny speck against infinity. He could already feel it draining out and feeding on his energy. He felt like his whole body was dissolving, being digested from the outside. Weakly, he clung onto the stick weapon, determined not to drop it. But he doubted now if the puny weapon would do any damage to this seemingly boundless inner universe. And whatever power it had, he desperately hoped that it had not been completely depleted by Win as she used it to fell the Vasitterites.

Then suddenly he saw a solidness to the barrier. It was hurtling towards him. He had only seconds before a deadly impact ended his existence. What was left of his dissolving body would be scattered like dust, vapourised by the impact. He pointed the stick weapon at the ever increasing wall of blue and just hoped that his thumb would remain solid long enough to press the tiny button in the handle. A thin cane of light shot out of the point of the weapon, disappearing into the distance ahead of him. He hadn't realized he had still been so very far away but, eventually, as the light beam contacted, the blue wall turned white and rippled outwards from the centre of the impact. As he hurtled onward, ten times faster than a bullet, he fired the stick weapon again. The cane of light took little time to reach the wall this time. Once again, the wall rippled and shook as it distorted like an animal in pain. Once again, willing his thumb to press the button, he fired, as an opening began to appear. Still he felt his body dissolving as he hurtled through the gap and into the centre of the ergametron. It was worse than anything he could have imagined. He knew it was eating him, converting his whole being to energy. It had a nucleus, a vast, bright, shimmering, golden centre of light, getting bigger as he was dragged towards it. He could still see his hand but it seemed detached; a long way away. Then he saw the rest of his body, faint and transparent and dismembered as he gazed down at himself from somewhere else. He willed his thumb to fire the weapon one last time. There was a pause while he watched the thumb move. He willed it to press the button, but his hand was no longer solid. It was being drawn away into the ergametron like dust in a gale.

Nothing happened.

With only seconds before everything was consumed, the stick weapon finally began to dissolve as it, too, the last remaining thing that Henri could see, tumbled and hurtled into oblivion. The casing of the weapon must have been made out of something really hard, but eventually, it yielded, and as it melted away, it was sucked off in a stream of particles.

Henri watched on for a brief moment, as the interior of the weapon escaped from its eroded outer shell. But, unlike the hard casing, the soft centre didn't evaporate as it hurtled onwards. Instead, it floated and wobbled like a soft white bag, half full of milky liquid. Instead of dissolving, its shape became rounder and harder, the closer it was drawn to the core. Whatever the power source inside the stick; whatever it was that blasted out those unstoppable, devastating, relentless light beams, it hurtled on, getting smaller and firmer.

The flash of light was blinding as the fuel pod from the weapon collided with the core of the giant cell.

Then there was nothing.

No time. No space. No hand. No body. Just light.

❖

Epilogue

THE LAST SPELL

Her black cloak floated smoothly behind her as she walked across the Room. To the seven witches watching it looked as if she were hovering over the floor, inches above it. Perhaps she was. Win had explained to all of them what had happened and she had told them about Barmough. Now the old witch was concentrating, and to do that she paced the floor backwards and forwards and back again.

'What good is The Seal without *The One*?' she muttered over and over again. 'We are saved. You are saved,' she said, sweeping her arm towards the coven of seven. 'But what use is that? Ah, you might say that the human race will need us one day. Well that is true, and that day is not so far off that we can afford to make any mistakes. The Seal,' she said, lifting it in her hand and presenting it to all. 'This is what you were after, and it was to save the race of witches, no one else. But now things have changed. You knew about the legend, *The Prophesy*, but you overlooked one simple thing.'

All The Seven watched her and waited for her to continue. Barmough was three times older than any of them. She had returned and she had magic that even the coven as one could not equal.

'Oh, no doubt I am much to blame, for it was I who brought our race to the edge of extinction. But that was not my intention. And now we… we have been saved by a human.'

All the other witches nodded.

'And that human was *The One*.' She looked into Win's eyes.

'Yes, I realized that soon after we met,' Win said sadly. 'I didn't realize that we were leading him to his death.' Her lip began to shake but she bit it firmly. Now was no time for self pity.

'And The Seal,' Barmough added. 'We were saved by a human and The Seal.'

'That's true,' some of The Seven concurred.

'The human and The Seal. They are one. Oh, you used The Seal, Winifred, but it was working for Henri Dubois. It was working for you on his instructions. And Henri Dubois is in *The Prophesy*. He should be here to fulfil it.' She stared hard at The Seven.

The coven waited, hoping that she had the answer.

'Henri didn't just stop the ergametron, he destroyed it completely,' Win stated. 'He didn't just set it back in time; he prevented it from existing in our future ever again.'

'True; and we helped him do that.'

'Yes, and he was grateful for your help, you know that, don't you?'

'Huh, that was nothing!'

'Your turning up just at the right time was a bit of a surprise, though, I must admit,' Win said with an appreciative nod. 'We thought you'd been killed when we saw blood on the console where you'd been working.'

'Oh, that was Ruskin's. He was trying to stop them arresting me. He seemed to have made a choice whose friend he wanted to be. It gave me the chance to disappear and come to find you.'

'But how did you know how far to travel back in time to meet us there?'

'We call it remote viewing, dear,' Barmough replied derisively. 'It isn't so difficult really. Most witches can do that if they put their mind to it, not just ancient old things like me.'

The Seven all agreed, nodding.

'It's a pity about the Vasitterites, though,' Win contemplated. 'We weren't supposed to be wiping out an entire species.'

'They brought it on themselves. Greedy power-hungry beasts with their crocodolves. Henri Dubois simply stopped them wiping out everything and everybody else at the same time. The Graftians are better off without them.'

'They have blue skies and green fields once again,' Win said proudly. 'Henri did that.'

'Oh stop moping girl,' Barmough scolded. 'Of course he did it. He was *The One*! How many times do I have to tell you? He was destined to do what he did. It's all in The Golden Book.'

'He wasn't destined to die,' Win sniffled.

'That was before he took it upon himself to rid us of that dangerous thing permanently. You think that The Golden Book explains four different futures. We had overlooked the one we are in now. We were settling for second best!'

'And The Golden Book said that Henri exists no more, does it?'

Barmough thought for a moment. 'Not exactly, no. What it says is:

'A future more enjoyed, plans the evil power destroyed.

'A future needing more re-healing, plans a past left evil reeling.

'A future devoid, completely empty, plans a past with evil plenty.

'A future always stumbling, plans a past with motives fumbling.'

'So where does that leave us?' Win said dejectedly.

'Ah, well there's a fifth future outlined,' Barmough went on.

'Four futures, the scholars said.'

'Well they are not as clever as they think they are then,' Barmough said derisively. 'If they'd given me The Golden Book then it wouldn't have taken me five minutes to translate it, never mind five long and tedious years! And then they didn't finish it!'

'How do I get the feeling you are going to surprise us again?' Win asked, now curious. 'But I don't suppose there were any scholars with over five hundred years experience,' she added, which rather perked Barmough up a little.

'The world is a different place when one is given a different face.'

Barmough quoted. 'But the transcript does not get as far as saying what that future is like and who is in it. It merely explains that The Seal is important and exists in all but one of those futures.'

'Obviously The Seal is not in the future where it is devoid,' Win argued. 'It means that evil reigns supreme.'

'Possibly. But I suspect that our future could be either the first or the last of those listed.'

'How will we know for sure?'

'There's only one way to find out, Winifred. That is to buy it and try it. Whichever one you pick you will have to live out. As far as I can see we have a choice here, but whatever that choice is, we will not be able to go back and change it again.'

'Haven't we already made that choice? Are we not already in the future where the ergametron has been destroyed? I presume that the ergametron is the evil in that respect.'

'I like to think we are still making the past for our future,' Barmough said lightly. 'I think we have yet to do whatever it is to not only secure our future but to secure that of your Henri.'

'*My* Henri!'

'Pah! You haven't been fooling anybody Winifred. You are smitten. You've been moping about like a child that lost her sweets, these past weeks. You fell hook line and sinker for that man, admit it.'

Win didn't need to consider for long what Barmough had said. A small sob escaped from deep inside her chest. She shrugged. 'Too late to do anything about it now,' she said, letting a tear fill each eye. She was past caring what anybody thought now.

'Your sorrow is blinding you,' Barmough scolded. 'The past of the fifth future is yet to be rolled out. *The world is a different place when the one is given a different face.*

'*The* one. The text missed out the definite article.'

'What do you mean?' asked Win, frowning. 'Could we possibly have saved him? Could there be any way he might have survived the destruction of a universe, one to which he had gone to the very centre to annihilate?'

'Could he?' Barmough repeated. She smiled. 'I have a confession to make, but before I do, I have to be sure you all agree that we choose the same future, the fifth one.'

'Yes,' all The Seven answered together.'

'The fifth one?' Win said, seeking total agreement. She looked into the eyes of all her companions.

'Yes,' they confirmed emphatically.

'Well it works like this,' Barmough began. 'While you were entombed in the tunnels leading to the core of the ergametron, I knew that the Vasitterites couldn't reach you. I saw how, by some means which I don't really understand, that they had begun to close the tunnels up. Once they had done that then I knew you were safe from them. So I disappeared. There was no more I could do there.'

'But I didn't leave,' she continued. 'I went to an empty space. I have no idea where it was, but it enabled me to remain visible and to use all my powers to cast a final spell.'

'A spell?' Win asked, cautiously. She knew how calamitous Barmough's spells had been in the past. She wasn't too sure what the old witch was going to say she had done this time.

'I was watching you. Well, not just you. I was watching you, and Henri Dubois and those curious little things that live in this thing,' she said, still holding The Seal out in her right hand. 'And I saw what was happening. I was remote viewing again.'

The Seven nodded again but remained totally engrossed in what Barmough was saying.

'I saw you take The Seal and it did as Henri commanded. It carried you back to your own time safely. He on the other hand was determined to stop the ergametron. He knew he was going to die. He is very brave.' She paused and thought for a long minute. 'If only I were five hundred years younger,' she said, a tinge of sadness showing on her inscrutable face for the first time.

'You're not though,' Win put in quickly.

'Eh? Oh, no, that's true,' Barmough said, coming back to her explanation with a deep sigh. 'Well, I watched as the wall was drawn in by the immense force of the gravitational pull of the ergametron. I saw it cracking and then giving way. I followed Henri with my mind, watching as he travelled like a musket ball towards the centre of the ergametron. He had no way of escape. I could see it was feeding on him, taking not just his energy but every particle of his body to use to feed its hunger for more and more power.'

Win cradled her face in her hands but remained silent.

Barmough continued. 'I saw his body dissolving. He was marvellous, still firing that wand weapon even as his body was being dispersed into a million particles. If I hated human kind before, then he was the one man that showed me there was goodness and courage in that vindictive and puny race.'

'So that's it,' Win said quietly. 'He was eaten up by the ergametron.'

'Yes, completely,' Barmough said, still excited with the vision she was still now recalling.

'That's just great then,' Win chuntered.

'But that's when I used my magic,' Barmough carried on. She had probably developed a thick skin over the last few centuries, Win thought. Sarcasm certainly wasn't working any spells on her. 'The remote viewing was nothing. The magic I had to use next took every ounce of my power. At one moment

I really thought that the ergametron was going to suck me through to its own space time and eat me up as well, I was so far inside it with my mind. But then, somehow, Henri fired the wand again and he did it! He broke through the outer layers of the ergametron allowing the fuel cell of his weapon to reach the core. It totally destroyed the thing that had eaten him. Killed it dead! The ergametron subsided like a deflated ball. And although his body did not exist any more, I could see his aura, his spirit, his subconscious mind hovering there, watching everything from a distance, watching everything that was happening to his once solid form. He seemed content with his superhuman achievement.'

'And so he should be,' Win said, still holding her cynical tone. 'Not every man can boast that they saved their universe.'

'You can be very childish sometimes, Winifred,' Barmough scolded. 'Are you going to let me finish or what?'

Win looked at her totally bereft of feeling. She shrugged. 'You might as well since you have started,' she said churlishly.

Barmough grunted her disapproval. 'The gravity of the ergametron had no effect on his being. It could only affect the solid matter. And it was the antimatter in his wand that destroyed the cell at the centre of the evil ergametron. Until then, I didn't realize what the source of power in the wand was. But it would never have reached its target if Henri hadn't opened up a way through.'

'Antimatter?'

'That's right. Of course,' Barmough added, 'it's unlikely that humans will rediscover that for some time.'

'Right.'

'But anyway, cutting a long story short...'

'Oh, don't mind us,' Win said, sad but nevertheless now intrigued.

'Well, I used my remaining strength to carry Henri, or should I say his being back to our time.' She looked at Win and waited for her to respond.

'What exactly are you telling me here, Barmough. Are you saying he's a ghost now?'

'Er, sort of. But not in another place or another time.'

'So he's a ghost here?'

'I put him in a jar for the time being. Just so that I didn't mislay him. Couldn't do with him wandering about. Free spirits and all that.'

'A jar? You kept Henri in a jar!'

'You can't keep a spirit in a jar!' one of the other witches exclaimed. 'They pass through them. They pass through anything solid.'

'Not if I've cast a spell on it to seal it they don't,' Barmough chuckled.

The old witch was looking around rather furtively, Win thought. She looked directly into the eyes of the old witch and said, 'You aren't joking, are you?'

'I never joke, you know that, Winifred,' Barmough retorted, still keeping her patience with Win. She understood all too well how she was feeling. 'You see I could converse with him,' Barmough continued, totally unperturbed, 'as I can converse with you telepathically if you wanted to reciprocate. I asked him if I could take him back to his own world. Eventually he understood that he couldn't remain where he was.'

'That's true,' Win confirmed. 'He would have been a lost soul for sure.'

'Quite. So then when I got him back here, I told him I would find him another body.'

'Another body!'

'Well he didn't much like the idea at…'

'I can't possibly understand why,' Win said sarcastically.

Barmough ploughed on. '*At first*. But I eventually persuaded him that you would miss him terribly and you wanted to be with him, you know, as couples do?'

'You told him what? I never said that…'

Barmough shrugged. 'And so he agreed.'

'He agreed?'

'Yes, and I found him a body.'

'You found him a body!' Win parroted.

'Oh, yes, Winifred, I have done all that.'

There was along silence. Nobody spoke while they watched the old witch turn over in her mind what she was about to say.

'It took a little time,' Barmough stated eventually. 'I thought the best place to look was where there was some fighting going on. I was right of course. But then, there is always some fighting going on somewhere in the world. I soon found a young soldier in Crimea, that looked very much like him and he was dying so when he passed over I took Henri to his body and, with my very last spell, I put him in it. Had to do a bit of healing on the body of course, but that sort of thing is as easy as growing rushes in a wet meadow. We can all do that, even the younger witches.' She paused as she recollected what she had done. Then she added, 'You ought to have seen the look on the field surgeon's face!'

THE END